STEADFAST COLLECTION

6 Novellas in 1 Volume

D.I. Telbat

In Season Publications
U.S.A.

Dedication

To those who know they must begin
to stand for Christ right now, not later.

Acknowledgements

Every book requires a team,
and every series requires commitment,
so, thanks to the individuals who bless me,
and strive alongside me,
by correcting, editing, and advising:
Dee, Sharon, Mountainman Ed,
and my Beta Reading friends.
Most of all, I acknowledge the finished work
of Jesus Christ for us,
and the saving work of God in us.
May the work of our hands bring Him glory.

Table of Contents

Note from the Author

Dear Friend,

The Steadfast Series is a story that takes place in the mountains of Wyoming. Originally, these were the Laramie Mountains with Casper in the north and Cheyenne in the south. But I have taken fictional license with the geography and presented a hypothetical mountain range and river system within the Rockies, in central and eastern Wyoming.

The Meridia Virus, which kills one hundred million people across America, is a fictional virus, though I modeled it after the Ebola Virus of Western Africa.

The edible plants and roots mentioned in the story are real and accurate for the region.

Though I believe Christ will return soon for His Church before the collapse of America, I have presented a "what if" scenario in the immediate future. But if Christ doesn't return to judge the world as soon as we believe, will we remain steadfast and uncompromising in our faith?

Please tell me what you think of *The Steadfast Series* through your reviews.

For the King,
David Telbat

STEADFAST BOOK ONE

America's Last Days

D.I. Telbat

~*~

2021 Fiction Novella Bronze Medal Winner
International Readers' Favorite Book Award Contest

Chapter 1, Book One

Eric Radner was starving to death. It had been weeks since he'd eaten an actual meal. Like a wild animal, he'd begun to eat grass and insects, even worms and snails. The only thing that scared him more than starving to death was the possibility of dying by the virus.

Now, a cold rain chilled his shriveled skeleton. The Wyoming forest was quiet except for the static of falling rain and Eric's chattering teeth. This was the end, Eric thought, as he sat on the ground and leaned against a tree. In a couple of days, he'd fall asleep and never wake up. His body couldn't take much more torment from the elements.

The thought of death saddened him most of all because he never understood why he'd been born in the first place. What was the point of life? It all seemed so insignificant. His malnourishment mixed with hopelessness brought upon him an overwhelming depression. There seemed no escape from the pending doom.

He tightened his designer belt around his midsection, but his belt wouldn't fasten any smaller. His clothes hung off him in tatters. The sole of one shoe had fallen off, and two of his toes had been cut on rocks while crossing a creek a week earlier. Though he knew nothing about living in the wilderness, he decided it was still better this way. In his imagination, he saw mountains of bodies in every city—infected, rotting, discarded . . . No, he wouldn't die from the virus.

Using the tree to stand, he studied the terrain around him. The movies always made it seem like the mountains were plentiful with caves, but he hadn't found a single one in weeks. His nights had been spent at the base of trees, covering himself with leaves and branches, restless from bug bites and nightmares of coyotes tearing at his corpse. Living like this, he'd never survive the winter.

Above the tree tops, he glimpsed a steep mountain slope, rocky and jagged. It seemed like a potential place for a cave—or to cast himself off a cliff to end his suffering. Why was he prolonging the inevitable? An instant later, he answered his own thoughts. He wasn't rushing into eternity because he didn't know what eternity held. He'd never taken the time to find out.

Using his hands, Eric climbed the mountain slope. In his city footwear, he slipped many times in the first few minutes, bloodying his knees and even his brow. He paused after ten minutes to scan the terrain behind him. Now above the trees, he looked down on the still green and gray forest, a sheet of rain barring him from seeing beyond a mile.

The world was finished, he guessed. Humanity, at least, would be wiped out by the virus. It all seemed so pointless—births and weddings, barbeques and vacations. Eric felt that he'd never done anything significant for anyone but himself, and even if he'd used his money to build homes for earthquake victims or fed the homeless, what would it all matter if everyone was to die now by a contagion?

To his right, Eric spotted a ridge that angled upward. On the spine of the mountain, the climbing was easier. In his pursuit for a cave to hide and die in, he exposed his thin frame not only to the pelting rain but now to a driving wind. A cliff face stretched beside and below him, and he contemplated a hasty end. His soul was pierced by defeat, deeper even than his fear of the virus or of the eternal unknown.

As he crawled over a boulder the size of a van, he slipped and tumbled off sideways. He landed a few feet below on his back, breathless, staring up at the cloudy afternoon sky. The rain stung his eyes. Slowly, he sat up and noticed he'd landed on a narrow ledge above the cliff. He'd heard of mountain goats and deer that had game trails where people couldn't safely walk.

Too dazed and weak to stand, he crawled along the cliff as a barely discernible trail cut up the mountainside. His knees were numb from the gashes. His head hung heavily, his untrimmed hair filthy and matted against his sopping skull.

His head bumped into something. He lifted his eyes to find not a tree, but flat boards. Several seconds passed before his mind recognized a manmade structure. A door and a wall were disguised by bark and slabs of rock set up against a small cabin, as if to hold it upright against the wind. An antique latch clicked under his thumb, and the door swung inward on modern though rusty hinges.

Was this real? A dark interior welcomed Eric, and he crawled out of the rain to roll onto his side on the plank flooring. Tilting his head, he looked up at a one-room habitat, large enough for a wide kitchen counter, a narrow bed, and a small wooden table. Open shelves lined the walls with books, charts, and cans of food. A rifle hung on a sling by the doorframe, and a closed trunk sat under the bed.

Eric drew his tired bones upright, leaning heavily on the kitchen counter, and hesitantly selected a can from one shelf. His deliverance was here before him. Through gasps and sobs, he fumbled for a manual can opener amongst a set of knives. After three attempts with the can opener, he tossed it aside and went for a sturdy kitchen blade. Impatiently, he stabbed weakly at the top of the can until he could pry open the top. His knees nearly buckled at the aroma of shredded beef in thick gravy.

For a man who'd eaten worms and insects for days, eating beef with his filthy fingers straight from the can was still a banquet.

Halfway through his feast, he clutched his midsection as cramps seized him. His stomach had shrunk. He was already stuffed. Setting the can aside, he took three hasty steps, then lunged at the bed. Facedown, he slept where he fell, one leg and arm hanging off the rustic structure.

#######

The following day, Eric woke to a chill on his back. He rolled off the bed and stood upright. Though weak, he felt rested. The cabin still seemed like an illusion, but the cold morning breeze was real. With a nudge, he closed the door and more thoroughly studied the interior of his sanctuary.

Miles from civilization, the mountainside cabin overlooked a vast, dense forest. Thick plastic windows had been set into the sturdy walls. The roof was angled sharply to avoid snow accumulation. Binoculars sat on the table next to a late generation radio and transmitter. A plaque on the wall confirmed what Eric had already surmised—it was a U.S. Forest Service cabin.

He'd found a forest ranger lookout post, probably only manned during fire season. Maybe occasionally by hunters. The lack of much dust indicated someone had been there within the last few months, but vacated, Eric guessed, when news of the virus had been heard.

"Why me?" Eric asked aloud.

Never before had he asked that question for anything but bad circumstances. But now, he understood he was being blessed, or honored, and he didn't know why. This wasn't luck. Death had surrounded him. Now, he stood in a mountain shack that contained everything he needed to survive.

In the trunk under the bed, he found men's jeans and flannel shirts. On one shelf, a row of books leaned against boxes of rifle cartridges. There were volumes on survival, hunting, and North American herbs, as well as a musty collection of crime novels and a set of encyclopedias—yet missing several volumes. And a Bible. Eric reached out and touched the binding of the Bible. None of this was an accident. Though he'd never read the Bible, he knew he was about to. He needed answers—about life and death and the end of the world.

The radio! He sat on a wooden chair at the table. After a moment, he found the power switch and turned it on. Using a dial, he clicked through static only briefly before he heard voices. With startled attention, he listened as reports poured in from around the country. Most of what was said were recordings. When the tapes looped for a second time, Eric changed the frequency to hear another.

Only weeks before—maybe four—he'd run to hide in the Wyoming mountains. Now, whole cities were closed off. The virus had spread to every metropolitan area. Half of Atlanta had burned. New Orleans was a ghost town from the dead and dying, or those who'd run for safety. Los Angeles was a war zone of looting survivors and a military force trying to regain control. Martial Law had been initiated nationwide, but the virus had depleted the National Guard ranks. Or soldiers had left their posts to care for their own families.

For the next several days, Eric ate canned food and listened to the radio. Something they called the Meridia Virus had swept across America like a vengeful wind. Some said it was a biological weapon accidentally loosed. Others said it was intentionally released by the Russians, or Chinese, or jihadists. No one knew where it had started, or if it would end. The nation's infrastructure was collapsing, and the death count hadn't even peaked.

While the Internet was still online and radio stations were still broadcasting, one hundred million had been reported as infected. Rumor had it, once infected, no one lived beyond two weeks. Death came after symptoms of skin boils, rashes, and dehydration.

The public, as a whole, seemed to accept the virus as an evolutionary response to overpopulation and unrestrained chemical consumption. Therefore, people reacted passively, with no desire to pursue ways of survival. Hopelessness prevailed.

Apocalyptic theorists boasted in their own reasonings for the pandemic, and offered numerous ways to overcome. None of them agreed, Eric found, and as the days passed, they went silent. Or died.

There was even a religious report that looped nonstop. The Christians were looking toward the heavens for answers. Many guessed that Christ would have returned while America was still eating and drinking, marrying and partying, texting and gaming. But the clouds seemed silent. So, believers understood the virus to be a warning, a final flag for all to repent. The wealthiest nation, the proudest people, had been brought to its knees. But while on its knees, would the remnant call upon the Lord?

Two live operators broadcasted what they knew or suspected—one from Denver and the other from Chicago. But after another week, only one remained, then the last operator went quiet as well. All that was left for Eric to listen to were announcements and warnings he'd already heard about the virus: avoid contact with everyone, even family. The virus could be airborne, or it could be transmitted by touch. No one knew for sure.

Eric finally turned off the radio and walked outside. The early autumn sky was blue. Below his cabin, the forest stretched like a blanket to the south. Lakes and ridges interrupted the green trees, but he was otherwise isolated. Yet, for how long? He couldn't stay in the ranger cabin. Someone might return, someone with the virus. Or someone with murderous intent for survival. They'd take his remaining possessions and he'd be starving in the wilderness again.

If he were to survive, he'd need to relocate in secret. Shielding his eyes, he gazed to the east. He was pretty sure he'd abandoned his car in that direction. The forest was dense there, and the mountains high. There was plenty of water, and trees to build a cabin, and game to hunt.

But he had much to learn first. He'd never hunted deer, let alone cut meat off a carcass. Reaching for the survival book, his fingers brushed the Bible again. How to gut a deer would have to wait.

Opening the Bible, he paged through its crisp pages. Someone had made notes in pen in the margins of almost every page. This was someone's personal Bible, the object of untold hours of attention and devotion. Where were the answers he sought? He flipped to the beginning and started reading.

Over the next two weeks, Eric turned on the radio only twice more, but found the same looped recordings. His Bible reading was interrupted only by meals, sleep, and studying the survival guide. As his strength grew, he considered which items he would take from the ranger's lookout, and which items he would leave behind for someone if they returned. However, it seemed no one was coming back to that mountain.

From the Bible, he found the truth of a just God, wrathful against rebellion and sin, but gracious toward repentant sinners. Eric was forced each evening to look honestly at his own heart. The words in the Bible had awakened something inside him. The fear of the virus and his concern of being around other people remained, but it lessened in the face of God's apparent plan for all of humanity. Even him. Mankind had entered a path of destruction. God alone promised to show Himself as Victor. Jesus, God in the flesh, had proven Himself as that Victor, and man was meant to be His followers and ambassadors to bring Jesus glory. It began by faith, Eric read.

He didn't see how he could possibly obey much of how the Bible guided him to live, since he was isolated from other people. But there were steps he could take now, privately, between himself and God. Faith, for the first time in his life, came alive. And he believed.

#######

"The following announcement is a pre-recorded statement in coordination with the Public Broadcasting System, in case of emergency. State and federal authorities are asking all citizens to remain in their homes. Because of the current health risk, specialists are advising all citizens to refrain from contact with your neighbors. Do not share food. Do not shake hands. Do not touch.

"The virus seems to have a long incubation period. Eight to ten days after exposure, the symptoms begin to show. Fever is the primary symptom, followed by other extreme flu-like symptoms. Due to dehydration, dry patches or sores may appear on the skin, possibly erupting as boils that may make transmission more possible. If someone has a fever, then they are contagious by touch, though airborne particles haven't been ruled out. Tylenol may be taken to reduce the fever, but the infected will still be contagious.

"Hospitals are not trained or equipped for this emergency. Do not bring your symptomatic loved ones to a hospital or any public treatment facility. You'll only be endangering others. At this moment, a vaccine is being prepared for distribution.

"You are encouraged to use sanitation services sparingly. As you accumulate trash, do not place it in front of your home. The piling up of trash will hinder emergency personnel in the cleanup effort. It's advised that community volunteers coordinate neighborhood burn factories, to eliminate trash. Burn factories and related furnaces should have a chimney that extends a minimum of thirty feet above the ground or street level to disperse toxic particles safely.

"In the event of the death of family members or neighbors, a quick private burial is necessary, unless an immediate cremation is possible. If cremation is not feasible, a grave in the ground should be dug at least five feet deep. Do not wrap the body in any material so that it may decompose quickly. If you need assistance in urban centers with body disposal or contaminated waste removal, hang a black flag or large dark-colored cloth outside your front door. Sanitation volunteers are asked to proceed with caution, with bio-hazard suits whenever available.

"Water shortage requires careful rationing. Fill sealable containers only, and never drink dirty or discolored water. Boil any water you collect from a source outside of your tap water if your tap water ceases to work. During rain storms, place water containers outside to collect rain water, but only five minutes after the rain begins. The first few minutes of rain may be contaminated or toxic, depending on your locality to a neighborhood burn zone.

"Food shortage also requires careful rationing. In rural areas, garden produce grown under the soil is recommended and safe for consumption. In urban areas, roofs and windowsills may be utilized for gardening space. Potatoes, carrots, turnips, onions, and radishes are advised. Do not eat meat without cooking it well.

"In cold months, or for cooking purposes, you may require a private source of heat, especially if electrical power restoration is delayed. All burning restrictions have been lifted in all counties. However, it is advisable that you burn wood and wood products only inside your private residence. Wood that is painted should not be burned unless the paint is first removed. The interior framing of your house, inside the walls, may contain wood that you can burn safely. If you do not have a stove, a fire below a window is acceptable, but it is not advisable to light fires near or inside ventilation systems. When not cooking, the fire should be extinguished to preserve fuel and decrease possible fire hazard.

"As specialists and government agencies restore utilities and management, it is advisable that you find pastimes that do not require physical contact. Reading books aloud with a mask is acceptable in the vicinity of family members. Board and card games are discouraged, due to accidental virus transmission. Exercising indoors is encouraged.

"Due to the threat of accidental transmission and virus carrier potentials, all family pets should be put down and buried immediately. The limiting of animals within residences will extend the availability of water and food resources, as well as diminish the threat of disease transmission.

"Patience and understanding are necessary through this difficult time. Depending on access to your community, utilities and services should be restored within weeks rather than months. In the meantime, under all circumstances, do not make physical contact with anyone until the contagion is better identified and a vaccine can be implemented nationwide.

"The following announcement is a pre-recorded statement in coordination with the Public Broadcasting System, in case of emergency . . ."

Chapter 2

There was a rumor that the virus was gone. But Eric Radner hadn't stayed alive for the last five years by listening to rumors. His gut told him there was still danger in Adderthorn, Wyoming, whether the contagion had passed or not.

His boots crunched on twigs and wind-blown dirt that now covered the highway pavement. He came to a stop at the end of Main Street. No vehicle had rolled on that road for five years, not since the fuel had run out.

Looking at what was left of the town of five hundred, Eric prayed for safety. God had kept him conflict-free during every supply run so far, but trouble in those days was always near.

The wind gusted and a door flapped on its rusty hinges. Farther up the street, two men were leaning on the porch of Adderthorn Deluxe Hotel. They looked familiar to Eric from his last run, as did the semi-automatic sidearms holstered on their belts. Maybe they noticed his own weapons—a revolver on his hip and a bolt-action hunting rifle in his hands. The difference between their pistols was that the two men probably had bullets for theirs, and Eric's was purely for show. He only had cartridges for his .223 deer rifle, taken from the ranger station years earlier.

Walking to the opposite side of the street, he approached the General Store with his head down, but his eyes were darting. Two hound dogs chased a stray cat up the sidewalk. A child of about ten years old pedaled his bike up the middle of the street. Then, at the sight of Eric, he skidded to a stop. No doubt, everyone was trained to avoid strangers passing through. Strangers might be carrying the virus. The virus meant death, therefore, strangers meant death. The child turned his back and pedaled quickly away.

Eric pushed open the front door of the General Store, all the while eyeing the two men on the porch across the street. Their clothes showed wear, like his own jeans and flannel shirt, but their faces were clean-shaven while Eric had grown a beard.

"Eric Radner!" Gordon Irwin slapped his hand on the counter next to an open bow hunting magazine. It looked worn, probably from being read a hundred times. The man rubbed his bald head. "I was never a doubter, but I did wonder if you'd survived the winter."

"I was snowed in for a couple months." They didn't shake hands. No one shook hands anymore. Touching was too dangerous, since the virus was transmitted by bodily fluids, including sweat. "You take care of the list I left with you?"

"Sure! Right here." Gordon rummaged through a shoebox held together by duct tape. "Yep. I was never one to throw away a faithful customer's paperwork, even if I ain't seen you since last fall. Let's see here . . . Blanket? I got half of a woolly. Best I could do. Matches? Nope. Got flint, though. You want flint? The neighbor kids found a deposit last spring."

"Sure. Give me a bullet's worth," Eric said.

"Okay. Also got an axe head, one shovel handle . . ."

As the man compiled the shopping list items, Eric faced the rest of the store. The shelves were empty and dusty. All that Gordon owned remained behind his counter, and it wasn't too organized, as if he removed it every night for safekeeping and reassembled it every morning for trade. Since the collapse of America five years earlier, everyone lived by the barter system.

"You hear the latest?" Gordon pushed the merchandise toward his customer, but kept a hand on the supplies until he was paid. "Sheriff Leo shot four blacks walking into town three days ago. Infected, all of them."

"How were they walking if they were infected?" Eric swung off his backpack and unzipped a front pouch to count cartridges. "How much?"

"The tarp cost me, Eric. I've got to say twelve rounds for everything."

"How am I supposed to hunt deer if you take all my bullets, Gordon?" Eric shook his head, but his frustration was only feigned. Eric's stash of .223 bullets was about the only thing he had a decent quantity of at his cabin. "And when did you guys get a sheriff?"

"Around Christmas. Mastover's had some violence, and Cheyenne had a raid last month, a trader said."

"So, what about these four people your sheriff shot?" Eric loaded his supplies into his pack.

"He said they had bad skin, black skin, or something. Maybe patches of black? You know, the infected get those blotches on the skin."

"Didn't you say they were African-American?" Eric clenched his jaw. Wyoming had a history of prejudice. "Gordon, how'd four infected people walk all the way from the next town if they had Meridia Virus symptoms bad enough to show on their skin?"

"Well, I never thought about it like that." He picked at a stray hair on his ear. "The sheriff's right out there—Sheriff Leo Pickford. His brother Milton, too. You can ask them. They shot them. There's a fifth infected in the jail, still alive, they say."

Eric contemplated criticizing Gordon's attitude, but Adderthorn wasn't his town. The town would have to live with its own shame if they were killing innocent travelers passing through. His business in town was finished. If he started back now, he could reach his mountain cabin by dark. He'd survived this long by avoiding everyone. Since the first day, hiding had been the safest response to the chaos.

After leaving Gordon a list for his next visit, Eric exited the store and tightened the chest strap on his pack for a fast pace through the forest. Every time he ventured to the east side of the Sharrock Mountains, he chose a different route. There were no trails to his cabin, and he meant to keep it that way.

"Hey!" one of the two men from the hotel yelled at him. Now that Eric knew to look for it, he noticed a star on the shorter brother's breast pocket. "You been here before?"

The taller brother's hand was on the butt of his sidearm. Eric now knew that was Milton Pickford. His cheeks were pockmarked and he held a piece of wood between his teeth like a toothpick.

"I come in every few months for supplies. Gordon knows me." Eric kept his rifle muzzle aimed at the dirt. "I live alone and I don't touch people when I see them. I'm clean."

"You're that crazy guy that lives down Cheyenne way." Sheriff Leo Pickford wagged his finger. He had a smirk on his face, or maybe it was a scar beside his nose. "Yeah, they say you eat raw bear meat, still warm. No fire. Live like a caveman, too. You're a wild man, huh?"

"I may or may not have eaten raw meat before." Consistent with rumors Eric had started himself in the early years, he picked at his teeth as if his gums were diseased. "Can I borrow your toothpick?"

"You're insane!" Milton recoiled, clutching his piece of wood.

"He's playing with you, Milt!" Leo punched his brother's shoulder, then addressed Eric. "You live however you want up in those mountains. You bring business here, that's fine. But in this town, you follow the law, understand?"

"What's the law?" Eric wiped his finger on his jeans. The sheriff wasn't buying the act, even if it had kept some hunters from straying to the back side of the mountain.

"No stealing. No killing. No judge. No jury. Just a sheriff."

"You'll hear no arguments from me." Eric took a step toward the street.

"You leaving already?" Leo asked.

"This town's too civilized for me, Sheriff. I wouldn't want to corrupt it with my wild ways."

"Go on, then." Leo waved him on. "One more thing. No Bibles allowed in Adderthorn, either. We don't want what happened in Mastover to happen here."

"What happened in Mastover?"

"Some Bible-thumpers tried to reestablish order. The locals wouldn't stand for it. They'd had enough of that before Pan-Day. Rounded up the Christians and killed them all." Leo was speaking, but Milton felt it necessary to draw his thumb across his throat. "Yep, didn't even waste a bullet on them. Something like twenty men and women. Burned their Bibles, too. Then they went over to Hilltower and Weighmouth, and did the same. They don't want anyone getting any more of those crazy ideas from the past."

"Help me understand," Eric said, taking a chance that his question would betray that he was also a Christian. He was carrying a pocket Bible that very moment, bought from Gordon in the early years. "A mob killed a bunch of Christians and burned their Bibles, and you're siding with the mob?"

"We just don't want any problems, got it? As soon as we heard about what happened in Mastover, we sent word up there so they know we'll keep the peace between us by policing ourselves. It's simple—no Bibles in Adderthorn."

"I understand your position," Eric said, but he couldn't accept their logic. "So, did the four African-Americans have Bibles? Is that the real reason they were killed three days ago?"

"No, they were killed because they were infected and had blotches on their skin. We did them a favor."

"That's what Gordon said. But blotches only appear from dehydration the last few days of infection. Being that advanced, they couldn't have stood upright, let alone travel. The four of them—maybe they were just thirsty, parched. The skin can get dry-looking."

"I said they were infected!" Sheriff Leo's smirk grew. "What are you, a doctor? The fifth one's up in the jail dying right now. I'm no murderer. I know infected when I see it!"

Taking a deep breath, Eric looked up the street by which he yearned to retreat. His cabin was waiting for him. He had meat to smoke and a water system to perfect. The gear he'd come for was already in his pack. Adderthorn was the only town within a day's walk that could supply him occasionally. Burning bridges in the town wasn't only careless, it would be stupid.

"Show me." Eric could tell they sensed his challenge to their authority by their stiffened posture. "Show me the infected one. Hysteria killed more people than the virus did the first year. If we have the infected still roaming around, I want to see it for myself. Look at it this way: the sooner I see the infected, the sooner I leave. You don't want a mad man walking around your town any longer than you have to, right?"

Eric started walking towards the sheriff's building. They could've shot him in the back, and probably no one in Adderthorn would've raised an eyebrow. After all, he was the crazy man who lived off raw meat up in the mountains. But a moment later, they joined him on the sidewalk. Leo led him into his office.

"She's back here." He shoved a chair aside and they walked past three dusty desks and an empty gun case on their way to another open door. "I checked on her last night. She was still alive."

"It's a woman?"

They entered a corridor with three holding cells that faced a cinder block wall. The sheriff stopped at the third cell. The steel door had a narrow window.

Cautiously, Eric peered through the pane. Sunlight from a high window on the outer wall illuminated a motionless heap of something on the slab of cement that accounted for a bunk. Unsure of what he'd discover, Eric knocked on the door. The body inside stirred. A dark face looked up at him from under what seemed to be a winter coat.

"Can you hear me?" Eric called. She didn't respond. "Stand up. Let me see you. Are you infected?"

She rolled off the bunk and drew her coat around her. When she stood, he saw she was barely five feet tall. Was this a child? As she shuffled toward the door, he prepared himself for the worst. Five years earlier, he'd driven into the mountains to hide the first day multiple cities went on quarantine, so he'd never actually seen an infected person. He may have been the only person in America not to have seen one.

Leo and Milton drew back as her face stopped a breath away from the glass. Eric wasn't all that tall himself, so he didn't need to crouch much to look into her eyes, to examine the skin of her face. Her skin was clear.

The woman wasn't infected. Eric had to consider at that moment how he would respond. He wasn't alive because he'd been courageous during the pandemic. Instead, he'd run and hid, abandoning everyone he knew in another state to lay low in Wyoming. Now, he could be safe and walk away, or be bold and risk his own life at the hands of the irrational law enforcement. His conscience won out, and he drew his empty revolver as he turned toward the two men.

"I may or may not shoot the two of you right now." Eric stepped away from the door. "All that depends on how quickly you open this cell door."

Before they rallied the nerve to fight back, he jerked their sidearms from their holsters. Disarmed, Leo conceded and unlocked the woman's cell door.

"It's your death, Mad Man."

"I'd rather be a mad man than a murderer. I bet if we examined this woman's travel companions, we wouldn't find the virus on them, either. She's not infected; she's just old!"

Leo opened the door and leaped back as the woman walked out, clutching her coat and a homemade pack complete with shoulder straps. She appeared to be about eighty or more. No doubt, she'd stayed alive for three days in the cell by rationing whatever she'd had in her pack.

"Drop your keys on the floor, Leo. Both of you—into the cell. Now!"

But neither of them moved.

"No way," Milton said around his toothpick, shaking his pockmarked head. "I'm not dying of the Meridia Virus in there!"

It took thirty seconds more for Eric to open the next cell and force the two men inside.

"I'll tell Gordon to unlock you later," Eric said to Leo through the cell door window. The sheriff's smirk had turned into a snarl. Eric set their guns on the corridor floor with the keys. "Killing healthy, innocent travelers coming through town? That's what you should really be concerned about, Leo. If Mastover's travelers keep coming up dead by your hand, that mob will come for you next."

Eric holstered his empty revolver and took the old lady by the arm to lead her into the office area. Her legs faltered and he caught her to set her on a dusty chair.

"How're you doing?" He knelt in front of the woman, his hand clutching hers. It was the first human contact he'd had in years. "You gonna make it?"

"I'm a little weak." Her voice was scratchy and she had no teeth. "Hearing you talk to them, I guess you already know what those two did to my family."

"I do, and I think they know it, too. They did it because they were scared and now they feel they have to cover it up." Reaching into his shirt pocket, Eric produced a piece of meat that looked like a gnarled stick. "Start on that. It's smoked deer." She immediately began to gum the stick. "Well, you can't stay in town. Everyone's convinced you're infected."

"I'm not infected. I know the rules. Last year, we left Seattle since there was a fresh outbreak. We wintered in Cody, and we've been on the road for three weeks, until here."

"Where were you headed?"

"Somewhere south. Anywhere."

"I see." Looking away, Eric sought God's guidance. He hadn't been a praying man for long, but God had impressed upon him a million little things over the past few years in his solitude. Why couldn't he expect God's guidance on something this big? "I'm not too interested in traveling farther south, and no offense, but you're in no condition to travel alone. I live in a cabin surrounded by trees up in the mountains. Once you get your strength back, we can go down to the highway and find safe travelers who can take you on your—"

"The cabin sounds fine. I was tired of the road, anyway. By the way, my name is Talia Wiseman."

"Well then, Talia Wiseman, the cabin it is. I'm Eric Radner." He rose to his feet, willing to accept in confidence what he'd just left in God's hands—even if it meant he'd have a new roommate. "But it's still about a ten-mile hike, and after what I just did to those two fellas, we need to cover some bad terrain fast."

"I'll do my best."

"Well, your best is going to be on my back." He unfastened his pack. "What're you, eighty pounds?"

"I don't know." She chuckled. "What do you have in mind?"

He hadn't heard anyone laugh in years, but it was a good sound. With her help, he fastened his thirty-pound pack to his front, then she climbed onto his back to ride piggy-back style. Behind his ear, she sucked on her meat stick. It was meant to be his dinner, but she needed it more than he did.

Eric entered the woods behind the General Store and angled east into the dense forest. Either Talia wasn't much of a talker, or she sensed the seriousness of the moment to let him march without conversing. After two miles, Talia relaxed, so Eric bowed his back and adjusted her weight to prevent the sleeping woman from slipping off.

When all alone in the mountains, he'd thought being a Christian was harmless enough, but he could see that learning to think and care for others like God cared had made him an enemy of Adderthorn. And now there was the massacre in Mastover to think about. Christians had been killed and Bibles had been burned. It was another type of virus that had begun to spread, and he wasn't sure how much longer until the contagion would reach his peaceful cabin in the woods.

With the added weight, it was dark when he finally approached the last ridge before reaching his cabin. First, he had to pass over a deep gorge by sidestepping on the tree-bridge he'd fallen across the expanse two years earlier. Cresting the final ridge, he paused and looked back down the mountain. He sensed something or someone was back there, moving in the forest. Mountain lions had stalked him while hunting in the past, but usually they were silent predators. This was something different—a human. Someone from Adderthorn must've tracked him up the mountain.

With his passenger, and in the dark of night, Eric's options to respond to this new threat were limited. He reached his cabin and fixed up his bunk for Talia. For himself, he laid out a blanket on the floor, but he didn't go to sleep. Instead, he walked out into the night and listened to the mountain that had become his home. In his old life—the ignorant and modernized man who'd first come to the wilderness—it all seemed like someone else's life now. His friends and business associates, his neighbors, and even a couple of loose girlfriends—none of them had cared enough to tell him the truth about his lost soul. No, God had driven him up to those mountains to teach him and to help him grow.

And now, it seemed God was drawing him back to humanity, but Eric wasn't certain he wanted what humanity had to offer. This was his mountain and his forest. He'd saved an old woman from dying in a jail cell, but what would that mercy cost him?

As he prayed that question to the night sky, the sky was silent, but he'd been reading the Bible for enough years now. He knew the truth—showing mercy always came with a price.

Chapter 3

The following morning, Eric knelt at the edge of the deep gorge in the Sharrock Forest. In forgotten years past, the Rocky Mountains had shaken and split open the chasm many miles long below the eastern ridge of the mountain. The aftereffect was a forty-foot-deep natural barrier between his cabin and the town of Adderthorn. The steep walls, averaging seventy feet across, squeezed upon a creek, causing it to boil with the ferocity of a river.

It wasn't the water or the gorge that troubled Eric now. What concerned him was that someone had cut and pushed his tree-bridge into the gorge. Far below, the bridge lay splintered against boulders. The water cascaded over it with fury. He'd kept spiked boots in the bushes on the cabin side just for crossing the slippery log. As far as he knew, no one had been that close to his cabin as long as he'd lived there. But someone from the town side had evidently found the bridge overnight. Because of his boldness in the town the day before, and his aiding the escape of a suspected Meridia Virus carrier, it seemed Adderthorn now meant to permanently cut him off from them. The Pickford brothers were certain to be behind it, but there were surely other woodsmen and hunters in Adderthorn as well, maybe experienced trackers who could find him if they wanted to.

Since his provisions were adequate for the time being, Eric wasn't complaining about being cut off from town— at least cut off from the shortest way to town. He could always hike down to the highway or climb farther into the Sharrock Mountains to circumvent the gorge, but both routes would require a full day's journey. If they really wanted him gone, they could burn the forest down, since all he had to do was fall another tree across the gorge to make an easy route for himself again. But apparently, he wasn't welcome in Adderthorn any longer, so he didn't have any intentions of being unpleasant toward them.

One thing for sure, he thought as he marched back toward the cabin, God was shaking his protected world from under him. Most significantly, he had another soul to care for now, an elderly black woman who was so feared by the locals of Adderthorn, they'd left her in a cell to die. And his more distant concerns were the stirrings in Mastover to the northwest, thirty miles away. If Mastover's massacre of Christians was true, the country was still on the decline, regardless of whispers in the east and west of infant governments being established. Of course, Eric guessed Wyoming had always found its own way of doing things, no matter the country's currents.

Reaching his cabin, he leaned his rifle against a stump and took up a telescope meant for observing the stars. Instead, he crouched and trained the scope down the ridge to the southeast. A column of smoke had been rising at the edge of the plain, which he'd noticed on his return from Adderthorn the day before. Now, it was a dwindling wisp, barely noticeable. Tree tops hindered his view of the smoke's immediate source, but he still hoped to spot some sign of the source or perpetrators—or spot anyone approaching the mountain heights before they could surprise him. The chances of someone climbing a rugged mountain covered in thick brush was remote, but he hadn't thought anyone would track him to the gorge, either.

At least from the east, no one could approach by bicycle, or by vehicle, even if they had fuel. Eric had fallen trees across the old logging road years earlier to discourage visitors. His own car, driven from his Nebraska home, was hidden in a ditch far below, abandoned and rusted, the plates removed.

"What do you see?"

Talia Wiseman's scratchy voice interrupted his focus. She crouched next to him, the wool blanket he'd purchased the day before draped over her shoulders.

"Somebody was burning something." Eric kept the glass to his eye. "It's a little unnerving. We might start wood fires nowadays to stay warm, but burning something to make that much smoke—it probably means renegades. Common people, survivors, don't burn things like that anymore. We refurbish, reuse, and rebuild."

"I don't see anything." She squinted her ancient eyes, so he passed her the telescope. "Where do I look?"

"There's an alley cleared of trees down that direction so I could keep an eye on a small section of the highway, about seven miles away."

Still seeing nothing, she passed the scope back to him. If there were something farther out on the plain rather than against the mountain and trees, she probably would've been able to easily see it.

"Thank you for allowing me to sleep in your bed." Her presence was comforting as they stared at the forest together, where birds fought with squirrels over seeds. "If you show me the tools, I'll build myself a bed frame. You can't sleep on the floor every night."

"I don't mind." He glanced at her. "You might like to know our friends from Adderthorn may not know exactly where we are, but they cut off our most direct route to town. They destroyed a log we crossed last night."

"That was fast."

"Probably Sheriff Leo and his brother." Eric disassembled the scope and stowed it in a black case. "I've tried to keep routes to the cabin closed to others, though accessible to me, of course. I'm not worried now that Adderthorn cut us off. It means they'll stay away. But I need to look into that smoke. There are some homesteads down there."

"You know them?"

"No, but travelers on the highway have stopped there to camp off and on for a few years. There's been a chance that someone would climb the mountain to see what lies up here."

"So, you've never made contact with anyone down there, your closest neighbors?" She clucked her tongue. "You should know your neighbors, Mr. Radner."

He grunted but didn't respond further. After the way she'd been treated by strangers, was she still open to contact with others?

Inside the cabin, she watched as Eric shouldered his pack that he'd repacked with essentials for an extended hike. He also attached the empty revolver to his belt. It was clumsy against his hip, but he felt that just the appearance of it might discourage aggression, if someone felt ornery towards him.

"What about breakfast?" she asked. "You shouldn't travel without eating something."

Eric picked up a tin cup and swished black liquid that was still warm from heating before she'd awoken.

"The jars there—coffee from chicory in that one, chufa there, and dandelion or pine needle tea there. Sorry, ran out of sweetener. There's lotus biscuits and oak bread. No yeast, so it's flat. More smoked meat in this jar—same as you had last night, but it'll soften more if you boil it. There's salted meat in the cupboard, but we'll save that for dinner tonight. I should be back mid-afternoon. Oh, and the hammer and nails are behind the bed. Some boards in the shed out back. Why are you smiling?"

"You've been alone up here a long time, Mr. Radner. I think you've forgotten how to talk to people."

"Did I say something wrong?" He touched his jaw, wondering if he should trim his overgrown beard to be a little more presentable as well. "You weren't exactly expected."

"I'll busy myself." She dismissed him with a wave and turned toward the coffee and tea in glass jars. "We'll talk when you get back."

For another moment, he watched her pick out green pine needles from a jar and pour steaming water from the kettle on the stove. Though she'd been there only a few hours, she seemed at home already. In those days, adaptation was key to survival, and to reach her age, Talia Wiseman must've adjusted to a lot of scenarios through the years.

Outside, Eric slung his rifle over his shoulder and descended the ridge to the east. Most of the way, he zigzagged to throw off anyone intent on backtracking his sign to the cabin. An hour later, he reached level ground.

Since the logging road to the highway was dirt, he didn't walk on it. His footprints would've been too obvious. But he eased up to the log-strewn road to examine the soft ground, now overgrown with weeds. He found only deer and wild turkey tracks since the last rain.

The thought of turkey meat made his mouth water, and he gazed in the direction of the recent tracks. Most of his days were spent hunting and gathering, so his mind naturally went to the prospect of catching turkeys, even though he'd intended to investigate the smoke this day. He preferred to trap turkeys rather than shoot them. His turkey coop had been emptied over the harsh winter, but he'd already begun to put out juniper berries on the ground to bait the birds closer to the cabin. Turkey eggs had been a good supplement to his diet, but he'd opted to eat the birds outright during the cold months rather than starve on mere egg rations. It was only spring, but in his mind, it was never too early to make preparations for the next winter. This was especially important now with another mouth to feed.

Remaining in the trees, he decided to hunt turkeys another day. He continued alongside the logging road, creeping toward the highway. He hadn't been to the edge of the forest for months. Though he'd fashioned snowshoes to use atop the several feet of snow the mountain received each winter, snowshoe tracks were a sure way to attract attention, so he'd remained in the higher elevations, venturing out only for wood or to hunt deer during breaks in the weather.

Leaving the logging road, Eric followed the highway south to where a little smoke was still visible. He eyed the highway cautiously, not comfortable with the prospect of meeting travelers moving up or down the road. In the early years, travelers had been a source of news and even a few supplies for him. Now, he believed his survival depended on total secrecy.

From a rocky outcropping protruding toward the highway, he hesitantly peered through the bushes to spy on a smoking homestead—or what was left of a homestead. At one time, it had been a gas station with a couple of buildings. Farther to the east and across the highway, was a ranch-style home, though he saw no sign of life over there.

It was possible a careless traveler had accidentally burned down the house, but that was unlikely. Eric felt this was an intentional fire, and his renegade theory seemed the likeliest idea. He hadn't known there were inhabited buildings on this side of the mountain, or he would've relied on them for supplies rather than the more populated town of Adderthorn. Normally, people chose the safety of numbers against roaming thieves and killers. Three years earlier, he'd foraged here, collecting loose boards and old nails left behind by the previous owners.

After watching the smoldering structure for thirty minutes, he finally emerged from his cover. The place was abandoned, or the owners had been killed, so he considered it fair game for him. Tools and materials were his priorities, even solar panels, batteries and wires, if he could find them, for a project he'd hidden above the cabin.

He circled the ashes once before stepping into the soot to search for metal. Even his untrained eye could see at least three spots where the fire had originated. Glass bottles suggested Molotov cocktails. What kind of people had firebombed peaceful homesteaders? His eyes narrowed as he checked the highway. There was a chance that others would be drawn to the smoke, too, or the bandits could return to their crime.

Under a collapsed roof timber, he found a blackened body pinned in the ashes, which were still hot to the touch. From the size of the body, he guessed it was a man, with a gun in a charred leather gun belt on his waist. But in those days, women were just as likely to be armed as men, especially in remote Wyoming.

"Who are you?"

It was a woman's voice, harsh and bold, coming from behind him. Guessing her voice was backed by a firearm, Eric raised his hands. With his mind on the highway, she'd approached from somewhere else and gotten the drop on him.

"My name is Eric Radner. I'm just passing through. Saw the smoke and turned off to check it out."

"Liar. You came from the trees. Let me see you. Slowly!"

He turned toward her, holding his hands wide. The sun was behind him, so he could see her better than she could see him, twenty feet away. The shotgun she held would cut him in two if she fired. She looked to be about thirty-five, and below curly brown hair, a streak of dried blood ran from her brow down the side of her small nose.

"Where are you from, Eric Radner?" Her shotgun barrel didn't waiver. "Your pack is light. Your boots have been patched. Talk!"

The question caught him unprepared. The only people he'd ever crossed since the pandemic were in Adderthorn or on the highway, and they'd always known he came from somewhere in the mountains.

"Originally, I'm from Lincoln. I got caught in Wyoming when the outbreak struck. I just stayed here."

"Stayed? Where?"

"There." He pointed vaguely with the pinky of his left hand. "Up there."

"You're the crazy mountain guy?" She frowned. "You got infected, didn't you, but lived?"

Eric glanced around. There was no cover to dive behind, which would've been preferable to telling her all his secrets. But she was no fool, having noticed his patched boots and light pack already. She knew he was a scavenger from nearby.

"Those were just rumors I started about myself during the first year. I'd join travelers for a mile or two on the highway, to trade with and warn them to stay out of the woods since there was a mad man up there."

"So those people would go to the next town and pass on your myth? I get it. Clever." She lowered the shotgun. "You're standing on my husband."

He leapt aside and almost fell in the ashes. Daring her diverted barrel, he stepped out of the burnt remains to her side of the house.

"Sorry." He remembered what Talia had said about his conversation skills, and tried to think of the appropriate thing to say. "Did you see who did it?"

"Some maniacs on mountain bikes. I guess they're the new road warriors, huh? They wanted our tools." She bowed her head. "I guess Brad should've listened to them, but they looked like they wanted me as well."

Eric nodded. Tools were more valuable than gold since equipment was always breaking down. And she was a beautiful woman. With men who had no scruples to steal valuable tools, it was a small step further to assault a woman.

"Well, if you can point me to a shovel, I can help you bury him."

She looked at him for a moment, then seemed to resign from shooting him as she cradled the shotgun in her arms.

"Just you saying that, I guess it means you're all right. But no, that beam on him weighs probably three hundred pounds. And he's already burnt to a crisp. We couldn't even move him without him falling apart. There's no sense."

A few years earlier, such words would've sounded cold, Eric thought, but these were hard times, and toughened people had to make hard, rational choices.

She walked through the ash as Eric gazed at his mountain. Even after sawing down trees and thinning his yard for more sunshine, the cabin was still hidden.

The woman sifted through ash for anything metal that hadn't burned up. She found cutlery, the wooden handles burnt, and a screwdriver with a melted handle. At the corner of the house, she kicked at a metal box to free it from debris, then dragged it aside.

"Could this be the last thing I own in the world?" She stood over the metal box, her hands on her hips. "I guess it's only right that I inherit the tools Brad died for."

She lifted the lid and Eric moved closer to gaze inside. He'd learned to be content with much or with little, as the Bible said, but that day, he coveted those tools. They were probably car garage tools originally, but a saw and hammer had been added to the weathered collection. Inside the metal box, they'd been preserved from the flames and much heat.

"Uh, no offense," he said, "but I'm not real comfortable about being this close to the highway. And I'm even less comfortable about leaving you here alone. Can I walk you to Rosenkern? It's not far to the south, I think."

She stared at the ashes as if she hadn't heard him.

"What were you before Pan-Day?" she asked.

From the radio, Eric knew Pan-Day was when the nation had reached a tipping point with so many cities quarantined from the pandemic, causing the banks to close, and civil panic to reach its peak.

"I was a blogger. Wasn't much good at anything else." The thought made him smile. "People paid me to review things, then I'd blog about it. I reviewed merchandise and tourist sights. Had a decent following, so the money was good. I was on my way to Jackson to visit and review a new resort. But I pulled off here."

"Brad was in real estate. I didn't know him before Pan-Day, but afterward, he was always talking about turning this place into a new community, based on trade and human kindness. I guess his dream was five years too late, huh?"

"I don't know." Eric sighed. "Five years ago, the country wasn't any better on human kindness. Your husband was just hoping for something better, I guess. So, anyway, Rosenkern is probably less than ten miles away. Or maybe you know other homesteaders nearby?"

"No. There's no one between here and Gaultridge to the south. Rosenkern burned four years ago. No one lives there now."

"Okay, then Adderthorn is—"

"No, I'd rather die than return to Adderthorn."

"Gaultridge is farther away than Adderthorn," Eric said.

"Those bikers went south." She shook her curls. "I'm not going south."

Eric rolled his eyes to the heavens. What was God doing?

"I'm sorry, but neither one of us is prepared to spend the night out here. Wherever you're going, you need to get started."

"Do you believe in God?" She looked far out at the plain. "I used to think I was chosen. Chosen to survive the virus. Chosen to marry a man like Brad. Chosen to have Andy."

"Andy?" Eric cringed at the ashes. Was there another body, maybe a child he hadn't noticed?

"I was hiding in the woods all night, thinking I was cursed instead. If there is a God, He must hate me. I don't even have another set of clothes. I actually begged God for help. I've never done that, but all I got was silence all night."

"I don't think you're cursed. My experiences aren't that—"

"And now you're here." She turned toward Eric. "I prayed for help, and you showed up. If I let you have the tools, will you take us with you—up there?"

"The tools?" He shook his head. "No, I don't need tools that badly. I'm not set up for more people."

"You have others? Who lives with you?"

"Look, I'm not alone, all right? I have enough mouths to—"

"You have a woman?"

"Actually, yes. Her name is Talia. There's just no room for—"

"We won't be a bother. Andy's good about chores. I can chop wood or whatever." She closed the lid on the tool box. "You want me to carry your pack so you can carry the tools?"

"No, listen!" He held up his hand. This was moving way too fast. "My place is in no condition to host a— Who's Andy?"

"My son." She put her fingers to her mouth and blew a shrill whistle, then waved at the tree line. "He can carry your rifle."

Numbly, Eric gazed at the edge of the clearing. A blond head emerged from the trees, then a golden retriever next to him. Together, they ran toward the woman.

"I just might have a heart attack right now," Eric said.

"You'll hardly notice us." She shaded her eyes with her hand and gazed up at the mountain. "That's just the kind of safe place we need right now. There's still too much violence around."

The boy named Andy, no older than five, skidded to a halt in front of his mother. He brushed shaggy hair from his eyes as the retriever ignored Eric to sniff the edges of the ashes.

"I have a one-room cabin. Seriously, this isn't going to work. I'm taking you both to Adderthorn."

"They won't take us in." She raised her chin. "They threw us out already, on account of Brad. He fought with one of the leaders. We were out here alone. Your cabin will be fine. We'll build another one for me and Andy. You and your wife can live in your own cabin."

"Talia isn't my—" Eric took a deep breath. Arguing with this woman wasn't working, especially not with the shotgun still in her hands. "Hello, Andy. My name's Eric."

"He'll call you Mr. Radner." His mother nudged him. "Shake his hand, Andy."

The youngster stepped up and thrust out a small, rigid hand. He was thin but appeared healthy.

"You ever carry a rifle, Andy?" Eric asked as he swung it off his shoulder.

"Keep the barrel out of the dirt," Andy recited, "and don't knock the scope on any branches."

"Told you." The woman smirked at Eric. "Now, give me your pack."

"I hope I don't regret this."

She took his pack and Eric stooped to pick up the tool case.

"Just think of it as a business deal," she said, "and the tools are payment for our rent."

"At least Talia will have someone else to fuss over." Eric groaned under the weight of the tools on his shoulder, easily forty pounds. "Step where I step, and try not to leave footprints anywhere. And I should probably know your name."

"Joyce. Joyce Adkins. I guess I'll be keeping my husband's name."

"And that's Runner." Andy carried the rifle over one shoulder like a little soldier, and pointed at the retriever charging the clearing in front of them.

Joyce fit the pack on her back, the straps a bit loose, and gripped her shotgun in her hands. By her stern look, she was a survivor, but the mountain had a way of testing a person's mettle.

"How many shells do you have for that thing?" Eric gestured at her shotgun. "There's a meadow I know that has some quail."

"I guess I just ran out of the house when Brad told us to run. It's not even loaded."

Chapter 4

The next morning, Eric was a bystander as Talia gave Joyce Adkins a tour of the inside and outside of the cabin. Although Talia had arrived only a day before Joyce and Andy, in Eric's absence down the mountain, the older woman had explored what had been his habitat for five years.

"The best I can figure," Talia said, pointing at rows of sprouting plants on the east side of the cabin, where the sun could hit most of the day, "this is his garden. But nothing's labeled, so we either have to ask him what's what, or use a book in the cabin that has pictures of each plant. Some are vegetables. Some are for tea or vitamins or medicine. Wild onion there, and we know that's garlic. The growing season just started, so we have time to learn."

Talia led Joyce to the west side of the cabin where the water tank overflowed into a stream Eric had channeled to the south. Fifty yards away, he'd carved a wide bowl out of the mountain slope for a pond where he bathed. The deer and elk also watered there.

"I'm guessing," Talia said, "there's a spring farther up the mountain somewhere. These logs have been split down the middle, hollowed out, then put back together to make pipes. They carry the water here. This outside tank drains into the hot water tank. I have no idea how he keeps all this from freezing during the winter, though. Now, the cabin addition we'll need to build will go here, on the north side next to the shed . . ."

Andy ran past them and stopped at the stream with Runner to drink from the clear water. Talia may have described the mechanics of Eric's home in a few minutes, but it had taken years to engineer—and he was still improving it. Adding onto the cabin would require more adjustments, all to provide additional sleeping space for his house guests, who were quickly becoming the chief proprietors of his estate.

By God's hand, Eric's concern at having company was being replaced with a warmth for the new residents. He'd read in the Bible that only a fool isolates himself, so, he'd been a fool for some time, living in fear of discovery, exposure, and of contracting the virus. As long as their mark in the woods didn't extend beyond the ridge, he guessed they'd remain hidden and safe.

"So, Mr. Radner," Talia called to him, "are you going to show us the source of all this water or is that a secret?"

He did have his secrets, but the water source wasn't one of them.

"It's a short hike." He picked up his rifle and handed it to Joyce, then nodded at Talia. "Shall I assume my role as mule?"

"My hips aren't what they used to be." She frowned, then climbed onto his back. "It's this uneven ground. By the way, how often do you relocate the outhouse?"

"We'll have to make it every three months now." He eyed the hastily-built single board wall he'd erected with women now on the property. "I'll build four walls on that thing tomorrow."

"By tonight," she said.

"Yes, ma'am."

Andy had acquired a stout club that he used to whack on tree trunks as he and Runner scouted ahead. They set off to the west, following the wooden aqueduct into the trees. It didn't take them long to realize they were moving downhill, not uphill.

"You push water uphill, against gravity?" Joyce looked back at the cabin to study the angle. "How does that work?"

"Water pressure." Eric paused to tighten a leather bind around a leaky wooden pipe. "From the spring, the water runs down into a large hollow log. Then it's connected to successively smaller pipes, which pushes a steady stream into the tank outside the cabin. It doesn't take much since it runs all the time."

"How do you keep it from freezing in the winter?" Talia asked in his ear, her arms clasped under his chin.

"I don't. I detach the log from the spring and let the whole thing drain out after the first freeze. For water during the winter, we'll rely on melted snow, which isn't a problem. We get about ten feet at this elevation."

"Ten feet!" Andy reached skyward with his stick, trying to gauge such a height. "How will we live?"

"Lots of cabin time with only short trips outside."

"What'll we do all winter?" Andy asked.

"School work." Joyce nodded at Eric. "Mr. Radner has a pile of notebooks just waiting to be filled with grammar and math lessons."

"We'll design our own curriculum," Talia said. "You'll be the smartest boy in Wyoming after a couple winters with us!"

"Poor kid," Eric mumbled, drawing a critical glance from Joyce, but he privately wondered how he would endure such a winter with two women fussing over him and Andy. Perhaps more hunting excursions were in order to make himself scarce.

They reached the spring, a bubbling emergence straight out of the hillside, tapped into by a thirty-inch log, anchored by stakes and leather thongs. Some water still spilled out of the end of the log to cascade down a natural streambed to the south.

"I'll put a roof and walls over all this," Eric said, "since pine needles fall into the water and collect in the pipes. I have a rough screen of wires to catch debris, but it's been getting clogged too often."

"Hey, what's this?" Andy called from above them. Eric hadn't realized he'd strayed toward the mountain summit.

"What's up there, Mr. Radner?" Talia asked as she urged him by a kick of her heels on his thighs. Joyce was already climbing to the summit of the mountain. "You have more mysteries besides water that runs uphill?"

Reluctantly, he followed Joyce, not willing to admit to anyone that he'd intended to keep the matter a secret.

A panoramic view opened before them of the whole world, it seemed. The highest point of the mountain afforded them a look down at most of Adderthorn, and to the east, there was farm and range land as far as the eye could see.

No one spoke for a few moments as they took in the sight. Not far up the Sharrock Range, a taller mountain, over ten thousand feet, slightly obscured their view of the west. If he would've used his telescope, Eric could've viewed the ranger station on the taller mountain, where his life had been saved.

"It's beautiful." Joyce panted in the thinner air and fell to her knees. "We're above the world. Brad would've loved this. He talked about climbing this mountain someday, but he just hunted the lower forest. He would've found you, Mr. Radner."

"The question is," Talia said, "what is this?"

There was a manmade box the size of a washing machine, which sat on the immediate sheltered side of the peak, protected from the worst winds.

"It's the reason I don't get more hunting done and projects finished." Eric set Talia on her own legs, and knelt with Andy to remove the box by lifting the cover completely off to expose a radio beneath. "Sit on this box, Talia. This wasn't part of the tour, but now that we're here . . ."

From the console, Eric picked up a handheld windmill and unfolded its three wings to lock them into place. It started to spin in the wind, and the twelve-inch wings became a blur.

"Andy, this job is for you." He gave him the windmill. "Keep it aimed into the wind."

The windmill wires ran back to the generator on which the radio sat. Eric handed Joyce a telescoping antenna that he usually shoved into a crack in the rock, but her height would give them better reception.

Eric saw wonder on their faces. Contact with the outside world was rare those days, except for occasional traders who came through town, but their word was only barely reliable.

"Don't get too excited." He sat cross-legged and touched the frequency dial. "Most days, I don't hear anything but old recordings."

"But you hear talking on some days?" Joyce shook her head. "Where did you get this?"

"There was a Forest Service lookout tower to the west. It had been abandoned for a while. Listen . . ."

When he unplugged a headset, static crackled from its hand-sized speaker, and he turned up the volume since they were pulling decent power from Andy. Eric figured the days he'd spent crouched and shivering on the mountaintop with the radio was comparable to a geek on his laptop before Pan-Day.

Turning the frequency dial, Eric first checked frequencies he knew by memory where he'd previously heard chatter.

"Where's your mic?" Joyce asked.

"No, we should never transmit!" He frowned. "They could track our transmission and find us."

"Who?" Talia jabbed a crooked finger into his shoulder. "There's people out there with technology? What aren't you telling us?"

The static broke with a man's voice, indiscernible at first.

"Hold real still, Joyce," Eric said, touching other dials to filter out the white noise. "There should be someone right . . . there . . ."

The voices were chaotic, sometimes overlapping, sometimes in succession. They could only catch pieces.

"They're falling back!" one voice announced.

"Someone take care of that fifty on the east flank!" another ordered.

"This is Vasquez. I've got too many casualties. I'm pulling out! Commander Morris, I've got to pull out!"

"Unit Two, push through the center. Break them! Break them!"

Eric turned the volume down as vulgarity, screams, and explosions intensified. His amazing secret had brought an awful truth to the ears of his small clan. Joyce slowly lowered the antenna.

"Andy, honey, you can give the windmill back to Mr. Radner." Without another look at Eric, she turned and walked down the mountain. "Come on, Andy."

Perhaps Andy didn't understand what he'd heard, but he understood enough to know not to question his mother right then. He gave Eric the windmill and ran after Joyce.

Holding the antenna and windmill in his lap, Eric looked at Talia, who clutched her winter coat against the brisk wind.

"Her husband believed the nation was being restored, and the improvements would soon reach here, where they could raise Andy in peace and quiet." The old woman frowned, her lower lip touching her small nose since she had no teeth. "That was a military unit attacking someone, wasn't it?"

"Yeah." Eric gazed to the east. "I've heard them off and on for months. They're pushing west mostly, taking towns and strongholds as they advance."

"Who are they?"

"From what I can tell from their communications, they're remnants of the US military. I haven't heard of any real authority behind them. They're after fuel depots and ammo, I think. There's talk about freedom, but they just keep killing. The whole Mississippi Valley is vulnerable. They're cleaning out everyone who resists, more or less enslaving others to join them for the spoils. The east and west coasts may be banding together, but everything in between, like us—it's every town for itself."

"How far away are they?"

"Last month, they were in Kansas City, probably draining the last fuel the people had there. Without fuel, their advance stalls, until they find more gas for their vehicles. I don't know how many vehicles they have, though."

Talia stood and Eric placed the protective box back over the radio. As he carried her down the slope, she cleared her throat.

"They could be taking Lincoln or Omaha," she said. "Or even Denver or Colorado Springs. Could they come through Wyoming?"

"If they hear Mastover still has resources, it's probable they'll come this far. I'm not the only one with a radio, though. When some are foolish enough to transmit, then they can be found. Great Falls has an Air Force base, so this army might come through Wyoming just to access Montana. But we'll be safe up on this mountain."

They didn't speak for the rest of the walk back to the cabin. Perhaps they were both trying to believe what he'd said about being safe.

#######

The next few days, they were each consumed with hard work. Talia was willing, but she was confined to her failing body. She was tasked with food preparation, which initially consisted of learning the young plants in the garden. She referred to the survival book Eric had found in the Forest Service station, but she confirmed each plant with him when he was near the cabin as he dragged tree lengths into the yard. The extra logs were for the cabin addition they needed.

Andy was earning his blisters on a peeler as he straddled each log Eric dropped into the yard. Joyce was up the ridge with the saw, cutting thirty-foot fallen trees into manageable lengths to build with. For several days, he didn't know whether to attribute her silence to her late-night tailoring to make herself and Andy buckskin clothing, or to what she'd heard on the radio. It was one thing to survive the virus, but then there was the attack that had killed her husband. Perhaps the idea of a renegade army plowing through the country was too much for her mind.

"I've seen you these last few days, you know," Joyce said to Eric two weeks after the radio incident. Midday, they knelt at the spring to drink water and gnaw on smoked deer meat. Her hair was tied back in a ponytail, but some wisps hung in her face. Eric was reminded of how long he'd been alone on the mountain. "I've seen you go into the woods, and when you think no one is watching, you read."

He touched his breast pocket where he kept a small New Testament, purchased from Adderthorn in the early years. In the cabin, there was a dictionary, three large Bibles, an atlas, and a few encyclopedias and novels.

"This isn't the first time a powerful nation has collapsed," Eric said. "The Bible has hope for these times. I could probably survive without God, but He gives me a promise that there's more after this. I've lived in fear of discovery up here, but I stay sane, or mostly sane, by feeding my soul."

"That's what you're doing?" She eyed him suspiciously. "Feeding your soul?"

"My life before Pan-Day was all about living a vacation. The closest I ever came to camping was buying a Patagonia coat and standing around a bonfire after a hockey game in Minnesota. Otherwise, it's been gluttony and hedonism. Samuel Hubbard sneakers and touch screens. All that stuff now—gone. Life is about more than what we had back then, and about more than what we see around us here—the stuff that passes away. The Bible has reordered my life and my dead heart, and helped me set new priorities. I'm a new person in here." He touched his chest.

"You think the Bible can help me?" She looked away, ringing water from her hands. "God let our world fall apart. How's He supposed to help me make sense of that?"

"I don't know how. He just does." He picked up his axe. "I actually didn't know you needed help. You seem so independent."

"You have a lot to learn about women, Mr. Radner."

That night, she took one of the Bibles off the shelf and started reading. As Eric made candlewicks using animal fat and thistle twine, Talia and Andy went to bed. Talia slept in a small bed she'd made for herself, and for now, Andy slept in the larger bed with his mother. Eric had been sleeping on the floor, tolerating a mouse that may or may not have thought his ear was a piece of cheese.

Candles not only provided light in the windowless cabin, but he kept one burning continuously to heat water in the indoor tank. Without matches, a ready flame made starting a cooking fire or fire for warmth a simpler matter.

Late into the night, when his eyelids were sagging, Joyce approached his bench next to the stove. She smelled of sawdust and leather.

"I've been reading about Jesus," she whispered. "What we heard on the radio—He would want us to warn the others about what's coming, about the danger."

"Hell?"

"Yes, but more immediate—the army." She gripped his arm with such strength, he almost winced in pain. "We must tell them, Mr. Radner!"

Because of the personal risks, Eric had never considered interacting with people who threatened his own preservation. But her personal sorrow had helped Joyce see Christ's compassion where Eric had overlooked it.

"Who would we tell?" he asked.

"Adderthorn needs to know. My brothers live there, Leo and Milton."

"The Pickford brothers? I thought your name was Adkins."

"Pickford was my maiden name."

"Of course." He set aside his candle materials and wiped his hands on his jeans. "I don't know about your troubles back in Adderthorn, but mine are pretty troubling, believe me!"

"I know. Talia told me what you did for her. But the Bible's right. We have to warn them. They have to get ready for an invasion. Even if it's risky for us."

"Your brothers aren't going to be too happy to see me."

"I'll go with you." She smiled and squeezed his hand. By her touch, Eric guessed she could convince him of just about anything right then. "They can be unhappy with both of us. But we have to get through to them, for the sake of the people!"

Chapter 5

Joyce and Eric left for Adderthorn two days later. The distant military force, approaching ever closer from somewhere to the south, had been doing so for months. But it had taken Joyce's compassion for the people who had dismissed her to stir up Eric's own sensitivity and willingness to warn the town. Danger of the worst sort was coming. A brutality of Armageddon-like proportions was about to rumble up the highway. Being a Christian meant expressing Christ's attitude toward others. Eric could see that God was using Joyce to teach this to him.

Together, they chose to save several hours by crossing the gorge rather than circling the mountain to reach the town. Thus, Eric carried his spiked boots and a tree saw to fall a new tree across the gorge. Since Joyce was coming with him, he didn't organize any speech for the people of Adderthorn. She would be the one to convince them of the danger. After all, she'd lived with the people, up until a few years earlier.

They selected a tree of the right height and girth near the southern edge of the deep gorge. On the warm, spring day, Eric began sawing the notch cut to guide the direction the tree would fall. Halfway through the tree, he stopped to allow Joyce to make the final horizontal cut.

Watching her work in her new buckskin clothing, Eric wondered what kind of man Brad must've been to win a woman like her. Eric had met her under fierce circumstances, and she'd placed herself at risk for her son to meet him, and then to entrust Andy and herself to his care. Now, after two nights of reading the Bible, she was willing to sacrifice everything to care for other people. He wondered if he had that same love for the souls of others. He hadn't had such compassion, but hers was rubbing off on him, growing inside his lonely heart.

"Here," she said. "You finish it."

Though she'd helped cut down dozens of trees on the ridge for the cabin addition, none of those could've killed her if they'd bounced wrong upon falling. This was a pine tree, over one hundred and fifty feet tall. Wiping her brow from the labor, she stepped back and let Eric have the saw. He finished the horizontal cut, but the tree didn't fall. Since he'd brought no axe or wedges from the cabin, they stood back and waited for the wind. Together, they watched the pine's upper reaches for a sturdy breeze to finish the job.

"I don't want to be away from Andy overnight," she said without looking at him. "What's the longest we can stay in Adderthorn to still get back by nightfall?"

"If we get there around noon, we can stay an hour, but no more."

"I'll expect you to hold us to that." She looked away from the tree and into his face. "No matter what kind of drama my brothers draw me into, make sure we leave on time."

"You're expecting problems?" He touched his revolver on his hip. It was still empty, but he also had his hunting rifle. "My guns are just for show, you know. I'm not a killer."

"Talia said you stood up to my brothers to get her out. That's all I'm asking. We'll warn them of the danger, then leave. If they gloat over Brad's death, I might lose it. Brad should've run Adderthorn, but my brothers wouldn't have it. They even threatened to kill him. That's why we left."

"Okay. We'll just tell them, then leave."

He wanted to ask her more, but her face seemed to plead for understanding. Besides, the tree creaked right then, and he grabbed her arm to pull her farther out of harm's way. The giant trunk twisted from the wind in the branches, and groaned as it leaned farther and farther over the gorge. Finally, the trunk snapped, and it flopped violently across the seventy-foot gorge. It was several seconds before it settled on the wet rock and lay still.

Since Eric was experienced at crossing logs, he gave Joyce the cork boots to wear. The pine still had its bark, and there were plenty of branches for handholds along the length, if they needed them.

Carrying his pack and rifle, he walked up the tree's first few yards, out across the gorge's expanse, and reached the lowest branches. Easing through the boughs, not trusting them with much of his weight, he moved onto the middle section.

In the middle, he held firmly to a vertical branch and bounced on the log to test its resting place. It didn't move, though he was only one hundred and eighty pounds against the several tons of mass.

Finally, he reached the north ledge and hopped onto solid ground. Joyce carried her own boots with the laces tied over her neck. She had no pack since Eric had their gear for the day. With only a few yards to go before the first branches, she was too hurried and stepped wrong. Instead of returning to the ledge to catch her balance, she dove for the nearest branch. Her fingertips brushed pine needles on the end of the branch, but otherwise, her dive was soundless. In a whisper of wind, without even a scream, she was gone.

Eric dropped to his knees to look into the throat of the chasm at the raging creek below. Her body lay broken across jagged granite boulders, halfway in the water. No amount of staring down forty feet into the dim wetness could reverse the shocking suddenness of her departure. Protests seemed in order. Anger seemed justified, but all he could do was gape down at this fearless woman he had certainly begun to fall in love with.

Pushing away from the wet moss that could cause him to slip, he set his pack and rifle against a tree. Too shaken to respond otherwise, he stomped this way and that, ringing his hands and grinding his teeth. Was this God's way of telling him not to go to Adderthorn to warn the town? Was God protecting Joyce from a worse fate? Was He taking her from him so she didn't become an object of worship for him?

Every imaginable doubt and reasoning flooded his battered mind, but nothing seemed to explain the horror that had just occurred. The cork boots had fit her well enough. The log was thicker than a man, more than adequate for crossing without a safety line. There were precautions they could have taken, as he thought back, but there was no reason they would've suspected her faulty footing at such a crucial moment.

Next, he was filled with fear. How would he explain this to Andy? Who would take care of him now? Joyce was to tutor Andy, to start him on his education. Now, Andy was an orphan.

And then there was the matter of Adderthorn, and the danger of an advancing army. And the Pickford brothers. They wouldn't listen to Eric. The last time he'd seen them, he'd forced them at gunpoint into a cell!

He couldn't deal with all these things that day. Even Adderthorn would have to wait. Joyce was his first priority now.

Picking up his pack and rifle, he re-crossed the log and reached the south side. It was a short hike up and over the ridge to reach the cabin, where Runner greeted him by leaping with muddy paws onto him. Andy was playing in the stream, his pant legs rolled up, so Eric slipped into the cabin without being seen. He caught Talia mid-page in her Bible reading. She closed the Bible and slipped it under the bed blankets at his sudden entry. With her head down, she busied her hands with a pine bough, plucking the needles to place in their tea jar.

"You're a little old to pretend you're not interested in the afterlife, aren't you?" Eric hung his pack on a peg and set his rifle on a rack above the door. "Find anything interesting?"

She shook her head and took up the Bible again.

"I'm just trying to make sense of what you and Joyce are doing."

"Well, going to Adderthorn has been postponed." He dug under his old bed for a dozen deer skins bundled in a roll. Joyce had selected four of the softest ones for pants and shirts for herself and Andy. Talia still had clothes of her own in her pack. After finding the largest, coarsest skin that he'd probably never use except for rope or belts, he knelt on the floor. "Joyce took a fall in the gorge. I figured I'd bury her in this."

"What?" Talia set the Bible on the bed. "She fell? Mr. Radner, you tell me what happened!"

He described the whole scene—the tree they fell together, then the fateful crossing.

They were quiet as his fingers played with the edge of Joyce's burial wrap.

"She's still in the gorge?"

"Yeah."

"You should bury her here."

"But Andy will see—"

"Bury her here, below the pond. You think about it, and you'll know it's the right thing for Andy. He'll grow up and hate you if you hide this from him."

At that moment, Eric wanted to climb onto the bed and sleep. No work, no hunting, no death, no burial. The last two weeks with Joyce, Andy, and Talia had been the best weeks of his life. They'd been building a home, becoming a family. A family?

"Andy's now my son," he said suddenly. "Would Joyce approve? She still called me Mr. Radner."

"She'd approve. And maybe this will mean something more." She opened the front cover of the Bible to show a few words penciled there. It was new writing in a Bible Eric had used a thousand times. "It says, 'I believe.' And she signed her name. I'm not a Christian, but that should comfort you, right?"

Eric smiled, thinking of Paul's second letter to the Thessalonians. For a Christian, for a believer, death wasn't the end. In eternity, he would see Joyce again. And he would present to her the man her son would become, the son he would raise.

"Now, you go get her and bring her back. My three children and grandchild didn't receive a proper burial in Adderthorn, but we can do better for Joyce."

Outside, with the deer wrap under his arm, Eric almost ran over Andy as he carried sticks across the yard to the stream. Eric didn't doubt that he was about to dam the stream—and flood the cabin with it.

"Andy? Come here." Eric knelt on the ground. "Set your sticks down and listen." He took the hand Andy had bravely offered him the first day they'd met. "Your mother had an accident. She fell while crossing a creek. She's dead, Andy. She went to heaven. I'm going to bring her back right now, and we'll bury her together."

Andy took a deep breath, and his face wrinkled.

"She's dead?" Runner stopped next to them. Andy's little shoulders trembled, and Runner whined at his master's turmoil. "But she's my mom."

"I know. You and me are family now. And Grandma Talia. We're gonna find a way to keep going." Eric looked up to see Talia at the door. She held a shovel. "I'm gonna go get your mother, then we'll bury her down by the pond. You think she'd like that?"

He nodded and smeared dirt across a wet cheek. Turning away, Andy accepted the shovel from Talia. Dragging the tool, he crossed the stream, and left the yard.

"I didn't mean for him to start digging now," Talia said. "I brought it out for you for when you got back."

"Well, maybe it's something he wants to do."

Fifty yards away, Andy reached the pond and stood there looking at the water.

"I'll be late," Eric told Talia. "I need to climb down to her."

"Be careful. I'll watch him." She nodded at Andy.

"I know you will." He set a hand on her shoulder and kissed her wrinkled cheek. She patted his hand like he imagined his own grandmother would've done, then he left, fetching a length of climbing rope on his way.

At the gorge, he tied the nylon rope to a healthy pine tree and lowered himself over the ledge. Forty feet later, he reached Joyce amongst rocks and knee-deep water. Forcing past rigor mortis, he wrapped her broken body in the deer hide, then wound the rope around her bundled form.

Climbing back up, his feet slipped often on the damp rocks. He reached the top out of breath, but stood, prepared to haul Joyce up, when a thousand birds around him in the forest took flight.

He crouched, wishing he'd brought his rifle to guard against some new danger. What was happening? The ground didn't seem to be shaking, so it wasn't an earthquake.

The flapping of wings and cries of birds settled, and then he heard it—explosions, or detonations. Adderthorn was too far away for him to hear small arms gunfire, so this was something more than rifle shots. Heavy artillery, he guessed, like thunder delayed over the miles, distorted by the mountain forest—but explosions nonetheless.

He checked the sun. It was almost noon. If he and Joyce had marched swiftly to Adderthorn, they would've nearly been there about now, walking into—what? Had the rogue army already attacked? It could also be militants from Mastover, he reasoned, who were expressing their authority across Wyoming. What had God protected him from?

Heaving against the rope, he drew Joyce up from the creek. Her death had very likely bought him his own life. Because of her fall, they hadn't stumbled into a battle in which they were terribly overpowered.

When he pulled Joyce over the edge, he clung to her in his arms and wept. He couldn't imagine a deeper sadness, wanting to share with her that she'd spared them a much worse confrontation in Adderthorn. But she was gone now. And he felt so alone.

Back at the cabin, he carried Joyce to the pond and laid her down to dig the grave that Andy had begun. Andy knelt next to his mother and pet the deer skin. Runner sat next to Talia as she read Psalm 23 aloud from the Bible over and over again. Eric stopped digging to let his tears pass.

He removed his cork boots from Joyce's feet, then lowered her into the deep grave. Andy helped him cover her with dirt as Talia wept. They limbed a sapling together, and pounded it into the ground as a marker. Using a hide strap, Eric tied a branch horizontally to make a cross, then the three of them stood rather formally in silence for a few moments.

"The world around us got wicked," Eric said softly. "Joyce Pickford left Adderthorn, then lived with her husband, Brad Adkins, hoping to trade peacefully with travelers on the highway. But he was killed just three weeks ago. She came up here to the mountain to live, and our lives are better for it. She met Jesus here."

Talia sobbed louder as he continued.

"She died in the process of trying to warn others of danger. Her son, Andy, can be proud of that. His mother died doing good for other people. I'll live the rest of my life believing her death kept me from my own death a little while later. And now we live with her in our memories. Good memories of a strong woman. She's in a place of peace with God now. We'll see her again."

"We will?" Andy lifted his tear-streaked face to the setting sun.

"We will." Eric smiled and held out his hand. Andy took it.

"You need to teach that boy the Bible," Talia said. "Joyce would want that. Along with his schooling."

"Yes, Grandma Talia." Eric laughed.

Then they all laughed, though Eric wasn't sure why. Maybe it was another way of releasing their grief. Or maybe it was at the prospect of him trying to teach a young man his academics.

Chapter 6

The morning after the funeral of Joyce Adkins, Eric took Andy to the summit of their mountain. In one hand, Eric held Andy's hand, and under his other arm he carried his telescope meant to gaze at distant stars. Together, they sat down on the rock, facing the northerly wind. Far below them, the town of Adderthorn was a distant mirage, a smoldering ruin between mountain and plain. And through its midst, to the left and right, tiny dots of vehicles moved up and down the highway.

"Whatever we see," Eric said to Andy as he assembled the telescope, "our Lord God is still good and strong. We don't need to be afraid."

Andy nodded, but Eric could see he was shivering, even under the deer jacket his mother had made for him. He knew it wasn't the cold that shook his little body. They had sat with Talia late into the night talking about what the explosions could mean. Evil men were near. That meant their lives were probably about to change again.

Finally, Eric held the glass to his eye. Not many of the buildings of Adderthorn remained standing. The General Store was still there, which probably brought some sense of comfort to Gordon Irwin, if he was still alive, but the hotel had been demolished. Armored personnel carriers rolled through town. Uniformed men in the turrets ignored the townspeople lined alongside the road. Whatever resistance Sheriff Leo Pickford had organized had been utterly destroyed. As far as Eric could see to the north, rolling on the highway to Mastover, was an armored unit that seemed large enough to mobilize against a foreign country.

On one end of Adderthorn's Main Street, two men carried a body and laid it in a row with a dozen others. The survivors would rebuild, but the town had been broken, and perhaps raided for all remaining supplies. Before Pan-Day, the town's population was five hundred. Afterward, it had dwindled to about one hundred. Now, Eric guessed it was much less.

A gunshot, then another, made Andy and Eric jump, and Eric searched the town for additional violence. But they were too far away from Adderthorn to hear small arms fire—this had to be much closer!

"Andy, can you tell where it's coming from?"

"There!"

He pointed at a clearing a mile below them, on the other side of the gorge. Movement! Eric focused the scope on the clearing to catch a flash of dark clothing, then it was gone. Suddenly, five figures wearing black and gray fatigues entered the clearing, shouldering rifles. A volley of gunshots cracked through the crisp air.

Eric leapt to his feet and tugged the telescope apart.

"They're coming, Andy!" He shoved the scope and case into Andy's arms. "Get to the cabin and help Grandma Talia get into the woods to hide!"

Leaving the boy, Eric flew down the mountain to the cabin. In the yard, Talia was tending the garden.

"Soldiers coming!" he shouted. "Get blankets for a night in the woods and hide with Andy! I'm going to the gorge to hold them off!"

From the cabin, he grabbed his rifle and pack, in which he kept a pouch of .223 shells. His legs pumped up the ridge and over the crest. For years, he'd hiked the mountain, living amongst the trees and wildlife, careful not to disturb more than he had to, to survive. Though he'd lived in solitude those years, God had suddenly brought souls into his care. He couldn't allow their fragile existence to be broken by soldiers with a misplaced zeal to conquer and kill for fuel, food, and ammunition!

When he reached the gorge, no one was in sight yet. How did anyone know where he was? He had no idea, but with the pine tree bridging their land to his own, he wouldn't be able to stop them.

He ran across the length of the tree, stumbled through the branches, and leaped onto solid ground on the far side. Sliding his pack off, he fumbled for his flint and started striking his knife in a heap of dry pine needles. His heart thudded and he had trouble focusing through the panic.

Not far away, he heard branches breaking as bodies charged through the underbrush. A flame leaped at his hands. Eric would never be able to burn the thick trunk in time, but where the dry branches rested on the north edge of the gorge, it was a fire hazard. With twigs and needles now aflame, he pushed the burning heap under the tree boughs. For good measure, he clutched a handful of rifle bullets and tossed them into the flames.

Smoke made him cough as he hooked his arm around his pack and stepped through the flames to the log.

"Mad Man!" someone yelled.

Eric paused and looked back as fire licked at his pant legs. From the bushes came Milton Pickford, the sheriff's older and larger brother. He was hobbling on a bleeding leg. The soldiers weren't charging the mountain; they were chasing Milton!

Jumping out of the flames, Eric ran to him. Whatever their past, here was a man in need. This was Joyce's brother. Positioning himself under Milton's arm, Eric half carried him to the roaring treetop. The bullets would begin to explode any moment, and the soldiers behind them were seconds from emerging from the trees.

"You'll never make it across!" Eric tossed his backpack into the gorge. Since the rope still hung over the other ledge from his previous endeavor, he could recover his pack later. But he kept his rifle on his left shoulder. "Take a deep breath!"

By Milton's arm, Eric pulled the heavy man over his right shoulder. If Eric hadn't been hiking the mountains for five years, he would've collapsed under the weight. He turned with determination into the fire once again. Through the flames, he felt for the tree. Milton screamed as heat licked at his head.

Five steps later, they were beyond the flames. The deadly expanse yawned at Eric, his adrenalin rushing. He didn't dare look back as men shouted and a volley of gunfire burst from the trees. Bullets zipped past his head as he concentrated on planting one foot after the other with the weight of a gorilla on his back.

A loud pop from the tree fire blew embers in every direction. The bullets in the flames had finally reached a critical temperature. Another two burst, and Eric imagined the soldiers behind him scrambling for cover as they tried to locate the source of gunfire.

Eric and Milton tumbled onto the ground on the south side. A quick glance at Milton's head told Eric his screams hadn't been unwarranted; his eyebrows and half his hair were singed off, but his skin seemed only superficially burned. Gripping his arm, Eric dragged him behind brush and deadfall twenty feet from the edge of the gorge.

Kneeling, he chambered a round into his rifle and aimed at the far side. The fire and popping bullets were keeping the soldiers away from the bridge, but they were still in sight. One man stood partly behind a tree, shielded from the exploding ammunition, but his rifle stock was framed perfectly in Eric's open sights one hundred feet away. Eric had never killed a man, and he wasn't about to start that day. The Lord had made him a fine enough shot to send a message without killing.

He put a round into the soldier's rifle stock, which sent the man sprawling one way and his rifle another. His buddies lay down cover fire as Eric ducked behind his tree. Their bullets rattled the branches overhead like hail.

"That'll keep them busy." Eric grinned at Milt. "I may or may not be the mad man you think I am."

"They killed Leo, and hunted down the rest of us." He held his seeping leg wound. "Somehow, I knew if I could make it this far, you'd help me. You helped that old lady. You . . . were my only hope."

"The way the world is now, you may just get a chance to repay me. And that old lady's name is Talia. You'd better watch the way you speak about her." Eric winced as a ricochet careened off a boulder. "She'll be the one doctoring your leg back at the cabin."

Eric dared a peek over the deadfall. The heat of the fire had reached the thick of the wood, destabilizing the bridge altogether. The soldiers backed into the forest away from the gorge. They'd never reach the south side now, and they knew it.

"I've got nothing left." Milton moaned. "They got Leo! Those animals didn't even want to talk! Leo would've made peace. They just said they were going to make an example of Adderthorn, and started killing us!"

A few minutes passed as the last of the bullets exploded. Eric took a couple deep breaths, trying to steady his nerves and think straight. For the enemy, it was a three-hour hike, minimum, around the downhill side of the gorge, and twice that if they decided to come up the mountain after them. But Eric and Milt had a few hours head start, as long as the invaders didn't chop down a tree of their own to make another bridge. However, a unit on the move probably didn't have time to deal with locals in a mountain refuge. Lord willing, they wouldn't bother at all with their little group at the cabin. Eric hoped they weren't worth the expenditure of lives and resources.

"I lived in Adderthorn my whole life." Milton shook his head. "That's the first night I ever spent on the run from my own home."

"We need to get you to the cabin, and take care of that leg."

"You got a whole spread up here, huh?"

"You didn't really think I lived off raw meat while hiding in a cave, did you?"

"There were a lot of rumors. I'm just . . . thankful."

"Let's hope that army listens to the rumors from someone still alive, and they stay far away from us."

As Eric helped Milton stand, the tree-bridge cracked and splintered, then folded in flames into the gorge. There was an angry clatter below as the huge pine tree came to rest—hopefully not burying Eric's pack completely.

It was a strange twist, bringing Milton into Eric's life that way. He saw God's hand in it immediately. Eric knew there were no accidents with God.

#######

Two days later, Eric had recovered his pack from the gorge and the army had moved beyond Adderthorn. Talia and Andy had hidden in the woods as ordered, but now they were all once again living in the cabin. Twice since the gorge incident, Eric had made wide circles around the mountain, checking possible entry points or back routes to the cabin. There was no sign that anyone was searching for Milton, and no sign of more survivors in the woods.

Once again on the mountain summit, Andy and Eric listened to the radio, now directing the antenna to the northwest. Runner sat mesmerized by the windmill that spun almost silently in Andy's two hands. They listened to men's voices, their imaginations wild at the kind of heartless men they belonged to.

Though Andy was young, Eric allowed him to listen to commanders giving orders and scouts transmitting reports. This was Andy's world now. It was a harsh world where men killed as indiscriminately as a virus did. On the mountain, Eric had found God. Andy's mother had also become a believer, and Talia was near to surrendering to her Lord. So, it was only natural that along with Andy's schooling, he learn what his Savior had done for them all. Eric prayed that Andy's heart might repel the evils he was being exposed to at such a young age. Even Milton was getting his dose of Jesus as Eric read from the Bible each night by candlelight.

"That's enough for today." Eric turned off the radio. They had discovered that Mastover had radioed the army before they'd arrived, and had agreed on concessions. Their cause and forces had now merged. Thirty miles up the highway, an outpost had been established, while the main force continued its rampage into Montana, killing potential aggressors along the way. "We'd better get back to the cabin to make sure Grandma Talia hasn't scolded Milton to tears."

"It's better than her scolding me!" Andy said as they started downhill.

Eric laughed as Andy's small hand found his own. Even through the suffering and uncertainty, there was still joy. A man with no family had a son, and a boy with no father now had a father. They were the only family they had left.

The Lord's return seemed past due in those days of carnage, but Eric taught Andy that God's delay was out of love for those yet to turn to Him. With this hope, they would live on their mountain, remember Andy's courageous mother, and remain prayerful and vigilant against sin in their own lives.

Milton was already talking about returning to Adderthorn and organizing a band of resistance fighters. Apparently, Talia's forgiveness toward him, and Eric's Bible reading, hadn't cracked his hardened heart. He only wanted revenge.

The mountain had seemed so safe when Eric had been alone. Now, he knew the reality of his existence. In the world, there would be trials and suffering and viruses and armies. But they didn't need to lose heart, for their Lord had overcome the world!

###

~End of STEADFAST Book One~

Bonus Chapter SF1

Who are the Wyoming invaders? What do they want? Read this Bonus Chapter to discover behind-the-scenes intel on the bad guys!

~

Commander Kelly Morris of the Liberation Organization gazed across the bridge that linked Iowa to Nebraska. Council Bluffs, Iowa, had fallen after a hard fight that morning. His message to them had been the same as to dozens of other cities: conform or die. They'd responded with silence, so they had died. But he suspected Omaha would be even more resilient.

"Sir!" A captain of one of his forward units saluted. He was a short man, an owner of a chain of laundromats in Atlanta, if Morris remembered right. Anyone with such leadership experience had been given some sort of command under him. "The wounded are too many for our medics. We don't have enough medical supplies to care for them. We're overwhelmed!"

"Treat our own wounded first, Captain, and the enemy's injured second, or not at all."

"But the enemy surrendered, sir. The wounded are among those who surrendered to us."

"Yes, but they waited until the end of battle to surrender, so we'll let them surrender now—to death." Morris saluted his man. "Nothing must slow our advance, Captain. You're dismissed."

Morris inhaled deeply, his feet set firmly on the pavement of Interstate 80. Behind him, Council Bluffs burned, but the smoke didn't erase the more favorable lingering scent of spent artillery. America needed to be cleansed, toughened, and set free. The days of its weak conservatism were over. Within a year, he expected to reach Seattle. Radio reports from the West confirmed that cities along the coasts of Oregon and California were already pledging allegiance and support to his martial efforts. America was being reborn!

"Except for these blasted fools!" He spat.

His aide stepped forward.

"What's that, sir?"

"This is a war of renewal, Sergeant. These Midwesterners are fools for fighting against us."

"Yes, sir."

"Before the virus, most of these people were still devoted to the idea that some God watched over them—that He created them. They've rejected the call to arms to protect our planet from man's destruction. Instead, they've taken up arms to fight against change. It's the twenty-first century! What's wrong with America, with people like this, holding to their expired traditions and beliefs?"

"Yes, sir, they're not living in reality."

"That's what religion does to weak minds, Sergeant. We need to be firmer in our discouragement of it. America is finished with the assault on science and conformity. How many cities are holding out against our liberation?"

"After Omaha, we're clear along Interstate 80 all the way to San Francisco. We'll now need to decide whether to turn north or south, if we want to continue to liberate cities."

"We can fight in the south this winter. We'll go north while it's warm."

"Then we need to move through Wyoming to reach Montana and Interstate 90," the sergeant said. "There are a lot of little towns between here and there who don't have radios—small towns with armed civilians, our bicycle scouts tell us."

"If towns don't have radios, then they won't know we're coming. We can catch them sleeping, unguarded. By the time we sweep through their communities, half their buildings will be burning. I don't want to stop rolling if we don't have to. We don't have time to pacify the locals of these insignificant towns."

"Rebellions could start by that method, sir. They could harass our supply lines."

Morris observed several artillery batteries positioned for firing at Omaha. Every city he took by force or surrender was a win for America. He had no political ambitions, only a vision of an America without boundaries or limitations. That meant those who opposed him would need to go.

"If they stand against us, they die, Sergeant. That's the law."

"Yes, sir. I'll pass the word before we roll through Omaha tomorrow."

His aide scampered off. The captain of the Liberation Organization's elite troops stepped up and saluted. The man's armband had a lightning bolt on it.

"Ready to commence firing, sir."

"Get on with it, Captain. Two cities in one day." Morris smiled and rubbed his balding head. "We're breaking our own records."

"Yes, sir!"

Morris watched his freedom fighters in their gray and black uniforms prepare for the ground assault upon Omaha. Taking the city by nightfall was unlikely, but they would pound them with ordnance, and hope for a surrender. The Liberation Organization was low on diesel, and Omaha was rumored to have stores of fuel. Omaha had to fall if Morris and his army were to continue west.

Suddenly, an explosion blinded Morris and knocked him onto his back. Fifty of his elite troops had been surveilling the city from the interstate bridge before it exploded. Omaha had put dynamite on the bridge! His soldiers retreated through the dust to the line of artillery batteries behind Morris. They were carrying a dozen wounded and dead with them.

Defiantly, Morris rose to his feet and dusted off his uniform. So, Omaha was committed to an actual battle. Blowing the bridge would indeed slow Morris down. His engineers were few. Now, he'd have to wait for barges downriver to arrive and carry his two-thousand-man force and their vehicles across the Missouri River.

Leaving the front line in the capable hands of his captains, Morris returned to his command trailer and took off his uniform. Years earlier, he'd been a two-star general. After his inflammatory remarks and criticisms against his superiors, Morris had been forced into retirement mere months before the virus erupted. His wife had committed suicide, and the future had seemed bleak. But then he'd gone to Atlanta's military base to help organize quarantine units. It had been in disarray—ripe for his leadership. That had been the beginning of the Liberation Organization.

Morris lathered his face to shave, then paused to stare at his image in the mirror. They'd called him weak before pushing him into retirement. But he'd never been weak. He simply hadn't agreed with the White House about the battles America needed to fight. If they could see him now, they'd see he wasn't weak at all! The masses needed firm regulation in every part of their lives—business, schooling, even family life. Individuals weren't able to decide for themselves how to cooperate with the whole diverse country. The Christian infestation was just one example of ignorance, though certainly one of the strongest and most dangerous movements. They continually fought his vision: true liberty was enjoyed only by true uniformity. Dissension had to be cut out and burned down.

After shaving, Morris walked outside to mingle with the men. Until they could cross the river, everything was on hold. Besides his two thousand soldiers, one thousand support personnel had been conscripted to keep his advance forces fueled and fed. Vehicles in the rear of the company were constantly arriving from and departing to liberated cities to the east, bringing in and dropping off arms, ammunition, and gear. Even years after the virus outbreak, America was still rich in resources, if one knew where to look and how to confiscate them.

"We'll get 'em tomorrow, Commander!" a provisions officer said with a smile and a salute as he passed.

Arriving at a Humvee dedicated to communications, Morris paused to listen to an argument between two radio operators. One claimed that threats wouldn't move the hearts of those in the western towns. The other insisted that fierce words followed by brutal action would send a warning all the way to Seattle that the Liberation Organization needed to be obeyed. Both operators looked to Morris for an assessment.

"We're not enemies of the obedient," Morris stated proudly, a message he'd repeated often the past two years. "Violence is necessary to crush the defiant and secure the stability of this liberating force. A household, a town, a city, or a state mustn't be left to itself. If we are to unite America again, better than it was, force must be used to break the backs of selfishness and privatization.

"Sometimes, that force will be in words. Other times, that force will be by war. The sooner this country is unified, the sooner we can live in peace. This is emphasized by the confiscation of civilian firearms and the proclamation of the rights of all citizens. If anyone encroaches or condemns the rights of others, they will be swiftly prosecuted—by us until a new government is in place. These ideals are the building blocks for our new nation.

"So, tell me, what wouldn't you do or say to reach this goal?"

The operators glanced at one another. The one who'd sought a softer approach shrugged.

"I guess I'll be tougher, sir."

"Of course, you will," Morris said. "Soon, we'll be in the mountains of Wyoming and Montana. Now, those people are tough, but they must still be broken. That means we must be tougher. I want more reports from you two that towns are pacified before we ever reach them. Bring them to their knees by the radio, or I'll bring them to their knees by the gun. You have time. Omaha will take a few days. When necessary, tell people up the road about our time in Ohio. Burning dissidents at the stake always gets people's attention. We're a liberation force. Tell them. They'll conform, or they'll die."

As the shelling of Omaha continued at the front, Morris weaved through the troops, their tents, and vehicles. This was a force used to moving, but now they had to sit idle for three weeks, or more. Even Morris secretly craved the next step of the battle for Omaha—the invasion. He yearned to walk onto the scene, his weapon in hand, to give the victory speech he'd given in dozens of cities and towns all the way back to Atlanta. That show of power touched his heart every time. Casualties in Omaha would be high since they were resisting, but he would leave a remnant alive to spread his message—conform or die.

A young soldier ran through a division of riflemen to reach Morris. Breathlessly, the man saluted, exposing an ear that was missing flesh, still bloody from the battle that morning. Many of the men had wounds, but they kept fighting, sharing Morris' same vision for true liberty.

The soldier's armband identified him as belonging to one of the gas depot units who was responsible for fuel.

"Yes, what is it, Private?"

"Back in Ohio, sir, you told us all to report any, um, overt Christianizing, right?"

"Among other things, yes, I said to report Christian proselytizing. It means forcing your beliefs on someone else. Well?"

"My sergeant has a Bible. I saw it. His name is Sergeant Landis. I took the liberty of having him arrested."

"Take me to him." Morris joined the Sergeant. The whole interstate was crammed with vehicles, and now that news of the delay was spreading, people were getting comfortable, even poking around in the debris of Council Bluffs. "Where are you from, son?"

"New York City, sir. I joined you in Charleston, West Virginia, after you burned down that church ten months ago."

"Do you enjoy your station?"

"I just want to liberate America from its cancer, sir."

"Good man."

They arrived at a tanker truck where a sergeant in uniform was on his knees against the front bumper, his hands handcuffed behind him. Two other depot soldiers held rifles on their captive. On the pavement in front of the sergeant was the man's open Bible, the wind blowing and fluttering its pages.

A crowd began to gather, so Morris waited for people to draw close. Teachable moments such as this didn't happen often. He needed to take advantage of opportunities to instill in the new generation of Americans what true liberty really meant.

"Are you Sergeant Landis?" Morris spoke loudly for his students. Often, his officers handled such internal situations when he wasn't available. "Speak up!"

"Yes, I'm Landis." The man lifted his bowed head a little, and Morris saw he was about thirty, too young to understand the offense he'd committed, probably, but he would pay for it, nonetheless. The arresting officers had already bloodied his lip. "What have I done wrong, sir?"

"Do you claim to be a Christian?"

"Yes, I do. I've never hidden that fact."

"And there's nothing wrong with claiming to be a Christian." Morris faced the circle of soldiers and paced in front of them. "You hear that? We celebrate our diversity, even in the things we believe about ourselves. We may identify ourselves with anything we choose. That's the joy of true liberty. No one should hinder anyone else from identifying with whatever they desire to be identified with. That's your right. That's everything we're fighting for out here. Do you agree, Sergeant Landis?"

"I agree that . . . we all have a choice, sir."

"I see." Morris crouched in front of the accused. "And you have chosen to be identified as a Christian. Is that correct?"

"Yes, sir."

"You're free to do that, Sergeant. But let me ask you: according to you, am I wrong if I choose another religion, or no religion at all? Would that be wrong or right?"

"I believe, sir, that what we trust in determines our eternal destiny."

"You're not answering my question, Sergeant." Morris acknowledged the crowd pressing in to see and hear better. They would remember this moment for the rest of their lives. He hoped they repeated his questions and challenged anyone who claimed to belong to a mutually-exclusive religion. "Am I wrong or right to choose a god besides the God of your Bible—according to you?"

"I believe there's only one God, sir."

"Answer the question!" Morris felt his anger rise, but he checked it. This was a moment for gentleness. He obviously had the perfect subject before him, to make his point. If he were viewed as a bully, his attitude rather than justice would be remembered. "If I reject your God and identify with another god who allows me different desires, do you condemn me or embrace me?"

"It's not my place to condemn you, sir." Sergeant Landis lifted his head higher. Morris looked into eyes that he expected to contain fear, but instead, they contained fire. This was the most dangerous kind of enemy—the one who truly believed what he said. For an instant, Morris envied the man's passion. Morris had zeal, but he'd never had whatever was showing through this man's eyes. "But the Bible says that without receiving by faith Jesus Christ's sacrifice for your sins, you'll stand condemned on Judgement Day."

"That's what your Bible says. But what do you say for yourself?"

"I have a tendency, sir, to believe the Bible."

Morris rose to his feet and paced amongst the gathering. He felt like a courtroom prosecutor who was about to win a case, knowing that the jury would side with him.

"I see. You admit that I would be condemned, even knowing where I stand against such bigotry?"

"I'm no better that you, sir," Landis said.

"Oh, we know that, Sergeant!" Morris laughed. "But do you know that?"

"I know I'm not better than you or anyone else, sir. I've just chosen a different path. Don't I have the liberty to believe what I choose to believe? Isn't that really what we're fighting for?"

"Not at the discrimination of another person's beliefs, Sergeant. That's what ruined America from what it was meant to be. By your own admission, your commanding officer, me, stands condemned by your God. How could you possibly remain a soldier under me? Impossible."

"I'm just a truck driver, sir."

"And I need every driver we have." Morris reflected on the sincerity in his voice. The men and women around him seemed mesmerized by his compassionate approach. In view of what was about to happen, he hoped they remembered him most of all as being tolerant. "That's why I ask you to say you withdraw your condemning beliefs against those of us who aren't Christians. What would your Jesus want you to do—accept us with love, or condemn us with hatred?"

"With love, sir, I reject the idea that there is any other way to be saved from condemnation, except through Jesus Christ."

"Then with your own words, before all these witnesses, on the eve of a great victory, you have condemned yourself." Morris rose to his full height. "Bring wood! Justice against bigotry and religious discrimination must be carried out!"

The crowd chatted excitedly as they lingered. A few men darted away to fetch firewood.

"Commander Morris." A messenger on a bicycle braked to a stop and saluted. "Word on the wire from Kansas City. The barges we need to transport the trucks across the river are blocked by debris in the river. It's a real mess, sir."

"How long until they arrive? We can't rebuild the bridge."

"It could take three weeks for them to reach us. Bridges up and down the Missouri have been burned or blown up. There's no other way west except by barge at this point. It seems people knew we were coming ahead of time. They've tried to stop us, sir!"

Morris clenched his teeth. Three weeks? He'd never reach Seattle by the New Year at this rate!

"Very well. Their attempt to stop us will only add to their own suffering when we roll onto their streets. Tell the engineers to have everything ready on the river bank the instant the barges arrive."

The messenger saluted and pedaled away.

The men who left for wood returned instead with old truck tires.

"We're low on wood, sir," they reported. "But these will burn with a little help."

"Do it."

Morris stepped back and watched as Sergeant Landis was forced to his feet. Five truck tires were shoved over his head, one on top of the other, stacking up to his midtorso. A soldier squirted kerosene over the tires. Another with a lighter stepped forward and looked to Commander Morris.

When he looked into the faces of his followers, Morris was filled with pride, and they seemed to be proud as well. Yes, discipline had brought them together before, like in Ohio. This was the new face of America—zeal for liberty—especially when that liberty was defended to the death. In Ohio, they had burned dozens at the stake, almost all of them Christians who insisted on their way being the only way. Sergeant Landis was one of their own, but they were still willing to administer punishment. No one had stepped up to defend the sergeant because they all knew better. They wanted to please their commander, and they wanted to see their nation restored.

After his troops finished scouring the nation in a couple years, they would be received as heroes by every city that endured. These were the liberators of an antiquated America. By the look on their faces at this moment, they foresaw the glory of their goal as well.

But then Morris noticed Sergeant Landis' face. It was peaceful, even upward gazing. He wasn't responding with threats for his God or cursing those about to execute him. In fact, his lips moved as he stared up at the sky, as if praying! All the pride Morris felt from the hundreds of admiring soldiers was ruined by Landis' single face of contentment. The traitor seemed almost willing to die for his God! It was this insanity Morris was determined to stomp out of America. Or burn it out, as often as necessary.

"Light it!" he ordered.

As the flames grew, someone threw the discarded Bible into the heat. In a year, Morris guessed Christianity would be merely a vague memory in America. After all, it had been dying off steadily for decades.

At other burnings, his soldiers had cheered in victory. Each fire had been a flame representing the new heart of a unified America. But that day, no one cheered. Everyone had seen the face of this Christian, who didn't scream at all. He simply expired in silence.

Morris turned and walked away. There would be other Christians and more Bibles. He would burn them all, in every town, as often as he crossed them!

Returning to his trailer, Morris lay on his portable bed and stared at the ceiling. Something terrible plagued his mind. Logically, killing the Christian was the right thing to do. It made sense. The troops seemed behind it, but he knew that region had a history of avoiding violence when given the choice. If he wasn't careful, he'd create martyrs. What he needed were small towns of people who stood with him, who would cleanse their own counties of anti-conformists. Only then could he step in front of the liberating force of his dreams, as the people themselves took the lead in discipline. That would require him leaving some powers in the hands of towns that pledged their loyalties.

Using his handheld radio, he called a messenger and shared his thoughts to pass on to the intelligence officers.

"We have to use the people, or we will fail," Morris relayed. "If we are seen only as conquerors, we will fail. The Northwest isn't densely populated, so we can very easily become burdened with squabbles."

"No one will stand against us, sir," the messenger stated.

"Not true. Ahead, in Wyoming and Montana, we'll be facing communities spread out, many of them armed, and not many towns. One community that doesn't submit to the liberation could derail our advance. Maybe even by one man."

"One man, sir? One man can't disrupt this beast. Thousands have already fallen to our mission. One man can't defeat hundreds of guns."

"Ah, but he can. He may even be out there right now." Morris held up his finger. "One man. Do you know why?"

"Why?"

"Because guns and bullets and tanks and grenades can't destroy an idea." Even as Morris said it, he knew he didn't have the answer for Jesus Christ, except to keep putting away His stubborn followers. "And it only takes one man to reignite an idea."

"No one is that bold, sir. Or that invincible."

"Listen to me, you fool!" Morris saw the messenger withdraw in fear on his seat. "It's not the man we need to fear. It's the idea! Of course, men aren't invincible, but an idea is. We have to destroy it before it spreads."

"Forgive me, sir, but let me ask you how will we do that? I'll need to tell the captains of the forward units."

"How?" Morris exhaled slowly. "Yes. That is the question. When we come to a town that wants to work with us, we'll embrace them, even if we still question their loyalties. Only then, by holding them closely, will we discern their intentions. If they are contrary, then we strike quickly and silently. We have to erase the idea from the people before it can spread."

"I'm sorry, sir. I'm not following. What exactly is the idea we're so concerned about?"

"Oh, never mind. I'll speak directly to the intelligence officers myself. And the radio operators. Never before have we needed to advance with more caution. We're far from Atlanta. One mistake, and we could get stuck in the Rocky Mountains."

"Sir, I just don't understand. We always destroy our enemies—anyone who's against your vision of America. How is what you're proposing any different?"

"This isn't about America." Morris dismissed the messenger with a wave of his hand. "Leave me. I need to think more on this. And speak to no one about what we've talked about."

"I . . . wouldn't think of it, sir."

The messenger left, and Morris looked at a map of the United States that he'd taped to his trailer wall. He wished he would've thought of the possibility of making martyrs long before that day. If his greatest fears were real, then he'd already ignited a simmering revolt. And if he hadn't, then it was a threat for tomorrow, or the next day. He may have even done it that day, by killing Sergeant Landis. Faith and beliefs and gods were beyond him. If he wasn't careful, the imaginations of America's devoted would bring his own vision to ruin.

~End of Bonus Chapter SF1~

STEADFAST BOOK TWO

America's Last Days

D.I. Telbat

Prologue, Book Two

North America has been ravaged by a virus that killed one hundred million people. Pockets of civilization hold out after the collapse of technology and government. The pandemic event, mixed with mindless panic, was labeled Pan-Day, the day that an overwhelming number of quarantined cities pushed society over the edge.

But now, as dreadful as the Meridia Virus has been, a rogue military division releases its fury upon all who resist its control. Towns are demolished. Civilians are massacred. Survivors are hunted—all in the name of freedom. Only those who declare loyalty will escape ruin.

Deep in Wyoming's Sharrock Mountains, Eric Radner's life has become unsettled by visitors. Once hidden in his secret mountain refuge, he is now thrust into the very events that challenge what little stability remains in America. Doing nothing is no longer an option, but to do anything will mean grave danger. Only a steadfast faith will carry him through, and by the grace of God, it will touch the few lives God has placed near him . . .

"The wicked flee when no man pursueth, but the righteous are bold as a lion." Proverbs 28:1 KJV

Chapter 1, Book Two

The town of Adderthorn, Wyoming, was sleeping as Eric Radner eased up to the back wall of the General Store. One year earlier, half the buildings had been demolished by the invading military unit, but Gordon Irwin's General Store had been one of those left standing. For months, from the peak above Eric's mountain cabin, he'd spied on the town to monitor troop movements, as well as to see how the citizens were faring. Finally, on this still night, he prowled down to the quiet, oppressed town.

Moving around the side of the store, he froze as headlights shined on a garbage heap, then swept on. Military trucks frequently passed through the town, but few stopped. Adderthorn had been broken, its people unable to resist or provide anything of value to the invaders. But if soldiers saw Eric skulking around in the dark, he had no doubt they'd investigate.

When the highway seemed quiet, he ran to the front door of the General Store and paused. A year earlier he'd stood in that very place, his life about to drastically change. Now, he wondered if God had something more for him than the latest news from the town gossip.

The door was locked, so he knocked gently, then louder when no one answered. Finally, a weak flashlight beamed in his eyes from inside. Eric recognized Gordon's bald head beyond the light. The man hurriedly unlocked the door.

"Quick, inside!" Gordon grabbed Eric's shoulder and pulled him through the door. "Move! They're coming!"

Pushing the door closed, they both lunged aside as two military personnel carriers rumbled past on the highway. Slowly, the two men moved away from the door and Eric followed Gordon past the empty store counter into a storage room. Gordon turned on a small LED light, which Eric stared at in awe. The rest of America was using kerosene lamps and candles, but Gordon had a functioning flashlight and an electrical source!

"Batteries," Gordon said as he seated himself on an unmade cot. "I recharge them on a wind generator. Have a seat."

He gestured to a precarious stack of hunting magazines three feet high. Next to them, a refrigerator, now converted into a pantry, displayed shelves stacked full of canned food.

"I was never one to hoard," he said behind eyes of shame, "but a man needs to stay alive."

Gordon's food stores could feed an army for a week—or a single family for a year. Eric understood, however, that not everyone had his own ability to hunt deer in the mountains.

"How many are still alive in Adderthorn?" Eric asked.

"About fifty. Some left to join the resistance. Others were recruited by the Liberation Organization. Rumor has it the fighting is fierce just up the highway. Speaking of which, Major Milton said you might come for a visit."

"Major?" Eric frowned, realizing that spying on Adderthorn through a telescope wasn't the same as getting news first-hand. "There's an actual resistance?"

"Sure. It started up in the fall. Milton is leading it. Homesteaders across the country are flocking to him and other militia units. They're making a real mess of the Liberation Organization's advance. We think the Lib-Org stalled out in Montana. Somebody up there is harassing their front as the Wyoming resistance harasses their supply lines through here."

The Liberation Organization was a name Eric knew from his secret radio monitoring on the mountain. They were a force of two thousand soldiers, supported by another thousand personnel—cooks, mechanics, and their families.

"I need thread, Gordon. The tough stuff." Eric squinted through the dim room at shelves of survival supplies. The military and the resistance alike would've stolen everything Gordon had if they knew he stocked such things. "Andy's growing like a sprout. I need to make him new clothes every few months."

"Milton said you took in the Adkins boy." Gordon reached into a cabinet, then offered Eric two spools of dark nylon. "Four bullets, Eric. That's a bargain these days."

Eric reached into his pack and the pouch of .223 shells.

"How about kids' books for schooling?"

"A mad man teaching a kid?" Gordon moved aside a plastic container to expose a shelf of books and more magazines. The smell of mildew reached Eric's nose. "Not many interested in education nowadays. This is all I've got for kids. One bullet."

After paying him, Eric studied what he'd just bought. Two used booklets—one coloring book, and one word-find. It wasn't much, but Andy knew how to get along with little.

"Did Milton tell you about the old lady we have living with us? Talia?"

"Sure. She fixed his leg, he said."

"She's been a great help to me. That's who Andy's staying with now." Eric sighed, settling into the welcome casual conversation with someone besides God or Andy for a change.

"We've buried a bunch of folks down here this past year." Gordon shook his head and leaned back on his cot. "You should know, Major Milton wants to see you. He said to tell you that when you came off the mountain. He needs you for something."

"What's he want with me?" Eric wondered if it had anything to do with the urge God had been putting within him to interact more with survivors. "He wants me to join the resistance."

"He mentioned it. I'm not one to push a man where he doesn't want to go, but someone like you could make a difference in this war."

"Someone like me?"

"A woodsman. A mad man." Gordon smiled. "The Liberation Organization drops by once in a while. I'm obliged to still share stories about you."

"What're you saying now?"

"The same—that you live like a wild man, half-insane from the virus. You're a carrier, but you didn't die. You attack hunters who enter the forest on the south side of the mountain. Civilians, travelers, locals—you don't discriminate."

"Sounds gruesome, Gordon. They believe this?" Eric frowned. "Well, we haven't seen any trace of strangers up there. The rumors do keep people at bay, I guess."

"Fear keeps them at bay. What do you want me to tell Major Milton?"

"Where's he hiding out?"

"South of Rawlings in the trees, about twenty miles northwest of us here. He bothers the Liberation Organization supply line just about every day, and he's been attacking the town of Mastover every few nights. He uses snipers, deer hunters, marksmen like yourself. He sends a runner once a week here to drop off and pick up rechargeable batteries for their walkie-talkies. Major Milton is getting more organized by the week, recruiting by the day. We're gonna win this!"

Eric thought about the offer to help Milton, and wondered if it had anything to do with a Scripture he couldn't shake from his mind—Joshua 3:11. It was about the Israelites crossing the Jordan River—that God was going before them. But Eric felt an unexplainable attachment to the passage. He knew God was going before him, calling him out to trust Him. Did Major Milton and the resistance have something to do with it?

"You say we'll win, Gordon, but what'll we win?" Eric tried to hide his distaste for the violent world in which they now lived. "Before we were invaded, Mastover outlawed Bibles and killed a bunch of Christians, and Milton's brother was enforcing that law here in Adderthorn. Moving from one aggressor to another isn't winning, Gordon."

"I suspect Major Milton will tell you what he's fighting for when you talk to him. Unless you don't go to him. You want me to tell him you refused his invitation?"

There was no subtlety in Gordon's voice. The man had joined the resistance, though covertly, and Eric was expected to join as well. He didn't owe Milton, especially since Eric had saved his life. But from Milton's perspective, his fight was securing Eric's safety.

"Show me on a map where I can find him."

Twenty minutes later, Eric had retrieved his rifle from the woods and was hiking through the darkness toward the resistance camp. His mind lingered on six-year-old Andy back at the cabin. He was again thankful for Talia being with them, being a grandmother to the boy, and watching over him. They would be fine, he was sure. Andy had been born since Pan-Day and was being raised to be a brave and helpful little man. And though Runner wasn't a large golden retriever, any dog that chased squirrels with her master would stand her ground against a larger predator. If Eric wasn't delayed with Milton, he hoped to be back at the cabin within two days. Eric had lined up several chores for Andy to work on in his absence, besides whatever Talia had for him to do.

As Eric walked, he prayed for a way out of whatever Milton was probably about to propose to him, but his curiosity was driving him on. Like Israel, Eric sensed God wanted him to trust Him, like the verse on his mind. *Trust*

God at the river. Eric wasn't a killer; he couldn't join the resistance. Milton surely remembered the weeks he'd spent healing at the cabin, listening to the Bible each night as Eric read to his cabin guests.

After dawn, he made a fireless camp in the trees. The highway was in sight out on the plain. The traffic had picked up—Humvees, ambulances, and even a few tanks moved to and from Mastover. As Eric's eyelids drooped from weariness, he considered the great deception of that day. Americans were fighting Americans, when they should've been fighting their ultimate enemies of deeper spiritual evils. Instead of preparing for Jesus Christ to receive them in the clouds, they were preparing to fight each other over fuel and food. Was there really that much food and fuel left?

Around noon, he woke with the same Scripture strongly on his mind. *Trust God at the river*.

Rested, he chewed on deer jerky and continued his trek until he suddenly stumbled upon a sentry posted in a tree, the man's rifle cradled in his arms. Before he was spotted, Eric stealthily moved directly below the guard's tree stand thirty feet above. As a game hunter, Eric had approached too quietly for the lookout to notice. The camp was close, and Eric had arrived undetected.

When Eric walked into the resistance camp, he was surprised to find over three hundred men. Along a creek, a dozen wall tents were set up where women and children washed clothes and prepared meals. A corral held twenty riding horses. The muddy trails between the tents smelled like sewage. Everyone he saw wore a red, white, and blue armband on their right arm.

He stood outside the command tent—which had been slightly charred from a stove fire—and watched the desperate scene, until a man with an assault rifle stopped in front of him. The man looked at his arm to see that Eric wore no armband.

"Who are you?" The man placed his hand on a pistol on his hip. "Where'd you come from?"

"I'm—"

"Mad Man!" Milton Pickford stepped through the tent flap and set a hand on his man's shoulder. "Easy, Hank. This is the guy I was telling you about. Mad Man himself, Eric Radner. Eric, this is Hank Worcester, a man I trust with my life daily."

"He doesn't look like a mad man." Hank Worcester sported a beard as Eric did, but his flannel shirt had more patches on it than Eric's. "We need a lot more than a wild man from the woods to help us, Major."

Milton grinned and placed a piece of wood between his teeth. He wore a green beret with a one-star emblem on the front. His frame was lean and his eyes more fierce than Eric recalled.

"It seems war has awakened something inside you, Milton."

"Not war. Revenge!" He turned to Hank. "Excuse us, Hank. We need to talk privately."

Eric walked into the roomy command tent, complete with table and war map. He waited for Milton to begin. Milton tossed his beret onto a wooden peg on a post and sat on a round, which was surely soon to become firewood. He gestured to another identical seat and the two men looked at one another in silence. Milton's face, now away from his men, became grim, and there was pain in his eyes.

"We're losing, Eric." He shifted the twig in his mouth. "People arrive almost every day and expect me to lead them to victory. All I do is get men killed. My brother, Leo, was the smart one. That's why he was sheriff. I'm no general."

"And I'm no war room advisor." Eric shrugged. "What am I doing here?"

"I can fight." He leaned toward Eric, his voice low. "But I can't fight with all these people. You're still a Christian, right?"

"Yes, you know I am. That's not something that gets turned on and off, Milton."

"So, I can trust you to take these people—the women, children, and wounded—to a safe place?"

"A safe place?" Eric shook his head. "Milton, for one, there's no such place. And two, you seem confused about my own abilities. I was a blogger before Pan-Day. I wore expensive watches and drove nice cars. Six years ago, I learned to skin a deer by reading a book I found at a forest ranger's lookout. Even if I did agree to join your army, there's no way your people would be safer with me. Honestly, I wouldn't even shoot to kill the enemy. You and me—our priorities about life are much different."

"I'm not asking you to kill. Look, I'll give you Hank, the guy you just met. He's one of the best fighting men I've ever seen. If I've got Hank and you keeping those people alive, the men will trust me to lead them into battle. Their families will be in good hands, I know. But we can't put all the men into the field while they're taking care of their families."

"There's nowhere to go, Milt."

"Just take them farther back in the mountains. Keep them fed. Half these men were from the city. It takes ten of them to bag a deer—once a week. I've seen you bring in a deer and an elk in the same day. Listen, I have a plan to take the town of Mastover, to get rid of the invaders, but I need the men! As soon as—"

"Don't tell me your strategy." Eric held up his hand. They sat in silence for a moment. "How's your leg?"

"I don't even limp. That Talia did a good job. Let her know, will you?"

"Sure, I will. She's looking out for Andy for me right now. She's been a real help."

Milton rose to his feet and went to the front of the tent.

"If I can't organize a fighting force, we'll have to disband by the fall. Otherwise, we'll die of starvation through the winter. If that happens, Eric, the Liberation Organization will overrun everyone all the way to Seattle. This isn't just about my brother, anymore." He faced Eric. "This is about America. It's about freedom. You want to read your Bible, but how would that be possible unless I fight and win that freedom?"

Eric didn't have an answer for Milton right then, but he knew more killing wasn't the answer from God. God had used the outcome of the horrors of war, but was war the calling for His obedient and loving servants?

"There's a small valley, hardly more than a canyon, with a river, about ten miles southeast of us, but it's hard to get to." Eric shifted his rifle in his hands. "It would take a hard day to reach. It's a narrow trail."

"Even better, if it's protected by the terrain." Milton chewed on his piece of wood. "So, you'll take them? You'll help me?"

"I'm not one of your soldiers, Milt."

"I know. I don't expect anything else from you, except to do for them what you did for me."

Eric foresaw the burdens ahead, and they weren't favorable. There would be danger, and hardship, but he couldn't turn down people who were close to starvation and disease. From what Eric had seen outside, the people really did need help, war or no war.

"Leadership doesn't appeal to me, Milt, but these people will need to follow my orders. That wilderness is no playground."

"You'll be in command. Hank will enforce it." He pulled Eric to his feet and shook his hand, which was a rare gesture in those days, since few touched one another while rumors of the Meridia Virus still circulated. "It's a welcome thing to have a good heart in the middle of all this madness."

"Madness and mad men apparently go well together." Eric smiled sadly, already regretting the commission he'd received. "How many do I need to relocate?"

"About a hundred. It's all that's left of these men's lives. It's everything they're fighting for—their families."

"Just promise me one thing, Milt."

"And that is?"

"As soon as the enemy realizes you're a worthy opponent, accept a sit-down and talk out something peaceful. We'll have nothing left at all if this war goes on much longer."

"I mean to make them pay, Eric."

"From what God tells us, revenge never works out that way. You'll be the one who pays in the end."

"You do your job, Eric Radner, and I'll do mine. Just because you and Talia took care of me doesn't mean your sensitivities toward the enemy rubbed off on me. If I need you, I'll send for you. Otherwise, keep these people alive."

Eric clenched his teeth as he glared at Milton. Perhaps Eric would've been filled with wrath as well if he'd lost as much as Milton had. But it was easy to justify war and death. It would take a steadfast compassion and much prayer to continue to see God's side of matters. Evil had to be stood against. Eric was just one man, but God had set him in a place to do some good. If caring for women, children, and the wounded was his calling, then he would do so, even while the rest of the world ripped itself apart.

Chapter 2

There was a time in Eric's life that he thought he would be content to live alone and isolated on the mountain until Christ came in the clouds. But God had driven him off his high mountain and into the valleys of life to extend a hand of mercy to others. First, he'd been directed to Grandma Talia Wiseman, and given her a home. Then, Joyce and Andy had come to live with him. Thankfully, they'd each been exposed to the gospel of Jesus, and Joyce had died as a believer—forgiven rather than condemned.

So, it was only natural that as Eric accepted the charge over Milton's people, he began to pray for a way to be true to God in the midst of this seeming precarious position. A civil war was being fought, and the reasons for the fighting were confusing, but he didn't need to concern himself with the fighting or confusion. The job he'd been given, apparently, was to care for those under his charge, and show them the compassion of Jesus. Perhaps twenty years earlier, he would've preferred to fight for honor or certain rights, pride or land, but God had opened his eyes. Life on earth was preparation for eternity. Anything that interfered with that perspective simply wasn't worthy of pursuit.

But that didn't mean his charge from God would be without trials, tragedies, and challenges. The narrow canyon he had in mind as a refuge had a river running through it, but it was no paradise. Maybe trusting God at the river would make sense there.

The morning after Major Milton appointed him as provisions officer, Eric led one hundred people south. They followed a mere deer trail into the mountains, a trail wide enough only for a pack horse. Behind him, women and children marched, some as young as infants in their mothers' arms. A few wounded soldiers were being dragged on travois behind ten horses Major Milton had given them. The trail was riddled with bogs that late spring, and an occasional deadfall tree. Women who didn't have their hands full guided the pack horses and wounded men through or around the obstacles.

Initially, Hank Worcester was assigned to the back of the long procession, to keep stragglers moving. However, their pace was so slow that he moved up the line to find Eric at the head, then scouted cautiously up the trail for the best route southward.

"Do you have a plan to keep all these people alive?" Hank asked as they climbed over a log that crossed the trail. "We're lucky it's almost summer, but winter will be here in a few months."

"What were you before Pan-Day, Hank?" Eric took the hand of a redheaded woman with an infant on her hip, and helped her over the log. The woman was beautiful, her eyes fierce and bold, but Eric wasn't there to court a future wife. "Let me guess. You were a laborer—carpentry or construction, right?"

Hank's face showed surprise.

"How'd you know? I was a building foreman. Pan-Day happened after my fiftieth birthday. I was planning my retirement."

"You've got the hands and shoulders that show you've got the experience. Besides, Major Milton said you'd be helpful when it came to building log cabins in the little valley I have in mind."

"No offense, but why are we following you instead of me? You're not even a soldier, just a crazy survivalist no one but the major believes in."

"All that may or may not be true, Hank, but this crazy survivalist knows these mountains after six years of hiking and hunting and gathering in them. The way Major Milton put it, you'll be in charge of the building, and I'll sort out the provisions, which means hunting and gathering. You and I are the only two able-bodied men here, so we need to start picking out women who can help with the work. We need builders who can swing an axe for log cabins, and diggers for latrines, and skinners for the game we bring in. And there's the matter of security as well. There's bound to be squabbles amongst us and new arrivals from Major Milton. Everyone needs to be recorded, and even interviewed and assigned to a responsibility."

"So, you do understand this is no small venture." Together, they lifted a travois over a log as the horse walked slowly on. A sleeping wounded man lay on the transport device, his head bandaged. "Maybe I should see the good side. At least I'm back here with my family instead of marching on Mastover where I'd be getting shot at."

"Your family is here?"

"Wife and daughter. They're toward the front of this parade." He moved to Eric's side of the trail and lowered his voice. "You mentioned security. The major will want a guard posted around our campsite, and we need to vet strangers who wander in. Could be spies for the Lib-Org."

"I'll leave the security to you," Eric said. "Just keep in mind we're not the army. These are women and kids."

They reached the hidden river valley after dark. Everyone was exhausted. Hank and Eric started several fires and set up the wall tents, with the help of several useful women.

Hank and Eric picketed the horses, then sat down at a fire with the new citizens of River Camp, and shared their jerky made from deer meat. Hank spoke quietly with his wife, a stout blond woman named Sara, but Eric saw no sign of the daughter he'd mentioned.

Many of the people—both men and women—were too tired to leave the fires, even after the tents were erected, so they simply slept under the stars, collapsing in sleeping bags, tarps, or blankets next to the fires.

As Eric fell asleep, he prayed for strength, wisdom, and faith to lead, now that he was at the river. *Trust God at the river.*

The rest of the night would've been uneventful if it hadn't been for the redheaded woman who rolled over and threw her arm across Eric's face. The blow startled him awake, but he realized he wasn't actually being attacked. The night was cool, and the woman, about Eric's age, had snuggled under the edge of his tarp for warmth.

Careful not to wake her, he used two fingers to lift her arm off his face and set it aside. Only then did he sit up to see the sprawling camp around him—one hundred lives committed to his care. He could be a useful caregiver to them because of the skills he'd learned, but he wouldn't be a meaningful and effective follower of Christ unless he remained steadfast in the Lord through the coming months. The people needed a shepherd, not just a provisions officer.

Slipping out from under his tarp, he pulled on his boots and gently pushed several half-burnt logs onto the fire. Dawn was an hour away, and the people would wake to a cold morning. And they'd be hungry. Hank was a soldier and builder, but Eric could tell by the way he'd walked the day before that he was no woodsman. His feet fell heavily and noisily. A hunter needed to be a prowler, a tracker, silent and deadly. Therefore, meat would be largely Eric's responsibility.

The gentle river flowed with barely a ripple below the ridge on the edge of their camp. It was shallow and rocky, but Eric had seen trout swim in its shadows in years past. He knelt and took a long drink, praying through the decisions for that day. He'd cared only for himself for so long. His mind was reeling at the number of people gathered around seven fires that early morning.

"It'll be a busy day." Hank crouched next to him and filled a tin pitcher of water. "What do you think we should do first, Provisions Officer?"

"My adopted son and grandma were left at my cabin to the east. Whatever needs to be done today is in your hands while I go get them. Can you handle things?"

"After our talk yesterday, I thought you had everything planned out." The big man frowned. "I haven't really put any consideration into what needs to be done myself."

"Call a meeting with everyone. Let them know that latrines need to be dug and the tents need to be moved away from the river to a little higher ground. I'll hunt on the way back from my cabin. Anyone with fishing line should get started on breakfast. I'll build a fish trap soon. And gather some of the women with axes and saws. We'll need logs for the lodges and firewood for cooking and warmth. If everyone has a purpose, no one will have time for despair."

"What about the enemy seeing our smoke from our fires?"

"We should put a couple guards on that ridge there. Maybe a couple of the older women who can pair up to keep each other company."

"That'll keep them out of my hair, too." Hank chuckled. It was a good sound to hear his banter. "I'll set my wife, Sara, over some of the women. She's bossy. How do you expect to fetch food for everyone here?"

"There's tubers, like potatoes, all along this shaded area west of the river. The fish from the river will supplement our diet, but we shouldn't over-fish. So, we'll need a hunting troop, maybe three healthy women who can hike, shoot, and pack meat with me. It'll be hard work. Two teams of two should do the job."

"Well, my daughter seems to already have taken a liking to you. She can shoot and she's strong."

"Your daughter?" Eric felt his body go rigid. So far, he'd been able to think of the River Camp situation as a professional and Christian responsibility. But the whole camp had more than a dozen women who were single and possibly searching for healthy suitors. "Which one is your daughter?"

"Gretchen. You were snuggling with her this morning. I thought you knew."

Eric felt his face get warm.

"Hank, I didn't— I mean, there was nothing—"

"Relax, Provisions Officer." He nudged Eric hard, knocking him off-balance. "She's a grown woman. I'm just glad to see she's comfortable around you. She usually steers clear of the soldier-types. Cares for the children more than anyone, but she doesn't smile much, anymore. If you need a hunter, I taught her to shoot, and Gretchen's a hard worker. Maybe with that kind of responsibility, it'll bring her back to the smiling girl we used to know before Pan-Day."

Before the camp woke, Eric waded the river and set off toward Andy and Talia at the cabin. He'd been gone three days, and it was a hard ten miles to the homestead, through deep valleys and up steep slopes.

Moving alone, he could cover forty miles a day, with a pack, so when he reached the cabin before noon, he took time for a swim in the pond below the cabin. All this business about being around attractive women suddenly made him feel self-conscious. A bath seemed in order.

He was pulling on his clothes next to Joyce's grave when Runner barked and ran up to him. Andy was a few steps behind, grinning broadly. Though he was mature for his age, he still didn't hesitate to run into Eric's embrace, and laugh as they ruffled each other's shaggy hair.

"No bears?" Eric asked as they hiked toward the cabin.

"Nah. I yelled and screamed during the nights, so I scared them away."

"Good man." Eric smiled. "There's no shame in dealing with your fear. You get those poles peeled? They'll make good logs for a larger cabin someday."

"Yeah, they're finished." He ran ahead and laid a hand on the handle of one of their axes. "This got stuck when I was trying to chop wood. I couldn't get it out."

"That's okay." Eric took the handle in one hand and yanked hard. The head had rusted around the wood through a couple dewy mornings, but he knew Andy had been trying to help. The axe easily came free. "Where's Grandma Talia?" He looked toward the cabin. He was surprised she hadn't come outside to welcome him back. She'd been uncomfortable about him leaving in the first place.

"Yesterday, Grandma Talia didn't get out of bed."

"Is she feeling better today?" Eric asked.

"I don't think she feels anything anymore." Andy patted Runner on the head rather casually. "She hasn't moved. And she's cold."

"I see." Eric felt a little nauseous suddenly. He turned and looked at the pond where one grave already lay. It wasn't like Talia to remain in bed—or remain still and cold. Andy was young, but he knew about mortality better than most. "Did she say she wasn't feeling well?"

"I don't think so." Andy shrugged. "Her hip was always sore. But maybe her pain is gone now."

"Come on inside, Andy." Eric walked to the cabin. "I have some news." Inside, he found the small woman's still form on the bed. Her eyes were closed and her face looked peaceful. He prepared Talia for burial, like he'd done with Joyce, wrapping her in a deer hide. Andy stood watching nearby, Runner whining next to him.

At the gravesite, Eric saw Andy wipe at his eyes, but trying to be brave, as Eric dug the grave. They'd both grown close to Talia through that winter. They would miss her very much.

When it came time to speak over the new grave next to Joyce's, Eric's words were few.

"Talia went peacefully in her sleep, her body simply worn out. What makes it all less sad, is that she came to

Christ around last Christmas. She knew the love of Jesus, and now she's face to face with Him. One day soon, we'll all be together again. Thank You, Lord, for bringing her into our lives. Amen."

Back in the cabin, he began packing as he told Andy about the commission he'd received. Andy's lower lip trembled as the news hit him much harder than Eric had figured it would.

"How long will you be gone?" Andy's little shoulders slumped and Runner whined. "I don't want to be alone forever."

"Oh, Andy." Eric knelt in front of the boy. "I'd like you to come with me, if you want. You can help with the plants and building. You have a good eye for purslane and water lily, and your hands are already as calloused as a man's from hard work, so I know you'll be helpful when it comes to firewood. I don't want anyone else as my partner on this next adventure. And I don't think God wants you and me to part ways just yet, either."

"What if they take you away from me? There's a lot of people, you said."

"Andy, you and I have history. We're like family. No one can replace what you and I have. There'll be a lot of people and they'll have lots of needs. We'll have to share ourselves with them to help them, but at the end of the day, it's you and me eating around the campfire and swapping stories."

"I don't really want a bigger family, Eric."

"I understand." Looking away, Eric thought about the redhead, but it was probably just wishful thinking. "How about this: you and I have to meet and agree if one of us wants to add anyone else to our family. Agreed?"

Andy tapped a finger on his chin, while Runner and Eric waited for a response.

"Agreed! What do I need to pack?"

Chapter 3

Instead of starting back to River Camp that afternoon, Eric and Andy spent the night in the cabin and readied the shack for their coming extended absence. Eric disconnected the water system to dry out, then tightly rolled up any hides they were leaving behind to discourage mice as much as possible. The place had been Eric's home for six years, so he was somber about leaving the cabin to the elements, but he and Andy both understood that God was leading them elsewhere. That made the change for them acceptable, especially since they were staying together.

The next morning, they set off before dawn, both with packs piled high and arms full of tools and gear. Since the way to River Camp was mostly downhill, Eric laid upon Andy more than he was used to carrying. But the young man seemed game for anything he could do with Eric, to show him he was indeed worthy of hard work without complaining.

About midway between the cabin and River Camp, they were crossing a flowery meadow when Eric noticed movement along the tree line. Movement itself wasn't too rare, since the whole forest was alive with wildlife. Spotting deer and the occasional elk wasn't abnormal. Rabbits and squirrels were everywhere, and birds fluttered about constantly. The movement he noticed was something of mass, something solid and lumbering.

He took a knee in the tall grass and eased his rifle off his shoulder. Andy, familiar with his body language from hunting trips, crawled up to Eric's side.

"Bear," Eric whispered, and pointed to their right. "Stay low."

Andy nodded, his eyes wide, as he hugged Runner to the ground. Eric was surprised Runner hadn't caught the scent of the beast already. Normally, they would've given a bear space to move along, but Eric's mind was on the prospect of meat. One hundred hungry people were five miles away.

Sliding his pack from his back, Eric steadied his nerves against fear. His rifle was a deer rifle, not a bear gun. The .223 cartridge had little stopping power against a charging bear. But the bullet was adequate enough if he could place it carefully in a vital organ. Such a shot would take precision, which wasn't something he could do if he were panicked.

After signaling for Andy to remain there, he stalked straight into the trees to approach the bear from the side. If it hadn't sensed him yet, he could take his time and place a shot without damaging meat or risking his life.

This area was full of young growth trees, burned and reseeded in the last twenty years, so there were no trees for several hundred yards large enough to climb if something went wrong.

Eric halted his advance as he heard the bear ahead, perhaps eating or digging, but definitely distracted by something on the ground. The trees weren't hindering his view of the animal, now only thirty yards away, but the foxtail grass was waist high and thick. Swallowing past terror, Eric realized he'd have to get closer to get a clear shot.

Suddenly, on his left, Runner bolted across the meadow! She'd broken free from Andy, and bounded straight west, yipping as she went. Whether chasing a squirrel or a bird, she ignored the bear. Andy's blond head popped above the grass, focused on his loose dog.

Just as startling, the beast Eric was hunting rose up to a stand. It wasn't a bear at all, but a man! The man held a bow with an arrow aimed at the field. An instant later, he loosed his arrow and Runner yelped.

Andy jumped to his feet in his hiding place and screamed as he ran toward his dog. The man, with half his face visible to Eric, appeared shocked by this turn of events. Eric quietly moved up behind the stranger and noticed a dead deer at his feet. The bow hunter had been gutting a deer. When he took a step toward the meadow, Eric raised his rifle and aimed it at the man.

"Stay where you are," Eric said.

The man froze, then turned slowly, his hands raised. Though he still held his bow, he didn't hold any arrows, but his quiver was full on his back. Andy wailed from the meadow as he found Runner.

"I thought it was a coyote," the bow hunter said. He wore black and gray fatigues and worn-out boots. His face was shaved and his hair was cropped short, like a soldier. Eric didn't recognize him from Major Milton's resistance fighters, and the man wore no armband. "I honestly didn't know there were other people out here. I'd heard there was a mad man somewhere in the mountains, maybe farther east."

"I've heard of the mad man as well." Eric aimed his rifle at his feet, easing the tension, but the bow hunter kept his hands up. "So, where are you from? I know for a fact you don't live out here."

"That's true. I'm just hunting. I live in Mastover."

"Mastover's a long way from here."

"Most of the other men go antelope hunting out on the range." He licked his lips nervously. Eric wondered if he would try to attack him, using a knife or reach for another arrow. "But I'm a bow hunter. I come down here and hunt deer a couple times a year for my wife and kid."

"You said the other men. From Mastover?"

"Yeah, the other—" He hesitated, then glanced northward. "You probably know who I'm with."

"I do. Your uniform says a lot." Eric cradled his rifle across his chest and the hunter lowered his arms. "I also know if you live in Mastover, you guys joined the Liberation Organization when it rolled through here last year."

"Everybody in Mastover works for them now." He shrugged and Eric noticed he was missing a front tooth. "For years, we barely survived. We had no gear to even fight the Meridia Virus. Now, we wear military surplus, and I do what I want when I'm not on patrol. We all have someone to take care of."

Andy walked up then, a bloody arrow in his hand, tears streaking his face.

"She's dead, Eric." He wiped his cheeks. "I didn't even get to say goodbye."

"It was an accident, Andy." Eric knelt down. "I wish it hadn't happened. This man thought she was a coyote. He really didn't mean to hurt her. Runner was a good, loyal dog."

Andy looked up at the man. The boy's fists were clenched. Pain etched his face, and grief pooled in his red eyes. He was about to say something, but then he turned and walked back to Runner.

The bow hunter sighed and glanced at the deer half-gutted.

"I don't think you could say anything more to make me regret what I did." He leaned his bow against a tree. "The look on your boy's face was more than enough."

"He lost his father to bandits last year, then his mother to a mountain fall." Eric frowned. "No boy should witness this much blood."

"I know it's not much, but can I give you a quarter?" He motioned at the deer. Eric noticed the arrow wound just behind the animal's left shoulder—a perfect shot.

"We could use the meat." Eric drew a buck knife from his belt and helped the stranger carve up the carcass.

The man's name was Joel Grayport. He'd lived his whole twenty-eight years in Mastover, and was now married to a neighbor girl named Lena. Perhaps Joel's regret opened his heart to speak freely to a stranger, so Eric let him talk. Eric's own feelings were mixed about the run-in. On one hand, Runner, Andy's closest friend, was dead. The boy he considered his son had been horribly hurt. On the other hand, a man who could be considered an enemy was now indebted to Eric. God was working out something, but what?

A hindquarter of the deer was cut off, and Joel cut a sapling to help skid the rest of his kill out to a Humvee he said was parked on the highway a few miles north.

"So, who are you?" Joel asked, wiping his bloody hands on the grass. "I've been doing all the talking."

Eric considered what he could say to a man who belonged to the Liberation Organization. Such a soldier would want to know all that was going on in those woods. Major Milton Pickford was staging an offensive against the Lib-Org's oppressive presence in Mastover. Not far away, the major's forces were gathering, and Eric had assumed charge over the families of the resistance.

"Just a man who needs to bury a dog."

"Well, take care."

Joel left, skidding his carcass through the trees. Eric looked down at the haunch of meat at his feet. It seemed a poor consolation for the loss caused by their meeting. The meat was needed back at River Camp, but nothing could replace Runner. From his gear, Eric drew a short shovel and joined Andy in the meadow where he was sitting next to his friend.

Kneeling next to Andy, Eric put his arm around his shoulder, and tried to find the right words to comfort the boy.

"She knew how much you loved her." Eric placed his hand on Runner's head. "We will always remember what a good friend she was to you."

When Eric and Andy reached River Camp, they were met with more death. One of the wounded soldiers of the resistance had died that morning, and a brief funeral was underway. A burial site under a stand of trees downriver had been selected, but only a few people gathered—Eric, Hank, and a woman who'd been the soldier's nurse. The fact that the whole camp didn't attend told Eric much about the weary hearts around him. They'd already seen too much death. Attending a funeral would simply remind them about the death that seemed to stalk them all.

"I think his name was Bill," the nurse said. Her hair looked like it hadn't been brushed in months.

"Someone said he was from North Dakota," Hank said, leaning on a shovel near the mound of earth. "He came to fight for us, but none of us really know anything about him."

Gazing back at camp, Eric saw the people had been busy over the past twenty-four hours. The tents had been moved off the riverbank, and women were at the river washing clothes. Others were in the trees, digging latrine pits. Andy had joined other youths who were stacking tree branches for firewood.

"God didn't design us for death," Eric said softly. "We chose to sin, which brought death. Every death around us reminds us of our own mortality. Eternity is a gaping mouth, and we all must enter it through the grave. May we entrust our lives to the Creator while we're still alive, because death on this side is so very final."

"You sound like a preacher," the nurse said. "I knew a preacher once."

"Major Milton warned me that you were a man of the Bible." Hank's voice sounded bitter, and Eric was reminded that there'd been a movement to remove Christians and Bibles a year earlier in Mastover. "Is there any truth in that?"

"Any truth in what?" Eric smiled. "That I'm a man of the Bible, or that there's truth in the Bible?"

"Both." He snarled, revealing his stained teeth through his beard.

"God's Word settles my heart about all this, and about eternity. If everything in our lives is stripped away, and we look closely, we see our need for God to save us from our sinful condition. That's the truth."

They stood in silence for a few minutes, then left the grave one at a time.

In camp, several women assigned as camp cooks chatted casually as they sliced into the deer haunch Eric had brought.

Between the tents, an older woman instructed three younger women how to tie line from pole to pole for a clothesline. Several youths collected rocks, piling them in a semi-circle as a boundary for the camp. The boundary served no practical purpose, Eric guessed, but the people needed to mark their new home. The boundary of rocks gave River Camp a sense of possession.

Near the river, three women waited for him, cradling hunting rifles in their arms. One of them was Gretchen, even more attractive in the full light of the afternoon sun. She wore a leather belt with a skinning knife on it, and her fiery hair was tied back in a loose ponytail.

Eric sat cross-legged on the ground and created a model of the area with rocks and river sand. The three women understood and knelt around the model.

"This is the river, and here's River Camp. The mountain range runs along here, and we're about in the middle of it all. The highway is along here, ten miles to our north. Never get any closer to the highway than you are right now, including when you shoot game. Otherwise, people in Mastover or travelers on the highway will hear your gunshots.

"Now, you have three mountain peaks to remember. None of you know this wilderness, so pay attention, or I'll be tracking down lost hunters instead of wild game."

After Eric's instructions for hunting and getting back to camp alive, he studied the other two women hunters, eyeing their rifles and gear. Both were brunettes. One was stocky and strong-looking, and the other was tall and slim. Each wore patched jeans and hiking boots, like Gretchen, and their faces seemed determined to accomplish the hard work ahead of them.

"Well, you three know each other," Eric said. "The last thing to sort out for an afternoon hunt is—who pairs up with me?"

"She already told us she's going with you." The stocky one pointed at Gretchen. "It's fine with us. We both have men already. They're fighting for Major Milton."

Rather than meet Gretchen's gaze and get swept up in the coupling idea that seemed to permeate the survival atmosphere, Eric stood and signaled to Hank. He was helping two women build a turkey coop.

"We'll be back by nightfall," Eric yelled. Andy heard, and waved. He had a stick in his hand, and was teaching several older boys and girls how to trap turkeys for the coop. Runner would've been a pleasant companion at his side, but such were the tragedies of those last days in America.

"Dad said you've lived in these mountains since Pan-Day." Gretchen matched Eric's pace as they crossed the river and headed south. The other hunting pair worked their way up the ridge to the east. "You lived alone, or did you have a wife?"

He stopped suddenly and smiled at her, remembering what Hank had said about her sadness for years. The world had changed, and worry had lined the young woman's face. Before Pan-Day, marriages and divorces were frequent and careless. Now, he hoped the strife would cause marriage to return to its rightful place—as an enduring and endearing relationship. Gretchen was husband-hunting while they were supposed to be deer hunting. Eric was flattered, but he had a job to do.

"Let's bag a deer before dusk, okay?" He nodded briefly. "We can talk back at camp as much as we want."

"Okay. Sorry."

"No apologies necessary." He climbed the ridge that overlooked a clearing to the south. "It's only natural to want to know the people we're supposed to work with."

From the top of the ridge, Eric used binoculars to scope the clearing, then directed Gretchen to sneak down to the edge of the expanse. Meanwhile, Eric intended to make a wide circle around the clearing, hoping to drive an animal or two into her range.

Suddenly, Eric saw several bounding white-tailed deer fleeing into the clearing from the forest where Gretchen had just entered. If he and the other hunters were successful this early on their first hunting attempt, packing the meat the two miles back to camp would be a quick trek. It looked like this would be an early night.

Less than a minute later, Eric heard a gunshot. He froze. The echo of the blast bounced off the mountains around him. A second shot sounded, and he measured the possibility of an enemy hearing the noise. But miles of forest, hills, and mountains separated them from the highway, and there'd been no inhabitants in the rugged land except him, as far as he knew.

Rather than continue his drive around the clearing, he walked directly toward where he figured Gretchen would be. Nearing the meadow, he stumbled upon a deer hiding in a thicket. It hesitated to run, and Eric aimed his rifle to quickly conclude the hunt.

Reaching the clearing, he found Gretchen standing over another deer.

"You got the other one?" She was grinning proudly, a small buck at her feet. "I did it. I mean, we did it. Three shots and we got two deer. That's not bad, right?"

"Not bad, Miss Worcester."

"So, we make a good pair, don't we?"

Eric sighed as she winked, apparently sensing his discomfort, but flirting anyway. She drew her skinning knife and knelt to gut the animal as he returned to his kill. By the time he dragged his doe to the clearing, the other two hunters had reached them and readied to help haul the deer back to camp. After cutting two poles with a compact hatchet from Eric's pack, they started the trip back to camp with the day's provision from God.

The other two women, Liz and Joy, chattered excitedly over the successful hunt, which pleased Eric. Their kills were viewed as success for all of River Camp. It seemed they were growing closer already.

But as they reached the river and started across, Eric could see that River Camp was far from rejoicing with them, as they stood near the tents. In the few hours they'd been gone, something had happened. The campfires were out and no one was moving about preparing the evening meal. The four hunters lay the two deer beside the cold coals of a fire circle, then Eric and Gretchen walked briskly toward the gathered crowd.

Eric wondered if calm would ever reach River Camp.

Chapter 4

Leaving the two deer in the care of Liz and Joy for skinning and butchering, Eric led Gretchen through the crowd gathered near the wall tents. They found Hank in the center, sitting next to a soldier Eric recognized from the resistance army. He had blood on his cheek, and his assault rifle stock was broken, perhaps smashed by a bullet.

Everyone waited for Eric's reaction, so he took his time assessing the situation. They all knew if fighting men were ever found in their camp by the Lib-Org soldiers, they would be targeted as the enemy, and attacked. For that reason, no one even wore the red, white, and blue armbands in camp, not even Hank.

"Whatever happened," Eric said loudly for the hundred people to hear, "we still need to eat tonight. It's dark now, so get the fires going and go about your business. Go on now. I'll hear what the man has to say, and you'll all know soon enough."

The crowd reluctantly dispersed, except for Gretchen, who sat on a log with Eric. Andy also remained and set his hand on Eric's shoulder. Hank gestured at the newcomer.

"This is Sergeant Zellick of the Resistance. He was part of an offensive against Mastover." Hank held up his hand. "I already told him, Eric. He knows he's got to leave as soon as he gets patched up."

Eric studied the man, who was a little younger than himself, with soft features and sad eyes.

"Tell me what happened."

"We took the bridge south of Mastover." He sipped from a dented canteen. "We were trying to cut off the supply route through town. The Liberation Organization continues to traffic supplies up from Denver. Most of us used to live in Mastover. We just want our homes back and freedoms restored. We don't want any part of this Liberation Organization. They're butchers!"

"I understand."

"How'd you take the bridge?" Hank asked.

"We were dug in with a couple RPGs and machine guns on the west and east flanks. Then we just blocked the bridge. We didn't even fire on the first convoy that met us. They rolled up, we told them the bridge was closed, and they turned around. One was even a tank. We thought we were finally making a point."

"They probably radioed Mastover," Eric guessed.

"Yeah, they must have. They hit us from the north, then got around us somehow. We took heavy losses on the south side before we pulled back. That's where I was. When we were retreating into the trees, the north side of the bridge had fallen. Major Milton was there. No one got out, but some were still alive."

"Prisoners of war," Hank growled and struck his knee with a fist. "They got the major. That blasted Judge Grayport will hang him!"

"Grayport?" Eric frowned, remembering his meeting with a bow hunter name Joel Grayport. "Who's that?"

"The traitor of Mastover, Zachary Grayport, the honorable judge himself." Hank spit on the ground. "He's ruled Mastover since Pan-Day. He was running for political office, anyway. Pan-Day just gave him the chance to rule like a tyrant. At first, he was an organizer, then he turned on his own people. He got us all killing each other, finding any excuse to turn in anyone with opposing views."

"Opposing views?" Eric asked. "Like being a Christian?"

"We were all responsible for last year's massacre." Hank lowered his gaze. "I admit it was wrong, even if I don't like them." He crossed his arms. "The judge joined up with the Organization the minute they drove into town. That's when most of us left. We wouldn't join arms with the invading army. It's un-American, even if they are made up mostly of our old military."

"Grayport still runs Mastover," Sergeant Zellick said, "but he runs it for the Organization, not for the people of Mastover. He'll torture Major Milton until he talks. The judge will know where all of you people are in no time. Torture. It happened last year when—"

"We've got to rescue the major," Hank said, leveling his gaze at Eric. The nearest firelight flickered off his face, punctuating his features. "I've got to leave, Eric. I have to find what's left of the resistance and reorganize them."

"They've scattered." Zellick struggled with his emotions. "It'll be weeks before we pull together again. After we left the bridge, we agreed I should come here and tell you what's happened. No one followed me. I was careful."

"Let me think a minute," Eric said.

Eric stood and walked away from them. The campfires were blazing now, and meat and wild vegetables were being cooked. Crushed cattail, like flour, was added to the water that the youths had gathered. Chufa, a type of tuber, could be smelled in the thick stew, mixed with the fresh meat. The aroma made his mouth water as he stooped at the river's edge and picked up a couple of stones to toss at the water. Was this it? Was this where God wanted him to trust at the river, like Joshua had trusted Him at the Jordan?

"Lord, give me Your guidance here," he mumbled to the blinking starlight. "The safety of so many under my care is under threat. I beg You, show me what to do. Please show Yourself mighty against—"

"You're praying at a time like this?"

Hank joined Eric at the water.

"I'm praying especially at a time like this."

"If you didn't hear me earlier, let me say it again: I was part of that Christian cleansing last year in Mastover."

He crossed his thick arms. "I'm not proud of the lives we took, but no religion is going to dictate my liberties."

"It's God, not religion, who gives us liberty," Eric said. "Liberty is found because of God. God wants us to be set free from the things that destroy our lives. I used to think that God spoiled all the fun I wanted to have. Now I understand He was trying to show me that He cares for me enough to warn me about the consequences of the wicked ways my old nature wanted to live for."

"Whatever. Just so you know, I don't need some religious nut's permission to leave and rescue Major Milton."

"That may be. But you'll need your wife's permission, and you'll never hear the end of it once I tell her you left to die in Mastover when God provided another way to get Major Milton set free."

"What do you know, Provisions Officer? You've lived on a mountain for years."

"Do you know Joel Grayport?"

"Sure, everybody knows Junior, daddy's spoiled brat. Quarterback and prom king ten years ago."

"What's his status under Judge Grayport?"

"He's a captain. When I left Mastover, he was in charge of security patrols around town, like the military police. Curfew and stuff."

"Mastover has a curfew?"

"I suspect every city in America has a curfew, since Pan-Day."

"So, to move around at night, people use a pass?"

"Not in Mastover. Everybody knows everybody. Strangers would be noticed immediately." He cocked his head. "What's this about?"

"I know Joel Grayport. He sort of . . . owes me."

"Well, that—" He glanced back toward the tents. "I have no love for any Grayport, but if you have something on Junior, that changes everything."

"Can you describe to me where he lives in Mastover?"

"I can do you one better." He chuckled. "I can walk you to his back door. He lives in a quiet part of Mastover with his wife—some rich girl from across town."

"Lena."

"You really do know him." A quiet moment passed. "I'd love to ruin the lives of the Grayports. The debt that Junior owes you—will it work for this?"

"It's something like a life for a life. But listen, Hank. We can't both go. You need to stay here. We can't leave these people without a leader. Is there anyone else you trust who can guide me to Joel Grayport's house? How about this Sergeant Zellick?"

"You've seen the man. He's weak and skittish. I don't think I'd trust him under pressure. And make no mistake: where you're going, there'll be plenty of pressure. Mastover was already a cesspool when we left. A year's passed, and that place literally stinks from miles away. And I haven't even gotten to the scumbags who live there!"

"I understand. Listen, I agree that we've got to get Milton free before he's forced to talk and tell them where we are."

"Judge Grayport is crazy enough to hunt us down and kill us all, just to make a point. He's afraid of that Liberation Organization." Hank cursed. "Gretchen knows where Junior lives. She catered their wedding, if I recall. But she can't go back. Everyone there knows us. They'll kill her."

"It's either her or someone less capable. She has good instincts, Hank." Eric patted him on the shoulder. "This is one of those places to trust God. Come on. Let's keep this quiet and go eat with the others. I'll talk to Gretchen when it's time."

That evening, Eric slurped deer venison stew while seated next to Andy at one of the fires. The boy barely ate, however, since he was so busy telling Eric about all of his new friends and responsibilities. Knowing everything a boy could know about staying alive in the wilderness had made him popular. Even at such a young age, he seemed to be a natural leader. He even had innovative ideas for catching wild turkeys that made Eric's own traps seem medieval. By gently corralling a whole flock of turkeys into a fenced funnel, dozens of the birds could be caught at once, supplying River Camp with eggs and the occasional turkey dinner.

That night, before Eric bedded down next to Andy, Hank approached him and spoke quietly.

"You haven't spoken to Gretchen yet about the rescue!" His anger surprised Eric. "What are you playing at, Provisions Officer?"

"I'm not playing." He smiled at the older man, though it wasn't his intention to provoke him. "I'm thinking of you."

"Me?"

"Yeah. Imagine if your wife knew ahead of time that you were allowing your daughter to guide me into the enemy's territory."

"Oh."

"Besides, the less I show myself actively concerned in this rescue, the more you'll see that it's God who has already provided us with the means to speak to Joel Grayport about the prisoners. I believe God has gone before us in this matter."

"You're so sure of this God, huh?" The man ran his fingers through his beard.

"I've been following Him for nearly six years, Hank. He doesn't speak to us in words, but by our circumstances, thoughts, and situations. It's a language that's pretty loud if we open our ears to it. He just wants us to trust Him."

"I don't know if you're crazy or brilliant." He kicked at a rock on the ground. "We can't keep this rescue from everyone for long. You'd better return with good news, or we're ruined, one way or another."

"As far as anyone knows, Gretchen and I are going hunting at dawn." Eric slapped Hank on the shoulder. "Just do me a favor and pray for us while we're gone."

Hank guffawed and shook his head as he walked up to the wall tent in which he and his wife had claimed a small corner. Only a few of the younger women slept outside the ten tents. The wounded and children had priority space inside, then the oldest women. Tarps were laid out and lean-tos had been erected for the rest. Gretchen stayed at Eric's fire, laying a sleeping bag under a folded tarp. As a primary provider for the camp, she was quickly rising in influence among the campers. Andy shared Eric's tarp, and before the fire started to diminish, they all fell asleep.

#######

Gretchen wasn't disappointed in the least the next morning when Eric told her they were headed into Mastover rather than going hunting. She listened to his plan and maintained a brisk pace northward.

"Together, we have to convince Joel Grayport and his wife, Lena, to help us," Eric said. "If they don't, River Camp may be raided."

"Won't breaking resistance fighters out of lockup automatically bring the fight to our doorstep?"

"It would, if the resistance fighters weren't free to continue their fight. A good offense is a good defense."

"You sound an awful lot like a resistance fighter," she said.

"I guess I do. But I think there's a difference between attacking and protecting, or hating and caring. If it were up to me, I would host a peace accord, but I haven't seen how God has opened that door yet. I made it clear to Major Milton that I'm not a fighter. I'll adjust tactics toward peaceful results the minute I see a better path to loving my neighbor."

"I don't think God is paying much attention to us here, Eric. Imagine the damage we could do to Judge

Grayport's forces if we put our marksmanship up against theirs. Then they'd see we're not worth bothering."

"Wait and see," Eric said. He felt God's reassuring hand of comfort—that trusting Him for what lay ahead wouldn't be wasted trust. God was about to do something unmistakably obvious.

By noon, they reached the highway. They hid in the trees until the highway was clear, then crossed it at a run. On the north side of the highway, there was only rolling rangeland, so they didn't slow their walk until they were a mile beyond the highway. If they would've been noticed, an all-terrain vehicle could've run them down, but like Eric had been telling both Hank and Gretchen, God was moving the situation in their favor.

Fifteen miles later, dusk overtook them, and the back side of Mastover came into sight. Exhausted, they lay on a bluff and looked down at the partially inhabited settlement.

"The virus killed most of the citizens six years ago," Gretchen explained between bites of spatterdock biscuits and dried deer meat. "People running from the east arrived weeks later and settled here, living in the houses of those who'd died. The fighting has killed more, mostly men. The Liberation Organization promised stability, but they only left equipment, temporary representatives, and laws to make sure the Organization's interests were maintained here. Mainly, that meant their vehicles could pass through unhindered, to keep the supply line open to the fighting up north."

"So, there's not a Lib-Org battalion here?"

"Not when we were here a year ago. It's all locals fighting for the Lib-Org. Half the people, I suspect, are caught in the middle. If they side with the resistance, then they have to face the Lib-Org. I guess the locals would rather fight us than them. And you haven't met Judge Zachary Grayport. The man's possessed by power. If we're going downtown, I'm sure we'll see his handiwork. He regularly hangs people who voice opposition to the Lib-Org. The Organization burns people at the stake, but the judge prefers hanging. I'm not sure which is worse."

"Are there people down there who aren't fully behind the judge and the Lib-Org?"

"Of course. But they still side with the judge, and the judge only sides with the Lib-Org to keep their commander from destroying Mastover. They're at peace with the Organization, so that makes them as bad as the Lib-Org."

When darkness had fully blanketed the terrain, they prowled down into the town. This was a true time of testing for Eric's faith. He'd spoken boldly about his God when there was no cost. Now, his life was in the balance with many others. He could rely on his own schemes, or he could believe God really had orchestrated his meeting with Joel Grayport.

The town they entered was a habitation of refuse. Stinking garbage was piled along every street and avenue. Only a narrow lane was provided down the center of roads for the rare vehicle to patrol through the rotting trash. No electricity had been restored to the outskirts of town, or the resistance had cut the power, so Eric's trek from house to house was in the twilight.

Through this stage, Eric followed Gretchen. She darted through yards where few dogs barked and no cats prowled; he guessed they'd mostly been eaten. Gretchen climbed through fences where boards had been removed for firewood. The town was no longer a town, but a cesspool under siege by its own hunger and garbage.

No one confronted them, and Eric began to wonder if Mastover was the fierce, invulnerable town he'd imagined. Whole neighborhoods stood without guard or patrol as they passed through them. If there were people inside the homes, they were sleeping or hiding. And starving.

Finally, they crouched behind a burned-out SUV. Around its flattened tires, weeds grew up through the cracked pavement. The vehicle probably hadn't budged since the riots of Pan-Day.

"That's his house." Gretchen pointed at a two-story dwelling, a green Humvee out front. "The judge lives across town in a mansion. He has electricity and demands tons of firewood in the winter. Joel didn't want special privileges that other people didn't get, so he distanced himself from his father by moving his family out here. It was a big controversy a few years ago between father and son."

"But Joel still fights for his father to remain in power here?"

"Of course." Her teeth shined in the moonlight. "You think he's crazy enough to go live in the woods? Besides, Lena was pregnant a year ago when we all pulled out in defiance against the Lib-Org."

Eric led the way around the house and approached a back door. It was locked, but he used his knife to punch through the rotting wood frame, and the deadbolt was freed with a muffled nudge. He would've liked to have one of Gordon Irwin's flashlights as he prowled inside, but instead, he quietly closed the door and crept into the dark with Gretchen behind him, her rifle leveled.

Silently, they approached a smoldering fireplace that crowded a cooking stove. Joel may have been a bow hunter, but living in the town had made him careless and without vigilance, just as Eric had hoped.

"Get comfortable," he said to Gretchen. "We'll wait for him to come to us."

Feeding the fire with a few scavenged boards, Eric lit the cooking stove and sat in a chair, his pack on the floor. He even leaned his rifle against the wall, which Gretchen did only grudgingly. It was all part of their plan to welcome Joel. To disarm the man they needed, they needed to be disarmed themselves.

But doubt began to plague Eric as the minutes passed. Would the plan work? He had no contingency besides what God had first given him—to meet and talk to Joel for his help. Then, a floorboard creaked above. A baby cried and Eric tensed, praying through his uncertainty.

"He's going to kill us!" Gretchen whispered and reached for her rifle.

"Stay still. He's not going to kill us." Eric's voice was normal, no longer a whisper. "There's a reason why the judge put his son on town patrol rather than on the frontlines of the fight. I don't think he's a killer."

They heard footsteps beyond the kitchen as someone padded in bare feet down the stairs, then paused. Gretchen eyed her rifle again, and Eric wondered if he hadn't dared death itself. What if Joel didn't even live there anymore? The fire flickered on his face, and the light stole his vision to see into the shadows of the living room where a shape stood.

Finally, unable to do anything through the tension, he waved toward the darkened staircase.

"Come on in, Joel. It's just me, the man who buried a dog a couple days ago."

"What does that mean?" Gretchen asked with a frown.

The shape emerged from the darkness. It was Joel, shirtless, shoeless, and holding a handgun. He studied Eric, acknowledging their rifles against the wall, then focused on Gretchen.

"I know you. You were a friend of Lena's." He looked back at Eric. "You didn't say a couple days ago that you were a resistance fighter."

"I wasn't a resistance fighter, and I'm still not a resistance fighter." Eric nodded at a chair that faced him. "But that doesn't mean I'm a supporter of those who slaughter innocents, either."

Joel eased into the chair, his gun resting on his knee. He wore jeans, but since he wore no shirt, he probably wished he were closer to the fire's heat.

"There's been slaughter on both sides," Joel said.

"That's not true!" Gretchen scowled. "The resistance has standards. They're fighting invaders who want to suck their lives dry. How can you be helping them? Look what they've done to this town! This isn't a caring government, Joel."

"That's not important right now." Eric held up his hand. "Willingly or not, we're on the side we're on. Joel, I believe we're both in a position to help one another. Our meeting out in the woods was no accident. I need your help, and you need my help."

"You planned the meeting in the woods? I don't believe it."

"No, I didn't plan it. God did." Eric shrugged. "That's right. If you and I hadn't met, I wouldn't know that you're the one to help us, and I wouldn't be here to help you."

"So you said. How do I need your help?" He scoffed, his missing tooth more prominent in the firelight. "The nerve of you two coming here, breaking into my home!"

The baby finally stopped crying upstairs.

"I don't believe we're enemies, Joel. At a time when we need one another for the sake of our families, I'm looking for more friends. How about you?"

"Say what you came to say."

Eric read Joel's expression and posture, remembering what the others had said about his past as quarterback and prom king. In a toe-to-toe fight, he could whip Eric. He was taller and broader and probably adept at fighting hand-to-hand. Except for his missing front tooth, he looked like a flawless warrior, especially while he still held the handgun.

"This civil war with the Lib-Org will make conditions worse in Mastover real soon. I'd like you, your wife, and your child to come live safely with us in the mountains."

"That's ridiculous. You don't even know me, and you don't know who my father is. Besides, we're perfectly safe here."

"For how long? The neighborhood is a garbage dump. An army could walk right through town and attack you— if the Lib-Org wanted to return in force, after the judge defies them for some reason. You hunt miles away for meat, and you burn fences to cook and stay warm. Winter will be here in a few months. Are things really that great where you are?"

"I can't leave." He looked at the floor. "My wife is sick."

"We have women to care for the ill."

"I don't mean she has the flu. I mean she's sick in the head. She just shut down since Shawna was born. I have to stay and take care of her most days. I was even demoted—to lieutenant."

"There's nothing left for you here, Joel," Eric pressed. "You and your wife will be very welcome in our camp. The change of environment and friendship may be just what Lena needs to return to her old self."

"The world is such a mess." He wiped at his eyes. "There's just no more hope. We're all just waiting to die."

"Not out at River Camp. We're alive. We're fishing and hunting. We're laughing and living in God's creation, enjoying one another's company. The war is far away from us. And you should be out there, too. That's one of the reasons I came here tonight."

"So, there's a catch?" His eyes narrowed.

"No catch. Just a responsibility. If the resistance falls apart, there'll never be stability in Wyoming. Your dad took prisoners a few days ago. We need to free them before we leave town. Unless they're free to continue their fight, hope for liberty in Wyoming can't be achieved. The Lib-Org will never meet to discuss terms for peace unless there's an opposition. We need to balance that power tonight."

"My father would kill me!"

"Where are the prisoners held?"

Joel shook his head.

"Are they at the courthouse?" Gretchen asked. "If they're there, the cells are in the basement."

"You can't free them." Joel glared at Eric. "How could you do this to me? We could've stayed here and died in peace! Why did you have to come? Why?"

"Because you matter." Eric rose to his feet. "Gretchen, go upstairs and pack for Lena and the baby. You'll be hiking back with them the way we came. Joel and I will be going through town."

She left the room, not even taking her rifle with her. They were a good team, Eric felt, but the last woman he'd favored had fallen down a cliff. He wasn't too keen on losing someone else he cared for, even if she did continue to drop hints about marriage.

Eric accompanied Joel as he collected his hunting gear and bow from the garage. Though it felt harsh to squeeze him between two choices, Eric still believed God was going before them, teaching him to trust . . .

Thirty minutes later, they were all gathered in the living room. Lena, a downcast blond, stood with a large pack on her back. Gretchen had attached a baby-carrier pack to her own front, while Shawna wiggled wide-eyed.

"They'll be chasing Joel and me," Eric said to Gretchen, "so you'll have some liberty with your pace, but you'll need to keep moving. It's fifteen miles the long way around the town back to the highway. If we can get out free, we'll meet you at the edge of the forest. Otherwise, get Lena to River Camp."

"How're you going to free the captives?" Gretchen asked.

Since he didn't have an answer, Eric gently crowded the four of them close, one arm around Lena and one arm around Joel, who stood stiffly next to him.

"Let's pray. Dear God, we are afraid and alone. Please show us Your favor and wisdom in this hard time. And please watch over us as we go into the dark night. We pray this because of what Your Son has already done for us. Amen."

No one said amen with him, but Gretchen nodded at Eric in the dim lighting as the fire died out.

She led Lena by the hand out the back door about two in the morning. Eric prayed he would see Gretchen again, that he would be given the opportunity to lead her to Christ. He felt she did hold some promise of a possible life partner, and he hoped he'd be able to pursue that thought.

Then, with their own packs, Joel and Eric walked out the front door and climbed into the Humvee.

Chapter 5

Lieutenant Joel Grayport drove his Humvee through two check points on their way to the courthouse. Heavily-armed soldiers let him pass without more than a wave, even with Eric, a bearded stranger, as a passenger. All around them, many buildings had remained half-burnt or in disrepair for years. There'd been no rebuilding, no recovery, no rising from the ashes of civil fighting. For six years, surviving had been the goal. Fear had been their driving emotion. How grateful Eric felt in that moment that God had directed him on Pan-Day to drive up that lonely mountain road and build a cabin. He hadn't seen half the misery these people had, but that didn't mean he could stand aside now that people in need required what he had—spiritually and logistically.

Joel halted the Humvee two blocks from the centrally-located courthouse. Soldiers on night patrol stood against a partially-demolished tech store, smoking cigarettes. On a low platform in the middle of the square were wooden gallows. Four bodies hung by their necks. One was even a child. Eric thought one of the dead moved, but it was a scavenger bird. It was a gruesome sight. The citizens of Mastover were forced to see what consequences they faced if one turned against Judge Grayport and the Lib-Org government.

The courthouse beyond the gallows seemed formidable, and Eric suddenly wanted to be anywhere but in Mastover, Wyoming. He wanted to be in the mountains, hiking beside Gretchen, Andy's hand in his, Runner dashing about as she chased squirrels. But, no. Runner was dead, and Gretchen was already far away. Before him stood a courthouse that housed soldiers with whom he had nothing in common, but he still desperately needed them to be free so balance could return to the land.

"There are about a dozen guards inside." Joel squinted through the windshield, then frowned at Eric. "I'll never be able to get you past them. We'd have to get downstairs. Only one holding cell has a functioning toilet, so that's where the resistance fighters are held."

"How many?"

"Seven."

"Is Major Milton Pickford with them?"

"He is. My father said that with his capture, he broke the resistance. He'll be furious if the major escapes, but it's impossible, anyway—if we want to get out alive."

"Exactly where in the basement are they being held?"

He drove the Humvee around the square and parked facing another wall of the courthouse, his headlights on the structure.

"There. That's where the cell is. The top of the cell has a small window at ground level. See it at the bottom of the wall along the ground there?"

"I see it." Eric licked his lips. This was a lot harder than springing Grandma Talia from Adderthorn's jail the year before. "Does the cell extend to the corner of the building?"

"Yeah, the cell fills that whole part of the basement."

"Let's get out. I have an idea."

They both climbed out of the Humvee. The odor in the air reminded Eric of Major Milton's resistance camp that had run with sewage.

"What now?" Joel asked.

"Meet me on the other side of the courthouse." Eric handed him his pack and bow. "I have to do this part. Go. If anything happens to me, get Lena and Gretchen back to camp."

As Joel walked briskly away, Eric went to the front of the vehicle and kicked the grill. It seemed made for ramming. He sat in the driver's seat—his first time in six years—and flashed the headlights at the courthouse three times, waited, then flashed three more times. If anyone was awake behind the cell windows, they'd be paying attention now.

Joel was out of sight. Both men would've liked to take the Humvee as far as they could out of town, but Eric's whole mission was meant to secure River Camp. Anywhere they took the vehicle, the Lib-Org troops could follow them.

"Lord, please help me." Eric revved the engine and buckled the seatbelt. Gripping the steering wheel, he punched the gas. The multi-ton vehicle roared forward, faster, faster. The speedometer said sixty when he jumped the curb, aiming at the corner of the building, intent on swiping through and beyond the edge of the structure.

The impact caused the seatbelt to bruise his collarbone, but the Humvee pushed through the debris, causing the courthouse corner to crumble. As soon as his brain recovered from the collision, he hit the brakes and skidded to a stop on a patch of uncut grass.

Running from the vehicle, he approached the demolished corner of the building. He imagined the soldiers would be rapidly approaching from inside, but he only needed ninety seconds.

The building material was still crumbling when he reached the damaged corner. Wires and rebar hung tangled in the settling dust. A gaping hole extended down into the basement cell. Eric stared at it, realizing it wasn't large enough for a man to escape through. His rescue attempt had failed!

Suddenly, a hand burst through the hole. Eric leapt back, then knelt and dug with his hands to enlarge the gap. Men from inside yelled incoherent instructions with panicked voices, as hands clawed at the hole from their side.

The first one out was a familiar face—Major Milton Pickford. The red, white, and blue armband was still on his arm. Barely did he acknowledge Eric when he reached back into the hole and pulled out another man. They wore their own clothes, some bloodstained. They were on their own now. Eric's job was finished.

Hearing gunshots to his right, Eric ran to the Humvee to shoulder his pack and rifle. Then he saw men running and firing from his left, and realized the soldiers were shooting at one another in the chaos! God was answering his prayer for help!

Within seconds, Eric had slipped from the confusion and was jogging into the darkness. A shape ran toward him. He'd nearly forgotten that Joel had been waiting for him. The bow hunter took Eric's arm and guided him down a dark street. They moved next to storefronts and down quiet sidewalks. Behind them, another burst of gunfire erupted, then silence.

They stopped in the moon shadow of a tree on someone's front lawn and tightened their packs for a prolonged hike.

"I can't believe that worked!" Joel panted and drank water from a canteen. "How long until we reach my wife? She needs a lot of . . . care."

"Gretchen's no stranger to helping people. Get down!"

They dropped flat on the grass and hid their faces as two pair of headlights rushed past them toward the courthouse. Major Milton had his hands full, but Eric knew he wouldn't go down easily.

When the way seemed clear, they jumped to their feet and dashed between two houses to leave the main thoroughfare behind. For an hour, they weaved their way through Mastover until the highway bridge south of town came into sight. Fifty feet below, the river boiled at its runoff stage, muddy and filled with debris.

"We can't swim it." Joel knelt off the highway. "But if we can cross the bridge, we can get into the forest. That's our goal, right?"

Only then did Eric see his concern. The bridge was guarded by four men inside a sandbagged nest in the center of the structure. The guards had certainly been radioed by now, and were waiting for the enemy—Eric and Joel. At any time, reinforcements could arrive to help hold the bridge.

"We have to swim the river," Eric said.

"No way." Joel took off his pack and drew an arrow for his bow. "If we get close enough, I can take out one or two. You can kill the others."

Eric looked back at the town. They didn't have time to discuss his moral and spiritual conscience against killing the enemy. Returning through town wasn't an option since it was nearly dawn and Mastover was crawling with soldiers. Nor was swimming the river really possible—not if they wanted to live. The logs and bushes floating in the swift rapids would batter a swimmer to death.

"You've heard me talk about God, right?"

"It's not a subject I care to talk about, I should tell you."

"Well, now we're about to find out if it's all just talk or not."

"What do you mean? We need to cross this river!"

"Are you ready?" Eric asked. "Because we're not beating four riflemen across that bridge, even if we were willing to kill them. They have machine guns. You have a bow and I have a bolt action hunting rifle. We're outmatched."

"What else can we do?"

"Nothing. That's the point. Nothing, except trust God." Eric felt something rise inside of him, growing, swelling. "We're dead if we go forward, and we're dead if we go back. So, it seems now might be a good time for us to place it all in God's hands. We need to trust God at this river."

"Well, we die if we stay here, too! I want to see my family again!"

Eric looked at the sky. This was it. This was the moment God had been communicating to him for days—to trust right now. This was the river. Now was the time, when trusting seemed impossible and useless and hopeless . . .

"What're they doing?" Joel grabbed Eric's arm and pulled him flat. "Where are they going?"

Together, the two men watched as the four bridge defenders climbed over their sandbags and ran up the bridge toward them. But instead of charging across the ditch to attack them, the four continued up the highway toward the town.

Their reasons for abandoning the bridge made little sense, since it was this very bridge that had caused such a problem a few days earlier. But Eric wasn't about to argue with what God had orchestrated at exactly that moment.

He and Joel crawled onto the highway and looked both ways. Sure enough, the four soldiers were out of sight and earshot. This time, Eric drew Joel upright.

"It seems," he said, "that God has provided a way across the river."

For a moment, Joel didn't move, as if he were still accepting what he'd just witnessed. Then, they walked across the bridge. It was riddled with signs of the previous battle. Mortar rounds had blown away sections of the railing. In the middle of the bridge, a portable radio system sat inside the sandbag formation. It had a recharger crank handle, much more versatile than Eric's bulky mountaintop system. In its collapsible form, the radio appeared more like a bulky thermos, and it slid nicely into the top of his pack as they continued to the south side of the bridge.

The impossible had been made possible by God. Eric had witnessed a miracle, and he couldn't celebrate until he was safely in the woods a half-mile later. A distance into the trees, he slipped off his pack and collapsed onto his knees, his hands raised to the sky. From his heart, he spoke to God, his lips moving, tears forming, his soul soaring. God had saved them from more than a longer trek east or west to cross the river elsewhere. The Lord had kept him alive to serve Him more, to be His spokesman, to reach the lost at River Camp with the truth of who God is, to stand steadfast against the deteriorating situation sweeping their nation.

Kneeling on the forest floor that night, Eric vowed to God as He corrected his humbled heart, that he would place River Camp's spiritual needs as a higher priority. Though he'd been mindful of God's presence and working, he'd not yet openly testified to all those under his charge. That had to change, especially in light of those final days when Christians everywhere expected Christ to catch them up in the clouds at any moment. He couldn't waste any more time!

"How long should we remain like this?"

Eric opened his eyes to see that Joel had shed his bow and pack, and had knelt beside him as well.

"That depends if our hearts have sufficiently been settled about what's happened."

"All I know is one minute, the bridge was blocked, and you were talking about God. And the next minute, the enemy was running away from the bridge like they saw an army coming. They must've been called back to town to hunt the escapees."

"Moments like this shouldn't pass without acknowledging God." Eric took a deep breath and sighed. "God moves around us all the time, and we ignore Him. We need to be more mindful about what He's done for us and what He continues to do for us—regardless of the mess man makes of everything."

"I've . . . never really cared for religion."

"Me neither, Joel." Eric clapped him on the shoulder and they stood facing each other in the moonlight breaking through the tree branches. "Let's forget about religion and just care about the God who made us."

"Apparently, you know Him better than me. I've killed your kind before, for my dad." He and Eric walked together back toward the tree line, leaving their packs behind them. "I've been thinking all the way back to our first meeting in these woods when I shot your boy's dog. Your reaction—I knew there was something different about you even then."

"As we wait for Lena and Gretchen to arrive, we'll have time to talk about it." They reached the tree line and stopped. The rising sun's rays illuminated the rolling hills, the clouds like wisps of smoke against the fading stars. "If we weren't being hunted, and if our women weren't running for their lives to meet us, and if that highway out there didn't traffic death every few minutes—I'd say that's a beautiful view."

"It is beautiful." Joel leaned against a tree. "Any view that's different from that rotting town of garbage is beautiful. I owe you, you know. If you hadn't come, me and my family would've died in that stinking house. And my dad wouldn't have cared."

"I risked your lives."

"But you risked your life, too." They were silent for a moment. "All of this—I can tell it'll be worth the risk."

#######

Just before sundown, Joel nudged Eric awake. Rolling over, Eric looked into Joel's smiling face.

"They're here. Come on!"

Eric groaned as he climbed to his sore feet and returned to the tree line. The highway was clear, so he followed Joel into the open. Gretchen came into sight first, the infant strapped to her front, and the large pack on her back. Regardless of his own weariness, Eric ran to her. Joel took the baby girl, and Gretchen and Eric embraced with relief, like they'd been a couple for years. Her arms felt natural around him, and he didn't want to let her go.

But they had to get out of sight. Joel called a warning, and Eric took Gretchen's pack as they hustled into the trees. Lena sat down and rocked back and forth, seemingly oblivious to their situation.

"Every time we stop to rest, she does that," Gretchen said. "She just rocks, and sometimes mumbles."

"Can you make it back to River Camp?" Eric asked Gretchen.

"If you want to carry me back!" She scoffed. "Remember, we took the long way here."

Eric smiled.

"Okay, we'll make camp here, then start back in the morning."

"Tell her what God did," Joel said as they weaved through the trees. "I'll never forget it as long as I live."

As they made a fireless camp a mile from the highway, Eric described the jail break, then the bridge miracle. He showed her the radio as evidence, taken without firing a shot.

"Who are you, Eric Radner?" Gretchen asked as she settled into a groove in the ground that he'd dug for her. She reached out and squeezed his hand. "And who are we to be so lucky to get someone like you?"

In the morning, they hiked the remaining miles into the mountains to River Camp. As they neared the canyon, they heard a warning shout from Lookout Ridge. At least the people had remained vigilant. Hank Worcester led the procession out to receive their gear and sweep them to a campfire and hot pine tea sweetened with crushed juniper berries.

"Major Milton?" Hank asked. His eyes warily acknowledged Joel and Lena.

"Last I saw, he was on his feet and free," Eric reported, then tensed as full attention shifted to Joel. "We have lots to tell you about. This is Joel, as you know. We would've failed without him."

"I remember you, young man." Hank nodded at the bow hunter. The throng around them waited through the tension. "I hear you're a fine shot with a bow."

Joel relaxed, and Eric with him, as the newcomer was accepted. At least until Hank told Eric to watch him closely. Joel Grayport wasn't his vicious father, but his old reputation would certainly not pass quickly.

That evening, as the camp women fussed over Lena and the baby, the few men in camp sat with Eric and Andy around their fire. Eric told about their adventure into Mastover and how they'd crossed the bridge. As if on cue, Andy chose that moment to hand Eric one of the Bibles they'd brought from the cabin. The fire crackled as he read from Psalm 143. The cry of the psalmist seemed like a prayer for them all, especially since most of those around the fire weren't believers. But Eric was planting the seed, and God would grow that seed, where faith was applied.

"But why did the four guards leave the bridge?" Hank pressed, though Eric thought they'd moved on.

When Eric was about to answer, Joel cleared his throat.

"Maybe it's not for us to ask why," the bow hunter said. "Maybe we're just meant to receive what gifts we're given. As long as we're here to receive them."

Since Eric couldn't have said it better, he closed the Bible and put his arm around Andy. The night would be a clear but cold one. The coyotes were noisy, but for the camp, it was a sound that told them their enemies weren't lurking nearby.

Sitting in the firelight, Eric content with his new companions, it was hard to imagine that the rest of America was still in turmoil. The virus still plagued neighborhoods. Rogue militias rallied for control. Bandits preyed on homesteads. Families struggled for food. Strangers were suspected and avoided.

But River Camp was quiet, and Eric was thankful to be a part of its stability.

Gretchen came to their fire and sat on the log with Andy and Eric. In fact, she sat close enough to Eric to link her arm through his and found his hand.

"Want to go hunting at dawn?" she asked.

"You don't want a day to rest?"

"I don't if you don't."

"Sounds good." He smiled, then nudged Andy as he started to doze on the other side of Eric. "As long as we're back by noon. Andy and I need to build a fish trap. It seems we don't have as many fisherwomen in camp as I'd hoped."

"What would we do without you, Eric Radner?" She kissed him on his bearded cheek.

"That's the second time you've called me by my whole name." He looked at her in the firelight. "Should I be worried?"

"What? Maybe I've just taken a liking to your last name."

"Well, when you take a liking to the Person this is about," he said, passing her the Bible, "then we can talk more about the prospect of you using my last name."

She giggled, until Hank threw the rest of his tea into the fire and stalked away. His reaction to their flirting confused Eric. Hadn't the man wanted a husband for his daughter? Of course he had, Eric realized. But he didn't favor the idea of a Christian as a son-in-law. It would take time for him to realize that followers of Christ were an asset, not a deficit.

Eric stared up at the starry night a long time before he fell asleep. Andy lay on one side, and Gretchen lay on the other. Like Joel had said, it was their job to receive what God gave them. It wasn't the ideal environment in which to raise a new family, but Eric was thankful. However, life in those days was never peaceful for long. River Camp had become a refuge for many, but there was a sense that change was in the wind once again. There was almost a fear to accept the normal. The Liberation Organization was on a rampage, and Judge Zachary Grayport's forces were a day's hike to the north.

And yet, Eric fell into a peaceful sleep. God had taught him to trust Him at the river. He could trust Him with the uncertain future as well.

~End of *STEADFAST Book Two*~

Bonus Chapter SF2

Who are the Wyoming invaders? What do they want? Follow this Bonus Chapter to discover behind-the-scenes intel on the bad guys!

~

Commander Kelly Morris, the leader of the Liberation Organization, watched his soldiers frolic in the icy waters of Coeur d'Alene Lake in Northern Idaho. The late spring temperatures had offered the troops a brief respite from their duties, but Morris wasn't about to join his splashing men in the cool water. He did his best to fix a smile on his face, and pretend that all was well with the liberation of America from its traditional and crippling moral fabric.

The truth was, Morris didn't feel much like celebrating spring. Defeating Great Falls and its Air Force base had taken the better part of the winter, depleting his army by twenty percent. The fighting had been fierce, but the winter conditions had also been crippling. They'd won only by starving the Montanans after surrounding them. And now, just a few miles to the west, scouts were reporting that a Spokane, Washington, resistance was preparing for an extended fight.

The factors that had led to their slowed advance westward were many, Morris considered, but he shut them out of his mind for the moment. While his men enjoyed themselves in the water, he sat on the shore and closed his eyes in meditation. Consciously, he reached deep within his soul for comfort, stability, and safety. He'd always believed the answers to his problems existed within himself, that he had the power within to overcome any obstacle. All he needed was to focus his determination, project his will, and declare positively what he truly desired.

But Morris opened his eyes after only a few minutes of inner focus. It wasn't working. Inner peace was getting harder to achieve the more his circumstances seemed to rise up against him. If he were a religious person, he would've thought there was a spiritual force opposing his success. However, Morris didn't believe there was a God—except the god within himself. Proof that he was a god, he reasoned, was seen in the amazing feat of marching across America, liberating cities from coast to coast. Nearly.

His failures of late rushed back to his mind. They were months behind in reaching Seattle, which waited for him to celebrate his cause, his vision. So, why didn't they send reinforcements? He knew the answer—mostly because they had no transportation. Seattle had struggled with bouts of the Meridia Virus for years, while Morris had taught his people to refrain from all physical contact. When Seattle citizens had sat indoors using up resources, Morris had deployed scavenger teams, in hazmat suits when necessary. He'd even started up an oil refinery in Texas that had kept their advance from completely stalling.

"Sir?" A bike messenger arrived from the barracks, which had once been the town's local college dorms. "A radio message for you."

Accepting the paper, Morris read a short typed message from his radio operators—another bad report from Wyoming. A group of prisoners meant for execution had broken out and escaped into the night. A nothing town hadn't been able to squash a local resistance. For months, the fighting in and around Mastover had disrupted his convoys, even his fuel deliveries. If a bridge wasn't being blocked, then a highway blockade was hijacking shipments of food. Traveling through Mastover had been necessary to reach the northwest command, but a man who called himself Judge Zachary Grayport hadn't suppressed the locals. Now, he blamed it all on someone who lived in the woods, someone the locals called Mad Man.

Morris remembered the rumors of the mad man when they'd rampaged swiftly through Wyoming, so he knew the judge wasn't entirely making excuses. Supposedly, there was a wild man who lived south of the highway in the thick forested mountains, who was rumored to eat people. Or he ate raw meat. Morris couldn't recall all the details, but he remembered the superstitious concern his foragers had upon hearing such news. No one had wanted to go into the woods for firewood or game when they'd camped at Mastover, establishing the town as a Lib-Org authority in the region.

Doubt suddenly plagued Morris' strategies. He'd ruthlessly executed dissenters along the way. And as towns submitted, he gave their leadership the authority to be ruthless as well. Most chose to burn the rebels at the stake, but some had reverted to hanging or even stoning, since firewood was a limited resource. Ropes and rocks could be reused; wood couldn't be. But regardless, they couldn't seem to wipe out their adversaries.

The more they executed, the slower the Lib-Org advanced, due to increasing problems along its supply route. Since when did smashing a problem make it grow?

"Tell Mastover I'll return to set things right," Morris told the messenger, who scribbled the note on a tablet. "It's time I traveled personally and tended to our supporters."

"What about Spokane, sir?"

"We can't move forward while our own territory isn't fully involved in these efforts. If Mastover doesn't comply, then they will suffer. That's the law."

"I'll remind them, sir." The messenger jumped on his bicycle and peddled away.

Morris watched his men shiver, but continue to roughhouse in the lake. Their lives were simple. They obeyed as good citizens should obey. They didn't need to decide how to fight or when to fight. They just fought. Morris had to decide who lived and died at their hands, but the future of America wasn't in their hands. America was his burden.

He almost felt sorry for Judge Grayport. The poor old fool really wasn't to blame for his inability to pacify his region, but he was still responsible. Morris knew it was the Christians and other independent thinkers, along with this mad man, who encouraged people to cling to old standards of morality and antiquated forms of self-government. They believed they didn't need regulation in every part of their lives, but their thinking errors were obviously disruptive to progress. The longer it took them to comply, the more severe their defeat would be.

More people needed to be executed, he decided, and he would escalate with the subtle foundation of problems within every community: the Christians. The followers of Jesus would die first. The sooner their moral projections and self-righteousness was wiped out, the better off America would be!

~End of Bonus Chapter SF2~

STEADFAST BOOK THREE

America's Last Days

D.I. Telbat

Prologue, Book Three

As Christians await Christ to return for His Church, America struggles through its darkest hour. Six years after Pan-Day, the Meridia Virus still plagues the shadows of countless neighborhoods. Rogue militias rally for domination over food and fuel. Bandits prey upon homesteads. Families struggle for a morsel of meat. Strangers are suspected and avoided.

But deep in the Wyoming wilderness, Eric Radner, nicknamed Mad Man, has preserved a remnant of women and children—the families of resistance fighters who are battling the invading Liberation Organization and its allies. Though Eric has made an effort to stand steadfast for Christ in River Camp, the gospel has been resisted. Even beautiful Gretchen has found more comfort in the idea of Eric as a husband than in the idea of a Savior who yearns for her heart.

As River Camp's Provisions Officer, Eric prays for strength to remain steadfast for Jesus Christ, even as the future of America has never seemed so bleak . . .

"O death, where is thy sting? O grave, where is thy victory? The sting of death is sin, and the strength of sin is the law. But thanks be to God, who giveth us the victory through our Lord Jesus Christ."
I Corinthians 15:55-57 KJV

Chapter 1, Book Three

Eric Radner tripped over a root and tumbled into a steep ravine. He came to rest in a small bog, the smelly water warmed by the summer sun. As he stared up at the blue sky, his wits slowly returned after his brain had been rattled by the fall. Death had visited River Camp, and Eric felt responsible. While civil war raged along the rural highways of Wyoming against the invading Liberation Organization, a grizzly bear attacked a party of River Camp's food gatherers.

With a wince, Eric sat up and checked his .223 hunting rifle still in his right hand. He hunted with open sights, so he didn't have to worry about damaging a scope. Except for a little dirt he blew out of the barrel, the rifle seemed unharmed. Only then did he gasp and touch the finger-wide branch that protruded from his ribs. After panting three short breaths, he plucked the branch straight out. Blood flowed down his side, but the piece of wood, sharp and jagged, had only penetrated an inch deep. A couple ribs felt broken, but his arms and legs were functional. Shakily, he rose to his feet, mud from the bog clinging to his backside.

After climbing out of the ravine, he paused on the north side of a birch tree where moist moss grew at the base of the trunk. His fingernails clawed deeply at the green spongy moss, and he lifted clear a section as big as his hand. Pulling up his shirt, he painfully pressed the poultice onto his wound. Nature had its share of remedies to fight infection, but it was blood loss that was his immediate concern. With a grizzly on the rampage, Eric needed all of his strength to kill the beast that had already killed one youth.

"Hold me together, Lord," he prayed aloud.

Pressing the moss against his ribs with one hand, the blood flow slowed. With his rifle in his other hand, he started through the woods at a jog, though less recklessly now.

He was two miles from River Camp when he came to a small meadow where he and Gretchen often hunted. Kneeling at the edge of the clearing, Eric took in the scene. A youth's dead body lay in the middle of the meadow. Small flowers in the short grass were smeared with blood, telling the tale of violence only minutes old.

A whistle pierced the scene. Eric moved only his eyes, not wanting to alert the grizzly that he was on the scene. The whistle had come from Andy, his adopted son, now six years old. But where was he? Only weeks earlier, Andy had discovered his ability to make an ear-splitting, two-fingered whistle, and he'd been driving River Camp crazy ever since. But now, the whistle meant life—his son was alive!

Still, Eric waited. To move hastily now could mean death. The three other rifle hunters from River Camp were minutes behind him, but he intended to put the beast to rest before anyone else was placed at risk.

Andy whistled again, and this time, Eric saw the boy thirty feet up a white oak tree, its sparse, thin branches barely giving the boy a foothold. The bear could be waiting even then for his prey to fall.

Movement to Eric's right caught his eye. He almost raised his rifle, but then saw it was Joel Grayport, River Camp's recent addition. The man was a bow hunter and meat provider, but his past from the town of Mastover haunted him, making him a loner and solitary tracker. Few in River Camp besides Eric associated with the gap-toothed man. Joel's father had sided with the Lib-Org invaders and was the scourge of Wyoming. Eric had known the thirty-year-old bow hunter was out hunting that morning, so he hadn't expected him to respond to their bear threat.

Crouching as he moved, Eric angled across the meadow to Joel. The bow hunter saw him and stopped his advance. Together, the two knelt and whispered. The dead child lay a few paces away.

"The kids were out gathering amaranth vegetables," Eric said. "A few of them ran back to camp and said there was a bear that had attacked them. At least one dead, we confirm now. It's got to be that grizzly we saw tracks from last week."

"It's him, all right." Joel nodded, his eyes scanning the tress, his fingers pinching an aluminum arrow already in the bow string. "I put an arrow in his shoulder. That's what set him off. I didn't know the kids were this far out in the woods. Is that your boy whistling?"

"Yeah, in the tree, there." Eric checked behind them. He'd heard of bears sneaking up when no one was looking. Since Pan-Day, his experience at hunting had been focused on deer and the occasional elk. He'd hunted black bears, but grizzlies were a whole different challenge. "We should've hunted down that monster the first day we saw his tracks. You're already unpopular back in camp. I'm afraid this is going to send folks over the top."

"What do you suggest?"

"About camp or the bear?"

"Let's start with the bear." Joel frowned at Eric. "And don't say we should pray about it, or I'll run straight into the jaws of that beast just to stop my misery."

Eric didn't laugh at the jab. Not many at River Camp had taken kindly to the Sunday morning services he'd started for those who wanted to attend. Even Gretchen seemed to barely tolerate his faith as he casually resisted her urgings for them to become an official couple. Each Sunday, he read from the Bible, gave a short encouragement to follow after Jesus, then prayed for the camp. Only ten attended regularly. Two women had asked if they could sing a duet the following week, though only one of them had made a profession of faith. The dead boy had been the son of one of those women—the only other certain Christian in camp besides him and Andy.

"After all you've seen God do, you still doubt Him?"

As often as Eric could, he liked to remind Joel of God's deliverance of them at the river months earlier.

"I just shot a bear, and it turned on that kid and killed him." Joel cursed. "Where's your God in that?"

With a prayer on his lips, Eric turned away. He didn't judge Joel for his stubborn heart. Before Pan-Day, Eric had also blamed God for the evils and tragedies in the world. True, it hardly seemed that good could come from the death of a child, but Eric wasn't willing to doubt God before he waited for Him to work something spectacular out of the suffering.

The sound of footfalls from a runner made the two hunters pivot to the north. Gretchen Worcester, her red hair loose from its leather tie, skidded to a stop at the edge of the meadow. She didn't react to the carnage before her, merely studied the scene as the cautious hunter she'd become. Her hard exterior had bought her the nickname, "Grim," but those who knew her best took confidence in her no-nonsense attentiveness. Eric held up his palm for her to wait, and she nodded. Silently, she eased her rifle to her shoulder, ready to fire. Like the rest in camp, her attitude toward Joel had been cold and distant. Eric guessed this incident wouldn't improve matters any.

"Your bow and arrow can't do much in this fight now," Eric said to Joel. "You'll just make that beast angrier. But you can still help."

"What do you want me to do?" The man replaced his arrow in the quiver and swung his bow over his shoulder.

"Priority one: we get Andy to safety. Move up to his tree and get him out of here. Gretchen and I will cover you."

Like Eric, Gretchen used a bolt action .223—hardly a bear gun, but it was all they had.

"Don't miss," Joel said as he cautiously moved forward.

Eric waved at Gretchen to move ahead. She snuck into the meadow, her face stoic. No one would call her Gretchen the Grim, Eric considered, if they saw her that day—committed to protecting the camp, even in the face of a wounded predator. Parallel, she and Eric moved thirty paces behind Joel. Finally, Joel reached the foot of the white oak tree. Andy started down the tree as Gretchen and Eric calmly aimed their muzzles across the tree line.

When Andy's feet touched the ground, Eric risked speaking.

"Where's the bear, Andy?"

"I think it went south." He pointed into the heart of the wilderness where the mountains jutted into the sky, and pristine lakes hadn't been visited by anyone but Eric in years. "It killed Willy."

"I know. Walk slowly to me, Andy. Joel, can you pick up Willy and carry him back?"

Joel didn't respond, though he took off his jacket as he walked back to the body. When he reached Willy, he wrapped the boy's broken form in the jacket and lifted him into his arms. The boy had been only seven years old.

"Gretchen, take lead. Andy, follow Gretchen." Eric nodded at Joel. "Go ahead. Let's get back to camp. I'll bring up the rear."

Gretchen hesitated, then moved closer to Eric.

"I hope you see it now." Her face was pale but her eyes were fierce. "My dad was right. Bringing Joel into River Camp was a mistake."

"Get moving," Eric said, realizing suddenly that if he sided with Joel about the incident, he'd be facing a camp-wide insurrection. "This wasn't intentional, Gretchen."

She and Andy started off. When Joel passed Eric, he paused.

"The body wasn't eaten. That thing just killed him and moved on."

Eric understood. The bear was a serious threat now—a man-killer. It had tasted human blood. It would have to be put down, or the camp would lose more people.

The two miles back to camp wasn't long enough for Eric to decide what to say to the people of River Camp about the death of Willy. The morning had begun with the final logs being set into place for seven lodges—a day of celebration that had become a day of mourning. Instead of dancing, there would be a funeral. Three months of hard work at their canyon refuge next to the river seemed to have led to this one day of death. And Joel would be to blame.

The two other hunters, Liz and Joy, met the returning party outside camp and warned them that the camp was in a panic, due to the children arriving earlier with news that a bear had attacked their foraging party.

Eric saw no other option except to march directly into camp and present the dead child to his mother, Barb. The women and children were weeping as the hunters walked through the sadness and stopped at the northern-most lodge. Barb was there, a big-boned woman with rosy cheeks. In the midst of the wailing crowd, Joel lay the child in his mother's arms.

"Where's Hank?" Eric asked Sara Worcester about her husband, the camp's second in command.

Sara pointed up at Lookout Ridge, where two women were stationed day and night in eight-hour shifts, watching the northern trail.

"Someone's coming," she said, her eyes damp. "The lookout shouted a warning a minute before you returned."

Gretchen approached Eric, her rifle still on her shoulder.

"You need to get that looked at." She pointed at Eric's side, wet from fresh blood. "And then we need to do something about Joel. That bear is his fault!"

"It just needs a couple stitches." Eric touched his ribs, choosing to ignore her bitterness toward Joel. "Come with me." Together, they climbed the worn trail up the slope to Lookout Ridge. "As if we didn't have enough going on today, your mother just said we have outside company coming."

They reached the lookout, which was a station with a lean-to and an outhouse. Two women in their sixties sat on the bench where they often busied themselves with braiding horsehair or crushing purslane to make flour for baking. Hank Worcester stood at the highest point of the lookout, binoculars to his eyes.

"Who is it?" Eric tried to shut out the wailing from camp behind and below them. He knew better than anyone else all hundred people by name. This death would be hard on them all.

"Looks like two men." Hank passed the field glasses to Eric. "They're wearing Lib-Org uniforms, gray and black, but look what they're carrying."

"A white flag." Eric shook his head. "Whatever they want, we can't let them see our camp. Even a peaceful scouting party is still a scouting party. They know we're out here, apparently. You recognize them?"

"Nope. Could be new arrivals in Mastover, or from the Lib-Org's forward command, thinking we're more involved in the resistance with Major Milton than we really are." Hank drew his sidearm and checked the action. "We'd best kill them before they return to confirm to anyone that we're out here."

"That's not the way we communicate with the enemy, Hank." Eric touched Hank's weapon, gently pushing it downward. "You cover me as I talk to them. Gretchen, sneak into the trees and scout along the trail to the north. Make sure these boys aren't a forward party to a larger force coming to attack us."

Gretchen slipped into the woods and out of sight. Eric started down the ridge toward the strangers approaching on the game trail. Once, he looked back and saw Hank scowling, certainly not agreeing with Eric's decision, but Eric was glad God had given him just enough authority in camp to enforce decisions that preserved life rather than took it.

Close to the trail, Eric sat on the uphill slope of the path and waited. His side was still damp with blood, but the moss was in place, aiding in the long-term healing. He considered all that needed to be done in camp before winter closed upon them in a couple short months. At least the seven lodges had been completed. Next came sheds and a spud cellar, more firewood, a better corral for the horses, and a smoke house to cure meat. There was also a grizzly to hunt, and that could be potentially deadly since it had already killed once. And now the Lib-Org was on to them. Eric's spirits sank at the prospect of relocating the whole camp.

Two men rounded the bend in the trail and froze. Eric's rifle remained cradled in his right arm, aimed at the ground. He raised his left hand and waved at the visitors. The man on the left lifted the white cloth on a stick a little higher and glanced about nervously as they proceeded. Their assault rifles, which were meant for killing people, not hunting animals, remained slung over their shoulders. Five paces from Eric, they stopped in the trail.

"Nice day for a stroll." Eric smiled warmly, and realized he really had no ill will toward the puppet soldiers of wicked men. "The way you're holding that white flag, I'd say you're out here for a purpose."

The two men eyed the trees and bushes, but Eric figured Hank had remained up on the ridge, practically invisible from the trail at fifty paces. Both men appeared to be in their thirties, clean-shaven and wearing wrinkled uniforms. Their boots showed much wear. The Lib-Org elite troops would never be allowed to wear sub-par gear, so Eric guessed they were local militia from Mastover.

"We're looking for the one they call Mad Man." The spokesman was a shaggy-blond with narrow eyes and a permanent smirk. "Judge Grayport sent us."

Eric studied the second man, taller than the first. He was dark-haired with a cautious look to him. The flag-stick in his hand shook with what Eric read as nervous energy.

"I've heard of Mad Man," Eric said. "They say he's a carrier of the virus. He foams at the mouth and eats hunters raw. Of course, it could all just be rumors."

"You know him," the smirker said. "The judge wants an audience. Tomorrow night at sundown at the bridge south of town."

"I can tell Mad Man, but I doubt he'll want to walk into a trap." Eric looked past the two soldiers. Gretchen moved like a ghost across the trail and disappeared into the woods to the west. "What would Judge Grayport want to talk to Mad Man about?"

Eric remembered vividly the four who'd been hung on the judge's gallows in Mastover. One had been a child. A child! His anger rose, but he prayed that God in His justice would avenge the terrors of evil men.

"Commander Kelly Morris of the Lib-Org returned to Mastover for a visit," said the blond, his eyes fierce with accusation. "He's heard about the resistance fighting here. His supply lines have been disrupted, so he rounded up five and burned them at the stake."

"Five what?" Eric asked.

"Mastover men. My friends. Men who'd served the judge."

Eric felt a foreboding dread wash over his soul. Burning at the stake in America? It was sickening, but he wanted to show himself firm with the visitors, so he tried not to react visibly. Commander Morris was the Lib-Org's head, a man who fancied himself as a freedom fighter, but so far, he'd only dominated others by force. Killing Christians had become one of his hobbies, radio broadcasters had even joked.

"The judge joined Commander Morris and his troops," Eric said. "The commander has charged across America, killing civilians. Are you really surprised he's turned on you?"

"It's the fault of the resistance that those five men were burned at the stake!" The short one eyed the bushes suspiciously. "They died because the judge can't suppress Mad Man's resistance efforts. And Commander Morris will return from the front lines up north to execute more of us if the judge doesn't put an end to the resistance. The resistance needs to end, or more will die. It could be us next!"

Eric's knees felt weak.

"Mad Man isn't a resistance fighter. He's just a survivalist."

"The judge wants a meeting. That's all."

Eric didn't believe that was all, but he nodded anyway.

"I'll tell Mad Man, but I can't promise he'll show."

"Then more innocent people in Mastover will be burned at the stake!"

"There's hardly any innocent people in Mastover if you've all joined the Lib-Org," Eric said. "Go back to Mastover. You've delivered your message, now go."

The men hesitated, perhaps expecting a little hospitality after their long trek into the mountains. But Eric couldn't risk exposing the camp to spies. Finally, the two visitors turned away, their weariness apparent as they trudged down the trail—a long ten miles back to the highway.

Eric sighed once they were out of sight, and held his bleeding side. He wondered if he had compromised his faith in God by joining the resistance even in a passive role. Obviously, the enemy believed he was actively part of the resistance now, or they wouldn't have come and asked for him specifically. Someone had singled him out. Someone had lied, and now he was implicated.

Gretchen returned a few minutes later, reporting that there was no one else on the trail for a couple miles, at least. They joined Hank on Lookout Ridge to watch the trail as they talked.

"Why talk with you?" Hank asked after Eric repeated the conversation. "Why not Major Milton? He's the leader of the resistance in this region."

"Maybe Milt was captured again," Eric said. "Or they can't find him. Or he's dead."

"But how do they know about Mad Man being in charge out here?" Gretchen asked. "That's why we freed Milt and the prisoners three months ago—to keep this place a secret. All we have is women and children, except for you two men."

"No one from River Camp talked." Eric turned and looked down at the mourners. "I don't think anyone has a transmitter we don't know about, and no one's left camp long enough to get a message outside. It had to be a resistance fighter who talked, maybe someone who was captured and tortured, or who's defected."

The three were silent for a moment. Eric hadn't sensed the heavy weight of leadership as much as he did now. As busy as they'd been in River Camp, Eric had felt lonely for weeks. Though he'd been sharing the gospel of Jesus Christ openly whenever an opportunity presented itself in conversation, little ground had been gained. The sentiments of the camp mostly reflected what Hank felt: he didn't want "religion" pressing in on his choices to live and think as he wanted. He was among those who'd been part of the Christian persecutions and Bible burnings a year earlier. What Eric couldn't get through to him was that Christ sets free the soul from the bondage of bad choices. Hank's anger, cursing, and even cheating on his wife with a woman in camp, were the choices from which he couldn't liberate himself.

Andy was the only one Eric felt a true kinship with in the things of Christ. After their small Sunday fellowship in camp each time, the two hiked alone into the mountains, exploring, fishing, and throwing rocks. At hidden lakes and beside pristine glaciers, they sat and talked and prayed. They'd even prayed for Judge Grayport, but that kind of compassion for the enemy was completely foreign to Hank and even to Gretchen. Eric hated to think what the death of Willy could ignite if the people insisted on hating Joel because of his father.

Standing on Lookout Ridge, Eric suddenly wished he and Andy were back at their mountain cabin, away from the threat of invading armies and violent townsfolk.

"If my nickname is attached to the resistance," Eric said, "then I'll go to the bridge tomorrow and set the record straight. Whatever's going on with this latest burning at the stake, it's got to end."

"Don't sell us out just to make peace with Judge Grayport!" Hank growled. "You already brought his son here!"

"Hank," Eric held back the fire on his tongue, "has there ever been any indication whatsoever that I haven't sought for the greatest good for our people? Just because I'm interested in peace doesn't mean I'm trying to harm them."

"Like I said, you brought Joel here."

"And he's brought in more meat than me, remember? For everyone."

"Joel caused the death of that boy this morning," Gretchen said, then looked down at the ground. She opened her mouth again to say something, but chose not to.

"Thanks, Gretchen." Eric felt like she'd just betrayed him, but she'd spoken her heart, and now her feelings were out. "That's really helpful."

He marched away down the trail to camp. Gretchen had chosen to oppose him and instigate more bitterness. Eric sensed that all of their closeness had vanished in a single morning of testing.

Weepy and fearful faces of women and children peered up at him.

"Eric," a young mother asked, "what are we going to do?"

Unable to speak at the moment, he held up his hand, then passed her and the others without a word. He reached Lodge One and went to his pack, which was always stocked and ready for travel. But he wasn't leaving just yet. From a side pocket of the pack, he drew a sewing kit. Outside, he went to the bank of the river, sat on a log, and took off his shirt. Painfully, he cleaned his wound and started stitching his own skin. Inwardly, he grumbled about the discontentment of the people and the impossible situations he somehow had to find solutions for. Though he tried to place the problems into God's hands, the personal pain he felt for being alone in seeking what was right made the problems seem too large to think about clearly. And he felt he'd all but lost Gretchen.

Using his knife, he cut the thread and poked at his sensitive flesh. The blood had ceased, but a scar would remain, he guessed, to add to his others collected over the years since Pan-Day. Shrugging into his shirt, he looked at the sky.

"I may or may not be acting like a spoiled child, Lord." He scoffed at himself. "You've taken care of me and shown Yourself mighty before. I can trust You through the chaos again, even now."

He turned around and was startled to find the entire camp gathered behind him, only thirty paces away, sitting or standing, watching him. They were waiting on him. No one else could be depended on for these decisions. The whole camp had been arranged according to his specifications. They were still alive because of him, and they knew it. If he showed himself defeated by hardship or even by their own criticism, then the camp's morale would be defeated and their ability to prepare for the hard winter ahead would cease. Ultimately, Eric knew he was there to prepare their hearts to believe in Jesus Christ before He returned for His Church. And these people were far from prepared for winter, or for the coming of the Lord.

Andy walked forward and stood next to Eric. Eric set his hand on his adopted son's shoulder, and together they approached the people. The people hushed themselves for what he would say. Gretchen stood at the back with Hank. Her arms were crossed and she wouldn't meet his gaze.

"We're a community in turmoil, but we're not broken," he said loudly, more boldly than he felt inside. "Willy was our friend, brother, and son. First, we'll have a funeral for him. Then, the hunters will go after the bear that killed him. The bear is just a wild animal, but it's killed one of us now, and it needs to be put down. After that, I'll be going to Mastover to meet with Judge Grayport. He's sent word that he wants to end the strife between us. I need to find out what his intentions are."

A murmur passed through the hundred souls. Eric raised his hands.

"Quiet now. I keep telling you people to trust in God through our difficulties, and that's exactly what we need to do. We have a chance to rise from the pain and fear, but only if we rely on the Creator. That includes right now. Let's see to our brother, Willy, and we'll consider the things of faith as we go forward. Come on, Barb."

Eric held out his hand. The grieving mother stepped forward to accept it, and the two walked together to the cemetery that already held the dead. The crowd followed after, weeping. Joel carried Willy. Gretchen remained distant, whispering with her father. They were already planning to rid the camp of Joel and his family, Eric guessed. Though their anger ran deep toward the Grayports from long past, Eric couldn't go against what he knew was right in his heart. He would stand with Joel, even if the others didn't. And in the midst of the strife, he had to go to Mastover.

He was going to meet Judge Grayport. And by the grace of God, there would be peace.

Chapter 2

"Two bears!" Joel Grayport said to Eric in a harsh whisper. They were eight miles southwest of River Camp. "Have you ever heard of such a thing?"

Eric shook his head at the man who'd become the unofficial scout within the hunting troop. Joel's stealth of foot and ability to read sign rivaled Eric's own skills, if not surpassed them. The camp would certainly be weaker now that they were losing Joel the next day. He was leaving with his wife and infant. The people had spoken after the funeral the night before, and their decision had been unanimous. Even Gretchen had opposed him, siding with the mob and her father to send the judge's son away. Only Eric had objected to the bowman's departure. As the son of the judge, Joel had already been viewed as a threat. The accident with the bear and Willy's death had caused the people to make the irrational decision. They didn't see it as an accident, but as murder, and Eric couldn't sway them. It could mean their own deaths, though, if the four other hunters couldn't bring in enough meat to feed the whole camp through the winter.

"The trail continues to the west," Eric whispered to Joel and Gretchen as they examined the bear tracks together. Their heads were just inches apart, and Gretchen was breathing heavily since the three hunters had been traveling fast with only canteens and rifles. Gretchen hadn't mentioned the night before, or even spoken to Eric flirtatiously as she'd done for months. "I have to pull out of the hunt. It's already mid-morning, and I have to get to the bridge meeting."

"We can't get the bear without you!" Gretchen said with a bite to her words. Joel frowned. He carried a rifle, but he was a bowman, not a marksman, and Gretchen obviously didn't trust him. "And now we know there are two bears. What are we supposed to do?"

"Get back to River Camp," Eric said to her. "Protect the people. Keep them close to camp until the bears can be killed. One of these bears is a man-killer. That's dangerous, but two of them together is twice the threat."

"It's not natural," Joel said. Eric thought he seemed especially sad when he spoke. First, Joel had left Mastover. Now, he was about to leave all of the people he'd come to join. In River Camp, he'd served a purpose, even if he'd been scorned. The campers' words the night before hadn't been friendly. "Maybe the virus is affecting animals to act aggressively and out-of-sync. Maybe the bears are siblings. But normally, even siblings are territorial. They don't usually terrorize the same range and travel together."

"When I get back from the bridge meeting—"

"If you come back," Gretchen said, scowling.

"—we can continue the hunt," Eric finished.

"I wanted to kill the bear before I left River Camp," Joel said. "But I'm not willing to stay another day where I'm not welcome, even to fix what I may have started with this bear."

"We don't need your help," Gretchen spat, looking away. "You got Willy killed. You might just get more of us killed."

"Gretchen, you volunteered to come today, remember? Try to be constructive." Eric offered Joel his hand, and the two shook. "The cabin will be a nice place for a small family, and I'll be glad to have someone looking after the place. Andy and I will visit you before winter to see how things are going."

"You're not returning with us to River Camp?" Gretchen asked Eric.

"No." Eric took a drink from his canteen, holding back thoughts he didn't have words for. "I'll need to hike straight to the bridge to arrive on time."

"What if the judge takes you prisoner?" She looked pained, but Eric didn't know how to help her through her hatred of the Grayports, which he didn't share. "What do we do then?"

"River Camp made its decision last night. You can't have the security of me and Joel while pushing us away at the same time." Eric retied his boots as Gretchen stared speechlessly. "There's a reason why I'm insisting on going to the bridge alone."

"You're talking about us kicking Joel out of camp?" She looked like she was about to cry, like she knew that their months of growing friendship had been disrupted. "What? Now we can't disagree with you or have our own opinions?"

Joel took a step back, obviously uncomfortable at being the continuing source of division.

"This is more than an opinion," Eric said. "This is siding against what is right. The camp made a decision based on fear, not compassion. We've become like the people we're hiding from."

"How dare you!" She stomped her foot. "I thought you and I had something special!"

She turned away and headed toward camp.

"Wow. Things went bad fast, huh?" Joel frowned. Eric could only imagine the weight he felt from Willy's death, and now being set aside by the camp. "I'll make sure she gets back okay."

"It's their hearts, Joel," Eric said, hoping to soften any anger the man might feel toward Gretchen or the others. "Conflict always shows what's real inside of us. Without God, we're all doomed."

"That sounds like something from your Bible." Joel smiled. "See? I'm catching on."

"God is the only stability in this life, Joel. There's a Bible on the shelf in the cabin. I hope you check it out, and never forget what God did at the bridge."

"I'm sorry you're catching so much grief for bringing me to River Camp, and now for standing beside me through Willy's death."

"Joel, when you head to the cabin tomorrow morning, you'd better take Andy with you." As Eric looked after Gretchen, she turned back as if to say something more, perhaps to apologize for her words, but she continued her walk to camp. "Since the rest of the camp shares her attitude, Andy won't be any more welcome in camp than you or me."

"How will Andy know you want him to leave with me and my wife?"

"Tell him I said David needs to run from Saul to safety. He knows the story. It's from—"

"The Bible." Joel chuckled. "I get it. Stay safe at the bridge."

Eric saluted Joel as they parted ways. Once alone in the forest, Eric was immensely overwhelmed by the presence of God and the emotions from the last two days. The death of Willy had brought out the worst in River Camp. But Eric understood it was all that could be expected from people who weren't guided by God in their inner lives. Their worldly lives would naturally rule and cause damage as they thought primarily about themselves.

Kneeling next to a small brook of water, Eric prayed for strength. In Gretchen, he'd seen a potential wife, but not when she opposed the things of God that inspired him to act accordingly. So, he opened his soul that late morning, desperate for the clear comfort of God to embrace him. There was also a measure of self-pity inside, which he needed to repent from—as he walked into the unknown, perhaps even into death itself. And for what? For River Camp and one hundred souls who'd turned against him.

While at the brook, he topped off his canteen, then headed north. He stripped off his outer layer, a buckskin shirt he'd worn that morning to ward off the coolness and to guard against scraping branches. The summer day was warming quickly, but he left on his flannel shirt since he was barging through thickets and wanted no more wounds than he already carried.

By midafternoon, he reached the tree line a half-mile south of the bridge. He chewed on jerky and drank from his canteen as he prayed for wisdom in dealing with Judge Grayport and whatever deal was to be proposed. Eric had never intended to speak for the resistance, but he couldn't turn down the opportunity to somehow influence the peace process locally.

He left the trees and used his binoculars to study the bridge where he'd trusted God three months earlier. God had preserved him then. Celebrating that memory in his heart encouraged him to trust in God's preservation again. Or, if he were captured, he hoped God still allowed him to testify of Christ, even as he died.

The bridge was crowded with troops, some of them watching him through their own binoculars. It seemed the whole Mastover division of Lib-Org regulars expected to face off against what was left of the resistance. Obviously, the judge wasn't aware of the strife within River Camp that had convinced Eric that he needed to come alone to seek peace in the nearest town. But he wasn't about to indicate to the Lib-Org troops that he was indeed alone, either.

He walked back into the trees, donned his buckskin shirt, then tore off the bark of a fallen birch tree to cover and hide his rifle at the base of a tall pine. Going armed into the midst of two hundred soldiers would be foolish, especially since he wouldn't shoot to kill anyone.

Emerging from the trees again, he guessed that the lookouts at the bridge would report they'd seen at least two different people now, since Eric had shown himself wearing two different shirts. He was sure no one was expecting him to show up alone. If Judge Grayport suspected there were witnesses watching from the woods, Eric hoped he would be a little safer amongst the hostiles.

With his eyes on the first ranks of soldiers, Eric reached the highway, then approached them by walking down the middle of the road. Unfortunately, the judge wasn't among the first people. Instead, the troops, in their gray and black uniforms, stepped aside to allow him to walk up the bridge. Halfway across, Eric noticed two Humvees and a number of officers standing, waiting for him.

As he walked up the center, he glanced over the railing at the muddy water fifty feet below. It was no longer boiling with debris from spring runoff, but it was still flowing swiftly.

Ten paces from the officials, Eric stopped, his hands at his sides. Soldiers behind him closed ranks. There seemed no escape. He begged God to be his refuge and give him courage.

"You're Mad Man?" one of the officers asked. He was clothed in the finest uniform, though with no precise indication of rank, and he wore a sidearm. Though his eyes were dark under bushy eyebrows, Eric saw Joel's eyes in the man's face. This was Judge Zachary Grayport, the one many called the menace and traitor of Wyoming. "You're the one causing all this trouble?"

Eric steeled himself, hoping his face betrayed nothing. He wasn't shocked that the legend of his madness had been exaggerated, blamed, and at some point, used as an excuse for the resistance. After all, he'd spent considerable effort planting rumors six years earlier among travelers on the highway that there was a mad man in the mountains.

"If it were up to me," Eric said calmly, "we'd all be at peace, keeping our people safe, and preparing for the winter."

Looking at their faces, Eric wondered if he wasn't speaking directly to their hearts, since they were gaunt in their loose-fitting uniforms. The army at Mastover apparently wasn't eating too well, and it would only get worse with winter coming.

"We're way past peace and safety." The judge gestured to one of his men. A soldier opened a back door of a Humvee and drew out a hooded figure from the vehicle. "You've cost me enough headaches. The resistance ends today."

The hooded man was shoved forward. His hands were bound behind his back. He complied with a grunt as he was forced to his knees in front of Eric. The hood was yanked off, and Major Milton Pickford blinked at the late afternoon sunshine. His face was swollen and bruised from beatings, and he wore a blood-stained shirt. Instead of meeting Eric's eyes, Milton's gaze was downcast, and Eric understood the look of shame when he saw it. Milt was the one who'd talked; he was responsible for blaming the Wyoming Mad Man for the resistance. For his own welfare, Milt had endangered everyone at River Camp!

Eric felt pity rather than much anger over Milt's situation. Over a year earlier, Milt had fled to him for help, his leg wounded by the Lib-Org's first incursion. Then, Milt had asked for his assistance in helping the families of the resistance fighters. Again, Eric had given up his life at the cabin to ensure the safety of the women and children. Next had come the rescue of Milt from the jail. God continued to place their lives at intersecting points, and Eric couldn't help but extend his aid to the failed resistance fighter. But what now?

"This man only wants to secure a safe and free life for his people," Eric said. "From what your messengers said, he's not the true face of your enemy. The Lib-Org has started burning even your own people now."

"Anyone, yourself included, is my enemy if you make Commander Morris come and execute Mastover people."

"I'm not your enemy, Judge." Eric browsed the hard faces of the surrounding soldiers. He might never get another moment to speak to such cold hearts. "We're all seeking a common, responsible liberty. But there is no liberty until we begin to stand against evil. We've all made choices since Pan-Day that have hurt others. Before the resistance and before the Lib-Org rolled through our towns, our hearts were already selfish and proud. But that doesn't mean we can't turn around and draw our communities together again. When the resistance kills one of your men, Judge, they kill an American civilian. And when you kill a resistance fighter, you're just killing a Mastover citizen. We're fighting ourselves to the death, when we should be fighting together a more sinister enemy that has sway over our souls!"

"No one can fight the Lib-Org and survive." The judge's face showed no emotion. "We joined the Lib-Org to stay alive. There's no other way, even if we don't like it."

"I've been through your town and seen what you call existence." Eric shook his head. "Commander Morris brought Mastover to its knees, and now garbage and sickness rule your streets. Maybe even the virus! That's your existence. He never rescued you. He crippled you so badly that you don't even know who you are anymore. You're Americans! Quit killing each other!"

"I'll accept your terms for peace, since Commander Morris will return next week. He has demanded an execution—five of my own soldiers, or the execution of the resistance leader in Wyoming. An example needs to be made. You want peace? This is your opportunity."

Milt raised his face to Eric. There were tears on Milt's face.

"How can the resistance rest if you continue to regulate Lib-Org policy in Mastover?" Eric shifted his feet, trying to avoid thoughts of execution for the moment. "You ruled as a tyrant, Judge Grayport, even before the Lib-Org came to town, but they gave you a license to treat your people even worse now. There'll be a resistance until change is implemented. You have the ability to unite a people who will stand behind you—as soon as you stand behind them. Don't you understand? You need to stand with them!"

"I—" The judge's uncertainty finally showed on his face. There was a hint of weakness and doubt. He hardly seemed like the villain Eric had imagined. Instead, the judge was just a flawed man whose leadership had been trampled by stronger men. "I represent the Lib-Org now. A traitor needs to be presented to Commander Morris. Only then will I entertain considerations for further peace with the people of the resistance."

Eric sighed. The judge's heart was so hardened against alternatives, so contrary to God's moral urgings.

"It seems you have your resistance fighter," Eric said, "but you're looking for me. Is that what I'm to understand?"

"Everyone knows you've been operating for years in those mountains. You're Mad Man from south of Mastover."

"Mad Man from south of Mastover? Okay. I see."

His heart raced, and Eric realized there wasn't even an argument he could provide to defend himself. Too many travelers had moved up the highway in the beginning years, sowing seeds of concern about the rumored crazed man in the woods. With the rumors and subsequent forced confessions from the lips of tortured resistance fighters, no one but Mad Man would appease the demand for blood. The judge didn't even want Major Milton!

"The commander already has a file on you from us." The judge smirked. "With you gone, the resistance ends. Afterward, we can concentrate on cleaning up Mastover. If you care about the people, you'll come as peacefully as you talk."

"If you care about the people, you'd leave the Lib-Org."

"That's never going to happen."

Eric rested his hands on his hips. The bridge railing was two bounds and a leap away. In seconds, he could be in the water, flowing briskly away from the threat of execution. By dawn, he could be with Andy. They could leave River Camp with Joel and return to the cabin. Life could be calm again.

But his own safety would be costly. Milt would be executed instead. The resistance would continue regardless, Eric guessed, until the Lib-Org backed off. But the Lib-Org wouldn't let Mastover rest until Mad Man was caught and killed. And Commander Morris would pour his wrath upon the residents of Mastover. Unless Eric bought at least a temporary peace for the judge, more people would die.

"This man is to be set free," Eric said, indicating Milt. He hoped to leave at least one witness of what was happening.

Milt's mouth gaped in shock.

"That's understood." The judge pointed at Milt's hands. The nearby soldier stepped forward and cut Milt's binds. "Your mountain fighters need to lay down their arms and return to Mastover. If they don't comply, I'll be forced to hunt them out of the woods once and for all—or we'll face more executions from Commander Morris. I have no choice."

"I understand." Eric pulled the battered frame of Milt to his feet, embraced him, and whispered in his ear. "It's time for peace, Milt. Too many are dying. Bring the men in to talk."

"There's no one left out there," Milt said, holding Eric tightly. "All the women you've been watching for us—their men are dead. The only bargaining chip I had was to say we had a whole army still out there."

Eric held him at arm's length, trying to blink away his surprise.

"That . . . complicates things." Eric winced. "Can you swim?"

"Yeah. Why?"

"Because, if you're the last resistance fighter, I think swimming is the only way you're getting out of here alive."

"What?" Milt's eyes widened.

Eric wasn't as tall as Milt, but he was stronger. Gripping Milt by the shoulders, he pulled him suddenly to the right.

"Jump!" Eric yelled, then lifted Milt slightly to send the resistance fighter over the rail.

An instant later, Milt was gone. Eric turned slowly, his hands raised, as one hundred muzzles aimed at his head.

Judge Grayport had his resistance fighter.

Chapter 3

The basement level of the Mastover courthouse was deplorable. The cement cell walls were rotting with mold, and wherever metal once gleamed, it was now rusted. The building had certainly flooded in months and years past, and the damaged corner cell where Eric had instigated a prison break showed the neglect of the entire structure. Fortunately, the plumbing in Eric's small neighboring cell had been repaired enough for use.

Being taken into custody on the bridge by Judge Zachary Grayport would've been without incident, except when the soldiers searched his person, they found his pocket Bible. The Bible had been passed to the judge, who had thumbed through its pages briefly, then pitched it over the railing and into the water where Major Milton Pickford had disappeared moments before.

Now, Eric sat on his cement bunk, his hands folded, staring at the mold on the wall in front of him. Losing the weathered little Bible pained him, since he'd read from it daily for years in the woods. Its words nourished him after coming to trust in Christ six years earlier. Thankfully, he had large portions of Scripture committed to memory, hidden in his heart, comforting him even now.

The loss of the Bible was a stark signal to the turn his life had taken. In a week, he would be executed. Yes, Milt was a coward who'd broken under interrogation, betraying a man who not only saved his life twice but ensured his escape on the bridge. But Eric didn't hate the man he was going to die for. After all, Milt had been captive to Eric's Bible reading each night when he'd been at the cabin. Eric prayed that Milt would understand he was only doing for him what Christ had done for them all. Now, he would become Milt's scapegoat.

The guard outside the cell door was the tall man, Josh Hicks, one of the men who'd approached River Camp with a white flag. Eric had heard the guard's partner, Ed Newman, instruct Josh not to speak to the prisoner. It seemed it was going to be a long week.

The first couple hours of his captivity were a shock to Eric. He spent them in prayer and thanks as his fate sank into his mind. Burning to death would be horrible, but he focused on what would immediately follow: a face-to-face encounter with Jesus Christ. The horror of death seemed to pale in comparison to the honor of life eternal in the Creator's presence. A few minutes of misery and suffering, exchanged for an endless reality of joy and completion. Yes, he decided, he would end this life with steadfastness. The truth of all that followed death gave him the strength to endure the unimaginable.

He considered Andy and prayed that his six-year-old son truly had accompanied Joel Grayport out of River Camp and back to the cabin. Hopefully, Andy's bitterness had waned against Joel after Joel had accidentally killed his dog, Runner, that spring. Joel, Eric considered, the son of the evil judge, would become Andy's new father. God certainly used the base and unlikely things of the world to accomplish His will.

That evening, Eric was fed a bowl of broth and a biscuit. The broth was beef-flavored water, and the biscuit was rock hard. But it filled his stomach a little, so he was thankful. While pacing, Eric glanced out of the cell door window and saw that Josh, his guard, had received the same food ration. Life in Mastover had certainly gone downhill.

Eric spent a cold night hugging his ribs on the hard cement slab that served as his bunk. Breakfast was another biscuit, this time with honey-flavored tea—barely flavored. Midmorning, his cell door opened and both privates, Hicks and Newman, gestured for Eric to come with them.

He was escorted without restraints up three flights of stairs to an office that may have once been a prosecutor's lair. Now, the law books had been removed from the shelves, perhaps for fire fuel, but a photo of the outside of the courthouse in its glory days still hung on the wall.

Judge Grayport sat behind the desk. Eric was directed to a metal chair. He guessed the wooden chairs had been burned the previous hard winter. The two guards stood behind him at the door.

The judge's dark eyes glared at Eric, but Eric wasn't afraid. The man's face was drawn and slim, having lost the vigor that Eric had heard the tyrant once had. The stress of leadership, the annoying resistance fight, and a dwindling food supply had evidently brought the once proud man to his knees.

"Commander Morris will be here in five days." The judge leaned forward, the light of a window offering sunshine on the floor near Eric's feet. "You're my peace offering for better supplies from the Liberation Organization."

"I hope you get what you want," Eric said, "but we both know you won't, not indefinitely. Commanders of armies are rarely good providers."

"I guess we'll find out." The judge waved his hand. "Except you. You won't find out. You'll be dead."

"Being a native of Wyoming," Eric said, "I'm surprised you would depend on strangers so much."

"What's that supposed to mean?"

"This is Wyoming. You have everything you need all around you. God has provided everything. You don't need to compromise what you know is right to get supplied."

"God? Hmph! There's no God." He shook his head. "Would God allow all this to happen? That's the kind of psychobabble the Lib-Org wants to stamp out!"

"What'd you bring me up here for if not to hear what I know to be true?"

"How many resistance troops do you still have out in the woods?"

The man's face, though weary, showed a hint of triumph.

"I'm not aware of any resistance troops left alive."

The triumph left the judge's face just as quickly. He looked at his men, then back at Eric.

"They're out there," the judge stated. "A whole army."

"No, there's not. You won. The resistance has been demolished. If you continue to run with a cruel hand, you'll see more uprisings, but the present resistance seems to have been broken."

"What about your men?" He frowned. "That Major Milton said Mad Man's fighters are—"

"I'm Mad Man," Eric smiled sadly, "and I'm alone. I'm not a resistance leader. The major lied to you to save his own skin. I'm just a woodsman."

"But, you're about to die the death of a resistance fighter!"

"It seems so."

"You chose this? To die rather than to live?"

"Well, I'd rather live." Eric shrugged. "You're the one who's insisting that I die."

"But Major Milton was a real resistance fighter. You helped him escape!" The man rose in a huff and stood at the window, gazing out at the garbage-strewn street. Suddenly, he faced Eric. "You're a resistance fighter. You're lying to me. You said you're Mad Man."

"I abhor violence. I wouldn't shoot you if you gave me a loaded gun right now."

"Why . . . would you allow Major Milton to go free when you know I have to execute you now? Commander Morris will be here in less than a week! I have to execute someone."

"Major Milton has always been a weak man. He has his good qualities, but he isn't ready to die." Eric licked his lips. "What I'm about to say will explain everything."

"Is that right? Well then, speak!"

Eric hesitated. This was the man who'd massacred Christians and burned Bibles the previous year. If there was any chance of release, he was about to close that door permanently—unless the judge came to Christ . . .

"Right after Pan-Day, I realized if I would've died from the virus, I would've passed into an unknown eternity. That scared me. That's when I recognized I was a man with many sins, and I needed to get right with God. I received Jesus as my Savior and Deliverer. That's why I live a life of care for others. That's why I'm willing to die for Major Milton or even for you, Judge—because Jesus cared for me. Like Him, apparently, I'm about to die to keep others alive."

"You're a Christian." The judge shook his head. "Killing you won't break the spirit of the resistance. I'll just be creating a martyr for the other Christians to honor!"

"Naturally, I would hope you won't kill me."

"Oh, I'm killing you, for the good of us all. And you'll keep your mouth shut when Commander Morris gets here, or I'll make it worse for you!"

"Worse than death?" Eric chuckled, enjoying the closeness he felt to God with eternity so near. "Don't worry. One of my motivations to meet with you yesterday was to stop Commander Morris from burning more of your people at the stake. If you need a life to sacrifice so no others are killed, I'm okay with being that sacrifice. Death holds no terror for me."

The judge stared at Eric for a moment, his eyes actually showing sympathy. Eric imagined a tiny seed of love growing in the soil of the judge's heart. But then, the judge waved his hand.

"You're a mad man. Take him downstairs. I don't want to look at him again. Insane, that's what you are! Pure madness. Nobody dies for other people like this! You hear me? Nobody!"

Eric's escorts pulled him roughly from the room.

#######

Two days passed in the basement cell. Eric spent them pacing, praying, and sleeping. There were only the same two guards who rotated outside his cell. He tried to engage them in conversation, but their orders not to communicate must've come with threats.

One day, after being served a particularly watered-down broth and dry biscuit, Eric tried a new tactic.

"How come we eat this starvation diet when there's a whole herd of cattle not far away?" He waited, watching Josh Hicks read a dime novel outside his cell. The man didn't look up. "Can you imagine a full stomach of beef? Look at us. Eating nothing but flavored water, while I know where the cattle are. What, did Commander Morris order Mastover to starve itself to death? I guess so."

Hicks didn't respond, but at his shift change that afternoon, Newman arrived and both men unlocked his cell door and marched Eric upstairs to the judge's office.

"You know where a herd of cattle is?" the judge asked, acting disinterested as he stood again at the window that faced west. Eric wondered if he could see the highway far away—the route Commander Morris would take to return from the front lines when he visited Mastover again.

Eric considered his words carefully. Just because the American economy had collapsed didn't mean there wasn't still such a thing called leverage.

"I haven't kept my weight and strength up for six years by eating biscuits and water."

No one in the room moved. Eric believed he heard Newman's stomach growl. Since Eric did indeed have meat on his bones, and they were malnourished, his words carried weight.

"Nothing will delay your execution in a few days." The judge turned, sat down, and folded his hands. His eyes were hard as they bore into Eric. "But being burned at the stake can be less painful if we give you something to dull the pain beforehand. A narcotic. You also have my word that I'll offer asylum to whomever is left out in the woods who wishes to return to Mastover. All that depends on what you know that'll help the people here. Today."

"I don't need mercy from you." Eric smiled peacefully, confidently. "If I die soon, or not, it's really in God's hands, not yours. My choice to help you and the people of Mastover is because I don't want to see people suffer. If I tell you where the cattle are, it's because I care about you, Judge. The love of Christ Jesus compels me to help you. If you choose to treat me well or not, that's entirely on your own conscience. But how I live or die is not in your hands."

"Oh, you will die, you arrogant little gnat! You'll writhe and scream in the flames as they climb up your body! Your Jesus can't move the mountains necessary to stop that. Right now, I am god of your life and death!"

"The only reason you're killing me is because you're being pressured by the Lib-Org's commander. You're not in as much control as you say, and all your men know it. A puppet leader is what you are, too afraid of Morris to do what's best for the people. I'm your captive, but my conscience is free. Sure, you're a leader, but you're a captive of an evil man's vision. And your people are suffering for it."

"The more you say, the more you'll suffer." The judge spoke calmly now, the truth hopefully wounding him, perhaps making him reconsider. "Take him back to his cell."

The men didn't move.

"But, the cattle, Your Honor." Hicks glanced at Newman. "I think he's telling the truth about the herd."

"I am," Eric said. "All you have to do is ask."

"Shut up! All of you!" Judge Grayport rose to his feet and leaned on his hands over his desk. "Mastover doesn't negotiate with traitors! Especially not Jesus freaks! I will never beg, not even for the lives of my own people! Get out!"

Down in the basement again, Eric lay on his bunk and listened to the indiscernible whispers of Hicks and Newman outside the door. After a few minutes, the door opened and both men crowded the doorway. Eric sat up.

"You really know where cattle are?" Newman asked. His narrow eyes and smirk now appeared as pleading, even desperate. Hunger had broken through the man's cold heart. "If you tell us, Hicks and I will make sure you die quickly. We both have families. We can't keep living off what the scavengers bring in. They haven't even found any antelope in a month."

"I'll tell you two where the cattle are," Eric said, "but first, you're going to listen to me."

"Sure." Newman shrugged, moved deeper into the cell, and leaned against the wall. Hicks remained at the door.

"Hardship always shows who we really are." Eric nodded solemnly, thinking of River Camp as well as the people of Mastover. "We don't know what's really in us until we're tested by difficulties. We like to think of ourselves as honest and caring, or courageous and steadfast. But in the heat of the fire, like we've witnessed since the virus, most of us have realized we're selfish, proud, and cowardly. We've hoarded secretly, and maybe stolen and killed, for another desperate day. For what? We're in the middle of a garbage dump here, serving a man who thinks he's a god."

"You don't know Judge Grayport. He's ruthless." Hicks looked away. "He'll kill my whole family if I betray him. We shouldn't even be talking to him, Newman."

"I think we're past that." Eric took a deep breath. "The judge is already killing your families, and you've both clearly considered the consequences of talking to me about this."

"Just tell us where the cattle are," Newman pleaded.

"In a minute." Eric bowed his head. His only bargaining chip didn't seem to be the leverage he'd hoped. Rather than withhold the truth for his own sake, he had to help these starving people. "There comes a time when a man's loyalties must be questioned. Let's just look at the facts and measure them. You're starving in a town full of filth, serving a man who threatens your families to keep you loyal. And then there's me. I've eaten healthy for years, bathed in crystal-clear water, and served a God who provides for me. You still want to put your faith in the judge?"

"Your God got you caught," Newman said, "and now He's about to get you killed."

"I'm not dead yet." Eric smiled. "I'm here to speak to you two about putting your faith in the God who looks at our hearts. I may die in a few days, sure. I'm content with that. We all die. But I know where I'm going when I die, and you don't. You and your families will die a little slower, and every individual will stand before God. What will your excuse be then? You'll tell Him you sided with a tyrant out of fear, rather than cared for your neighbor out of love?"

"I've never seen any God do anything for me and my family," Hicks said, his face downcast.

"He's using me right now to speak to you. This is often how He works. If it's goodness and kindness—it's coming from God. Now, Judge Grayport is only as strong as his men agree to do what he says."

"The Lib-Org troops will demolish Mastover if we defect as a whole town." Newman shook his head, but Eric could see his words had penetrated his mind. "Just tell us where the cattle are."

Eric bit his lip. He'd be dead soon, anyway. Mastover didn't deserve to discover the cattle, but exercising grace was just that—offering favor that the recipients didn't deserve.

"I'll tell you, but only because you need to see God's hand of deliverance for something this simple." He took a deep breath. "About twenty miles south of here is a town called Adderthorn. It sits below the last mountain peak of the Sharrock Range. To the east is rangeland, all the way to the Mississippi. You with me so far?"

"Yeah. The rangeland." Newman nodded. "We follow."

"About ten miles east of Adderthorn, there's a wash or spring, with a small stand of oak trees." Eric didn't tell them he'd discovered the water source on a clear day using his telescope while sitting on top of his mountain. "A whole herd of cattle have used that place as a watering hole for years. They graze on the range around them, but they return to the water each day."

"You've seen this for yourself?" Newman asked. "That's a long way from Mastover, but if it's a guarantee, the judge will let us take a couple vehicles."

"It's a guarantee," Eric said, "but depending on how you manage the slaughter, you may or may not kill off the whole herd this year, and be back to starving to death next year."

"We know how to manage a herd," Hicks said. The quiet man seemed to have replaced the sharpness his partner once had.

"Just don't forget about me." Eric forced a smile, thinking of Joseph and the cupbearer. "When you're eating and filling your bellies in a couple days, it was a follower of Jesus Christ who guided you to the food."

"Yeah." Newman scoffed as he backed out the door. "Like we're telling the judge that!"

Once they were gone, Eric lay back and sighed contentedly. Maybe that was the last of his work on earth—to use his knowledge to keep the town alive for a little longer. He'd never gone after the cattle himself since the rangeland to the east had no cover, and he didn't want to be attacked by bandits or a military unit on the open plain. However, only someone from the mountaintop heights would be able to discover the thousand or so cattle grazing out there.

From thoughts of contentment, Eric's mind gradually drifted back to being burned at the stake. It was a harsh reality. Major Milton, the man he was dying for, was surely back at River Camp by now. Andy was probably up at the cabin with Joel and his wife. While Eric died in the midst of flames, the refugees of war would probably not even grieve for him. After all, they hadn't been too happy about his leadership. Gretchen hadn't been pleased with him, either. But Eric's conscience was clear, since he'd sought the inspiration of the Lord to make his decisions for the people.

A clear conscience, he considered, was more valuable than all the comfort in the world—when it came to standing before Jesus Christ. And he would certainly be facing the eternal realm sooner rather than later, so it was just as well he'd already been striving to live faithfully and pleasing in the sight of God. Yes, he was about to meet his Savior!

Chapter 4

The morning of his execution, Eric was fed a slim piece of salted beef and a mug of weak tea. Beef! So, they'd found the cattle he'd told them about, he thought somberly. He'd delivered them from starvation, so now they would deliver him to the fire.

On his knees, Eric prayed. He felt a gentle joy in his heart. The prospect of meeting God gave him a peace that transcended any fear of excruciating pain. The pain would last but a few minutes. Eternity would last—forever!

Even with the meat in his stomach, he hadn't been fed well for a week. He prayed he would remain strong enough to die with honor for God, and not in shame or defeat. His cell door suddenly opened and he stood up.

"The judge wants you to wear this." Hicks tossed Eric a red, white, and blue armband that the resistance fighters wore. "Put it on."

"I'm dying as a resistance fighter, so why not be clothed like one, huh?" Eric said, as he pulled the band up to his biceps.

"Keep your mouth shut about the resistance, or this'll go much worse for you." Newman looked at the floor. "That's what Judge Grayport said."

"So, Commander Morris is here?" Eric presented his wrists to be cuffed in front of him. Instead, Hicks turned him around and roughly cuffed his hands behind his back.

"He's here—with two squads of his best men." Newman took hold of Eric's left arm. "They thought they might be coming to burn five Mastover people at the stake, if we hadn't resolved the resistance problem. Nothing will interrupt that now."

"Good thing you're resolving it, huh?" Eric joked as they led him upstairs. "How disappointing it'll be for you all when the resistance reignites since you're not killing its actual leader."

"Shut up!" Hicks jabbed him in the ribs. "No talking now."

When they emerged into the sunshine, Eric squinted at the charred earth near the side of the courthouse where it had been cleared for executions. The hanging platform Eric had seen months earlier was gone now, and the platform wood was piled for feeding the fire. Around the courtyard, the gray town stood like something from a black and white movie. Its streets were choked by trash, and the tallest buildings seemed haunted by silence, tensed for more death.

A crowd was gathered—voluntarily or forced, Eric wasn't sure—with Commander Morris seated on a metal chair at the front. Eric was marched over to him, and Judge Grayport walked up with his private security guard of five local soldiers. Twenty of Commander Morris' troops wore the gray and black insignia of a lightning bolt on the shoulders of their uniforms, distinguishing them as the Lib-Org's elite forces—apart from the rag-tag and recently-starved militia of Mastover. About one hundred Mastover soldiers were present, and all eyes were on the visitors and Eric.

"This is the resistance leader." Judge Grayport presented Eric, and gestured at his armband. Eric noticed the judge averted his gaze often, like he didn't want to make eye contact with anyone for too long. "They call him Mad Man, like I wrote to you in the report. Sergeant?"

One of the judge's men stepped forward with rehearsed precision and drew a polished dagger. The knife slid roughly against Eric's arm, cutting him through his jacket, but slicing away the armband. The red, white, and blue band fell to the ground. With the pageantry completed, the judge nodded to Hicks and Newman. It was burning time.

"Wait." Commander Morris stood and stepped up to look into Eric's eyes. The commander was a balding man with broad shoulders and a thin waist. He portrayed a fighting man with daring eyes and hands at his sides that seemed frozen in mid-grip. "You're Mad Man?"

Shorter than the leader of the Lib-Org, Eric's head tilted up. Though the judge's bluff depended on Eric keeping his mouth shut, Eric also had a commitment to River Camp to continue the facade. If he didn't, the judge's troops would be forced to clear the woods of the remnants of the resistance—which were the women and children still living in safety.

"I am."

"This dog scared us from hunting for game in the woods to the south?" He turned and smiled at his men, drawing laughter. "Did you ever have the virus, like they said you did?"

"Not that I know of."

"How can we be sure he's the last of the resistance?" he asked the judge.

"No one else is left." The judge chuckled, but it came out as a nervous cackle. "The dump is filled with their bodies. He's the last threat."

"Hardly the last threat." Morris took out a handkerchief and mopped his forehead from the mid-morning heat. "The Christians are still out there, even living among us. They don't wear armbands or wave flags, but they hate the freedom the Liberation Organization seeks to reinstall across this fine land."

"We've executed our share of noncompliant citizens as well, Commander," Judge Grayport said. "Take him away, men."

As Eric was escorted from the commander's company, the judge's face showed relief that Eric had remained silent regarding his charges.

Hicks took Eric by the throat and forced his back against the tall stake posted in the ground. A simple cord was lashed around his neck. His hands remained cuffed behind him. Hicks and Newman commenced to tie his legs to the post as well. Then, the wood stacked nearby was moved, piece by piece, to lean against Eric's legs.

Eric was saddened by the silent stares of the people as they watched, their faces blank. Perhaps their hearts had become desensitized from the other executions. They seemed emotionless.

Above the people, the buildings around the courthouse square stood just as silently, their dark windows mostly absent of glass due to bullets and grenade concussions from past conflicts. The marks of fighting and turmoil scarred the structures. So much violence and pain. And loneliness.

Focusing his eyes above the buildings, Eric looked at the clouds. God was watching, and Eric was ready to go to Him. He'd lived a selfish life, until six years earlier. Then, Eric had taken God's side against his own sinfulness. Because he'd trusted in the sacrifice of Jesus, physical death didn't hold any great sting. Life would come from his death.

The wood was sufficiently piled around his legs. Eric did his best not to think about how the flames would leap up his body. Depending on where they started the wood on fire, he might even be unconscious from the smoke before the flames reached him. The thought made him crane his neck even more against the collar to see more of the sky. The tears on his cheeks weren't from sadness. But perhaps there was some sadness since he'd not been able to bring more of the River Camp people to see the gospel truth.

Thump!

Eric heard a murmur course through the gathering. Several people pointed at Eric in fear. But it wasn't at Eric they were pointing, he suddenly realized. Hicks and Newman backed away from an aluminum arrow shaft that had thudded deeply into the ground near the pile of wood.

Its angle was nearly vertical, as if it had been sent from heaven.

Thunk!

A second arrow stabbed into a board close to Eric's feet. Hicks dropped a box of matches and backed away from starting the fire. The Lib-Org troops and the commander swung rifles against their shoulders. But where was the unseen archer?

Staring at the aluminum arrows, Eric gasped. He might still die that day, but he wouldn't die anonymously. Those were Joel Grayport's arrows! Probably all of Mastover knew of the bow hunter's skill and trade. Eric prayed Joel didn't show himself and get caught. Who else would take care of Andy?

The eyes of Eric and the judge met. Yes, the man knew those were arrows belonging to his son. The judge's face showed confusion, but curiosity as well.

"People of Mastover!" a voice boomed into the square. Eric knew the voice. It was Hank Worcester! What was he doing here? "People of Mastover! When will the killing stop? Will you execute your own sons and daughters next? All because of Commander Morris? No more! No more! No more!"

The chant seemed to shake the ground, echoing off the structures surrounding the courtyard. The buildings around the courthouse came alive. Every window, every roof, was filled with people. Their clothing was drab and they were mostly women and children, but they were still a startling presence. Eric watched the soldiers near Morris stagger and try to organize themselves to aim their rifles at their elevated enemy. Gretchen was there, too. And Andy, who whistled a shrill whistle and waved at Eric. Some of the women held rifles, but most of them and the children held wooden spears, all aimed at the soldiers.

The people of River Camp had come for Eric!

"What is this, Judge?" Commander Morris bellowed over the chant. The chant slowly died away for the people to hear the words of the men. "This is what you call a smashed resistance?"

Again, the judge's eyes met Eric's. The old man's gaze was filled with defeat. He'd been moments away from making the resistance a thing of the past—at least as far as the town's military guest was concerned. But now, it was obvious the ruse was up, and the judge had been lying. The resistance was apparently alive and well, and it threatened the Lib-Org commander himself.

"Untie Eric Radner!" Hank shouted. He stood on the tallest building facing Eric. "Let him walk, Judge Grayport, or you'll have a massacre on your hands that the whole world will hear about and curse your name!"

There was more shuffling of the soldiers, each with a bead on a River Camp person who held a rifle. Judge Grayport frowned at his son's arrows in the ground. Everyone waited for him to decide—to choose the Lib-Org or the people.

"Maybe, for once," the judge said to Commander Morris, "I should listen to the people."

"You're afraid of this? I'm not afraid of them!" Morris sneered and cursed at the weakness above him. "A few hunting rifles and sticks in the hands of women and kids? I've slaughtered more aggressors for less reason than this."

"Maybe you have. But you won't today. My son is one of those people." The judge squared his shoulders and glanced at Eric. Then, he drew his own sidearm and aimed it at the commander. "No one else in Mastover dies for the Liberation Organization."

Following the judge's boldness, the Mastover troops swung their assault rifles from the River Camp people to Commander Morris' twenty soldiers.

"What are you doing?" Morris, even with all of his authority, held back the order to fire as he seemed to calculate the odds—one hundred against twenty, not counting the few marksmen on the roofs. "You are a Lib-

Org protectorate, Judge Grayport! You signed a treaty of allegiance to me! I am fighting for your freedom and the right to—"

"Enough!" The judge's handgun shook, but it was clearly aimed at the commander's chest. "You take your men and leave Mastover forever! If you return, it'll be an act of war!"

"You're making a mistake, Judge." Morris stepped toward the judge, but Grayport didn't back away. Instead, he pushed his gun muzzle directly into the commander's gut. Morris hesitated, perhaps gauging the judge's nerve. "Okay, I'll leave. But this isn't the end. No, the end will have you up there on that stake. You'll burn for this, Grayport! Burn!"

Commander Morris swatted the pistol aside and gestured to his seemingly invincible twenty men. They backed off slowly, rifles held ready, and walked toward their vehicles waiting yards away on the street.

No one else in the square moved until the vehicles roared away. Then, the judge holstered his sidearm and slowly approached Eric. Eric noticed a new light in the man's eyes, but the judge didn't move to release him.

"I probably should've done that a long time ago," the judge said.

"The timing seemed perfect to me." Eric felt fresh tears on his cheeks. "The people are just looking for a strong, benevolent leader. Is that you, Judge?"

"Benevolent?" The judge snorted and drew a pocket knife. "The Lib-Org will level Mastover for my benevolence."

The judge cut the tether around Eric's throat, then knelt to saw at the ropes around his legs. Once loosed, Eric kicked firewood away and stumbled free. Hicks uncuffed his wrists. Eric stood shoulder to shoulder with the judge, staring up at the people, who were silent again, but with a new radiance to their faces Eric hadn't seen before. He couldn't wait to hear how and why they'd suddenly rallied together to help him.

"They'll back you, Judge, if you stand up for them. Like you did today."

"I had a little inspiration." The judge looked at Eric out of the corner of his eye. "It didn't sit well with me that I was killing the only man who's helped us the most this past year. That beef saved us all. We'll make it through the winter now. Unless the Lib-Org attacks before the snow falls."

"You won't have to face Commander Morris at all," Eric said, "if you blow up the bridge west of town. And if you also destroy the bridge south of town, Mastover will be just plain inaccessible. The Lib-Org will have to find another route to supply their front lines."

"So, finding cattle out on the range isn't the only trick up your sleeve?" The judge eyed Eric suspiciously. "You'll help us?"

"I may or may not have more ideas." Eric gazed up at the River Camp people who still stood above them. "But I'll help keep your people safe and at peace. Your son is also someone who should be at your side, you know."

"Just keep that God stuff to yourself."

"You don't get me without my God, Judge Grayport." Eric waved at Gretchen, and she waved back, grinning, her red hair blowing in the wind. Since Joel Grayport was there, as well as Major Milton, there had obviously been some reconciling in Eric's absence. "It's my God who's going to continue to do mighty things for the people of Mastover, so you decide now: do you want to rely on yourself, or do you want the favor of God?"

"From one idiotic agreement to the next . . ." The judge cursed. "Do I have a choice?"

"I need to hear it."

"Okay. Let's figure out how to stay alive. Together." The judge hesitated, then offered his bony hand. "If you bring your imaginary deity with you, and you think that makes you stronger for the rest of us, I guess I'll just have to accept it."

Eric gripped the judge's hand.

"You stick with me, Judge. You'll find my God is far from imaginary."

The two shook hands, and a cheer erupted, a thunderous sound in the courtyard. The cheer wasn't only from the mouths of the River Camp people, but from the soldiers of Mastover as well.

#######

That night, the people of River Camp inhabited the town of Mastover, many of them moving back into homes they'd abandoned a year earlier when they'd joined Major Milton's resistance. After sunset, however, a few of Eric's companions from River Camp gathered next to the courthouse, and Hank Worcester started a fire using the wood meant to burn Eric alive. His wife, Sara, provided some deer steaks and the clan seemed oblivious to the reality that they were in the middle of town. A couple even laid out tarps to sleep on through the warm summer night.

"The judge still has a lot to answer for," Hank said as Eric sat on a tarp with Andy. "There needs to be more changes than he knows if we're all coming back to live here."

"I don't want to live here." Andy looked up at Eric, his eyes pleading. "Do we have to live in Mastover?"

"No, we don't have to." Eric nodded at Hank. "I'm all for change, but my place isn't here, Hank. Andy and I are going back to the mountains. A few of the others want to go back with us, too."

On the other side of the fire, Gretchen pushed a board from the old gallows into the flames.

"I don't know what we're going to do." Hank took his wife's hand. "I was a better soldier for a few months than I was a statesman in this dump."

"Compared to a month ago, it seems there's already been some changes for the good," Eric said. "Last I knew,

River Camp voted to push Joel out on his own. How did you all come to see things differently?"

"We were wrong," Gretchen blurted over the fire. "I mean, I was wrong. After you freed Major Milton at the bridge, he crawled out of the water and came back to River Camp. He told us that you were willing to die in his place, even for all of us, to keep us safe."

"That major is more of a coward than I thought!" Hank spit at the fire. "Letting you die for him? Unbelievable!"

"But he's the one who talked us into coming to Mastover for you." Gretchen walked halfway around the fire, closer to Eric. "After that, we realized we'd been wrong about Joel, even if he is the judge's son. We knew we'd need his help if we were coming here to get you."

"Gretchen went herself to your cabin to get Junior," Hank said, "and she brought Andy with them. We met out at the highway south of town, then entered Mastover before dawn."

"We were counting on the judge not wanting to kill his own son." Gretchen continued around the fire, then knelt on the tarp at Eric's feet. Eric was reminded of their first night together, when he hadn't known who she was. That cold night in the mountains, they'd shared a similar tarp. Now, like then, the firelight flickered on her face, making her hair seem aflame. "But the judge's heart was hard. We knew it would take more for him to turn away from the Lib-Org. But I had faith."

"Faith?" Eric smiled.

"Yes, faith. I believed you were praying. To God."

"I was." Eric sighed. "I was praying a lot, and God delivered with far more than I expected. Look at us, all here together. I even saw Joel and the judge talking before sundown."

"Can you ever forgive me?" She held her empty hands in front of her, palms up. "Eric, I've been miserable these last few days. So much was happening, and it was good.

But then Joel came to live at River Camp, and Willy's death, and the pressures of the resistance— I just wasn't thinking right. I should've stood with you."

"None of us were thinking right," Hank mumbled, then cleared his throat and lowered his head like he hadn't meant to admit wrongdoing.

"What do you think, Andy?" Eric nudged his son. "Should I forgive her?"

"She seems pretty sorry," Andy stated. "And she makes good deer stew."

They all laughed.

"It's settled, then." Eric stared intently into Gretchen's eyes. Something about all the conflict and reconciliation made him want her close to him more than ever. "You're forgiven."

"Just don't be offering yourself up to die for people anymore!" Hank scowled at the flames. "I'm getting tired of saving your life, Provisions Officer!"

Gretchen sat down next to Eric, facing the flames with him. Eric put his arm around her, and looked at the starry sky.

"Thank You, Lord," he said for all to hear.

For once, Hank didn't grumble.

Conclusion, Book Three

Eric crouched against a fir tree in a canyon deep in the Sharrock Mountains. Through the brush, he saw Gretchen do the same, her rifle held ready, waiting for the grizzly bears. Her father, Hank, was somewhere to his right, and Joel Grayport—armed with an assault rifle rather than his bow—was supposed to be farther up on the wall of the canyon, watching over them.

It had been one week since all of River Camp had turned up in the town of Mastover to spoil the Lib-Org's execution of Eric. They had defied the mighty army of Commander Morris. Hope could once again be sensed in the clear Wyoming air. But first, they had to kill the man-eaters to secure the safety of the few families who remained in River Camp.

Ahead, one of the bears snorted. Eric aimed at the rustling bushes. He had no desire to wound the predator. Joel had already made that mistake, and the bear's fury had turned on a child and killed Willy. Rather, a clean shot to the heart, one bullet for each bear, would do the job. But where was the other bear?

Without shooting, Eric edged closer to the brush. Hank waved him back, but Eric ignored him. After all, he was Mad Man.

Brown fur! Eric froze. The bear turned, the hump on its back prominent above the huckleberry bushes. The beast was only thirty feet away! It stopped moving. Eric frowned. Was that its snout?

He fired into its dark, left eye staring back at him. The noise of the gunshot echoed off the steep canyon walls. Another huge mass lunged over Eric from the left. Eric fell onto his shoulder and rolled as the second bear leapt from the dense forest and soared over him. The second bear had been stalking him as he'd been stalking the first bear!

A split second later, Eric was on his knees, a fresh round chambered in his rifle. He looked after the bear as it crashed through the foliage on a wild charge straight at Gretchen. Gretchen fired and a bullet zipped past Eric's head. Her panic won over. She dropped her rifle and scrambled for the nearest tree to climb.

Eric rose smoothly to his feet and gazed down his sights. The bear's tail was tucked in its reckless charge. Above the tail, facing away, was the back of the bear's bobbing head. Gretchen wasn't going to make it into the tree in time. Hank screamed. Joel fired and missed. There was only time for Eric to take one more shot.

He squeezed the trigger, aiming over the spine of the bear, at the back of its skull. The giant snapped upright, still moving forward, then fell limply in a tangle of tree branches and fur. Gretchen fell onto the bear at her feet, then hastily pushed off to stand over the kill that had nearly killed her.

No one moved for a few moments, except for Eric as he chambered another round, half-expecting another bear to charge.

"Everyone okay?" Eric asked, and remembered the first bear. He investigated by stepping through several feet of ferns and wild huckleberry bushes. When he rolled the gnarled skull aside, he saw the animal had indeed been shot through its left eye. "This one's dead!"

"This one, too!" Gretchen announced of the second bear.

"I'll get the horses." Joel started east to where they'd tethered the two remaining horses the people of Mastover had left in River Camp.

"Two shots for two bears?" Hank rested his rifle over his shoulder as he and Gretchen stood over the second bear. "If he keeps this up, I'm liable to start believing his God really does favor him."

"Both head shots, too." Gretchen beamed. "I think I'm actually starting to believe."

She kissed Eric on his bearded cheek as he joined them. Ever since his rescue at Mastover, she'd been clinging to him and claiming him as hers, as much as the first week they'd spent together in River Camp, months earlier.

Eric was elated at the attention of this beautiful woman. Not only was Gretchen making her matrimonial intentions clear once again, but she was also asking heartfelt questions, and seemed close to professing Christ. She'd even asked to read from one of his Bibles. Only two Bibles remained since the judge had thrown away Eric's pocket one.

"We'll get a couple decent bedspreads out of these bear skins." Eric took a handful of fur and felt the fat beneath. "We don't have enough horses to get all this meat out, though. It's eight miles back to camp, and the sun's nearly down. Get your knives out. We'd best skin them and take what we can before dark. River Camp won't sleep until we get back with the news.

"They're probably still on their knees!" Hank said in criticism, but then grumbled when it sounded like he'd meant it as a positive comment.

Eric smiled, guessing the hard man was only days away from coming to Christ himself, as several others had in camp.

Most of the River Camp residents had moved back to Mastover to live since Judge Grayport's heart had apparently turned. Living in the wilderness was harder, many had discovered, than living in even the garbage-infested town. But all that was due to change. Rumors of free elections and the appointment of sanitation teams had begun to circulate. Looking northward through a pair of binoculars, a trail of black smoke ten miles away could be seen reaching skyward. The sanitation crews were already at work.

Besides Hank and his wife and daughter, Joel had elected to stay at River Camp with his wife, Lena, and their infant. Since standing against the judge for Eric's sake, it had brought him into the good graces of the others in camp.

Major Milton Pickford had been more than delighted to bring out a stash of red, white, and blue armbands to distribute to everyone—even in Mastover. The resistance against Mastover might have died out, leaving many dead in the process, but now the stand for Mastover had begun. The major was remaining in the town, he said, to keep a close eye on the judge's newfound consideration for his people.

The bridges west and south of Mastover had been dynamited, ruining the Lib-Org's direct approaches to attack the town. But no one believed the Lib-Org and Commander Morris' violence had ended. He would be back.

It was nearly midnight when the hunting party crossed the river and reached River Camp. As expected, the few campers who had stayed ran out to the river to meet them. Eric eased his pack of bear meat off his back onto the river rocks. The rest of the people clamored around two fires burning high, and the story of the hunt began as quickly as Hank could settle everyone down to listen. Sara scolded Hank as he sniffed at a cooking pot, which he excused as the right of only the storyteller to do.

Barb was there as well. With her son Willy gone, in her grief, she'd taken to caring for Lena, Joel's ill wife, and Shawna, their infant child. A couple other women slept in one of the lodges with Barb. They were Christian converts and adoptive mothers of several orphaned children.

Since the judge had purged Mastover of Christians only a year earlier, these few believers chose to remain under Eric's care, still not trusting that the judge wouldn't have them killed next. But Eric had plans to foster the budding relationship he had with the judge. He did indeed have other plans and ideas for Mastover's well-being, and monthly visits into town had already been scheduled. Eric began to see them as evangelistic journeys. Though the judge wasn't a Christian yet, he'd stood against Commander Morris, so the judge couldn't afford to alienate any of his own people.

Andy had brought a young black lab puppy from Mastover. He'd immediately named her Runner. The man in Mastover who'd given her to Andy said it was doing the town a favor by taking the pup—she would be one less mouth to feed in town. Little Runner was nipping at Joel's blood-spattered boots, the smell of bear still strong.

Eric took a deep breath, praising God for the family he now beheld—his family.

"You look like a proud father," Gretchen said as she approached from the darkness. She hooked her arm around his. "What's on your mind?"

"I may or may not break out in song at all that Christ has blessed us with. I'm alive. My son is smiling. And the people around me are recognizing their Creator."

"It's more than we imagined, huh?" She leaned against him. "You really think He's coming soon?"

"Jesus? Yes! Most in America, I gather, thought He would've already come to collect His Church. But trusting Him as Lord includes believing His timing is always right."

"Speaking of timing, how much longer will you and Andy sleep all alone in that lodge of yours?" Gretchen asked.

Arm in arm, they approached the fires, the food, and Hank's tale of more bears than there actually were.

"Alone? We have Runner in there with us now, too." He chuckled. "I can't imagine who else we'd ask to join us."

"If you don't find us a preacher soon, I'm liable to tell Dad to stand in, if he'd agree to touch a Bible for a ceremony."

She shoved him playfully and went to help her mother with the stew.

Andy, playing with the other orphans, nearly plowed into Eric. Eric caught the boy and steadied him on his feet. He knelt in front of the six-year-old.

"I've been meaning to talk to you about something, Andy."

"What is it?" He set a hand on Eric's shoulder, the gesture taking the words from Eric for a moment.

"When we were still at the cabin, we agreed that we like our family just the way it is—you and me. Remember?"

"Yeah. Now we have a new cabin," Andy said.

"That's true. We also agreed that if we wanted to add anyone else to our family, we'd each need to approve of any additions."

"Who? Runner?"

"No, Runner's just fine. I was thinking more along the lines of Gretchen."

"The hunter? In our cabin?" He frowned and seemed to look at Gretchen in a new light. "I guess so. If she doesn't mind Runner."

"I think the whole camp enjoys having Runner here."

"It might be good to have another hunter in our cabin, I guess," Andy said. "That way, you won't have to wake up anyone else in camp when you want to get her to go out early for a hunt."

"That certainly would be an advantage." Eric nodded. "I was thinking along the lines of a wife as well."

"A wife? In our cabin?"

"A wife, yes. For me. I've never been married, and now I see she is coming along as a new believer. And maybe, if you accept, she could try to be a mother to you, too. She wouldn't replace your real mom, but your real mom would want you to have a mother, I think."

"Makes sense. Well, I guess if you like her." Andy cocked his head. "Joel said he brought back a big ol' bear bone for Runner. I think he feels bad for killing the other Runner."

"Could be." Eric patted the boy on the back. "Maybe it's best to let him know you appreciate it."

"I will."

Andy threw his arms around Eric's neck, then darted off to join the ruckus. Over the fire, Gretchen smiled at Eric. He winked at her, then faced the river. Everything seemed as right as it could be, but in those days, harmony was fleeting. Winter was coming, and wood needed to be gathered. Mastover hadn't seen the last of the Liberation Organization, and Mad Man south of Mastover would be one of Commander Morris' most hunted enemies. Yes, further danger was surely in the breeze . . .

But whatever might come, Eric was determined to remain steadfast on the path the Lord had prepared. He'd entrusted his soul to God, and through peril or even burning at the stake, he would anticipate being with Jesus Christ soon. Forever.

###

~End of *STEADFAST Book Three*~

Bonus Chapter SF3

Who are the Wyoming invaders? What do they want? Follow this Bonus Chapter to discover behind-the-scenes intel on the bad guys!

~

Commander Kelly Morris of the Liberation Organization drove into his Coeur d'Alene headquarters around midnight. His driver tapped the fuel gauge. The dial registered on empty. The five other Humvees his soldiers had driven to Wyoming were certain to have empty tanks as well. His army's fuel reserves were nearly depleted.

As exhausted as his body was, Morris' mind was racing. Anxiety had left him fidgeting in the front seat the whole day as they had driven back from Wyoming to Northern Idaho. Leaving his men, he climbed the stairs to his quarters in the old college dorm building, hoping for some time alone. He didn't want his men to sense his sour mood and discouragement from the wasted trip to Mastover. Morris was unaccustomed to defeat! However, a bike messenger was asleep on the floor in front of his door, so being alone wasn't yet an option.

Morris nudged the young man with the toe of his boot. The messenger leapt to his feet and saluted. If Morris remembered correctly, the man's name was Hoyle. He'd been hazed by some of the regular troops, so Morris had moved him to the bike messenger corps.

"At ease, soldier. What's so pressing at this time of night?"

"Bad news, sir."

"More, huh?" Morris unlocked his door and walked into a room that held only the essentials for an overnight stay, though he'd been living there for months. "Well, what is it? Out with it, and we can both get some sleep."

"Actually, sir . . ." Hoyle shuffled through several slips of paper in his hands. "I drew the low card this evening. The others left their communiques with me."

"Do any of them carry good news?"

"I'm sure you'll be able to find something worthwhile in some of these, sir." Hoyle studied one paper, then rearranged it to the back of his stack. "The lookout you left in Wyoming as you guys left this morning relayed a message already. I guess things didn't go well there, huh?"

"What's the message?"

"The town of Mastover has destroyed the two bridges leading in and out of town. There's only a rope bridge for pedestrians south of town remaining over the river, the side of town that faces the wilderness."

"That was expected. Our supply lines are now completely cut off. We'll have to send word through Southern Idaho to reroute trucks to reach us here."

"But how could Mastover force our hand, sir? I mean, we're the Lib-Org. They're just a little town. I remember when we drove through there a year ago. We liberated them from their backward, isolated thinking. They owe us."

"Not everyone is grateful, young man. Don't worry. They'll pay for their betrayal, eventually. What else?"

"Um, there were about twenty desertions while you were gone."

"Twenty?" Morris' knees felt weak. "So many, huh?"

"The MPs were on patrol, but they didn't see them leave. They think the deserters went south."

"Did they take any fuel or vehicles?"

"No, just bikes. You want to send some men after them?"

Morris sat down in a wooden chair and folded his hands. Desertions had been growing the last six months. People were losing hope in his vision for a liberated America. As fast as his fuel was running out, his personnel were fleeing. He didn't want to admit aloud that deserters reflected on his leadership, but he feared the men were already whispering.

"We have to get this army moving west again—at all costs!"

"Well, sir, that regards another message." Hoyle took a step back, and Morris read the involuntary action as a sign of the news. "Spokane has dug in better on the east and west sides of the freeway leading into the city. They look like homesteaders, reports say—people from the mountains. They've probably grown up hunting and they'll know how to use their rifles. One of your captains said that a head-on attack as you planned may not be wisest."

"Such small minds standing against progress. Homesteaders!" Morris drew his handkerchief and touched it to his forehead. It was going to be a long summer in the dorms if they had to continue holding out at Coeur d'Alene. "Such madness seems to be the new virus. First Mastover, now here."

"Speaking of the virus, there's been an outbreak in Vancouver. We have an outpost just south of the US-Canadian border in Bellingham. They say it's not good."

"So? There's been outbreaks before. We're equipped to avoid them." Morris stuffed his handkerchief back into his pocket. "How's this one any different?"

"This time, there's a mass exodus out of Canada. Vancouver residents are flooding on foot into Seattle. They're spreading the virus. Seattle's resources will be taxed, one of the scouts thinks. Bellingham forecasts that Seattle residents, those we were hoping to unite with, will be scattered."

"Those who aren't killed by the virus will be hard to rally together again." Morris cursed. "Our cause is just. We have to continue!"

"An Oregon scout says there's a new government rumored to have formed in San Diego. They're heavily armed and moving up the coast, gathering resources before we can get to them."

"Well, that's just great!" Morris rose to his feet and turned to his window. It faced the moonlit, calm lake. What a contrast to his tumultuous heart, he thought. He had so much to give America, but she kept resisting change and renewal. "What's the point of defeating Spokane if we have to meet an organized army coming up from California?"

"Maybe we could join them? Or they could join us? Maybe our cause is the same."

Morris felt pressure in his sinuses. He remembered the sensation as a child, an indication that he was about to cry. He hadn't wept for years, but he'd never felt such helplessness, either. Ever since they'd moved through Mastover, things had been falling apart. How could one town catapult such change to his whole organization?

"We need to change our strategy." He turned from the window and struck his palm with his fist. "Yes! We don't need to press west. We need to shore up what we've won. We need to occupy the hearts and minds of the towns we've already liberated. We need to ensure America doesn't revert to its old ways of faith and moral righteousness. If we are barred from moving farther west, then we'll reinforce what we've already taken."

"So, back to Montana?"

"And Wyoming and Iowa and Ohio—all the way back to Atlanta! We'll set up outposts everywhere—with our own people, this time, instead of hoping the locals can maintain their new liberty. Raise armies of liberators and loyalists, whole towns committed to the new purity of science without religious fiction, a proud America without the shame of condemning moralists. We need the regulation of calculating government without the mindless direction of individualistic beliefs. To survive, we must unite this country!"

"It sounds like a new vision, sir." Hoyle beamed. "A revival!"

"Yes! A revival!"

"Might Mastover be involved, sir?"

"Oh, yes, Mastover will be part of the revival, and part of the cleansing. We'll make an example out of them." Morris stared at a spot on the wall, remembering that morning. "There was a man in Mastover. He was willing to die for his empty ideas. If he could sway a whole town using his pointless convictions, just think what I could give the people with the glorious Liberation Organization and a revived government!"

"It sounds great, sir!"

"But there's work to be done, son, before we can meet our goals. We need to appeal more broadly to hearts and re-establish our supply lines. This new revival starts tonight!"

~End of Bonus Chapter SF3~

STEADFAST BOOK FOUR

America's Last Days

D.I. Telbat

Note from the Author for Book Four

Dear Friend,

In this fourth installment of *The Steadfast Series*, I have sought to portray not only the depraved condition of the unredeemed, but also the desperate need for God in all of our lives. In this writing endeavor, I have plummeted the story into the depths of sin's bondage and shame, and in these pages, a dreadful crime is committed in the heart of the Wyoming wilderness. We are meant to be appalled by this sin.

But in our distaste for such sin, we are reminded of the grace that Jesus Christ offers. Where we are tempted to judge a neighbor, and condemn beyond recovery—God forgives. Therefore, the shocking sin mentioned herein is not for our entertainment, but rather it is meant to highlight our Lord's great mercy, and our tremendous need for His offer of forgiveness.

May we all learn to call evil by its true name, then extend the hand of compassion to those who need to be rescued from its bondage. We all have this need.

Your brother,
David Telbat

Prologue, Book Four

Kelly Morris, commander of the Liberation Organization, stared at the gray wintery forest before him. Nothing moved—no birds, no deer, no wolves. It was too cold to move. Everything alive was burrowed deep inside forest dens or thickets, sheltered from the harsh Wyoming freeze.

A soldier in a white parka moved up beside him, panting and leaning on his ski poles.

"The men are exhausted, sir," Lieutenant Tesh said. The hood on his parka was drawn so tightly, his mouth was muffled and his ski goggles were pressed firmly against his face. "One of the men has what looks like the first stages of frostbite. I request permission to escort him back to the vehicles. He'll need two men to help him, or he'll die."

"We can't spare two men." Morris continued to stare ahead, searching for the best route through mounds of snow. Each mound was a tree. "This may be our last shot at rooting out rebels in this wilderness. Who has frostbite and how bad is it?"

"It's Private Hoyle. He was a bike messenger in Northern Idaho for us. He's been loyal. But if his foot isn't treated properly, he'll lose his leg, maybe even his life."

Morris cursed. He'd been losing men left and right for a year. If resistance snipers weren't killing them, then they were deserting their posts.

"We're not even fighting yet, and men are on death's door? No, I won't spare the men. We have to keep moving. Have you seen the sky to the west? A storm is coming."

"Private Hoyle can't continue."

"Then he can stop and shelter in place. We'll return for him after our raid is over."

"We can start him a fire, but he'll need someone to remain behind just to fetch wood for him. Otherwise, sir, he'll die long before we return."

Morris turned and looked at Lieutenant Tesh in the face—what he could see of it. The man in his early thirties pushed back on his ski poles to distance himself from the commander. Like the rest of the unit of fifty men, Tesh carried an eighty-pound pack and an assault rifle.

"Lieutenant, you're a competent soldier. You've campaigned with me for years. How far back do we go?"

"Atlanta, sir. I served under you when you were a two-star general before Pan-Day."

"And what is our chief directive?"

"True liberty is achieved by true uniformity, sir. We are liberators."

"There are whole states that have conformed to the vision I have for America, but those small pockets of resistance ruin everything we've achieved. Do you think our march west would've stopped if it weren't for this Wyoming nonsense—this Mad Man nonsense?"

"Of course not, sir, but one man isn't to blame. I don't see how—"

"This one man has created hope that doesn't conform to what the world view is, Lieutenant! He has inspired a movement that stands against this new society's progress. Mad Man is a cancer, a disease. Do I need to remind you that Mastover burned their bridges down, and we were forced to divert our entire frontline to the south? He must be hunted down, along with his forest followers, and killed like the mad dog he is!"

"I understand our mission, sir."

"Then how can we spare even one soldier? I like Hoyle, but he's a fool if he's become injured after just two days of travel. We have a whole wilderness to cross before we're in place. Approaching from the southwest will catch Mad Man unexpectedly, especially in this weather."

"So, you want us to leave Private Hoyle behind, sir?"

"This is a test for us all, Lieutenant. We can't be hindered by weakness."

"Permission to set up a quick shelter and gather wood for Hoyle if we have to leave him, sir."

"Permission denied, Lieutenant. We have to get over another mountain and make camp by sundown. That storm will be upon us in hours. Hoyle's on his own. Now, move out. You're on point."

Tesh hesitated. Morris saw doubt on the soldier's face. He was losing the men to weakness when he needed uncompromising resolve! All of the attitudes that had led up to Pan-Day were still infecting his men—complacency, sympathy, and lack of discipline. The more he sought to rid the world of Eric Radner and his Christian collaborators, the more his own men seemed to fail him.

After a look back at the column of skiers, Tesh started forward, making new cross-country ski tracks for the unit. Morris waited until all forty-nine men passed him, then he went back to the lone figure of Private Hoyle, who sat in the snow, his skis off and his pack set at his side.

"We have to keep moving, Private." Morris tried to sound concerned, but his obsession with Wyoming's religious holdouts was known to all. "It'll be another week before we're back this way, if the resistance camp is where I think it is."

"I don't think I can get back to the trucks, sir. Please I—"

"You're a soldier, aren't you? If you can't make it, then die like a soldier, understand?" Morris yanked the man's rifle from him and picked up Hoyle's pack. "It's for the liberation of America, Private. We'll remember your sacrifice."

Hoyle opened his mouth, but remained speechless. Morris skied away with his extra burdens. At the next tree well, where the snow angled steeply under a tree's branches, Morris tossed Hoyle's pack and rifle. There was no room for compassion, Morris thought, when conformity was the objective. America needed to learn that, beginning with his own men.

He skied after his unit, and focused his mind on the blood to be shed from their coming surprise attack. Perhaps this mission would break the curse over him that had stunted his liberating movement across the West.

Eric Radner had to die!

"Ye therefore, beloved, seeing that ye know these things before, beware lest ye also, being led away with the error of the wicked, fall from your own steadfastness. But grow in grace, and in the knowledge of our Lord and Savior, Jesus Christ. To Him be glory both now and forever. Amen." II Peter 3:17-18

Chapter 1, Book Four

Deep in the Sharrock Mountains of Wyoming, Eric Radner tracked an elk through three feet of snow. He'd never been this far away from River Camp hunting for game, especially not alone. A mid-morning hunt had become a thirty-mile hike.

He knelt to examine the elk tracks and to catch his breath. If he would've known the snow was this deep inside the next valley, he would've brought snowshoes. But he hadn't been able to turn back. Even with nightfall approaching, he was still moving away from River Camp and those he'd been tasked to watch over. This elk was too big to let go. The tracks it had left—it had to be the largest bull he'd ever hunted. It would be too big to pack back to camp. He'd have to return to fetch porters to help him carry the meat back.

Before he started forward again, he paused to study the forest. He smelled the air, felt the bitter cold, and rejoiced at the life God had given him in this world of trial and challenge. He saw that the hardships in his life were God's way of molding him to become more like Christ—and he'd known plenty of hardships. The environment that surrounded him was a sample of that hardship, and he'd grown to love it!

But as much as he loved the challenge of the hunt, he didn't forget how deadly such weather could be. The world around him was covered in a virtual white quilt. The tree branches bowed low, burdened with cotton-like mounds.

But such weather would kill him in hours if he weren't careful. He knew it wasn't as peaceful as it seemed.

As he started following the elk tracks again, he shifted his pack on his back and mentally inventoried its contents. If he'd planned to spend the night in the woods, he would've packed a sleeping bag instead of just a tarp, but a decent snow cave would provide sufficient shelter for the below-freezing night ahead. Also in his pack was a small hatchet, a spare wool shirt, and a little seasoned jerky. It wasn't much, but God had preserved him with less in more desperate times.

Movement to his right brought him to a stop. An instant later, he whipped his .223 open-sight hunting rifle off his shoulder, and aimed it steadily at the place where he'd seen motion. Barely breathing so his vaporous breath didn't blur his vision, he waited. Sometimes, branches became too heavy and would give way, causing snow to cascade to the ground. Was that what he'd seen? No. He decided to trust his instincts. What he'd seen was horizontal movement.

Turning his head slowly, he surveyed to his left. The virus that had plagued America had seemingly affected the wildlife as well. He'd witnessed mature grizzly bears working together to stalk and kill humans. Wolves had been prowling closer to River Camp, and a coyote had attacked Runner, his son Andy's black Labrador, a couple weeks earlier. Some of that aggression could be justified by the harsh winter and lack of food, but some of the aggression was too uncharacteristic to ignore. Predators were becoming bolder.

The stillness of the forest shadows created an eerie scene that seemed almost like a photograph, and Eric was held captive by its strangeness. Until he saw an animal move again—some sort of canine, maybe a mixed mutt or wild dog. The events leading up to and after Pan-Day had resulted in millions of pets being abandoned or loosed, their owners dead or too focused on personal survival to feed them. Pan-Day was the day an overwhelming number of cities across America went on quarantine because of the Meridia Virus. From coast to coast, one hundred million had died, but Eric had found refuge in Wyoming.

However, a forest overrun with predatory canines didn't feel much like a refuge right then. At least the dog he'd glimpsed seemed to be moving ahead of him, and not toward him. But there could be others.

Shadows grew as he waited for more indication of what to do. The sky was overcast. It could begin to snow any minute. Night was an hour away. If he was smart, he considered, he'd find a gentle hillside and build a snow cave while he could still see.

Instead, he continued after the elk tracks. He was surprised at himself for being this reckless with so much at stake. Back at River Camp, he had a fiancee waiting for him, and a wedding planned for spring. His best man would be his adopted son Andy, and his soon-to-be wife Gretchen was being handed off by her father, Hank Worcester. Since Hank had come to faith in Jesus Christ, the two men had grown close, and spent most evenings talking up on Lookout Ridge with Joel Grayport. Often, they prayed together, considering America's last days and the Bible's prophecies regarding the end of the world. They knew Christ was coming soon.

Twenty other people lived at River Camp as well, some of them new arrivals from the highway—men and women, travelers and pilgrims, each searching for answers and safety. Those who preferred the tougher life of River Camp remained there in the woods, and those who preferred the semblance of town life were escorted to Mastover, ten miles to the north. Eric had made four visits to Mastover since the bridges had been burned and the Liberation Organization had pulled out of Wyoming. But he appreciated the peace and solitude of the forest rather than the town.

Life had been pleasant at River Camp, and yet that evening, he plunged ahead into the unknown wilderness in pursuit of meat for his people—apparently in competition with other hunters of the forest.

He climbed a short hill to the top where the snow on the ground was only a few inches deep, but was trampled and windswept. There, thirty yards away, he found what was left of the elk, a monstrous and aged beast, slaughtered and now being devoured by a mixture of dogs and wolves. The carcass was in pieces, and the canines only growled at him as they continued to gnaw jealously on bones. Eric kept his rifle leveled, but the dogs seemed content to leave him be as much as he wished to be left alone.

The snow was awash with crimson, and Eric squatted down to study the scene. A few blackbirds and chickadees fluttered overhead, then dodged into the scene for a quick bite of leftovers. He was a little disappointed that he was too late to get a shot at the elk, maybe by only an hour or two.

Man had done this, Eric suddenly realized, and browsed the trees with concern. The elk was a fresh kill. If it had been brought down by animals, the carcass wouldn't have been devoured so completely already. No, the animal had been skinned and quartered. He saw no sign of the hide or the antlers. And the bloody snow was trampled, though in the fading light, he couldn't make out distinct human tracks. The dogs had been romping and fighting for a time, wiping out much of the sign Eric wished he could find so he might've seen the whole story.

He entered the trees to his left and made a wide circle around the kill zone. More dogs were in the woods, but they were too greedily chewing on bones to bother quarrelling with him as he passed.

On the far side of the hill, where dog tracks were fewer, Eric acknowledged a swath from human travel cut through the deeper snow. Their trail led southwest, and judging by the tracks and their ability to haul out five hundred pounds of meat and hide—it was a party of at least five people.

Eric checked the sky, then backed away from the trail. He used his gloved hand to lightly push snow into his tracks, erasing sign of his passing for a few yards. Then, he hiked straight into the woods a ways. Against a boulder, he piled up snow and carved into it with his hatchet. Inside the snow cave, he rolled up in his tarp to sleep. But sleep didn't come quickly, even as he prayed to God for wisdom in dealing with newcomers to the Sharrock Mountains.

River Camp was no longer alone.

Chapter 2

Eric awoke to thoughts of River Camp. He knew God had given him those people to watch over. They would be concerned that he hadn't returned from the hunt. With so many hidden crevices and logs beneath the quilt of snow, they might think he'd been injured. Even a resourceful man wouldn't survive long in this freezing weather, if he were injured. Surely, they would send out a search party to track his boot prints.

Gretchen would insist on joining the search, he guessed, as he shook out and folded up his tarp. Andy would want to go, too, but Hank wouldn't allow the nearly seven-year-old to join them on such a grueling hike. They would need to cover territory quickly, up high mountains and steep ridges. And with the possibility of newly falling snow covering his tracks, they may have already set off that morning to search for him.

Bow hunter Joel Grayport would join Gretchen, and perhaps Wendy Sullivan, another tough woman hunter who'd recently joined River Camp. She was in her mid-forties, an ex-truck driver from outside Billings, Montana, who'd outlived her two brothers. Though Wendy wasn't a Christian, she'd become a pleasant and useful addition to the River Camp Community. Since she'd survived on her own for several years, her skills in the wilderness made her a popular woman around camp.

As pressed as Eric was to return to River Camp to let them know he was safe, he felt a stronger need to assess the newcomers to the Sharrock Mountains. In the night, he'd woken to a puzzle: the slaughtered elk had been brought down by a group of people, not by one or two. Who hunted in a pack? Something didn't feel right about it. Before continuing to follow their tracks further southwest, he returned to the elk carcass.

Carnivores had fought further over the remaining bones, but Eric had already seen what the people had left behind. He ignored the animal tracks and varmints that were at the site itself, and instead focused on the area around the kill site. It was in the trees to the north and south of the dead elk that Eric found extensive sign of human presence. Boot tracks had trampled the snow around trees, and impressions in the snow indicated that several people had lain in wait for a period of time. A wall of branches shielded the position from the elk kill.

It had been an ambush, set by people in a blind. No hunter hunted this way, not with a whole group of people. But Eric couldn't argue with the results. They'd laid some trap and downed what he guessed was a thousand-pound bull elk. No one would lay such a trap unless they didn't have guns or ammunition. Someone with a rifle wouldn't want to spoil a shot by having so many partners around.

With the thought of approaching a camp of people who weren't armed, he set out at a fast pace after their deep trail through the snow. Those before him had trampled a clear path—maybe by as many as a dozen people, he guessed. He crossed a meadow, climbed a slope, and skirted a frozen creek that showed the ice had been chopped through recently. He deduced that they probably had hatchets, even if they didn't have firearms. No one could survive out there without axes or hatchets to chop and collect wood.

Three miles and thirty minutes later, he came upon them. He smelled their cook fires first, and slowed his gait. Ten makeshift shelters lay spread out amongst sparse twenty-year-old tree growth. None of the shelters were the same as the next. One was made up of smoke-blackened tent canvas draped over a diagonal pole. Another was a teepee with patched hides covering obvious fire damage. Another showed plastic trash bags layered over its roof, held in place by tree boughs. The most haphazard shelter was simply a lean-to facing a fire, sheltering its occupants from the northern breeze.

The people were gathered in twos and threes in front of individual smoking fires near their dwellings. Eric guessed there were more campers inside the shelters. No one gave warning upon his arrival, and no one moved to intercept him as he wandered about, taking in the despairing scene. They stared with bowed heads and empty eyes as he reached the middle of their camp and turned in a small circle. He estimated that fifty people lived there. Their source of wood was good, since there was a thick forest nearby, but he saw no fuel collected. Some of their shelters wouldn't stand a harsh wind, and several people wore tattered animal skins, their flesh visible beneath.

Still, no one approached him. He didn't attribute it to being inhospitable exactly, since he figured fear of the virus still permeated some communities.

Then he saw a body, frozen and half-buried in snow. It was a man. His beard was iced and his gaze was toward the treetops. He wore only a light shirt, and his lower body was anchored in a snowdrift. Someone had stripped him of his coat, Eric noticed—hopefully after the man had died.

Near a more prominently-built shelter was a tangled mesh of hide and rope hanging between two trees. The knots were thick and the braids were stringy. This was a net, he could see, and he understood that this was the weapon used to kill the elk. They'd probably buried the net before the last snowfall, then laid in wait for a day or two on the suspected game trail. But an elk would feed a camp this size for only a few weeks. River Camp had only twenty people residing there, and its hunters needed to bring in a deer every two or three weeks.

One dome-shaped shelter didn't have anyone out front, so Eric approached it cautiously. No one from the other shelters seemed to care or notice him, but he kept a wary eye on everyone, nevertheless. Though he wouldn't shoot anyone, he wasn't against firing his rifle into the air to warn someone from aggression.

He walked once around the dome of hide and tarps until he found a heavy flap door. Standing slightly to the side, he lifted one corner of the flap to let in some overcast sunlight. His eyes slowly adjusted to the dark interior. Six adults slept side-by-side. An unpleasant odor reached Eric's nose.

A woman lifted her head. She looked to be in her forties. Her eyes squinted at the brightness. Eric expected to see dark blotches on her skin, an advanced sign of the virus, but instead, her skin was smooth and pale.

She lay her head back and closed her eyes. Eric let down the flap and returned to the man frozen stiff in the snow. Without touching the body, he studied the skin. The lower part of his shirt front was barely stained with frozen blood. Leaning closer, Eric saw rugged slashes up the man's arms. Suicide.

"Lord, what is this place?" Eric prayed as he surveyed the camp with fresh eyes. "What hell have I entered into?"

Finding a camp plagued by the virus would've been manageable. There were rules to deal with the infected. But this was worse. The hollow faces and empty gazes that passively acknowledged him were more terrible than of those having the virus.

Eric walked over to a man in front of the shelter where the heavy net hung. The man had a balding head with skewed hair around his ears. Lifting his head, the man looked Eric in the eyes. The man's face held so much grief that Eric steeled himself before he choked on his own sobs of sorrow.

"What happened here, my friend?" Eric asked softly, holding out an empty palm to express his good will, regardless of his shouldered rifle. "Where are you from?"

The old man's eyes teared up, then he lowered his head and looked away. Such defeat and hopelessness—Eric had never seen such a condition up close.

"Go away. Leave us alone."

An overweight woman seated on a tree stump nearby, crawled into the nearest shelter. One by one, the rest of the people outside entered their dwellings. The old man was the last to disappear within his canvas tent. Eric was left alone with the campfires burning low and smoke drifting upward. The air was bitterly cold, and the sky, even mid-morning, was darkened.

It would snow soon, and not just a little flurry, either, he judged. A real blizzard was coming, and these people weren't prepared for heavy weather falling upon them.

Eric left the camp from the direction he'd arrived. The despair in the air clung to him. He had to help them, but he couldn't do it alone.

Chapter 3

It was noon before Eric covered fifteen miles, reaching the outer limits of River Camp's normal hunting grounds. The storm enveloped the region. Flakes as big as quarters fell in a fluffy curtain. The silence was startling as so much seemed to be happening. Not only was he out of food in the middle of a snowstorm, but his tracks leading home were being rapidly covered. Though he could find his way home without the tracks, he couldn't do so without visibility. He could see no landmarks.

His concern for himself became concern for those who may have set out to find him, thinking he'd fallen or become injured. Gretchen would insist to press on, and anyone with her would be threatened with exposure and a lost trail as well.

Though Eric would've normally found immediate shelter for himself, for their sake, he pressed on. Three feet of snow was added to by four inches an hour. The traveling was slow, every step an act of labor and eventually pain. His leg muscles were screaming for rest and warmth and sustenance.

He left what he thought was his trail home and turned to the less exposed terrain of the forested hillsides. The snow was only inches deep in most places amongst the thickest trees, but he still paused occasionally to scrape at the base of the trunks to check for moss or mushroom growth. Growths developed on the north sides of the bark. Though he had a compass on a shoestring around his neck, he had to pull a glove off each time he wanted to fish it out of the front of his coat. The temperature discouraged exposing his skin any longer than he had to. Besides, checking his northeasterly heading along the way by studying the trees kept his mind distracted from the cold.

When the wind started howling through the trees, he felt the wet snow on his shoulders chilling him to the bone. It was time to stop before he marched himself to hypothermia and death.

He traipsed straight north until he emerged from the trees into a small clearing. The snow was piled high against a fallen log, and it was here he piled it higher. His gloves were wet, along with his knees and most of his upper body, but to stop moving now would invite his demise. Next, he packed the snow pile down. As the pile settled, he took the hatchet from his pack and re-entered the trees to break off branches for a fire. With an armful of wood, he returned to his packed snow pile and went to work digging out a cave.

Each movement was difficult and exhausting, but he kept his wits by mumbling aloud his actions, like a narrator would.

"Dig a little out, pack it down. Make the ceiling higher. Poke a hole with a stick in the top. There's the log. Deep enough. Dig out the sides a little more . . ."

Everything was more difficult now because the cold had sapped his energy and concentration. Lack of food hadn't helped, either.

The opening to his snow cave faced south. Once he crawled inside, he pushed more snow toward the opening to make it smaller. The whole burrow was twice the width of his shoulders and only tall enough in which to sit, but he managed to shift his tarp underneath him and then used the wood to start a fire near the opening. The smoke rose to escape through the hole in the ceiling.

Outside, the day darkened as the snow fell more heavily, and afternoon turned into evening. He kept the fire small to conserve fuel. It was just large enough to warm his hands and dry his clothes. The cave's walls turned to ice and the heat was trapped inside.

Eric's stomach growled as his eyes burned from the close proximity to the wood smoke. His mind cleared as he warmed, and he thanked God that he'd had the brains to stop hiking when he had. Another hour, and he wouldn't have had the energy to make a good cave. Though he wasn't especially comfortable, he believed he'd passed the moment of danger. Now, he focused on what it would take to get back to River Camp.

He had no doubt that he was far from his trail back home, but with a few landmarks and mountain peaks in sight, he knew he'd quickly reorient himself. That was, if the storm ended in the next day or two.

From the side of his dwelling, he scraped ice into his canteen. Pure drinking water was plentiful. Food was the problem. Then he smiled. His first weeks in the mountains had been filled with starvation and wandering. Those had been fearful days of uncertainty immediately after Pan-Day. But since then, God had broken him down and brought him miraculously through so much, so many times.

Far to the east, where he and Gretchen still hunted deer sometimes, he'd built a cabin in the early days after Pan-Day. The coming of the Liberation Organization had disrupted life all over Wyoming, but God had kept Eric out of the thick of the fighting and the resistance conflict itself. Once in a while, he even visited the radio on the mountaintop above the cabin, and listened for a couple hours, either alone, or with Andy or Gretchen. As isolated as they felt in the wilderness, listening to the radio chatter always returned them to a feeling of concern.

The Lib-Org was still a threat across Colorado, but their influence had waned in the east where they'd originated. On the West Coast, a San Diego-based force called the Pacific States, complete with a president named Criswell, had started to push back on the Lib-Org and other rogue armies.

Meanwhile, far to the east, from New York to North Carolina, the Appalachian Federation had been formed. The territory in the middle was often referred to by radio operators as the Zone, or the Plains Zone. It was viewed as a no-man's land, where local militias barricaded themselves against roaming armies—of which Commander Morris' Lib-Org was only one of four more prominent groups. Each group claimed a cause, but they all killed whoever didn't view the collapsed country their way.

While the nation fought for balance, Eric continued to teach the River Camp residents the way of Jesus. The very act of Jesus coming as God in the flesh to save believers excited most of those who'd remained at River Camp. They knew He'd come once as prophesied, and that there was a second coming prophesied as well. River Camp anticipated the day when sin and fear and evil was dealt with finally by a Righteous King on earth.

But not everyone in River Camp had viewed their survival in the woods as a God-given paradise for their growth and preparation for eternity. When Hank had come to the Lord, his wife, Sara, had criticized him. Once, Hank had been an unfaithful husband and a violent man who had blasphemed God. Sara had tolerated him then, but she couldn't tolerate his new faith. His past was too offensive for her to accept him in the present. She'd moved back into Mastover, threatening to shoot him if he ever came into town. Those who knew the bossy lady believed she'd do it, too!

Sometime in the night, Eric's fire burned out, but his clothes had dried. He slept until dawn, wrapped in his tarp.

With daylight came chirping birds, and though Eric was famished and suffering from cramping muscles, he was smiling at God's goodness as he clawed barehanded at the cave mouth.

Praise the Lord, the sky was blue!

Chapter 4

Eric walked into River Camp just before noon. The river that wound through their narrow canyon refuge had frozen, except for a hole that Andy and the other youths in camp kept open for cooking and drinking water.

"Thank God, you're safe!" Eric gasped as he wrapped his arms around Gretchen.

"Me? How about you!" She pulled back and scowled. "Dad and I searched all day yesterday. Joel and Wendy were out there, too! Then the storm blew in. Why didn't you . . . you know!"

"What?" He laughed. She wasn't usually at a loss for words. "Why didn't I leave a message? Maybe a text? I think our smart phones are little lumps of rust and shriveled plastic by now."

Joel Grayport gave Eric a nod from a few feet away. He had two pair of snowshoes over one shoulder and his bow over the other.

"Wendy and I were getting ready to head out again. The man spoke softly, Eric had learned, to avoid a lisp from his missing front tooth. "Hank said your trail was heading southwest when they turned back. An elk, huh?"

"Yep. Big one, too!"

"Did you get him, Dad?" Andy asked as the boy wandered past. Runner, the boy's black Lab, stopped and waited patiently, though the two were clearly on a mission, hunting critters or building forts with a couple other youths in camp.

"No, it wasn't my turn to get him." Eric shook his boy's hand like the little man he was becoming. He remembered his own boyhood adventures, growing up in Lincoln, so he wasn't hurt that Andy didn't seem too concerned about his absence for two nights. "But I did come across a discovery. Camp meeting in ten minutes, okay?"

"Sure." Hank nodded. "I'll ask Barb to bring you some food. We'll all want to hear what Mad Man has gotten us into now."

"A meeting?" Andy's shoulders fell. "Aw, Dad, but me and Runner and Chuck found a badger den."

"A badger den?" Eric raised his eyebrows and realized the stout stick in Andy's hand was no mere walking stick. "Sounds serious. What're you going to do with a family of badgers?"

"Get 'em away from camp! They might be the ones scratching on the bread box door."

"All right." Eric waved his hand, and without hesitation, Andy bounded away, free from obligations. Still next to Gretchen, Eric took her hand in his. "Why do I have the feeling that boy is about to stir up a family of badgers against River Camp?"

"He takes after his father." She kissed his cheek. "Always willing to confront what everyone else is willing to ignore."

Hank and Gretchen walked to the farthest of the seven cabins, which had become the official meeting cabin when Eric, Andy, or Hank weren't sleeping in it. Joel walked closer to Eric as the two followed Hank.

"You find something out there?"

"Yeah, I found something." He tried to keep the dread out of his voice. "You think River Camp can spare you, me, Gretchen, and Wendy for a few days?"

"We're stocked up." The twenty-eight-year-old former prom king and high-school quarterback gazed southwest at the farthest ridge. "Trouble?"

"It's nothing God hasn't directed us to handle."

Eric waved at Barb, who'd lost her son the previous year to a bear attack. She was a hefty woman, but a true sister in the faith who sang a hymn at each Sunday assembly. In her arms she held Joel's baby girl, Shawna, since Lena Grayport remained in silent shock from the weight of tragedies in America's last days. In her free hand, Barb carried a sandwich meant for Eric.

Inside the cabin, the hearth was stoked and everyone shed their winter coats. Several couples were there as well, including Ben and Heidi Lawrence, and their teenage daughter, Annette, recent arrivals from Colorado. Eric was still praying for their salvation, but the family was fitting into the camp nicely. Safety for Annette had been their utmost concern in leaving Colorado, so they preferred the wooded community rather than Mastover, which was populated with several hundred people.

"I was tracking an elk forty miles southwest of here, and I came upon a camp of . . ." Eric paused. "I don't know what they were—refugees, perhaps? About fifty. They're in bad shape. Living in terribly-built shelters. I wouldn't be surprised if yesterday's storm didn't claim some of them. They have a little meat, but they need a lot more than food."

"Clothing?" Joel asked. Since he'd been meeting every other day with Eric and Hank in the evenings to read and study the Bible, it was no surprise the man was concerned for strangers. "We don't have a lot to share, but we'll stretch what we have."

"What we can spare, we must." Eric took a moment to look them all in the eyes. "They are dying from . . . something. Don't worry; it's not the virus. I think it might be from despair. If they're from the cities, then survival has been real tough for them. I'm surprised they made it this long, living like they are."

"Are they safe?" Ben asked, which was expected from him. He'd been a stock trader before Pan-Day, and he'd assumed the role as camp actuary, measuring risks and offering counsel against certain hazards. Since he was no woodsman, he and his wife had made themselves useful within camp, helping with cooking as well as teaching mathematics and grammar to the few who were of school age.

"They're not armed with guns, if that's what you're asking. Knives and axes maybe. I'm thinking they need people to show them how to live in this kind of environment. Whoever goes with me will be gone for a few days."

"But these are our woods," Hank said, then glowered. "I mean, we need to think about this."

"The only thinking we need to do is to figure out how best to help them," Gretchen said, which sounded like a scolding directed at her father. "What should we bring?"

"Pack our two game sleds with deer hides and food." Eric nodded at Joel. "Joel and I will pull the sleds, and Gretchen and Wendy, if they agree to go, will carry packs. Wendy?"

Wendy, one of the camp's dependable hunters, straightened her perpetually-tangled blond hair.

"You sure you want me to go?"

"The supplies and food will help them, but I saw a lost people out there. They need to be reminded of what it means to be loved."

"But," she grunted nervously, "I'm not what you'd call a Christian, like you guys. I can help with supplies, but I'm not sure what I'd have to offer them as far as hope goes— eternity and all that."

"If ever there was a time to learn how much you need God, Wendy," Eric said," this is that time. Besides, we might need to do some hunting while we're with them, to get them back on their feet, assuming they're still alive after that storm. Pack what we can. We leave before dawn. Joel, we'll need snowshoes for everyone. With all our supplies, it'll take us two hard days to reach them."

"Once again, I get left out of all the fun." Hank frowned.

"Someone has to keep the coyotes out of cabin four." Gretchen said, referring to the cabin where their food stores were kept. She pulled on her coat and kissed her father on his bushy cheek. "Besides, you complained all day yesterday about the hike while we were searching for my future husband. You've lost your hiking privileges."

"We could've covered more terrain with skis." He crossed his arms, glowering, though everyone in camp enjoyed Gretchen's scoldings aimed at her opinionated father. "That's all I'm saying. Skis are worth looking into."

Barb rose to her feet with the baby still in her arms.

"I'll get the others to pack some spuds from the cellar, and some flour and tea."

Eric left the cabin with the sandwich still in his hand. The bread was unleavened since they had no yeast. They made the dough from water lily or spatterdock plants. The deer meat had been smoked, seasoned with wild onion and crushed juniper berries, and sliced thin. In the middle of the sandwich, he bit into a leaf of chicory, then smiled to himself. They were out in the wilderness, but the Lord still made sure they ate well.

If River Camp hadn't risen above their own problems and become self-sufficient, they wouldn't have had enough to take care of others. With only half the winter past them, Eric hoped River Camp was indeed efficient enough to take care of two camps!

Chapter 5

Before sunup the next day, Eric prayed with Gretchen, Joel, and Wendy. Though Wendy wasn't a believer, she had voiced her curiosity about River Camp's unconditional concern for others, which included herself. Eric continued to expose her to the habits and inner joy that came from having God's Spirit living inside them. A mission of mercy to a distant people was the best exposure for the Montanan.

Since Eric knew their destination, and the weather was holding, he chose a different route over the mountains—one that offered him and Joel the least resistance up slopes and around cliffs. Their snowshoes puffed lightly with each step on the fresh powder, and the heavy sleds behind them whispered forward with each stride.

Gretchen and Wendy ranged ahead, scouting for favorable paths through forests and around fallen logs. Wendy seemed to be a private person in camp, even distant, but she and Gretchen had become friends. Eric guessed it was because they each shared skills that provided uniquely for the camp. Though Gretchen was almost tactical in her hunting approach, with a bit of her mother's bossiness, Eric was glad she'd found a similar spirit in the older woman.

They made camp well beyond the twenty-mile mark that evening. It was farther than Eric had hoped they'd manage the first day. That left only fifteen miles for the next day, which would permit them to begin their distribution of aid to the campers while it was still daylight.

The puzzle of the strangers' distraught and depressed behavior concerned Eric more as they drew closer, but he hoped River Camp's assistance would bring peace into their lives. Six and a half years earlier, Eric had experienced his own sense of panic and uncertainty about hardship, death, and eternity. He believed Christ would bring the necessary ointment to the newcomers as well.

Instead of a snow cave, the four erected a single wall tent that slept four comfortably. The dynamic of four unmarried adults, two men and two women, wasn't awkward since their minds were focused on their coming duty, and their bodies were exhausted from the day of travel.

Eric lit a small candle to read by as they lay in their sleeping bags that night. Joel and Wendy were breathing steadily when Gretchen leaned over, her face close to his Bible.

"You've been more quiet than usual," she said. "What aren't you telling us about what we're about to find?"

He closed the Bible and tried to block out the images of the camp of broken lives.

"Around Pan-Day, I was already out here in the mountains. I never saw the piles of dead bodies like you did. I didn't fight for my life for food and water in the city streets. But I think I've seen all that in the faces of the people we're about to help. Over six years have passed, but these campers are as lost as I've imagined helpless people were on Pan-Day. Without their cars and smart phones and fashion and entertainment, they've become hopeless."

"They've given up?" Gretchen rested her chin on his arm. "How could they survive almost seven years without hope?"

"I don't think they could." Eric blew out the candle. "I think something in the last few months has happened, which has broken their spirit. Maybe it's something they did. It could be guilt."

"Guilt?"

"Or shame. I sensed that. Like people caught taking more rations than they should've taken. I don't know.

That's the kind of look they had, like the weight of sin immobilized them. That's why I think we can help them. The cross deals with sin, and the Word of God cuts straight to the heart of the matter."

He tapped his hand on the Bible he usually kept inside his jacket.

"You're talking about evangelizing them." Gretchen shivered. "I've never really spoken to anyone outside River Camp about God. I don't think I'll be very good at it, Eric. I'm sorry."

"Don't think of it as a job. Let's just take care of them. When you sense their spiritual needs, God will give you the right words to comfort them, because your heart is right. God will give you words of hope and peace when it's time. Just love them, and you will naturally share Jesus with them."

The next morning, the temperature had risen enough to harden the surface of the snow. They were able to walk without snowshoes at a faster pace. The sled runners slid without resistance on top of the ice crystals, allowing the group of four to hurry ahead. Around midmorning, they came upon the site of the dead elk carcass. Barely any sign was left of the dead creature since the latest snowfall had covered the reddish snow.

Eric described how the campers had netted the elk by lying in wait, perhaps for days.

"It's primitive," Joel said, pulling off his glove from one hand to touch one of the carnivore prints that had prowled through the area since the blizzard. "That's how they hunted mammoths thousands of years ago. Traps and spears. You'd think modern people would at least use some modern means to survive."

"They're animals," Wendy said. "I mean, they're animalistic. They've got to be from a city somewhere, ignorant of the rural life. Watched too many caveman movies."

"Let's enter the camp together," Eric said, then eyed Gretchen and Wendy. "I don't want you two far from me and Joel at any time until we know what we're dealing with."

Three miles farther, they walked into the camp. It was eerily quiet and seemed to be abandoned. A foot of snow and deeper drifts had settled over all ten shelters.

"Eric!" Joel called as he crouched next to the lean-to Eric had guessed wouldn't last through a heavy storm. Together, they inspected the snow around the lean-to. A tarp was frozen stiff, half buried in snow, trailing out of the lean-to, as if wind-blown. "That's blood. And those are cat tracks. Mountain lion. Probably two hundred pounds."

"Cats are territorial." Eric glanced over his shoulder at Gretchen and Wendy as they advanced cautiously upon a dome-shaped shelter. "Food is scarce, but it's still pretty bold for a lion to come into a camp like this. A cat like that might be back. Scout around. See if you can dispose of it before it comes and kills again. And watch for game in the area. We'll get started while you look around."

Joel kept his pack on, but he left his sled with the other one as he moved stealthily into the brush, tracking the killer cat.

Eric threw back the hide doorway of one shelter. The odor of soiled clothing would've made him stagger backward, but he knew to expect it this time. The people hadn't been leaving their shelters even to answer nature's call. Indeed, Eric saw no structure that might resemble an outhouse.

"You have some friends out here," he called into the dim shelter. Several bundled forms moved and faces peered up. "We're here to help you. It's going to be okay. Let's get everyone up and outside so we can see what the damage is. Come on. It's not too cold today. I'll start a fire and get something hot for you to drink. Come on, everyone."

"We have eight in this one!" Gretchen shouted to him.

"Seven here," Eric said, then went to the next, where he found nine, then another eight in the next. The smaller shelters held fewer souls, and one was collapsed entirely by snow that had fallen from the trees above. Four people had perished where they lay, if they'd been alive during the collapse.

After rousing the occupants from every shelter, Eric returned to the central area of the sleds, and piled wood for a fire. As the flames grew, people trailed from their shelters, clutching wrinkled coats, hides, or blankets around their shoulders. Eric did his best not to stare as he set a pot of chufa coffee amidst the flames.

Those who approached were emaciated and dark-eyed. The men all had beards with hair askew, and the few women who emerged looked as if rats had made nests in their hair. Fingernails were chipped and filthy. Their clothing was soiled and stained. Their teeth were rotting and had turned dark like wood. Malnutrition was apparently rampant, but Eric smiled nonetheless, and helped a man probably in his thirties to sit on a log near the fire.

"That's right." Eric shook a few hands of the bewildered people. "Everyone gather around. There's room for everyone. Bring your cups and plates, if you have them. And your canteens."

Gretchen and Wendy were each escorting women to the central fire. Eric dragged another log into the growing crowd and lay it in the flames. He fetched another pot from a sled and filled it with snow and pine needles. The pine needle tea, full of vitamin C, would check the scurvy that had set in.

"We're going to get you fixed up," Gretchen told a young woman as she led her to a spot around the fire. Get warmed up and we'll have a little talk."

She looked at Eric and he nodded. Nothing they were doing was planned, but the central fire seemed like a good step forward. Something was terribly wrong with these people, much worse than the physical effects they could see, but Eric had to begin somewhere. Warming them up and filling their bellies with something hot was a start.

Wendy approached Eric as he unwrapped drop biscuits from a sack.

"There's a woman in that lodge." She pointed to a shelter with plastic bags layered on the roof. "She won't move. She might be—"

"I'll take care of it." He handed her the biscuits. "Break these in half and pass them out. Some haven't eaten in a few days, so we'll start them slow."

He marched to the shelter she'd indicated and peered inside. The interior smelled like an animal had died. Somehow, the people who'd emerged from that dwelling had grown accustomed to the odor.

Against his discomfort, Eric crawled inside while holding his breath and felt the cheek of the woman who lay there. She was cold. He drew her body out and gasped for fresh air. Underneath her sleeping bag were squirming maggots in the rotting fabric. The sleeping bag was a total loss, so he zipped her up inside and tied the top closed. There seemed no other option but to burn the shelter. More people would die if they were exposed to such filth and decay.

When he returned to the fire, Wendy was pouring steaming liquid into tin cups and bowls as Gretchen prodded a young woman to speak. Eric counted those who stood and sat around the fire. They were a crowd of forty-eight on death's door.

Wendy filled both the pots with fresh snow and approached Eric.

"There are no children, Eric," she whispered, her mouth hidden behind her mittens. "Where are the children?"

It was a sobering statement rather than a question. Eric didn't have an answer.

Joel walked briskly out of the woods on the west side of camp and signaled that he wanted to speak to Eric privately. They converged near an unnatural snowdrift where Eric knew lay the man who'd committed suicide.

"I tracked the cat almost straight west for a mile." Joel took a swallow from his canteen. "Ran into another camp like this one, abandoned. A couple dead, maybe a month or two old. I think it was from these people. They left it for the animals."

"So, instead of burying their dead or cleaning up, they just moved on." Eric looked back at the group. His eyes connected with Gretchen's and held long enough to see her concern. "Half these shelters have been used as an outhouse while sleeping inside them. We need to salvage what we can, then burn everything else. Maybe we should move the camp again, but where?"

"There's a stand of trees to the south of us." Joel pointed. "A whole strip of thicker growth. Definitely a stream or creek nearby."

"How far? These people can barely stand let alone walk far."

"Maybe four hundred yards."

"Running water would help what we need to do for them." Eric shook his head. "God help them. There's a tragic story behind all this. But I'm not sure I want to know what it is."

"It's no worse than our own stories," Joel said. "When you came for me and my family, I was living in a house in the middle of a garbage dump."

"We started from scratch at River Camp with half this many people. We can do it again here."

Together, they joined the gathering at the fire. It was noon, but Eric didn't feel like eating. If these people were going to survive the next winter storm, they'd need solid shelters within a day or two.

"Can I have everyone's attention, please?" Eric clapped his gloved hands and noticed that not everyone had gloves of their own. A couple people's eyes met his, but dropped immediately.

"Listen up. My name is Eric. We know you've been through a lot." He remembered Wendy's observation of there being no children in camp, and he wondered if that had something to do with their countenance. "There may have been unspeakable things you've done or witnessed. We're not here for anything but to help you. To help you, we need to move this camp to the south a little. Joel, wave your hand. This is Joel, everyone. Follow Joel to the new campsite a few hundred yards. There's running water there. We're going to get everyone cleaned up and build new shelters—real cabins for you to live in."

"It doesn't matter," a woman sneered. Her hair had tree bark clinging to it. "We're cursed. They'll come for us no matter what."

"You're not cursed!" Eric's voice broke at the depth of despair before him. "None of my friends are cursed. You hear me? And you're now our friends. So, listen: everyone pick up some wood to take with you. Collect firewood as you walk. We'll start a new fire after a short distance. Joel?"

"Come on, everyone!" The bow hunter took one of the sled ropes over his shoulder and led the way. "Follow me!"

One at a time, they pulled themselves away from the fire and walked single file after Joel.

Gretchen and Wendy joined Eric at the diminishing fire. Only about a dozen of the people had taken wood from around the fire.

"Search the shelters," Eric said. "Salvage what you can. Everything else, bring to the fire. We'll burn the dead here as well. We have to; we can't bury them in frozen ground."

"What did that woman mean?" Wendy asked. "Who will find them?"

"I don't know." Eric gazed up at the sky. "But whoever's out there, we're about to make an awful lot of smoke for them to see."

Chapter 6

Eric and Gretchen worked together to pull the second sled to the new campsite. It was piled with salvaged hides and tent canvas. At the new site, Joel had separated the people into three groups around three separate campfires. The campers stood or sat in the snow on the north bank of a frozen stream where Joel hacked with an axe to find running water. He found it six inches below the ice and snow.

"Bathing and washing clothes is our first priority," Eric said to Gretchen and Wendy. "Women first."

He and Joel erected the wall tent over the stream itself to offer privacy, but it would be cold business regardless. Ashes from the fire worked as soap, and extra hides were used as wraps until everyone's clothing could be dried on racks made from saplings.

The women finished mid-afternoon, then Eric and Joel took the men, two at a time, into the tent and had them strip naked. Standing shivering over the stream, they protested sometimes like whimpering children, but each man eventually surrendered to the much-needed dousing. Their clothes hadn't been washed probably in months. In the haste and cold, the washing wasn't ideal, but it was progress.

Before they bedded down in smoke-dried clothes, hot meat and potatoes were passed out. Many of the forty-eight people wept as they grasped warm spuds and a small portion of meat in their bare hands. They ate slowly, their rotten teeth making it clearly a painful task. They craved the nutrients, even if their bodies struggled to digest at first.

"There are only twelve women," Joel said to Gretchen. "Fit whomever you can into the tent. The men and the rest of the women will be comfortable enough around the fires. We'll pile tarps and furs on them."

Once everyone was bedded down and the fires were stoked high, Eric met with his River Camp friends twenty yards into the woods for a quick conference.

"They ate the children!" Wendy hissed. "It's the only answer!"

"No, that isn't the only answer." Eric couldn't see his friends too well in the dark, but they knew each other well enough for him to guess at the weariness they all felt after two days of travel and an afternoon of such labor. "There may be other reasons, but let's keep an open mind. Whatever's happened, it's probably nothing good since they're not speaking about it. Holding them in judgement for things we're not sure about helps nothing.

"Even if that is true, Wendy—and it very well could be—these aren't lost souls. Not yet. Whatever happened before our arrival is between them and God. It isn't our concern. In the next few days, I suspect they'll begin to open up to us, and we'll need to be ready to help them heal."

"How do you heal from—you know!" Wendy almost shrieked. "It's appalling!"

"There's all kinds of sin that's appalling. We're guilty of all kinds of sin ourselves. In danger of starvation in a faithless group of fear-stricken people—I can imagine adults giving in to hunger. But we don't know that's what's happened yet."

"They're cannibals!" Wendy rasped.

"Let's say they are," Eric said, not surprised that Wendy was the only one to protest helping the people since she wasn't relying on Jesus Christ to help her. "What should we do? What's our response? We wouldn't be the first people to reach out to people who've eaten others. This is hard for us, but it's harder for them. Look at them. Think about their consciences, if that's what they've done.

You know what I found underneath the snow back in their old camp?"

"What?" Gretchen held onto his arm.

"The meat from the elk they trapped and killed. They gorged themselves on the raw meat. I saw the teeth marks. Then they crawled into their tents and lodges to sleep or die. They had food. They have water from the snow. They could've had warmth from the fire, but they weren't even burning fires when we showed up. We need to find it within ourselves to teach them how to live again. That's our job. Let God deal with whatever they've done. We have bigger problems."

"Like what?" Gretchen asked.

"I've been thinking. They have no guns or weapons. Just some axes for wood. Hardly any personal possessions except what they have on them. I don't think they abandoned who they were. I think their identity has been stolen, and with it, their dignity and hope. Let me tell you this: after what I've witnessed in my life, no one around me is going to remain in Satan's grip of gloom if I can help it, no matter what they've done, or what's been done to them!"

"Okay, how are we supposed to help them then?" Wendy asked. "They won't even help themselves. We just hand-washed filth off forty-eight adults like they were three-year-old children, Eric!"

"I know, I know. But we can bring them back with this." Eric drew his Bible from his inner vest. "We read to them, and we don't stop reading to them until we see some light. And while one of us is reading to them, the rest of us will work and pray. And we keep our eyes open for whoever stole their humanity from them."

"I agree." Joel nodded. "This is more than a group of people falling apart. They're victims. They may even be on the run from something."

The next day, the camp woke slowly, but Eric was already awake, as were Joel and Gretchen. As the campers rolled out of tarps and hides to reach for the fire's warmth, Eric was there to greet them. One by one, he shook their hands.

"Today, we're going to grow a little together," he said to each of them, smiling from his heart.

He didn't insist on knowing their names, nor did he question them about their past. All that would come in time, he knew.

Spuds, meat, and pine tea were passed out again—carbohydrates, protein, and vitamin C. Eric rationed out some chicory for their next meal, just to keep some roughage in their diet.

When Wendy woke, Eric had her sit at the middle fire and handed her the Bible.

"Start reading here," he told her, opening to Matthew. "I'll spell you in an hour."

He and Joel built up the middle fire, and the others drifted over to join the main gathering and to hear the words. They stared passively at the flames as they chewed their food.

Joel left with his bow to scout and hunt for deer while Eric marked out space for three cabins. He had plans for the site, especially regarding the running water, but the winter weather and frozen ground hindered some of those plans. Gretchen was on firewood detail, so she came and went, dragging deadfalls to the edge of camp.

When it was Eric's turn to read, Wendy joined Gretchen in fetching wood. Eric used his reading time to study the people more closely. Most were listening, it seemed. Some remained distant or downcast, though the two other fires had dwindled to ashes since everyone had gathered at the central fire.

One particular man in his forties watched Eric's face as he read. Between sentences, Eric would pause and look up. Others were watching him, too. This was a good sign, he thought. The rest would soon follow. Progress had been made.

At the end of the Book of Mark, Eric closed the Bible and surveyed their faces. They'd heard the story of Jesus Christ from two perspectives, and he prayed that what had been planted inside their hearts would be watered by his care for them, and God would give the growth to something new.

"Starting over can be difficult," he said gently, yet loud enough for all to hear over the fire. "But God will show us how to work together and how to care for one another again. Now, I need a volunteer to continue reading. Come on. This is good for us. This reading will bring life into our souls. Just one person."

A big-boned woman in her fifties hesitantly raised her hand. Eric recalled that she had walked with a limp.

"Very good! What's your name, my friend?"

"Um, Doris." Her voice sounded strong.

"Wonderful, Doris. Here you are." He opened the Bible to the Psalms. "Start reading here with the first Psalm, and just read straight through."

Before she began, Eric went around the circle to the man who had been intently watching him read.

"Hello, I'm Eric. What's your name?"

"Neil." He had big hands and a direct, intense gaze.

"Neil, I need some help building us a couple cabins. Can you swing an axe? You'd be doing a lot of good for everyone here. We'd all appreciate it."

"Sure."

"And you come help when you're ready, too," Eric said as he walked by another man.

A moment later, Eric leaned his rifle against a large spruce tree and handed Neil the axe.

"I'll saw, and you limb," Eric said. "Got it?"

"Got it."

"All right! Let's build us a forest home out here. You never know—we might even get to know each other while we work."

Neil looked away, but Eric wasn't giving up.

Chapter 7

The truth about their despair came out in pieces, and Eric was the one to first pry it gently from their heavy hearts as he gradually, each hour, recruited more helpers for the chores. Neil was reluctant at first, but during a break from sawing and limbing logs, he opened up.

"It started three years ago, during a hard winter outside Boise. A group of armed men surrounded our camp and told us to lay down our weapons. We only had a few hunting rifles between us, and they had some serious machine guns."

"I understand." Eric drank from his canteen and shared it with Neil. "What'd they want?"

"They wanted three of our children." Neil looked away. His big hands clenched into fists. "They made us pick which three, saying it'd only be for chores in their camp. Cooking and laundry and whatnot. It felt wrong from the start, but what could we do? They had us at gunpoint."

"You gave them three kids?"

"We drew lots by family. One lot fell on my family. I chose my son instead of my daughter. I never saw him again. I'll never forget that day, the day they dragged my own son away from our camp. That was the last day my wife looked at me. I think that was the last day I was a man." Neil could say no more.

Eric recruited two other men to help gather firewood. In the woods, he loaned his saw to one of them as he spoke to the other named Geoff, a red-bearded, middle-aged man with a European accent.

"Those bullies kept coming back," Geoff said. "They made us fight amongst ourselves who would be given up next. One day, it fell to my family. My wife was chosen, and they gave her a choice."

"What was the choice?" Eric asked.

"They would take her or take me. It was her choice, they said. Of course, by this time we knew no one ever returned. I begged her to pick me. I'll never forget her face when she made her choice—pure love. It destroyed me. Love destroyed me. Look at us now; it's destroyed us all."

"The people you're talking about—they still do this?"

"Of course." Geoff hefted Eric's hatchet in his hand, taking a practice swing. "Every few weeks, more often in winter when food is scarce. You found us like this. We're done running. We can't run any longer. They've ruined us."

"I . . . see." Eric prayed in his heart, feeling inadequate to speak any words that could help, so he just listened.

"We've run. Some have fought. We tried to hide. Nothing works. They track us down and round us up. Besides, we're not woodsmen. I grew up in Prague. We're all civilized men. What do we know about fighting? I wish my wife would've saved herself. Living is worse, I tell you. Living like this is worse!"

Eric tried to rouse others from the central fire and Bible reading, but the few he'd put to work were the only ones who had the will or strength to labor, for now. He guessed those who'd hunted down the elk were among the same men now cutting logs for their cabins. Though their tools were limited, Eric found work for every person who pushed themselves, just to keep them productive, if they didn't mind leaving the fire for a spell.

The afternoon of day three with the people, one lodge was half-constructed. The walls were log, with the angled roof poles covered with hides and plastic, supported by interwoven branches. They were now calling the place Three Lodges. Joel brought in a deer, his second since arriving to help the strangers, and Wendy went to work butchering it. Eric took Joel up the stream a little, to speak to him privately.

"Someone's been kidnapping their families?" Joel's face turned white. He held his bow in front of him. "Who are they?"

"I don't know, but they must be within a few miles, following this lot every time they move camps, keeping them isolated."

"Like a herd of animals!" Joel closed his eyes. "No wonder these people are such a mess. They've been watching their families get picked apart. Culled!"

"These people are in no condition to travel, or run to Mastover. Neil's the strongest one, and he can barely swing an axe ten times without resting. This is up to us."

"So, we face down kidnappers with guns? Reminds me of a few other times we've seen God back us up when we were outnumbered."

"Scout around. Find out where they're camped, and we'll deal with them before they realize we only have four rifles."

"Hit them? But we're not killers." Joel tightened his bowstring. "Even before I came to Christ last fall, I didn't like killing for my dad. Now, knowing that people are made in God's image, and believing what He says about even my enemies—I can't kill, Eric. I won't, not even now. Listen to me. I'm starting to sound like you when we first met!"

"I'm not asking you to kill, Joel. My understanding of God's love is the same as yours. He instructs us to love even my enemies. All I'm asking of you is to scout around. Find them, then we can put together a plan. Like you said, this isn't the first time we've been outnumbered."

"No, it isn't." Joel grinned. "I see what you're saying. We don't have to kill the enemy to bring them to ruin."

"It'll be dangerous, but rewarding."

"Okay, I'll head out right now."

"Let's keep River Camp in mind as well." Eric imagined Andy in the hands of the wicked men. "They can't discover River Camp, so cover your tracks where necessary. We're only about forty miles from there."

"I'll die before they find River Camp," Joel vowed, "if they catch me."

"Don't get caught, Joel." Eric shook the bowman's hand. "You're the best hunter I know. God will guide you."

Joel set off with his bow, snowshoes, and a little food, then Eric returned to Three Lodges. He stood on the south side of the stream and surveyed the camp. The sky was overcast, looking like it could snow again that night. The camp was in the shade of tall trees that they were leaving in place as windbreaks, but that also meant when the sun was shining, there wouldn't be much warmth. However, the stream trickled across nearly level ground and there was good soil beneath the snow and ice. Before the snow melted, at least two dams should be built, he decided, to offer one pool for drinking water, and the other for laundry.

Gretchen hopped across the stream and joined him. She linked her arm through his.

"You don't approve?" she asked.

"Of the camp? No, I approve. It's a good site. Just lots to do." He watched Neil and Geoff guide two other men in the placement of logs. They'd participated in the building of the first cabin, so they knew how to complete the other two. "I need you and Wendy to return to River Camp. Take a sled and bring back all the spuds you can. And a pickaxe. These people need to dig their own spud cellar and a couple outhouses."

"Eric, it'll take us four days to go there and return." She turned him to face her. "You're trying to get rid of us. They told you something. They talked, didn't they? How bad is it? Don't protect me by sending me away."

"It's worse than we imagined." He took a deep breath, glancing at the near-comatose gathering around the central fire. "But we can't abandon them."

"Are we in danger?"

"More than a little."

"So, a lot?"

"Yeah, but not from these people." He gazed afar off, wishing he could see Joel's progress through the wintery land. "No, the enemy is out there. And after all the smoke from burning the previous camp, they might already know someone else has joined these campers. One thing we've got going for us is this unpredictable weather. And Joel's superior tracking skills. And the Lord, of course. That's three things."

"Then you need me and Wendy around for our rifles. Let me stay."

"The danger isn't our only concern, Gretchen. We need more food, anything River Camp can spare. Lord willing, by the time you return in four days, Joel and I will have this situation sorted out, then we'll have these people stocked up on food to get them into spring."

"What do I tell my dad?" She shivered. "I can't think about what's happened here. Look at these people. They're awake, but . . . asleep."

"I'll speak to them tonight. The gospel is all we have to bring them new life. Let's pray they've been listening to the reading."

"I don't want to leave you, Eric." She embraced him. "But I will because you asked me to."

He held her close, praying about the miles she needed to trek and the work Three Lodges needed to complete—both preferably before it snowed again.

Chapter 8

That night, Eric ate with the forty-eight survivors, seated shoulder to shoulder with them on log benches. He watched their faces as they stared at the flames. Neil occasionally glanced at him over the fire, and each time, Eric gave a single resolute nod to the man. After each nod from Eric, Neil nodded once back. It was a type of visual handshake, or like a boy checking to make sure his father was still there for him.

"I have something to say." Eric lifted his voice, but didn't stand up. He was reminded of the first weeks of the start of River Camp, but these people had been through much worse. "I know only a few of your names, but I'm bound to you by compassion. It's a strength that's not my own. The God of the Bible lives inside me."

Eric thumped his chest hard with his fist. A few campers looked up. Gretchen, holding the hands of two young women on Eric's left, smiled a sad smile that tugged at his heart. She seemed to understand how difficult the words came to him, but also how important the right words were at that moment.

"These last few years have been difficult for us all. After surviving the virus, maybe we expected to live peacefully, isolated from conflict. Instead, our sanity has been tested and our humanity has been threatened. We've been pressed to do unthinkable things, and to make choices that no one should ever have to make. At some point, we've made selfish choices. And we've made others our victims, or we've been victimized by others.

"With all this has come shame. We've seen civilization reach the heights of productivity and security and even beauty. But it only brought out our greed, loneliness, and ugliness. Our hearts have become ugly. Look at us. Look at what sin has brought us to."

Eric paused and sensed God's continued presence with him. He didn't want to speak or act without the Holy Spirit's guidance. Who else could heal such misery as this except God?

"Civilization has been pushing away from God since the beginning. Ever since Jesus came during Roman times, we've looked everywhere else for fulfillment. It got us nowhere but here. We can't ignore our dead spirits inside us any longer. We need to repent from our sins, and trust in who God is, even in this situation. This night, we're blessed to be able to look up from the very bottom and cry out to Him. We must now—"

"Stop!" a woman near Neil begged. She fell on her knees in front of her log seat. Her face was wet as if it had rained. "No more, please! I'll die if I live another minute like this!"

Gretchen opened her mouth and reached for the woman, but another at her side cried out as well. Like a wave, an indiscernible wail swept around the fire. Men wept aloud, their heads in their hands, and some of the women clung to one another as they mumbled pleas.

"What do we do?" Gretchen asked, having waded through the collapsed bodies to reach Eric's side.

"I think we just let God do His thing until it's time for us to guide them some more. One thing I know for sure is that we don't have enough Bibles."

"River Camp doesn't, either," Gretchen said. "Maybe Mastover can help us out."

She knelt to comfort a young mother whose children had been taken by the aggressors, and Eric edged to his right to approach Wendy, who stood aloof.

"They've gone insane," she said. "They've finally lost their minds completely now. Look at them!"

"No." Eric smiled. "This is how God heals us. He breaks us to the point of desperation. Only then are we ready for His healing touch. These people won't be the same tomorrow."

"It won't help them." Wendy crossed her arms, reminding Eric of Hank's hard heart the previous year, but God had still gotten through to him, eventually. "It won't help any of us. I've talked to some of them, too, you know. The murderers who did this to these people will find us, Eric. We have to make peace with them. We have to protect ourselves. We've already spent too long here. We're messing with people who are as good as dead already. You have to think about this!"

"Slow down, Wendy. You're jumping to conclusions."

"No, I'm not. How easy would it be for the people out there to reach River Camp? We have to let them know we're not their enemies! These people are."

"Wendy, we're forty miles away from River Camp." Eric shook his head as he stared at the fire. Wendy's words were beginning to scare him. "It wouldn't be easy to reach River Camp. This wilderness is huge. Besides, we have Mastover to flee to if we need to. Judge Grayport has extended an open invitation to us. You've never met him, but I assure you River Camp has friends. We're not alone, nor are we abandoned by God."

"The killers already may be looking for us. They'll know we're out here now, so they'll come for us. We have to make peace, Eric!"

"There's no peace-making with people who did this to their neighbors. They need to first stop what they're doing."

"Eric, listen, please! We don't need enemies like this. I don't want enemies like this!"

"We won't let them take down River Camp like they did these people. God won't let it happen." Eric wondered if he'd expected too much from Wendy. After all, she'd resisted the gospel since coming to River Camp. She didn't seem to have faith even in a God who didn't abandon His people. "If you hadn't noticed, God has made us kind of resourceful. We're a presence in Wyoming. God will preserve us until we have completed our work for Him out here. That's the way He works."

"Well, I can't be so sure." Wendy walked away from the fire, and into the growing shadows of the evening.

Eric returned his focus to the weeping and distraught supplicants all over camp. A people who'd rarely made eye contact earlier, now clung to one another, whispered confessions and shared their pain. A few days earlier, Eric had wondered if any of the forty-eight even knew each other. Now, he witnessed hearts as close as family being greatly moved. He watched them comfort one another, but he knew their real comfort was coming from the individual surrender of misery and guilt into the hands of a loving God who alone could lift such burdens and guide the lost into green pastures.

He tried to shake off Wendy's paranoia, but she'd planted fear in his mind that wouldn't go away. Had he responded too casually to the threat of aggressors? Had he endangered River Camp? Though he'd dispatched Joel to look into whoever was out there, it sounded like Wendy thought they should've abandoned the victims to their deaths, and run away to safety!

But no, he thought. God could save them all. He really could. But even if He didn't choose to, for some greater divine purpose, Eric could never turn away from souls in need. He knew their pain too well himself. And there was nothing better than what he was seeing right now—faith and repentance.

There was too much work to do for Christ than for Eric to focus unnecessarily on what schemes Satan was attempting. He prayed for God to guide him away from fear of the unknown, and that fear wouldn't dictate his obedience to his Father.

The seeming chaos that he'd caused by calling for repentance lasted nearly an hour. Soon, eyes were dried and seats were reclaimed. When Eric gazed over the fire into their faces, he no longer saw emptiness. He saw new beginnings, people ready to rise up. Death had nearly claimed them all, spirit and body, but they were now newly alive.

"Tell us what to do, Eric," Neil said for them all.

There was no apprehension in their eyes, only anticipation. Eric barely noticed that other than Joel, Wendy was the only one absent.

"We begin new lives," he said, "but for God now. And we rebuild."

Chapter 9

The next morning, Eric woke to a blowing wind. Since only two cabins had been completed, he'd slept outside next to the fire so the change in weather reached all the way inside his sleeping bag. For a moment, he listened to the wind and the mumblings of the few men around him as they slept. It was a cold wind from the north, gusting occasionally. He couldn't see stars, so the sky was still overcast. A terrible storm was on its way, and that meant more snow.

More snow would hamper his plans, but he threw off his tarp without grumbling, and climbed out of his sleeping bag. God had a hand in the weather, he knew, so if God was blowing in a weather system that hindered travel, He clearly didn't want Gretchen and Wendy to travel that day.

Trees groaned and swayed as Eric placed more wood on the fire. Massive clumps of snow fell from tree branches and blew in the wind as Eric dragged another log onto the smoldering fire. The others would rise as dawn reached them in an hour, so he wanted the fire stoked. No snow was falling from the sky yet, but the air all around him was filled with icy whiteness because of the wind. Visibility was diminishing by the minute. The sky brightened with the rising sun, but it only confirmed the dark clouds drawing closer from over the mountain range.

A hard storm could blow for days, and the Three Lodges' food supply was dwindling. But Eric smiled into the mounting blizzard at the thought of the previous evening's final moments. This camp could handle a storm. Those who had suffered through a death to their old lives were reborn to lives of promise and hope. They had parted late in the night, but not before embracing each other in newfound joy. Eric guessed he'd been hugged a hundred times before going to bed. That was remarkable since there were only fifty people in camp.

"Wendy came back in the night," Gretchen said as she approached the flames that whipped and rose in the wind, a pot in her hand. She nestled the pot into the edge of the coals. "But she left before I woke up this morning."

Eric's elation from the night before couldn't be destroyed, but it did suffer loss of some brightness at the thought of Wendy's departure.

"She didn't say where she was going?" He squinted at the curtain of white that seemed to surround them. "She'll never reach River Camp in this weather, and it'll be impossible to find her without visibility."

"All her gear is gone, too—pack, rifle, snowshoes. And she took some of our meat."

"Let me look around." Eric kissed Gretchen's worried face, then walked away from camp.

He started searching for fresh tracks on the east side of camp. If Wendy had left for River Camp, then he guessed he'd find her tracks there. With so many of the campers working in the woods the previous day, reading fresh sign was difficult with the many boot prints, so he moved farther from Three Lodges. The storm tugged at his coat as he studied the snow, working his way around to the north.

On the northwest side of the camp, he found her snowshoe tracks. He knelt and prayed. Wendy wasn't a believer, so she hadn't understood his calmness in the presence of danger. She hadn't been around the aggression of Mastover against Christians, or the threat of the Lib-Org against River Camp. But according to her sign, she'd gone northwest instead of attempting to return to River Camp. She was risking her life with strangers rather than remain with people she knew. If she survived the storm, Eric wondered if she would survive the company of evil men who'd tormented the Three Lodges survivors for years.

Sound and movement farther out in the forest brought Eric to a motionless crouch. He didn't have his rifle! Even though he would never shoot a human being, the presence of a rifle sometimes discouraged others from shooting at him.

"Please be Wendy," he whispered, hoping for one more opportunity to comfort her. But an instant later, he recognized the broad shoulders of Joel, with his bow over his shoulder. Eric put his cupped hand to his mouth. "Pssst!"

Joel stopped and scanned the hazy white air, then spotted him. The two approached one another and shook hands, about one hundred yards outside of camp.

"I found them." Joel checked his back trail, then rattled his canteen. By the sound of the container, half his water was frozen. He'd spent a chilly night out there in the woods. "Thirty men, heavily armed, and a few women. But there were no children."

"Did you see Wendy? She sort of panicked last night, and I think she ran off to join the enemy."

"I saw no one else, Eric, but make no mistake—they're enemies for sure. They have a ridiculous amount of supplies and gear for less than forty people. Their camp had no dogs, so I slipped up to a few lodges and looked inside. They have at least two lodges filled with coats and clothes—too much for a group their size to own. Get my point? It reminded me of old Holocaust photos of piles of clothes and boots."

"So, it's confirmed." Eric felt his heart ache. "Until now, we've been assuming the worst happening to those who were taken from the Three Lodges people. Now we know: the worst is a reality. The people who were taken are no longer alive."

"How could Wendy leave us?" Joel appeared pained. Since she'd arrived at River Camp the previous fall, he'd often been paired with Wendy to hunt deer. They'd become friends. "She didn't explain?"

"She'd been talking to some of the survivors. Someone must've indicated where the enemy is camped. We're outgunned here, vulnerable, under-supplied, and half these people are severely malnourished. She thought she needed to try to make peace with the stronger force."

"Not so strong any longer." Joel bit his lip, obviously holding back a smile. "They had about twenty pairs of snowshoes. But they don't have them anymore. I buried them in a gully. This blowing wind will cover up all sign of any tracks I left, so they'll never find them."

"You took their snowshoes?" Eric chuckled. "With new snow falling, they'll be immobilized for a while."

"I'm learning to think like you." Joel nudged Eric's shoulder. "I guess that means we're in trouble, huh?"

"Thinking like me isn't necessarily an improvement!" Eric rubbed his hands together, enjoying his friend's banter despite the wind-chill and threat of danger. "Maybe we should leave the thinking to God. Come on. I have to introduce you to some new people."

"We got new arrivals since I left yesterday?"

"More like new births, rather than new arrivals. I think God is reminding us that there is a purpose at work here that is greater than the threat of kidnappers."

Joel was welcomed back to camp by fully awakened campers. Person after person greeted him, introduced themselves, and embraced him, leaving him stunned and speechless. The excited talk and retelling of the previous night's events was overwhelming to Joel's emotions. Around the fire, he wiped at his eyes with his half-frozen sleeve as he ate hard biscuits and a stick of spiced jerky.

"You have a plan?" Gretchen asked Eric as they stood to one side of the celebration. He'd told her what he'd heard from Joel and discovered about Wendy's departure, and Gretchen's face showed fresh lines of worry. "She's turned against us, betrayed us. Eric, she'll lead them back to us. She'll deliver River Camp into their hands!"

"The group is about eight miles northwest of us through hard territory, Joel says." Eric waved back at a middle-aged woman who seemed to have eyes for him. Soon, he'd tell the whole camp that he and Gretchen were engaged and were planning a spring wedding. That would remove him from the eligible bachelor list. "As long as this storm is blowing, and without snowshoes, they won't reach us. But yes, I'm formulating a plan, though our only dependence needs to be on God. No one can plan for the unknowns we're facing."

"Don't go sacrificing yourself, Eric. Not like you've tried the other times. I won't allow it."

"Well, it looks like you're going to be here to enforce your will," he said, "since you won't be going back to River Camp for supplies in this storm, and definitely not alone."

At that moment, an accumulation of snow in a tall tree dropped and landed on the central fire, nearly extinguishing the flames. Eric and Joel started to respond, but others reached in and scooped the snow away. A couple men pushed tree branches into the diminished flames, and in minutes, the fire was back to its full height. Regardless of the location of the three cabins, the fire didn't seem as protected from the fierce gusts as Eric had intended.

"This won't do, everyone!" Eric yelled over the commotion. "We'll waste energy and firewood fighting this wind. Let's take it inside for the day and wait out this blizzard."

No one argued. They split themselves between the two completed cabins, within which was enough room for ten bodies to sleep side by side, or twice that when sitting up or standing. Once bunks were built, doubled occupancy would be possible. Fires were started in the rock fireplaces, which had only a hole in the roof since no chimney had been fashioned yet. Soon, the fire warmed the cabin to a sustainable temperature.

Eric was exhausted, and with the warmth of Gretchen's body sitting next to him, he dozed while leaning against the log wall. In his state of half-sleep, he heard angels singing Amazing Grace. It was a distant sound, some of the words whisked away by the wind, as if the hymn were being sung at a great distance.

Suddenly, he opened his eyes wide. There was indeed singing! It was coming from the cabin next door, where Joel was hunkered down with half the campers. A few people had apparently remembered the old hymn from long ago, and they sang it to honor their new God.

Eric and his cabin companions listened and were nourished by the sentiment. When the song from the cabin next door drifted to silence, those in Eric's cabin raised their voices and continued together. Where the people faltered with the words, Gretchen sang loudly, her clear voice sometimes the only one piercing the howl of the wind. All paused to listen, and soon they had learned the words. Beaming at her side, Eric rejoiced that in the few months she'd been a believer, she'd learned the song from their Sunday service when Sister Barb sang in River Camp.

Even crammed inside the cabin, it was a fine day. But Eric's thoughts occasionally returned to how he would deal with the nearby camp of aggressors. He couldn't avoid a face-to-face confrontation with the killers, once the storm was over. Until then, he would enjoy his fiancee's company and the delight that his new brothers and sisters now had in their Savior.

Chapter 10

The blizzard blew for two days. For hours at a stretch, snow fell in a great white wall of flakes. Then sometimes, only the wind would blow. The Three Lodges campers ventured outside only for visits to the nearby outhouse and to fetch wood. Otherwise, they passed the time sleeping, visiting, and reading from Eric's Bible.

Considering the time of forced immobility, Eric saw it as a blessing. Rather than the people becoming engulfed in the camp busy work, God had used the storm to confine them to a tight space where they were forced to speak of the unspeakable. No one was silent, and the healing that had begun from the night of change at the campfire, continued now inside the cabins.

Geoff, the middle-aged European, was the first to share more of his story. He'd come to America to visit a girlfriend in Oregon, whom he'd eventually married. Pan-Day had prevented him from returning to Prague. From the Oregon coast, he and his wife had joined survivors who were traveling inland. Eventually, they met up with outdoorsmen in Idaho. They kept moving east, living off the land with other nomadic campers, hunting and gathering, until they met this group.

Eric learned from Geoff that the Liberation Organization had harassed both campers and townsfolk in Idaho Falls and Pocatello two hundred and fifty miles to the west. Geoff had spoken to traders who had brought such news, which had inclined them to hide deeper in the mountains. But he and his wife had eventually suffered the depletion of supplies, then had become victims of the nearby aggressors.

After Geoff, others shared their stories of loss. Many wept and confessed their involvement when, in an effort to keep their own families alive, they'd allowed the enemy to force them to choose other campers to die. But the aggressors had simply come back for more. Of the forty-eight who remained, only a couple of them were actually related. Everyone else had been taken. Survivor's guilt had ensued. But the sadness of their past was met now with their renewed reliance upon Jesus' free gifts of grace and hope for their repentant souls. They were learning to consider their present conditions from God's perspective, and their future reality in His presence. Eric and Gretchen even taught them new songs, and by singing loud enough, they shared them with the cabin next door.

When they emerged from the cabin after two days, they found a blue sky and two more powdery feet of fresh snow upon the blanket already laid. Neil and Geoff set up firewood crews, as much of their fuel had been depleted. No one refused to work.

Since Geoff and Neil were the camp's natural leaders, Eric and Joel pulled them aside when they had a free moment. Eric explained his plan to return to River Camp to fetch more potatoes, as well as supplies to build a spud cellar and a better situated outhouse for Three Lodges. He also wanted to dam up the stream for a more permanent settlement. With a pickaxe and a strong man to swing it, some of the digging could begin before the ground thawed.

"But we can't focus on rebuilding without going to the aggressors' camp," Eric said. "We have to confront them."

"These aren't men you can confront." Neil lowered his head, his big hands clenched. "More than once, they held a gun to my head and made me choose their next victim. They don't negotiate."

"We can't fight them," Geoff said. "Even if we get our guns back, fighting them isn't in us any longer."

"Confronting them is better than staying here and waiting for them to attack." Eric saw the worry on their faces. "Look, I don't like our options, either, but none of your people can travel."

"This is Eric Radner." Joel placed a hand on Eric's shoulder. "The Lord is with him in a mighty way because he submits to God. This isn't his first confrontation."

"We're harmless as doves, sure." Eric smiled, sensing a godly confidence with a righteous mischievousness deep inside him. "But we're also sly as foxes. I have a plan."

"What is it?" Neil asked.

"We remind them of their crimes, then show them how their only path to survival is to give up or run away."

"Maybe it's worth a try." Geoff said. "Neil and I should be the ones to go."

"Perhaps you should," Eric said, "but your strength is still returning. It would be an honor for me to do this for you."

"Me, too," Joel said. "I can't wait to see how God is going to do His thing again!"

"But you've both done so much already." Neil sighed. "Okay, we'll stay here and work. And we'll pray. Can you leave your Bible so we can read it? I mean, if something were to happen to you . . ."

Eric drew his Bible from his coat. He'd lost count how many times he'd loaned the worn Bible to yearning hearts.

"We'll get more Bibles soon, or find a way to print them in Mastover. I'm sure we can arrange a deer-meat-for-Bibles deal at an old dusty print shop."

"I just want to be ready," Neil said. "Jesus must be coming soon, I believe."

"Yep, I'm convinced He's on His way." Eric shook their hands.

Gretchen was waiting for him as he swept snow off his snowshoes. Her face didn't show a great deal of understanding, so Eric avoided direct eye contact as he readied his pack.

"So, you're sacrificing yourself?" She stomped her foot in the trampled snow outside the central cabin. "Eric Radner, this is not wisdom or faith. This is madness! Do you expect me to round up all of River Camp and Mastover to come save you again?"

"Don't bother." Eric tightened his pack straps and placed his hands on her shoulders. "These men we're meeting aren't the kind to keep prisoners. If they take us, it won't be because they want to negotiate. Joel and I know that we may be walking in a one-way direction."

"Exactly! A one-way direction into a cooking pot!"

"Gretchen, they may be violent and murderous people, but they're not stupid. They want to survive, which is why they took all the rifles from these people. We can use their fear and self-preservation against them."

"There's no guarantee it's going to work. You know that!" She scowled. "I've almost lost you before. I still have plans for us, you know. Those plans don't work if you're dead!"

"Listen, if we're not back in a day or two, then Three Lodges should expect an attack. Be ready to run into the woods. Take who you can back to River Camp. Your dad will get everyone safely to Mastover."

"It's forty miles to River Camp—in five feet of snow!"

"The enemy will have the same conditions. But just think, Gretchen. We have no other option. Joel and I are going to try to help these people see reason, one way or another."

She opened her mouth to protest, but Eric pulled her into a tight embrace. He didn't let her go until he felt her arms around him in response. He loved her deeply, but he had to care for others as well.

Chapter 11

Eric and Joel strapped on their snowshoes and tromped straight northwest, with Joel leading since he knew the route. After a few miles, they stopped to rest. It was an hour before noon. Eric relayed his plan to Joel—to deal with the kidnappers, they would threaten that the news of their crimes would reach the nearby towns. He waited for Joel's reaction. In the silence, they both stuffed snow into their canteens. Clipped to their belts, their body heat kept the water mostly melted in the freezing temperature.

"It's a good bluff," Joel finally said, "if they don't kill us the minute we walk into their camp."

"It's not a bluff. This group is finished eating other humans. Too many people know now. Through the pressure of nearby townspeople, they'll stop their ways, or run for their lives from folks who will come for them."

"It could work," Joel said. "You're right. If my father gets word of cannibalism near his town, he'll put together a justice force and rampage through these woods."

"It's not my plan, really. I got it from the Bible."

"Where? Which story?"

"In Judges 19 and 20, all of Israel is called upon to bring about justice when a crime is committed. We can do the same, until a change is made."

"The Levite and the concubine." Joel nodded and started walking again. "Just remember: thousands of people died in that story in the end. Maybe your plan still needs some work."

Two hours later, Eric took point and approached the camp cautiously. Like the rest of the wilderness, the camp was buried under a couple feet of snow that hadn't been there when Joel had spied on them two nights earlier. It seemed no one in camp had been too swift about digging themselves out since the storm had ended overnight. And Joel's further caper of taking their snowshoes had certainly set them back from any plans to venture outside the camp.

Eric cradled his rifle as he walked into camp. Joel carried his bow, but he didn't put an arrow to the string. The point wasn't to invite conflict, only to show themselves as men who weren't intimidated.

They were both in the middle of the camp of a dozen dome-shaped shelters before a man outside one dwelling called out to them, then stumbled into his shelter. Eric and Joel held their positions, standing tall on their snowshoes, listening to men scrambling for their coats and assault rifles.

As the aggressors emerged from their shelters, they advanced and surrounded them. Eric tried not to dwell on the fact that these men were mass murderers who had pursued their fellow neighbors to the brink of hopeless shame.

The men who approached them yelled and threatened all at once. They demanded that Eric and Joel lay down their weapons, but Eric remained calm. He held up his empty gloved hand in greeting, but he didn't lay down his rifle.

But the aggressors' approach was cumbersome through the snow, since it was so deep, and their hate bordered on panic. Visitors hadn't been expected! They ended up wading through the fresh snow up to their thighs, giving Eric and Joel a two-foot height advantage over even their tallest men.

Finally, they had encircled the two men as close as they dared, and the yelling stopped.

"My name is Eric Radner." He noticed several women and a couple of elderly men near the shelters, but his main focus was on the nearly thirty muzzles aimed at him and Joel. "We have you outnumbered ten to one. I think you'll want to hear what we came to tell you."

"We know who you are, Radner!" a bald man with a gray beard said. "She told us!"

He gestured toward one shelter. Eric glanced to the left and saw Wendy. Defiantly, she stared back.

"You don't have any men," another aggressor said. He wore an eagle feather in his long black beard, though he didn't look Native American. "You don't even have any more guns!"

"I am Eric Radner, also called Mad Man, and this is Joel Grayport. His father is Judge Grayport, sovereign leader over the town of Mastover. We forced the Liberation Organization out of Wyoming last fall. Wendy Sullivan must've told you we're intimately connected to a resistance fighting force nearby, under Major Milton. Like I said, we have you outnumbered ten to one."

The men hesitated, unsure, and looked at Eagle Feather. Eagle Feather glanced back at Wendy, who nodded reluctantly, then ducked into a shelter.

Eagle Feather cursed.

"We'll talk, but leave your weapons with my men."

"No." Eric shook his head slightly. "We're not those kind of dinner guests."

Joel grunted at the not-so-vague charge, and the aggressors' faces turned a shade darker. Their sins were no secret.

"Follow me!" Eagle Feather turned as fast as he could turn in the deep snow, dragging one leg at a time in lunging steps, to the largest of the camp shelters.

Eric and Joel remained surrounded, though they quickly outmaneuvered the others, since they were the only two who could walk on top of the snow. They took off their packs and carried them, but for fear of losing their snowshoes, they wore them right into the shelter. Four men followed, facing them in a semicircle.

The ceiling was low. Eric crouched and moved to the left to squat on his haunches, facing Eagle Feather. A single kerosene lamp lit the interior. Since kerosene was not easy to obtain, Eric guessed they were burning oil from the fat of animals.

The four others peered from around a metal stove in the center, complete with a metal chimney up to the center of the ceiling.

"You're the cursed dogs who took our snowshoes!" Eagle Feather snapped.

"You're fortunate that's all we took." Eric smiled, wondering how many more retorts he would manage before they simply shot him. "You're resourceful people. I'm sure you'll manage to build new snowshoes as you leave Wyoming."

"Leave Wyoming?" Eagle Feather grinned, showing blackened teeth and diseased gums. His skin was pale and he scratched at sores on his hand and neck. "We're not leaving Wyoming."

"We know the method of your survival." Eric tilted his head. "We network with Mastover, and Mastover networks with traders north, east, south, and west of us. Within a week or two, everyone within two states will know about you. You'll be hunted and hung, if the Lib-Org doesn't get to you first. They're into burning people, I hear. But all that can be avoided, if . . ."

Eric paused and unclipped his canteen. Taking his time, he took two long swallows. His gulps were loud in the silence. He heard men mumble outside discontentedly as they listened for more. Men inside shifted nervously.

"If what?" Eagle Feather pressed him.

"If you change your ways, a violent end can be avoided." Eric clipped his canteen back onto his belt. "Have you ever seen a man burn at the stake? It's not pleasant. I'm not saying this is my desire for any of you, but if you insist on your barbaric methods of survival, it's one possible end for you."

"The woman who left you said—"

"Her name is Wendy."

"Wendy said you don't believe in killing." Eagle Feather leaned forward and sneered, his breath making Eric recoil. "You won't do anything to us. It's against your religion."

"Wendy doesn't know me that well. She only joined us a few months ago. She doesn't know all the horrible rumors about Mad Man Radner from the Sharrock Mountains. Of course, I wouldn't kill you, but there are worse things than death for some men."

"I'm not some men." He shrugged and unbuttoned his coat a few buttons in the warmth of the shelter. "I'm not afraid of your threats. None of us are."

"Oh, I'm not threatening you. Shall I be more specific? If you don't care, perhaps some of the others listening would like to hear."

"Go ahead."

"Okay. It begins and ends with this: you have been eating people. Homesteaders, travelers, and roaming militias will band together to put you down. Your only chance at survival is complete reform, beginning today."

"Or I kill you." Eagle Feather drew a long, thin butcher knife. "And our secret dies with you."

"It's too late. The forty-eight campers you left alive have recovered their senses. Killing us would only delay the inevitable. We have a radio back in our camp, and we call Mastover on a regular schedule. When word reaches them, hunters far and wide will come to massacre you in the most inventive ways they can imagine. We reap what we sow, that's how sin works. God makes sure of it. That's why we urge people to flee from sin before the consequences get worse."

"God? Wendy already told me about your God. Like I said, killing you seems like a good call, even if it's a short-term fix."

"I'm here to help you." Eric felt the conversation taking a turn for the worse, but he still had to try—for the sake of Three Lodges. "You've shown no mercy to countless victims, but God is rich in mercy. The gaping, rotting mouth of death is at the door. You and your people won't live out the winter if you don't turn from your evil. You are literally being offered the choice between life and death. If you live, it must be on my terms. If you die, it will be on your enemies' terms. I ask you, for the sake of your people, choose life."

Eagle Feather twirled the knife in his fingers. Eric resisted the thought of all that knife's victims. The look in the man's eyes was one of derangement. He was sick and brutal, but he'd provided food for a few weak people, so they had followed him.

"Before I kill," Eagle Feather said, "I ask people how they want to die. So, Eric Radner, how do you want to die? This will be your last request. Think carefully."

Eric stared into the man's eyes. They were emptier than the eyes of the forty-eight campers when they'd been at their worst. He really was about to kill them, and escaping out the door of the shelter was impossible. Half the camp was standing outside, listening.

He turned to Joel.

"I guess this wasn't such a good plan after all."

"I guess not." Joel frowned. "But it was worth a try."

The four men facing them drew handguns and aimed them at their guests.

"We want you to know we don't hate you," Eric said, resigning himself rather suddenly to meet the Lord in a moment. He laid down his rifle instead of holding it in his hands where he'd be tempted to use it. If he leapt just so, he guessed he could knock over the lantern, but then what? At the most, he might entangle the enemy enough to give Joel a chance to escape, but it seemed unlikely. "When Jesus Christ was murdered by wicked men, He could've fought back, but He didn't. He restrained Himself out of love, and we'll do the same. You'll be held accountable for what you're about to do, but because of our care for you, we won't try to kill you. Soon, you'll face the wrath of God, and that's why we are inclined to show you compassion now. However, I should mention, we have no intention of making this easy for you."

"Slaughtered animals never do." Eagle Feather raised up, his knife leveled to thrust. "Fight all you want!"

Chapter 12

Machine gunfire outside made everyone in the dome shelter freeze in motion for a moment. Eagle Feather's eyes widened as he seemed to recall the very warning Eric had spoken seconds earlier.

Eric and Joel glanced at one another. They'd seen God insert Himself in the final moments of desperate situations before, so they knew not to hesitate. Though Eagle Feather held a knife and the others held handguns, their faces showed confusion mixed with denial. In their enemies' distracted state, Eric and Joel tackled the aggressors, knocking them backwards. The lantern was kicked over, and flaming oil spread across a blanket. The stove pipe was dislodged and spewed soot.

Bullets fired from outside peppered one wall and passed clean through the shelter. Eric wrenched the knife from Eagle Feather's grip, then rolled over and stabbed at the back wall of the shelter, slashing it top to bottom. Only then did he realize he still wore his snowshoes, as did Joel. Using his snowshoes against one enemy, Joel grappled with another for a gun. One man crawled out the door as screams pierced the crisp air and dozens of guns were fired.

Eric grabbed up his rifle in one hand and Joel's collar with his other.

"Let's get out of here!"

As the enemy exited the front, Eric and Joel stepped awkwardly in their snowshoes through the gash Eric had cut in the back wall. Joel had his bow in his hand, but neither man had their packs.

Eric coughed at stove soot and smoke in his throat, and looked over the top of the shelter at the raging battle. Men in white parkas, with black patches on their shoulders, were charging on skis from the forest, firing as they screamed. Though the campers appeared to be outgunned and caught by surprise, they fired right back, hatred and curses spewing from their mouths. Because of Eric and Joel's recent arrivals, the camp had been on edge, armed and wary.

The attackers, it suddenly dawned on Eric, were the Liberation Organization! The black patches identified them as an elite fighting unit.

"Run!" Eric gasped over the screams and gunfire, but his own feet got tangled in his snowshoes, like crisscrossed skies.

Joel yanked him upright and dragged him forward. Their flight was mostly screened by the domed shelter. As they entered the trees, Eric was again moving on his own at a steady shuffle—as fast as anyone could move in snowshoes. They put as many trees behind them as they could, separating themselves from any visibility of the aggressors' camp.

Finally, they stopped and leaned against a tree to catch their breaths. Eric guessed he and Joel had fled only a quarter-mile. The gunfire continued, but seemed to fade in the distance as it moved out of the camp itself.

"That was the Lib-Org!" Eric said, the deep breaths of cold air hurting his lungs. He was sweating from fear, which was dangerous in those temperatures. "I hope Wendy made it out."

"She betrayed us, Eric." Joel checked his bow for damage. "She's better off to get her justice now."

"No, she's better off alive. She's not a believer. There's still hope for her if she's alive."

"Well, it doesn't sound like anyone's taking prisoners back there." Joel lowered his eyes. "Sorry. I'm not as forgiving as you. Wendy was one of us. She's responsible for what almost happened to us. I can't believe we got out alive. I thought we were going to become their evening feast!"

"The Lord keeps cutting it close for you and me." Eric laughed through his tense nerves. "I thought that was really it this time, too. It's hard to know whether I should cheer to stay here for Andy and Gretchen, or cheer for the Lord to let me go home to be with Him."

"Sometimes I wonder myself. Eric, look!" Joel pointed to Eric's leg. "You're bleeding!"

Only then did Eric feel the wetness from his belt down to his knee. He unclipped his canteen and shook the punctured container.

"It's just water." He stuck his little finger into the bullet hole. "That was close."

Joel took the canteen from his hand and examined it.

"God just doesn't stop with you, does He? This bottle may be useless to you now, but I'm keeping it—as a reminder. Back at River Camp, this is going on my shelf as a symbol of what God did for us today."

"We're a long ways from River Camp, and we have no gear." Eric listened to the forest. The gunshots dwindled to sporadic gunfire every few seconds. "Let's find high ground to see if we're being tracked before we head back to Three Lodges."

Their adrenalin ebbed as they trekked, and the forest silence was accompanied by the quiet shuffling of their snowshoes. Finally, they removed their snowshoes to climb a steep ridge of jutting rocks and sliding shale to the topmost peak for miles around. Using binoculars, they scanned their back trail to the south. They'd traveled about four miles to reach Shale Peak.

"I don't see any movement," Joel said. "You?"

"Nothing but smoke." Eric lowered his binoculars and held them in his lap. "They burned the camp. They were evil people, but I'd hoped to turn them around."

"It's almost biblical—two men of God call for repentance. The people refuse, then destruction strikes."

"But I wanted to save Wendy."

"You saw her face." Joel shared his canteen with Eric. "Sure, it would've been great to bring her back, but she chose her family, Eric."

Eric led the way off the east ridge of the peak. He wanted to return to the aggressors' camp, but it was too dangerous. The Lib-Org was apparently purging the forest. They might have posted a heavily-armed sentry on the site for a few days to wait for survivors to return.

It was nine miles back to Three Lodges. The two travelers were exhausted as they walked into a smokeless, vacant camp at sundown. The temperature had dropped to zero, but there was no fire burning and the cabins were empty. However, the third cabin had been roofed that day, so the campers hadn't been gone for long.

"I see no sign of an attack," Eric said after sweeping the perimeter of camp for tracks in the snow.

From across the stream and up the slope, a sapling rustled. Gretchen emerged in the fading light. The others crowded close behind her. Eric waved for them to return, and they hustled back into camp. Joel started a fire, and the others carried flaming branches to the other fire pits.

"We heard the thunder," Gretchen said after embracing Eric. "Thunder on a blue-sky day? We thought they'd killed you both. It sounded like a war!"

"It was, but not against us." He described their visit, their failed attempt at reconciliation, and the attack of Lib-Org troops. "We lost our packs, but not our skin."

"They're all dead?" Neil asked. He accepted food that was passed around by a couple of the women. "That's it, then. We're finally free from them."

"But if we escaped," Eric said, "others might have made it, too."

"I don't mean to belittle our escape from evil folks," Joel said, "but whoever survived back there today is going to be in bad shape. The camp shelters were burned, I think. People might freeze to death."

"You're not going back!" Gretchen gasped. "Eric said they tried to kill you! You were both nearly shot. They could track you and follow you back here!"

"There could be people suffering out there." Joel's face appeared peaceful as the light of the flames illuminated him. "They could be wounded. Besides, even if Wendy turned from us there at the end, I guess she was still one of us."

Eric saw a change in the bow hunter that he could only attribute to a miracle of God inside him. After a cruel people had nearly killed him, Joel still felt compassion, even a change of heart toward Wendy, their betrayer.

"They wouldn't help us if we were suffering," Neil said, then looked away, seeming to regret saying it an instant later.

"Someone needs to go back to scout out what the Lib-Org is up to," Eric said. "There are no roads this deep in the forest. Those soldiers must've hiked for days in some of the season's coldest weather to reach this far."

"From what I saw," Joel said, "the Lib-Org wasn't exactly winning, though. Both sides were giving and taking. What I'm saying is, maybe the Lib-Org's advance out here has been broken."

"If the Lib-Org is out here," Gretchen said to Eric, "they're after Mad Man."

"Who's Mad Man?" Neil asked.

"Just a legend," Eric said, then nodded at Joel. "Can you scout around for a couple days? See what the status is of both sides. Gretchen and I will take a sled back to River Camp and pick up more supplies. We'll be back in three and a half days, if all goes smoothly."

"What if Joel finds survivors?" Neil asked. "What if there are people still alive from the camp of the cannibals?"

"Well, that's something for us all to pray about." Eric said.

Neil didn't respond. He only stared into the flames. Many other campers had heard their discussion, but they were silent with their own thoughts as they recovered from their cold afternoon hiding in the woods.

Gretchen took Eric's hand in her own.

"I get you all to myself for a few days? I feel spoiled," she said.

"You won't feel too spoiled towing that sled back full of potatoes!" Joel joked.

They all laughed. Regardless of uncertainties and struggles of the Three Lodges' residents, Eric saw a new light in their faces. That light was the hope they now had in Jesus. And he knew they would all somehow endure whatever was to come.

Chapter 13

Their spud run back to River Camp was indeed no easy journey. It was a trip of necessity. If Three Lodges didn't become self-sufficient by spring, River Camp would be too overwhelmed even to support itself.

As much as Eric wanted to take his time and enjoy Gretchen's conversation and marriage planning, his mind was on the people's survival. God had once again given him a whole settlement to raise up for Himself. Eric had found them half-dead, and had led them back to life from a disease worse than the virus. They'd survived the torments of guilt and shame, but their fight to stay alive wasn't over.

The two made it back to River Camp in a day and a half, arriving before noon to an ecstatic welcome. A venison stew was thawed and put on the fire, and Hank announced an evening of tale-telling and lore-boasting. Andy had his own stories to tell around the campfire as well, but Eric held up his hand.

"We can't stay," he said. The camp groaned in disappointment. "Lives hang in the balance. We have brothers and sisters in Christ at another camp—forty-eight souls who are still too weak to care for themselves. Barb?"

The woman looked at him expectantly.

"We need all the spuds that River Camp can spare for the rest of the winter. And venison and flour and chicory leaves. Can you gather everything for us? We need to leave in an hour."

"We'll get started," the woman said, and hurried away, signaling for two youths to go with her to help.

While Gretchen packed food for them to eat on their journey back, Eric met with Hank in the first cabin. Andy and Runner stood at Eric's side, so Eric's details of the

Three Lodges situation and Lib-Org attack were accurate but somewhat censored. Hank seemed to understand the threat for what it was.

"I see." The big man's mended flannel shirt had a new patch on the arm. "So, we don't know if the Lib-Org is pushing east or not. Highway 191 is far to the west, but in this terrain, that's at least a week's march for troopers. Just to get vehicles up that highway, they'd need a fleet of snow plows."

"Joel is out there scouting, seeing what they're up to. That's one reason I want to get back. If we need to move everyone back here, and then on to Mastover, we will."

"And leave our homes?" Hank gazed at the log walls where he'd fixed hooks and shelves, skins and curtains. "I know we're strangers and pilgrims in this world, but I was starting to really like this place. Besides, Sara is in Mastover. She threatened to shoot me!"

"You have to reconcile with her someday, Hank," Eric said, petting Runner's head.

"Dad," Andy asked, his hand on Eric's shoulder, "would you say I'm a good hiker?"

"You hike better than some men, I think. Why?"

"Runner and I want to go to Three Lodges with you."

Eric's immediate thought was to deny his son's request. It was too dangerous, and they would be in a hurry. However, with the sled, they wouldn't be moving too swiftly, and Andy could snowshoe as well as anyone. There were still unknowns about the aggressors and the Lib-Org in the region, but having a youth and a pet at Three Lodges could offer much encouragement and normalcy to the encamped residents. Having Andy with them offered more advantages than disadvantages, though there was still one obstacle to overcome before he could join them.

"Gretchen's about to become your mother, so you'd better clear this with her. And then you'd better pack a backpack and let me inspect it before we leave."

"All right! Come on, Runner!"

The two dashed out of the cabin.

"You really want him to see those people?" Hank asked. "You describe them as still pretty weak and gloomy."

"Only in their appearance. Their spirits are remarkable. That's what Andy will notice. And that's what they'll notice about Andy."

The return trip to Three Lodges took two full days. Most of the way, Eric pulled the sled with Gretchen helping when needed. On steep trails, even Andy was tasked to steady the sled so it didn't topple down slopes into seemingly bottomless ravines. Eric pressed them all, since he was eager to hear news from Joel's scouting. This was also the first time the Three Lodges residents had been left alone. Building the three cabins and collecting firewood together were good exercises, but these people needed to learn to live together after unspeakable adversity.

Late on the second afternoon, Runner ran ahead of the sled and barked an announcement of their arrival. The last few miles had been otherwise level for the sled, so an exhausted Andy had found a perch for his weary young body high up on the sled gear.

But the campers at Three Lodges didn't emerge to greet them with the elation Eric had hoped for upon their return. Neil's face was downcast as he shook Eric's hand. At first, Eric thought someone had died. Many of the forty-eight had been malnourished, and good nutrients hadn't been very plentiful in Eric's first load of supplies.

"What's wrong?" Eric asked Neil quietly as others gathered to inventory the sled.

"Joel hasn't returned. I'm sorry, Eric."

"He hasn't been back since we left?" Eric tried to temper the worry in his voice. For the sake of those nearby, he forced a smile and clapped Neil on the back. "If I know Joel, he's probably trying to hunt down a big ol' elk and drag it back here all by himself. Come on. I want you to meet my son."

There was joy in their faces as they shook hands with Andy, though Andy wasn't the epitome of courtesy since he could barely keep his eyes open. Eric lost track of exactly when the boy disappeared into one of the cabins to sleep on one of the bunks.

A log shed had been erected in the four days of Eric's absence, so the supplies had a place indoors. In minutes, with everyone's help, the sled was emptied and the shed was filled with food, tools, and gear that River Camp was gifting their sister settlement.

As the people settled around the three campfires for stories and Bible reading—which had become an evening tradition already—Eric drew Neil and Gretchen aside.

"The moon is bright," he said. "I need to go look for Joel. Four days is too long. He's either been captured, killed, or—"

"Or what?" Gretchen asked.

"I don't know. It's just a hunch I have. That old camp of the aggressors is only eight miles away. I'll stop in there first. We'll never be able to rest here unless we know what's going on with our enemies."

"I'm going with you." Gretchen took a step closer as if daring Eric to refuse her. "Enough of this going-off-alone business. I'd rather die with you than wonder what happened to you. Just please don't tell me we have to drag that sled."

"No sled." Eric chuckled. "If you have the energy, I'd like the company. Neil, we probably won't be back by dawn. Andy's a good gatherer. Tell him to teach you how to catch wild turkeys."

"Wild turkeys?"

"Tastes like chicken." Eric shouldered his rifle and a new pack. "We have much to teach you. And keep Runner out of the biscuits!"

Their pace out of Three Lodges was slow, but the snow had a crusty surface after several sunny days, so they strapped their snowshoes onto their backs. Their boot soles squeaked on the snow with each step in the sub-zero temperatures.

Eric led them on a southerly arc toward the aggressors' camp, pausing often to listen to the night. Since Joel was missing, Eric thought it might mean Lib-Org troops could still be in the area, or that the aggressors had managed to regroup to become brutal survivors once again. But the night sounds were filled only with a few distant and certainly chilly coyotes.

Before midnight, Eric stopped and eased his pack off his shoulders. Gretchen followed his lead. Though they'd not been on many moonlit hunts together, they'd hunted countless deer over the months, and knew each other's abilities and signals, and the necessity for silence.

With only rifles in their hands, they eased through the woods where the glow of a fire was burning. Gretchen tugged on Eric's coat and brought him to a stop.

"Is this their camp?" Gretchen whispered into his ear.

"No," he whispered back. "This is someone else. The aggressors' camp is on a plain another mile farther northwest. Let's get closer, then sit and watch."

He didn't need to tell her to step carefully as they advanced another ten yards; Gretchen was lighter and placed her feet softly behind his.

They crept as close as they dared. Though it was the middle of the night, someone in a white parka with a hood on his head sat at the fire. From their angle, they couldn't see his face. By the light of the fire, they counted four sleeping masses around the fire. Even so close to the flames, sleeping outdoors in that temperature had to be a challenge.

Gretchen pulled Eric down to kneel together on the snow. Motionlessly, they watched the five individuals at the campfire. The woods were close all around the campsite, as if intentionally picked to use the trees to hide the fire's light from onlookers. Any other approach to the aggressors' camp, the two would've passed by and completely missed this campfire.

Ten minutes went by with no one moving. Eric recalled hunts with Gretchen when they'd waited like this, once for a full hour for a monster buck to leave a couple does in a thicket.

The hooded man leaned to his side and drew more firewood from a pile on top of the snow. He set it gently on the fire, then sat motionless again.

Eric had a choice to make. They could go around this camp and approach their intended destination, or they could introduce themselves here. The five in front of them didn't seem to possess the exact identifying gear as the Lib-Org raiders. Though the hooded man wore a white parka, the sleeping bags and tarps that they could see weren't Lib-Org surplus. Eric had no intention of advancing on people who meant them harm, but he wasn't about to pass up a potential lead to Joel's whereabouts.

Gretchen seemed to read his mind and peeled a chunk of bark off a fir tree next to them. She handed it to him and he underhanded it high over the fire. The bark soared to the other side of camp, clattered against a tree, then landed with a plop on the surface of the snow.

Much to Eric's surprise, the hooded man didn't lunge to his feet, though he did lift a stout stick and stare into the trees. Gretchen handed him another piece of bark, and he threw it in another direction. But again, the hooded man didn't rise to his feet or aim a gun. The others lying around the fire remained covered and unresponsive, though the two thrown objects had made loud, unnatural sounds in the night.

Eric rose to his feet and walked away from Gretchen.

"Eric!" she whispered as loudly as she dared. "Come back!"

He couldn't remain in the darkness all night, throwing wood at campers. Besides, he suspected he'd never get the response from these campers he and Gretchen had first expected.

Casually, he stepped into the light of the fire. No firearms were visible, but the campers could've been hiding their weapons under their coverings. The four sleeping masses appeared cozy in sleeping bags, lying on top of tarps on the snow. The hooded man gripped and regripped his stick, but Eric's gaze drifted to the bloody bandages around what had once been the man's left leg— now a stump. The crippled man appeared frightened, but that wasn't all. He had no beard!

"You're Liberation Organization?"

The hooded man's eyes darted about nervously, then settled on the snow in front of him. He lowered the club in his hands, then rested it on the snow.

Gretchen walked up then, and pulled back the corner of one sleeping bag to expose a pale, unconscious woman in flannel. After checking her pulse, Gretchen nodded at Eric.

"She's alive." Gretchen pulled the sleeping bag farther back to reveal that her torso was bandaged with a cloth dressing. "Gunshot through the side. Someone treated her. Cleaned and wrapped it."

"She was with the . . ." Eric realized he couldn't keep calling them cannibals. "The aggressors."

"What about him?" she asked of the hooded man who wouldn't raise his head.

"No, he was with the Lib-Org." Eric studied the camp more carefully, and couldn't withhold a smile. "Where's the person who helped you?"

The man looked up sharply.

"There is no one else. We're alone."

"I don't think so." Eric took three strides to open three packs of clothing and blankets. He smelled burnt cloth. "No, this mountain of stuff was salvaged after the attack on the camp. These four people are too sick to move, and you didn't amputate your own leg."

"It's Joel," Gretchen said proudly, then to the hooded man, "Don't worry. We're friends of Joel's. You don't need to protect him from us, but it's sweet that you would."

"My own unit left me to die." The stranger sighed. "I would've been wolf meat without Joel. Would've lost more than just my leg."

"Commander Morris was with you?" Eric asked. He moved aside as Gretchen quickly examined the three other sleeping figures. None of them were Wendy. "I know him a little bit."

"I was a lieutenant under him. We skied for a week to find some ghost he called Mad Man. Now look at me."

"Look at all of us." Eric crouched down and held out his hand. "We're all trying to stay alive, but only a few of us are realizing we need God and one another to make it. My name is Eric."

The man pushed back his hood to reveal a short-cropped military cut, then shook Eric's hand. He appeared to be in his early 30's.

"I used to be Lieutenant Tesh, but I guess you can just call me Alan now."

"And this is Gretchen, my fiancee. Where's Joel wandered off to?"

"Once he saw I was stable, he went back out to recover more supplies. He brought us all here while we were unconscious. Said we weren't safe to stay any closer to the ruined camp."

"Yep." Eric said to Gretchen. "That all sounds like about four-days-worth of work for Joel. The man's turned into a regular hero."

Chapter 14

Joel returned to his makeshift camp before dawn. Eric rose from his place by the fire to greet his friend in the trees while the others remained asleep. The two men embraced with smiles in the bitter cold, then stomped their feet in place to ward off the chill."

"Survivors, huh?" Eric said. "We wondered what kept you."

"I was just too busy to get back to Three Lodges yet." Joel gestured to a rope tied to a bundle of gear he'd dragged on top of the snow. "Had to avoid a bunch of wild dogs, but I collected about thirty rifles, ammunition, some coats, skis, and more blankets from the campsite, though most everything was burned if it was inside a shelter. The Lib-Org troopers had packs full of stuff."

"How many dead?"

"Total? Sixty or seventy from both sides. Judging by the tracks, I'd say only a few Lib-Org men made it out of the firefight. Those campers put up one furious fight!"

"Commander Morris?"

"As best as I could tell," Joel said, "he wasn't among the dead, but there's someone still out there."

"Out where?"

"A little to the north, near Shale Peak. I've seen campfire smoke."

"You didn't check it out?"

"I've had these five to take care of. Besides, anyone who can start a fire out there can probably take care of themselves. And they're steering clear of us, which is all I'm concerned about right now."

"Still, I'd like to know who's shadowing us." Eric picked up the rope to Joel's gear. "Come on. Rest for a few hours, then we'll see about getting back to Three Lodges."

"Even with these people?" Joel raised his eyebrows. "I mean, the four in sleeping bags were some of those who took family members from Three Lodges campers. And the one-legged guy was Lib-Org!"

"You saved their lives." Eric pulled the gear into camp. "Now, we have to keep them alive. There's nowhere else to take them but to Three Lodges."

Gretchen awoke briefly to greet Joel, but settled back next to the fire to sleep once she found out they weren't going anywhere until Joel rested some. Eric stoked the fire and checked the sky—blue, with no clouds, though it was below zero. Regardless of the recent violence, he believed their little camp was safe for the moment, and he desperately wanted to know who was still out there.

He shouldered a small pack, his rifle, and snowshoes, and headed northwest. As he hiked, he presented his plans to God and sought His wisdom.

Three Lodges wasn't his home. He missed River Camp. Once Three Lodges was set up in a week or two, he purposed to head home. He and Joel could occasionally visit Three Lodges and bring supplies and fellowship, but they would need to learn to grow independently from their humble restart. It was a pleasant thought to consider that he'd helped sculpt a couple mountain communities out of the unforgiving wilderness.

A mile later, he came upon the aggressors' camp, and stopped on the edge of the clearing. Wild dogs seemed to be in force, claiming the dead, so Eric kept to the edge of the tree line to reach the north side of the destruction. Gazing northward, he located Shale Peak, but even using his binoculars, he couldn't find any hint of smoke.

Pressing onward, he contemplated the misery he'd witnessed the last few weeks. Those woods had witnessed the unthinkable committed by unmerciful men and women. Though he kept waiting for the shock of it all to hit him, he wasn't surprised at the horrible nature of violence and selfishness. It was as biblical and sinful as the people under siege in Jerusalem had become in the sixth century before Christ. People had literally turned on one another to eat. When towns in America burned people alive for believing in Jesus, other shameful offenses against neighbors could be expected in these last days as well.

At the bottom of Shale Peak, where the valley floor met the mountain, Eric found boot prints that led to the east. The prints crossed his and Joel's tracks from days earlier, but had kept moving. Visibly smaller than his own, there was only one set of prints but they were days old.

He followed the prints for a mile before he came upon a lean-to and an empty camp. Firewood had been collected, but the fire had gone out. There was no sign that anyone would return there, since no gear had been left. When he scouted around the empty camp, he couldn't read through the dozens of coming and going boot tracks to determine which direction the person had gone when they'd finally departed. Silently, he prayed it wasn't someone cruel who'd continued east toward River Camp.

Though he was tempted to wait and hide to see who was out there, he had to get back to Gretchen and Joel. Thus, he walked away, leaving in God's hands the unknown person who'd survived the Lib-Org raid.

On his way back to the makeshift camp, his weariness set in, and it took him three hours to cover five miles. Gretchen was up and eager to know where he'd gone. Not wanting her to worry, he admitted he'd been scouting around, but Joel cast him a knowing glance as they prepared to depart.

Using tarps on which to pull the five wounded patients, the ride across the snow hardly disturbed them. They were conscious when the group started out, but not energetic enough to converse. Eric didn't recognize anyone among the wounded with whom he'd been inside the dome shelter. But their silence and downcast eyes spoke volumes. The four had been in the aggressors' camp, and that made them party to the horrors that had occurred.

Joel skidded one tarp across the snow, on which sat one-legged Alan, who held one of the wounded men. Eric pulled two men on another tarp, and Gretchen pulled the woman with the torso wound. They left the mounds of gear behind that Joel had collected from the demolished campsite and the dead. Someone could return for it later.

Their journey over several miles took the remainder of the day for the three able-bodied, since they stopped and rested often, avoiding strain that would cause them to sweat. During each break, Eric nonchalantly watched the trees and gaps in the forest to the north. On one occasion, Gretchen noticed.

"Who's out there?" she asked, following his gaze.

Before Eric could downplay her concern, Joel stepped closer.

"Whoever it is," Joel said, "they aren't a friend, or they would've approached us by now."

"Eric?" Gretchen looked worried. "What should we do?"

"Nothing. They don't want to be found out. It's a Lib-Org survivor or a survivor from the aggressors' camp. Either they'll approach or they won't."

"If it's someone from Commander Morris' command," Alan said from the ground, "they might try to kill me so I don't talk about the Lib-Org's command structure or plans."

"We won't let them kill you," Joel said with a sharp nod.

"Let's go," Eric said, breaking the theorizing about the unknown by picking up the corners of his tarp again. "Three Lodges is just ahead."

Eric continued to pray about the potential enemy behind them, but he was more concerned about the potential conflict in front of them. As they pulled their injured burdens into Three Lodges around sundown, the whole camp came out to greet them. But at the sight of the survivors from their most loathed enemies, everyone fell silent and stood facing the weary travelers. Panting from the toil, Eric glanced from Gretchen to Neil and then to the others.

"It's them," Doris said softly. Everyone knew what the woman meant.

Geoff took a step forward, but stopped, his face showing pain.

"What kind of people live in Three Lodges?" Eric asked as the shadows grew.

The fires behind the crowd of forty-eight popped and crackled. Andy pushed his way through the front of the crowd and stood watching with the rest.

"In a court of law," Neil said, "they'd be judged, Eric. And sentenced."

Several agreed, nodding. The sentiment grew.

"That's true." Eric browsed their faces. "But then again, so would all of us."

They fidgeted, the snow squeaking under their boots. Eric could see the old shame surface. He knew they were recalling how they were only alive because others had died in their place, people they themselves had chosen to die instead of their own families. No one was innocent.

"Well, what do we do with them now?" Neil asked.

"Your enemy was massacred by the Liberation Organization." Eric paused, realizing this was a decision they had to make themselves. "These people are wounded and in pain. They might even die, whether you decide to help them or not. I know that we are being tested right now, and in the days to come. What kind of followers of Jesus are we if He cared for His enemies, but we don't? What kind of gratitude toward God will we express by the way we treat men and women who once mistreated us?"

"It's not fair," a man in the back said, his voice breaking, "but we've agreed to trust God, Neil."

Neil nodded, and that seemed to be the signal for them all. Eric, Gretchen, and Joel stepped aside as the forty-eight carried the five wounded into camp.

"What happened?" Andy asked.

Runner's tail wagged against his leg. Gretchen linked her arm through Eric's.

"A miracle, I'd say." Eric put his other arm around Andy, pulling him closer. "A miracle just happened."

Conclusion, Book Four

A few months later, Eric and Gretchen were married on the first day of June, when puddles from melting snow still muddied the Wyoming wilderness. Early flowers from the meadows were abundant and plucked for the occasion. The ceremony took place in River Camp beside the swollen river, and a few old friends from Mastover, including Milton Pickford, returned to the forest for the celebration—or for the feast that followed.

Andy was Eric's best man, and Barb was Gretchen's maid of honor. Gretchen wanted her mother to be there, but when Sara heard that Hank was walking their daughter down the riverbank "aisle," she refused to relinquish her bitterness even for her daughter's special day. Hank and Sara had much to work out, about which Hank prayed often in private with Eric.

Joel brought in a trophy buck for the feast, and his wife, Lena, seemed to come out of her near-comatose existence a little bit for a slow dance with him next to the river. Hank played his harmonica while Runner barked and begged for a sliver of venison from any willing hand.

The slaughter of innocents and the shame of Three Lodges seemed like ancient history, but Eric felt there was still a pending threat. It remained a puzzle for him and the others who'd returned home to River Camp. Just who had survived the massacre of the Lib-Org raid? During some of his hunts in recent weeks, Eric had paused, sensing someone nearby watching, but he didn't notice any evidence that he was being stalked.

The morning after the wedding reception, Eric and Gretchen shouldered their packs and rifles for a week-long honeymoon up at the mountain cabin, ten miles to the east. Andy didn't like being left behind, but Joel promised to take the boy and Runner on a mountain lion hunt, so the seven-year-old relented.

The heavy winter snow had caved in one corner of Eric's cabin, but the newly married couple arrived early enough in the day to make simple repairs. Eric connected his wooden water pipes to the spring downhill, and in no time, the pond next to the grave sites nearby was rising to its previous level.

"Is it wrong to like it here more than in River Camp?" Gretchen asked as they lay beside one another in the cabin the next morning, sleeping in late. "It's away from the rest of the world. It's so peaceful, Eric."

"I don't think it's wrong to like this peacefulness." Eric felt the same way, but he wondered if God really wanted him to leave River Camp yet. Joel and Hank were quickly growing into strong Christian leaders, regardless that the fringes of their lives were still imperfect and unsettled. "We can pray about living up here, if you want. Andy will need his own addition, though. I can't picture him and Runner in here cuddling with us every morning."

Gretchen giggled.

The next day, Eric took a light pack and his rifle to scout the forest to the east, down to the highway. Gretchen opted to remain at the cabin to work on the garden, which was a patch of sprouting weeds.

On Eric's hike, he walked slowly, watching for sign that might tell if strangers had visited the mountain. He found only wild animal tracks and thick undergrowth that would hinder most casual adventurers from entering the forest.

At the highway, he chewed on dried meat as he waited for travelers, but no one came around the south bend near Andy's parents' old homestead, or around the northern ridge that hid Adderthorn from view.

Eric returned to the trees, but swung far south to approach the cabin from a different direction. Turkeys often roosted on the south slope of the mountain, and locating them now would save him some searching later.

He was midway up the mountain on a well-used deer trail when the wilderness air was pierced by an unnatural screech. Eric froze and shouldered his rifle. Some wild animals had seemed more aggressive since Pan-Day, as if the virus had altered their natural instinct to fear man. It was unnerving to think of a mutated creature from his nightmares this close to the cabin!

The screech had sounded something like a wild cat, but the sounds that followed were guttural, like a growling dog. The brush rustled as if two beasts were tangled in the undergrowth, fighting over a kill. Eric aimed his rifle at the disturbed saplings. Birds nearby chirped their aggravation at the disturbance. His finger remained on the trigger. He thought about running up to the cabin to get Gretchen for backup, but the creature might escape then, or attack him as he fled. There would be no sleeping in the cabin that night without knowing exactly what prowled out there in their woods.

Suddenly, a wild turkey escaped from the bushes and flew directly at Eric. The wings of the heavy bird beat loudly against the air as it sought altitude. By reflex, Eric aimed at the thick body, but he declined to pull the trigger as an instant thought directed his attention back to the dense woods. Something had scared the bird . . .

The turkey barely passed over his head, flapping noisily into the trees behind him. Then from the bushes arose a tattered and mangy horror. It screeched again and reached its gnarled talons for Eric's eyes. Eric understood he was merely in the path of this creature as it chased after the turkey, but he was about to be attacked regardless!

Without time to aim his barrel again, he swung the stock of his rifle at the animal, which stood as tall as him. Its mane was matted and greasy, smelling like a mildewed rug.

His rifle stock battered the thing on the side of its head, stunning it. Its size didn't seem as big as it had first appeared, as if its fur or skin gave it a thicker appearance. The creature tumbled sideways, tried to rise once, then lay still, staring at the sky with one visible eye.

Eric thought he'd killed it, but when he studied it from a few feet away, it blinked. The mud-streaked face was blotched with blood, whether from scratches from the bushes, or from the brawl with the turkey. In the one visible eye, Eric saw fear and confusion.

"It's okay." Eric backed away and set down his rifle, then approached empty-handed. "I'm not going to hurt you. I'm a friend. Can you understand me?"

He pushed a few bushes aside to see the limbs of the creature. It had human hands, with long nails like claws, darkened and stained from living like an animal. Its fur wasn't fur at all, but clothing, soiled and rotting, torn to the flesh in places. Its mane was actually matted blond hair, covering half its face. Eric reached out slowly.

"It's okay. You're safe. See?"

With his fingers, he brushed aside the creature's mangy bangs. Now he could see two blue eyes staring back at him, and he tried to connect what he saw with what he remembered. The eyes and face, even through the dirt and grime, were familiar, but the body was that of some wild animal. She'd lost much weight.

"Come on," he offered with an outstretched hand. "It's okay. It's me, Eric. Remember me? I'm your friend. Let me help you."

The creature hesitantly placed a grubby hand in his, and sat up.

"Eric?" the creature squeaked.

"Yeah." He smiled, and squeezed her hand warmly. "I always wondered what happened to my good friend."

The creature seemed to crumble in that instant, and become a human being once again. She fell into his arms and he held her as she desperately clung to him.

"I've got you." He patted her hair, plagued with beetles, pinecones, and twigs. "You're safe now."

She started to whimper, her face against his chest, then she sobbed loudly. It became a wail that upset the forest more than her screeches toward the turkey, but Eric held her through it all.

After some time, she settled into a peacefulness, and Eric thought she might have fallen asleep. Until she spoke again.

"How can you even touch me?" she asked.

"I'm not that squeamish about my friends." He held her at arm's length. Her tears left streaks down her muddy and scratched cheeks. "You're Wendy Sullivan, my friend."

"But I . . . betrayed you." Her gaze fell. "I wanted you to die. I told those people how to kill you, if they'd let me live."

Eric lifted her chin.

"That did hurt me, but I don't hate you. I have hoped for months that you were still alive, that it was you who'd survived the attack that day."

"Eric, I'm not worthy of this—of your forgiveness."

"That's okay. Forgiveness isn't based on your worthiness, Wendy. It's based on your need for it. None of us are worthy. That's why we all need God's free forgiveness once and for all."

"What will the others say?" She shook her head. "I can't face them. Are they mad at me?"

"Well, I think first they'll need to receive you back in their own way, and then they may have some questions for you."

"What questions?" She shrank back.

"For one, how are you going to hunt for River Camp again if a single turkey got the better of you?"

"Be serious, Eric Radner!" She feigned a pout.

"How about this: you're fifty miles east of where we last saw you. How did you survive the rest of winter and travel this far? Those are good questions. Where's your gear? Your camp?"

Wendy shook her head.

"I don't know." She looked down at her filthy hands and nails. "I think I lost my mind. I remember hiding a lot. And being really cold."

"Well, I've heard it said that we really don't find ourselves until we realize how lost we are."

"You always did make all that God stuff seem practical." She sighed. "Do you really think River Camp will have me back?"

"I think so, but you're miles away from River Camp."

"Really? Where are we?"

"You're actually interrupting my honeymoon at the mountain cabin I built years ago." Eric faked a frown. "Gretchen is going to be terribly disappointed when I bring home a house guest."

"Oh, Eric!" The older woman frowned and swatted at his arm. "How does Gretchen put up with you?"

She laughed as he pulled her to her feet. They started up the mountain together with Wendy leaning against him. He couldn't wait to bring Wendy back to his new wife, and he knew Gretchen would be as happy as he was to find her alive.

God had taught him much about forgiveness the past winter, and his heart was filled with thankfulness. The day had turned out to be a fine spring day. But he wasn't foolish enough to believe their hardships were over during America's last days.

###

~End of *STEADFAST Book Four*~

Bonus Chapter SF4

Who are the Wyoming invaders? What do they want? Follow this Bonus Chapter to discover behind-the-scenes intel on the bad guys!

~

Earlier that winter . . .

Commander Kelly Morris of the Liberation Organization skied down a small slope and onto the highway where they'd left the Humvees for his fifty-man invasion force. He fell against the lead Humvee and struggled with his ski boots to release himself from the cross-country skis. Once free, he waded through snow drifts that had accumulated halfway up the vehicle door in his absence.

He was alone, though injured. His shoulder wound was superficial, so it didn't hinder him from using both gloved hands to sweep away the snow from the Humvee door. With a groan from exertion, he opened the door and collapsed inside the cab. After losing his pack and rifle the day before in a mountain avalanche, he was surprised he'd made it back at all.

Still panting, and with some effort, he closed the door and rested his head against the back of the seat. Somehow, he was alive, but it had taken his own ruthlessness to remain that way. Privately, he believed his mission had failed. The camp his unit had attacked had fought back with beast-like ravenousness. Even outnumbered, the survivalists had chased Morris' troops into the woods as the Lib-Org had retreated. And Morris had seen no sign of Eric "Mad Man" Radner after they'd set the camp on fire.

But publicly, Morris had to return to his command as a hero. No one could know he'd left Private Hoyle to die from frostbite on day two. No one could know his army's best fighting men had been too exhausted to successfully implement a surprise attack. And no one could know he'd killed two more of his own men during the return trip, so he could eat their food rations.

He held up his arm and acknowledged the frozen blood on his white parka. Though he would boast about the wound as a battle trophy, the bullet hadn't come from an enemy, but from one of his own men, Lieutenant Tesh. The wounded soldier, once loyal, had shot at him after Morris had opted to leave him behind as well. Tesh had been shot in the calf—the wound too severe for the man to survive without medical care—so Morris had left him to die alone, to freeze to death in a merciless wilderness.

No one could know his sins, Morris told himself, and no one ever would know. The fifty soldiers he'd taken into the mountains had all died, he was certain. He would spin his failed campaign in such a way he'd become a legend of triumph and sacrifice. And he would recruit new troops in the spring, promising them such glory, with a vision of liberating America from moral rigidity and Christian absolutes. The people deserved to live free, to determine their own way, like he did. There was nothing wrong with that.

Morris dozed in the quiet Humvee, and when he woke completely, it was night. Gradually, his dilemma fully hit him. He was many miles up a deserted highway. Several feet of fresh snow trapped the vehicles in place. It was two hundred miles or more back to Southern Idaho to rejoin his army. Two hundred miles—on skis! With no pack or rifle. He'd need to search the vehicles for provisions, then set out. It would be a dreadful journey, possibly even deadly.

Before he realized he was weeping, he felt the tears rolling down the stubble on his cheeks. Hunting down Eric Radner had seemed more like an exercise in futility, as if forces Morris couldn't identify were working against him, mocking him. He wondered if Eric Radner's God, the God of the Christians, was real after all. Two hundred miles on skis in the dead of winter was close to impossible. He would need forces helping him, not working against him.

"I'm getting weak." Morris laughed at himself and dried his eyes. He'd spent six years fighting for America's liberty, away from gods and religion and moral demands. And now, in a desperate hour, he was praying to Someone? Never would he be that desperate again. Never! And to prove he didn't need Eric's God, Morris would continue to hunt down their kind. If he survived the winter, he would never give up his fight to liberate everyone, to make them as free as he was!

~End of Bonus Chapter SF4~

STEADFAST BOOK FIVE

America's Last Days

D.I. Telbat

Prologue, Book Five

Kelly Morris' stomach growled as he waited in the bushes beside the highway. The snow had melted, and spring had invaded southeastern Idaho with puddles and fluttering birds. And Kelly hated every bit of it. A wounded shoulder and the winter snow had hindered his return to his army wintering in Pocatello. Now, hunger and mud delayed his progress. He was only forty miles away from his men, his army, the Liberation Organization.

There was movement through the trees and up the highway. A lone man walked with a happy-go-lucky gait, perhaps as lighthearted as Kelly wished he were after a debilitating season. The traveler seemed to have no care in the world, and Kelly felt even more hatred toward the man. He hated weakness and unpreparedness, but this man's faults would be Kelly's deliverance! This wouldn't be the first traveler Kelly had ambushed for food. It was their own fault they were traveling alone and defenseless.

But this one was armed. As the man drew closer, Kelly contemplated how cautious he would need to be. Kelly's own strength was still returning and this approaching man was broader in the shoulder. But the man had a pack and a hunting rifle on a sling over his shoulder. As desperate as Kelly had become, there was nothing he wouldn't risk at this point for a full pack and a rifle.

The traveler's face was pale and his beard was patchy. But Kelly wondered if his own appearance looked even worse. Kelly's clothes were tattered, and he'd even eaten mice as he'd shivered through the last weeks of winter inside an abandoned Cadillac on a deserted roadside. The last twenty miles he'd hiked had taken him three days, so he knew he wasn't the strong marching soldier he'd once been. His men would probably barely recognize him once he reached Pocatello, but reach them he had to, for the Lib-Org's destiny was to unite America's survivors with his vision of freedom!

The traveler neared, close enough to talk to, but Kelly remained perfectly still. He had reinforced his blind in the thicket as close to the highway as he'd dared. Every advantage he could plot had been applied. After all, he'd been a general in the army for years—before and after the collapse of America. In his left fist, he held a rock. In his other, he clenched a thick tree branch as a club.

The instant the traveler passed Kelly was the moment Kelly chose to toss his rock over the man's head to the other side of the cracked pavement. The traveler's attention was briefly drawn to the opposite side of the road as Kelly sprang from his hiding place.

The traveler seemed to realize the trap before Kelly reached him, but by then, Kelly was close enough. He swung his club. The pale traveler crumbled onto the highway and lay still.

Kelly looked up suddenly at the sound of metal clanking against metal not far away—like a hammer striking a nail repeatedly, or two pots jangling against one another. Someone else was around the corner, coming up the highway!

He dropped his club and bowed over the unconscious traveler. The rifle and pack was all he needed. Without food, he wouldn't survive another day.

But the pack didn't have a buckle or clasp. It was tied in a knot at the front of the man's waist. Frantically, Kelly fumbled with the knot, then decided to cut it away. He drew a knife and sliced the strap. As he reached for the rifle, he glanced up, aware of movement and more jingling, now sounding like bells, from up the highway. A troop of horsemen and pack animals were walking toward him.

In panic, Kelly cried out as he tugged and wrestled with the rifle over the man's shoulder. Now he understood—he may have attacked a forward scout for a small convoy! If he couldn't get the rifle free and flee into the woods . . .

Two horsemen broke into a charge from up the road. The shod hooves sounded loud on the pavement. The men swung assault rifles off their shoulders and held them in one arm, clutching their reins in their other hands. Kelly abandoned his attempt to free the hunting rifle and grabbed up the pack. But the pack wasn't light, or he was too weak to easily carry it. He tumbled into the ditch, clutching the pack to his chest, and rolled to his knees.

The forest was just feet away. He tried to rise to walk, but the pack was too heavy. A horseman thundered past him and knocked him sprawling into the weeds. He lost his hold on the pack and he came to rest in a mud puddle at the bottom of the ditch. While staring up at the sky, he cursed his luck. First, he'd been wounded during the raid into Wyoming to crush Eric Radner's Christian resistance, and now he was too weak to fight off these scoundrels. If these horsemen only knew who he was!

After a moment, he caught his breath and sat up to see two bearded horsemen standing over him. These were hardened men, tough and fierce, nothing like the traveler he'd just attacked. Even their mounts appeared well-fed and powerful.

"He did us a favor by attacking that other guy," one with red hair said to his friend. "Two for one."

"What's going on?" a voice boomed from the highway. "Chain him up and let's keep moving. I want to get into Wyoming while it's still spring."

Kelly turned his head to acknowledge a heavy-set, bearded man on horseback. The brute wore a wool sweater that seemed to add to his already muscled arms and shoulders. A revolver was strapped to his belt and a black metal baton hung from his wrist on a tether.

The two men in the ditch with Kelly leapt from their mounts and easily wrestled his arms together. As one held his arms, the other shackled his wrists with chains. Suddenly, Kelly understood the sound he'd heard earlier. It hadn't been tools or cookware jangling—it had been chains!

Before he could rise to his feet himself, they hoisted him upright and dragged him onto the road. Twelve other men stood chained in a line beside another line of nine women. Kelly stood bewildered as he was added to the rear of the procession. Slavers!

The pale traveler on the highway was jostled awake, and he was also shackled, then added to a length of chain behind Kelly.

"Please!" the pale man pleaded. His scalp was bleeding from where Kelly had struck him. "I have to get to my family in—"

One of the slavers belted the man on the side of the head.

"Shut up and do what you're told!"

"Let's move out!" the man in the sweater ordered.

An instant later, Kelly was yanked forward by his wrists. His shackles cut into his skin and he thought about resisting the forward momentum, but there was no resisting. If he resisted, he would only be pulling against the men in front of him, and the front of the chain was anchored to the pack of a mule. A second pack mule led the women's length of prisoners.

"What's happening?" the man behind Kelly cried. "My supplies!"

"Shut up!" Kelly hissed, despising the man's weakness.

As they pulled away from the area where Kelly had so carefully staged his ambush, the two horsemen cut back to pick up the pale traveler's pack, then rummaged through it, searching for anything useful to them.

Two more gunmen and a man with a blue scarf rode at the front of the caravan—Kelly summed up six men on horseback, and twenty-three prisoners, including himself.

He'd been shanghaied, he understood, just for being vulnerable. They didn't know who he was, yet, but Kelly bitterly began to contemplate what might lie ahead. He wanted to go west, back to his command, but they were heading east, into Wyoming from where he'd fled. People to the east might recognize him, and then being a mere prisoner would be the least of his worries. People would try to kill him, and he had no way to defend himself.

No one would show him mercy, he knew, once they found out his true identity. He'd been a powerful force across the country, and sometimes power needed to show itself in merciless ways. Yes, he'd massacred thousands during the last seven years, campaigning across America from his base in Atlanta. No one would understand that his methods had been for the good of a new nation, that people who didn't conform needed to be sacrificed. Men, women, and children had even been burned at the stake for resisting his prescribed liberality, but it had been necessary in order to rebuild the country.

For now, he would need to keep silent. Somehow, he would get free, or get a message to his Lib-Org forces in Pocatello, if they were still there. They would rescue him, and then he would punish the men who dared to take advantage of him in a moment of weakness. He would teach them who he really was—but not yet. For now, somehow, even with barely enough strength to walk, he needed to survive.

Vengeance would come later . . .

"Be sober, be vigilant; because your adversary the devil walks about like a roaring lion, seeking whom he may devour. Resist him, steadfast in the faith, knowing that the same sufferings are experienced by your brotherhood in the world." 1 Peter 5:8-9 (NKJV)

Chapter 1, Book Five

Eric Radner saw them coming from a great distance. Even though he was far away, gazing through his binoculars, he felt the misery of the men and women in chains, led by horsemen through the plains of eastern Wyoming.

Dropping his binoculars to hang around his neck, he glanced north and south. There was nowhere for him to hide. His afternoon of scouting the range for sign of antelope that spring day had left him exposed on the rolling, grassy range. The mountains of River Camp were visible to the southwest, but it would take two hours of fast walking to reach them.

He noticed two horsemen separate from the rear of the detail and trot their mounts toward him. Eric inhaled deeply, mindful of all that God had preserved him through during the last seven years since Pan-Day. Though he was alone on the plains that day, he wasn't alone. God was there, watching, aware, and able to direct events even then.

As the two horsemen drew nearer, Eric prayed for the right words to say to them. He'd often spoken to travelers coming or going on the highway below his mountain camp, but this caravan wasn't made up of mere travelers. The prisoners' chains could be heard jingling even at a distance, as if announcing their suffering in the otherwise silence they endured.

With no sudden or alarming movements, Eric slid his rifle off his shoulder and cradled it in his right arm. He would never shoot another human being, and he only carried the bolt action hunting rifle, but even the presence of a firearm had deterred violence in the past. As the horsemen slowed to a walk, he squared his shoulders and stood with his feet planted apart. Men of violence and caution, as these men seemed to be, would recognize the readiness in him, and he hoped they would think twice about harming him. His lovely wife and their seven-year-old son waited for him at River Camp. Dying now seemed a most upsetting prospect!

The two stopped their horses. Their wide positioning spoke volumes of aggression to Eric, as did the assault rifles on their backs and the lengths of chains and shackles hanging off their saddles. Behind them, the caravan of other horsemen and chained prisoners approached, but Eric steadied his gaze first at one horseman in front of him, then at the other, a redheaded, bearded man.

"What're you doing out here all alone?" the redhead asked, then glanced at the nearby hills.

"Who says I'm alone?" Eric cocked his head. "We haven't seen you guys in this area before. We would've noticed. Headed east, huh?"

His intentional usage of the word "we" had a visible effect on their edginess. These men were vultures, preying on weaker travelers. But the threat of nearby company made them nervous.

"We're traveling through." The redhead's eyes lingered on Eric's rifle. "Out hunting? Any game around?"

"Not an antelope track for miles." Eric realized once the rest of the caravan caught up to them, he'd be outnumbered six to one, since there were four more horsemen riding in front of and alongside the prisoners. "We had a good winter, but we're always on the hunt for more game. You understand."

"Sure." The redhead turned in his saddle as the caravan stopped next to them. He addressed a sizeable man in a thick sweater. "He's hunting out here. Says he's not alone."

The man in the sweater took a long draw from a canteen, then eyed Eric with suspicion.

"That's what they all say."

A moment of silence passed between them. Eric felt anything but comfort. They were apparently deciding if he was really alone or not. And as they studied him, Eric studied them. The pack mules were sturdy animals, and their packs were weathered but full. Their clothes were faded but in good condition, and every man had a sidearm and a rifle, except a balding man who wore a blue scarf and seemed to ignore Eric altogether.

Then Eric's eyes strayed to the prisoners who swayed on their feet, certain to be thankful for the rest. Three feet of chain between each prisoner separated fourteen men in rags, with ripped pants, and raw skin showing where they'd fallen and had been dragged. There were ten women on the other side of the men. They had ratted hair and downcast, dirty faces.

"Criminals, all of them," the man in the sweater said, smiling at Eric. "Are you in the market for a working man, or maybe a woman to keep you warm at night? Or to cook your meals?"

Eric walked slowly behind the two men who'd reached him first, careful not to turn his back to them, and approached the prisoners for a closer look.

"I wasn't aware there was any law in the region." Eric did his best not to grimace at the condition of the captives. Several of them were thin, appearing half-alive with empty eyes. Such suffering! "Criminals, you say?"

"Thieves, murderers, indentured servants. They're mine to sell for a price."

Moving down the line, Eric realized the slavers would've added him to the length of chain if he hadn't appeared a threat with his rifle.

"What kind of price?"

"Guns, horses, meat." The head man scratched his brow with a metal baton. "Where's your camp?"

"It's a whole settlement of hunters," Eric said, "and it's not far away. As you see, I'm not carrying a pack for a night out here."

"Of course." The leader's voice sounded disappointed, as if his final hope to take Eric prisoner was dashed. "Trade me that rifle, and you can have your pick of the men."

Eric came to the last two men on the chain. He had to fight the urge to step back in shock as he recognized the second to the last man. It was Commander Kelly Morris, the slaughterer of innocents and persecutor of Christians! Kelly's face was drawn and unshaven. The man turned away from Eric, but Eric had seen him well enough. The last time they'd met, Kelly had tried to burn Eric alive in front of the citizens of Mastover! By the look of the general, he'd been on the chain for days, maybe even weeks.

"What would the Liberation Organization say about your train of slaves here?" Eric tested. "You came through their territory, didn't you?"

Everything in his soul screamed for him to say something, do something. They didn't know who they had on the chain!

"The Lib-Org?" the leader asked with a grunt. "You haven't heard? It dissolved over the winter. Most of its fighting force joined the Pacific States, led by President Criswell out of San Diego. The Lib-Org is no more. Nobody cares what we're doing. Do you see something you want, or are we wasting what remains of this daylight?"

Kelly turned his face back toward Eric, and any sympathy Eric felt for the bound man disappeared. The general's eyes were glaring and hateful, challenging or begging—Eric couldn't tell. All that flashed before Eric's memory were the reports of thousands being butchered by this very man. Just that winter, dozens had died in the mountains by his hand. This monster was getting what he deserved!

"No, I see nothing here that I want. Sorry to keep you."

Eric backed away.

The man in the sweater kicked his mount hard, jerking the caravan and pack horses forward. Kelly's mouth curled in a snarl as he was forced after the others. He pivoted his head and watched Eric as long as their eyes could see one another. Eric felt the man's hatred, and Eric hoped the murderer thought long and hard about this turn of events. Kelly was finally reaping what he'd sown.

"Next time, antelope hunter," the redhead said as his horse pranced in front of Eric, "maybe we'll get to know each other more intimately."

The man patted a length of chain and shackles hanging in front of his knee from his saddle horn. Then he and his partner laughed and charged their horses after the caravan of condemned souls.

Eric exhaled with relief as they disappeared over the next hilltop. The Lib-Org was no more! It was news he hadn't even picked up on the mountaintop radio yet, if it were even true. River Camp would be happy to hear the Lib-Org forces had finally been dissolved. And no wonder, if their commander was in chains!

Frowning at the horizon, Eric felt the shame of his interaction with the slavers. He hadn't actually protested the condition of the prisoners, and he'd offered no comfort or hope to the captives. River Camp didn't have many rifles, but Mastover had a whole armory at the courthouse, enough firearms to trade and free everyone in those chains.

But no one would be interested in freeing Kelly Morris. The Lib-Org commander was gone. That was all that mattered to the people of Wyoming. In a few days, the slavers would be out of Wyoming, and Eric would think nothing more of the incident. After all, he'd seen humanity treated worse just that very winter. It was none of his business to do anything more but pity a bunch of criminals.

However, as he started walking toward the mountains, his gut told him the captives weren't actually criminals. The head man and the redhead had been eager to put even him in chains—if they'd been more certain he were alone on the range, and if they could disarm him. Of course, the others had certainly been kidnapped as well when they'd been found alone fetching firewood or traveling unprotected.

The shame grew as Eric drew closer to River Camp, but he pushed it away. Commander Kelly Morris was out of his life forever. That was all that mattered.

As he walked into the settlement beside the river after dark, he realized that he hadn't spoken to God since the slave caravan had pulled away hours earlier. He hadn't even prayed to thank the Lord for keeping him safe from the slavers' intentions. But he pushed all these thoughts away. River Camp was safe. That was his only responsibility, he told himself. The starving, abused captives in chains were long gone now. There was nothing he could do for them.

In camp, he sat on a log and listened to Andy's report of his own adventures that day. His son was certain he and the other youths had found an abandoned gold mine. After seeing the boy to bed, he hugged his wife, Gretchen. He hoped his family never found out about the suffering people he'd ignored to avoid any conflicts. The word cowardice came to his mind, but he swallowed his self-condemnation and held his head up.

Chapter 2

"She's getting worse, Eric. You have to get her to the doctor in Mastover."

Eric moved up beside Barb, his wife's nurse for two days, and felt Gretchen's clammy forehead. She had moaned through the night as her fever continued.

"It's got to be appendicitis." He sat on the edge of the bed in their cabin in River Camp. "Gretchen, can you hear me? We need to take you into town."

"I'll saddle up two horses," Hank Worcester said, and he moved toward the door. "She'll just have to make the trip."

Eric left his wife's side and held the door open for Hank, Gretchen's father.

"Try fixing a stretcher between the two horses, suspended front to back. She'll never stay in the saddle in her condition, and a travois would be too rough."

"A stretcher? Show me."

Together, the two men left Barb with Gretchen and walked to the corral at the end of the row of cabins.

It had been two days since Eric had returned from the plains. Two miserable days of moping about in shame, telling no one that Kelly Morris was a prisoner of a gang of slaves on their way to Nebraska. When he'd shared the news about the Lib-Org dissolving to join the Pacific States, he'd told Hank, Joel Grayport, and Wendy Sullivan that he'd learned of it from the radio up at his cabin. The lie, to cover his inaction over the slaves, gnawed at him, grew inside him, and brought upon him more shame. He felt he could share the shame with no one, especially since they all looked up to him as a Christian leader.

At the corral, under the afternoon's overcast sky, the two men fashioned a stretcher between poles extended from one horse's flanks back to the breast of the second horse. The second horse's head would hang over Gretchen, but the suspended bed would travel much more comfortably than a sled or saddle.

Eric shook Andy's hand, and left his son in Hank's charge. The boy was almost eight years old. Looking at the boy that evening, Eric knew Andy would be ashamed that his father hadn't helped the slaves. Still, Eric kept his secret to himself. Kelly Morris deserved to suffer, he told himself. The captives couldn't be helped.

Joel returned with Wendy from a fruitless hunt and heard the news of Gretchen's worsening condition.

"I'm going, too," Joel said, his bow still in his hand. "I haven't seen Dad all winter. The two of us need to catch up."

"I'd be glad to have you, Joel," Eric said, slapping him on the shoulder. He knew Joel's father, Judge Zachary Grayport, one of the leaders of Mastover, would be glad to see his son, too. "We might be a week or two if she needs surgery."

"Well, someone better come back in a day or two!" Hank glowered. He'd grown more sentimental since coming to Christ, and more insecure since his wife had left him to live in Mastover. "I won't know what's going on with my daughter unless someone returns. Don't leave me in the dark, Eric!"

Gretchen didn't wake as they lay her in the sling and started up the ten-mile trail to town. Eric rode the lead horse, and as darkness closed, he felt the urge to pray for his wife's desperate condition, but he sensed no closeness to God right then. And how could he, he reasoned, since he'd turned his back on the chained captives? And God had turned His back on him, it seemed. Even his wife was on her deathbed. The miraculous hand of God through the winter, involving Three Lodges, seemed a distant memory. Circumstances had changed drastically and suddenly.

By midnight, after dwelling on the lack of antelope, the illness of his wife, and the burdens Eric felt from River Camp, a tinge of bitterness toward God had set in. His mood became sour as he and Joel crossed the swinging footbridge over the river into Mastover. Joel seemed to sense that something more was amiss with Eric than just his wife's illness, and he asked his friend about it, but Eric insisted things were fine, that he was just tired.

The town's Eternal Hope Hospital had been moderately staffed with one doctor from Colorado and three nurses. Medicine was scarce, and though power had been restored for some machines to function, the doctor used a flashlight to examine Gretchen in the early morning darkness in an empty waiting room.

"Yes, it seems to be appendicitis," the doctor agreed. "If it has burst, she's in a lot of trouble. I need to operate, and you can pray we find it intact."

"Pray?" Eric felt guilt resurface. "Right."

"You're the praying Mad Man from River Camp, aren't you?" The doctor wheeled Gretchen away with a nurse. "So, pray!"

"Come over to the house." Joel moved to his side. "I'm sure Dad would like to see you, too. I bet he has a list of Bible questions a mile long for you. Ever since you got him reading the Bible last fall, he's been so—"

"No, I'm staying here." Eric sat on the cold floor and leaned against the wall. "I need to be here for Gretchen."

"Okay." Joel lingered, standing over him. "Well, try to get some sleep. You're not yourself. Some sleep would help you."

Eric wanted to tell his friend that his mood had nothing to do with Gretchen's condition or even the lack of sleep, but Joel left without another comment. A moment later, Eric heard the horse's hooves trotting away on the pavement.

Toward dawn, Eric's head bowed, his chin resting on his chest, and he slept restlessly. He was startled awake when the hospital's front door opened. He hopped to his feet to greet Judge Zachary Grayport.

"Look at you!" Grayport frowned as he shook Eric's hand. The man had an oversized nose between bushy, graying eyebrows. "You look as gloomy as yesterday's storm clouds. Any word on your wife?"

"None. The doc's been in there for hours."

"He's the best anyone has for hundreds of miles around. We bribed him with all the amenities of Mastover just to keep him from traveling on. He's saved the lives of many others. Gretchen will pull through. She's tougher than both of us, right?"

Together, the two slid down the wall to sit and wait. Eric recognized the special moment they were sharing—two old enemies God had brought together through the pressures of strife. But instead of rejoicing in God's goodness and sovereign hand, Eric focused on how depressed he would become if he lost Gretchen. Three days ago, she'd been fine. Why now?

Eric was happy to see the judge, and if his shame hadn't been smothering him, he could've spoken plainly with the older man. But instead, the two sat in silence, and Eric's eyelids succumbed to heaviness once again until the judge spoke sometime later.

"I must admit to you," Grayport mumbled, "that I haven't been the best leader of Mastover lately, not as good as I wish I could be."

"To be honest," Eric sighed loudly, "I could say the same about myself and River Camp."

"The town has changed. It's clean, productive, and downright neighborly. Why, half the folks are even having weekly Bible studies, thanks to all the River Camp people who returned to live here." The judge paused. "But I've been staying separate from them all, reading that old Bible you left to me last year. I don't know what to make of it."

"You don't understand it?" Eric didn't feel very qualified to help anyone else with a spiritual need, since he was so burdened with guilt of his own, but he hadn't forgotten what he knew to be true. "God can help you with that."

"I have trouble believing that, even though I've seen God break down some barriers the last couple years." Grayport looked at the door, as if he were thinking about leaving, but then he continued. "A few days ago, some slavers came up to Mastover on the highway. Our border security called me out to talk to them. But I did nothing. I just sent them on their way."

Eric barely breathed. This conversation was God ordained, he understood now, meant to teach them both a profound lesson. They'd both done nothing!

"I saw them, too." Eric felt tears clouding his eyes at the memory of the captives' condition—their scabbed skin, their soiled and torn clothing, their looks of lost hope. "And I spoke to them."

"You did? I wouldn't even let them into town. They said they were from California, passing through. What happened with you?"

"Nothing." Eric shook his head, his teeth clenched. "Nothing at all. I just let them go, too."

Eric put his fist to his mouth as he choked through a sob. Admitting his weakness and sin was painful, but a relief as well.

"Oh." The judge was quiet as Eric recovered. "Doing nothing isn't like you, Eric. The people expect it from me, but not from you."

"It's worse than that." Eric took a deep breath. "What if your worst enemy was suffering and needed your help, but you kept your mouth shut and let him go on his way?"

"Well, from what I've learned from you, God supposedly orchestrates those moments to reconcile people, so we're not supposed to keep our mouths shut. It's why you and I are sitting together right now. You never did shut up. You always made yourself a thorn in my side!"

Eric chuckled, fresh joy rising in his heart as his faith was being restored. He knew what he had to do.

"I walked down the line of those slaves," Eric said, "and I recognized one of them, and I wanted him to suffer for what he's caused this country. That's why I walked away. I was like Jonah, refusing to help the Ninevites, when God had clearly opened the door for me to help this enemy. I've been in the belly of the fish since then, Zach—angry that I was such a coward, hating myself for doing nothing, even angry at God for putting me in this situation."

"Who was the enemy?" The judge faced him. "I didn't get a good look at the prisoners. I just talked to the slavers, then sent them around the town to the north."

"It was Commander Morris. They had Kelly Morris, Zach. He was in chains, the second to the last man."

"Morris!" The judge climbed to his feet and threw his hands in the air. "Commander Morris? The butcher of the Lib-Org? I killed people for that man! If his own troops sold him into slavery, then good riddance! You did the right thing, Eric! We both did the right thing. We can keep this quiet. That dog deserves one thousand lives of slavery and chains for what he's done."

"I'm not so sure, Judge." Eric winced as he climbed from the cold floor to his feet. "Now that we're talking this out, it makes me wonder if this is God's way of bringing Kelly to Christ. That would be something, wouldn't it?"

"He's killed babies, Eric!" Grayport turned away, wringing his hands. "This isn't a moment for intervention. This is a moment for celebration! The Lib-Org's got to be in shambles because of this."

"They are. The lead slaver, the one in the sweater, said the Lib-Org has merged with the Pacific States, that government out of San Diego we've been hearing about over the wire."

"Then, see?" The judge laughed. "Everything is as it should be. The Lib-Org is finished. That's the real miracle in all of this! Forget your so-called Christian responsibility for a minute. We've won something here. We've all won something!"

"And we just condemn those other captives, all because we don't want to help Kelly Morris?"

"You make it sound like we can still help him." Grayport growled under his breath. "No, they're long-gone, probably in Nebraska by now, deep in the Plains Zone. He tried to kill you, Eric. More than once! It's time to let this one go."

"You tried to kill me more than once as well, and look at us now." Eric smiled, sensing strength surging into his inner man. "I could catch them if I'm on horseback. They weren't traveling very fast with so many in chains."

"Insanity. Pure insanity, when you get like this." The judge crossed his arms and turned his back to Eric. "You're already working it all out, aren't you? You are still the Mad Man from the mountains. Insanity!"

"Yeah, I guess that's me." Eric took a step toward the man. "Alan Tesh is still here, right? He's been out east. He'll know what to expect, riding into the Plains Zone."

"But you can't take Alan Tesh." Grayport put his hands on his hips and eyed Eric. "Tesh has only one leg, Eric. Think, man! Do you know how he lost that leg?"

"He told me. Kelly shot him, and then Alan shot Kelly. Can you give me a couple extra horses? And maybe spare some medicine for the captives and a few supplies?"

"And an army? Those slavers were heavily armed. You'll need at least ten Mastover men, and Joel will probably want to help you with this mess, too."

"No." Eric frowned, sensing the mission of mercy before him. "Just me and Alan Tesh. Two horses apiece and a pack horse. That'll do."

"Pure insanity."

"If there's a chance that we can bring Kelly Morris to repentance, it'll all be worth it."

"I'm leaning toward despising you right now." The judge's voice softened. "Wyoming can't lose you, Eric. Forget your forgiveness and grace this once. I beg you! It could cost you everything."

"Believe me, I don't want to die, but if I would've done what was right—anything to make a difference a few days ago—we wouldn't be having this conversation. Kelly Morris is no more or less deserving of God's grace than you or me. I need to set this right, or try, at least. If all goes well, we'll rescue the rest of those slaves, too."

"And you'll bring them back here? What about Kelly Morris? The people will kill him. He won't be welcome anywhere. Eric, I don't want him here. I wouldn't trust him."

"We're a long ways from figuring all that out, Zach, but God will direct us with that, too."

The inner door to the hospital hallway swung open, and the doctor emerged. He slid off his surgical mask and rubbed his eyes.

"She'll be okay. We got it in time. She needs to heal, but she'll be moving around in a few days."

"Thanks, Doc." Eric embraced the surgeon, and clapped him heartily on the back. He then turned to Grayport. "Judge, I want to be on my way before noon. Can Gretchen stay with you and Joel until Alan and I get back? Once she's able to leave the hospital?"

"Sure, sure, it might do me some good to have a Radner under my roof for a few days. I could use the company. Just don't leave me with a widow on my hands, or I'm liable to regret I let you leave on this fool's errand at all!"

Eric shook the judge's hand, then slipped down the hall to see his wife.

Chapter 3

"I don't want to worry you, but I couldn't leave without telling you myself where I've gone."

Eric bit the inside of his cheek as he waited for Gretchen to respond. When she'd woken from her anesthesia, Eric had immediately told her his plans to go after Commander Morris. Her face showed she was still physically uncomfortable from her appendectomy, and now Eric was placing even more upon her weary heart. In the quiet ward, Gretchen seemed to study the ceiling for answers. Her red hair was loose and needed a wash, but Eric still thought she was beautiful—and that he must indeed be insane to leave her to search for the slaves.

"You mean you're telling me this," she said, "just in case you don't come back."

"It's a possibility." He squeezed her hand. "But I'm not blindly doing what God would have me to do. I know there are risks whenever we're obedient."

"But you were disobedient, you said."

"I was, but now, I'm righting that wrong. Those slaves need to be freed. I'm certain they were kidnapped, and Kelly Morris was picked up somewhere along the way, captured or sold out by his own people. God has set it all up, I believe, for us to respond."

"You owe that man nothing." She sighed loudly. "But I understand. He recognized you a few days ago. You can't let him die thinking that Christians abandon anyone, even him. Christ wouldn't abandon him."

"So, you do understand. I have to try, even if I fail. The judge even let me pack a little medicine to use for the slaves, once I catch up to them."

"I need to go with you. You'll need another gun-hand to watch your back, like I've had to do before."

"No, the doctor said it'll be a few days before you're able to move around much. And Alan and I will be riding hard as it is to catch the slavers before they get too far east."

"Alan—but you hardly know him."

"I know he's a Christian now. I'd say that's enough to know about him for a mission like this."

"Does he know he's doing this for Kelly Morris? He may not want to go."

"I haven't spoken to him about it, but the judge sent for him and arranged supplies. Alan will want to go for the same reason I want him to go."

"Which is? To die?"

"No, to reconcile Kelly to Christ, and then reconcile him with those of us he made his enemies. I think God will use me and Alan."

Gretchen touched his bearded cheek, and tears filled her eyes.

"You have such a good heart, Eric, much better than the rest of us."

"No, what I'm doing now is the opposite of what my flesh really wanted to do. Without God, I would abandon Kelly and those slaves to save my own skin. But with God, I believe we can do something meaningful for the slavers, for the slaves, and for Kelly."

"They won't be expecting you, that's for sure." She dried her eyes. "Okay, then, I'll heal up here. But if you're not back in ten days, I'm putting together a search party, and Joel and I are coming after you!"

"Fair enough." He chuckled. "Just make sure those stitches are out first. Wouldn't want them getting caught on any sagebrush while you're riding a tornado, coming to get me!"

"Oh! Don't make me laugh." She held her side. "Are you trying to injure me further? Just go. I know God. I've seen Him work enough to know you're in good hands, even though they're not my hands."

"Thanks, hon." He kissed her. "And don't let the judge push you around."

"Are you kidding? If I'm staying at his mansion, I'm going to milk my condition for all it's worth. I'll have him running errands for me every hour."

"That's my girl!"

#######

When Eric stepped outside the hospital, Alan Tesh sat on a riding horse waiting for him. He was leading three other horses and a tall mule with two full pack boxes straddling his spine.

"You got the invitation!" Eric said with a grin. He caught the reins to one horse as Alan tossed them to him. "That was quick."

"One-legged men aren't much use around here, so if someone's inviting me somewhere to do something, I'm going to jump on it—even if it's to where no one should be riding a horse!"

"Meaning?" Eric asked as he swung onto his mount.

"Meaning, I know what nightmare is out there in the Plains Zone. The Lib-Org stayed in our vehicles when we raided through Iowa and Nebraska because we had to. Any other way, we would've been killed."

"By the local resistance fighters?"

"No. People weren't our problem. No local militia ever successfully stood up to us until we reached Wyoming. No, I'm not talking about people keeping us in our vehicles, even at night. It was dogs. Thousands of them; maybe millions. Families let their dogs loose around Pan-Day. Couldn't feed them, so they just let them go. Cities like Chicago, Des Moines, Kansas City, Springfield—they all let go of hundreds of thousands of dogs. They've gone feral now, whole packs of them. Please tell me we're not going that far east!"

"I'm afraid we are—at least to central or eastern Nebraska."

"What for? The judge wouldn't say. He acted like it was some secret." They put their heels to their horses and headed down the street. Alan held onto the lead rope to the string of spare mounts and the pack mule. "All he said was that you needed me since I've been out there before."

Eric told him about the slaves, their condition, and the six gunmen with them. But he didn't mention Kelly Morris.

"We'll need a plan," Alan said after thinking about it for a minute. They reached the edge of town where a pit had been dug to dispose of garbage. They skirted the pit and rode out onto the range where the spring grass was already knee-high on the horses. "Regardless of God's provision, we'll need a good plan if it's just the two of us trying to free all those captives."

"The slavers are careful not to cross anyone who has a gun." Eric rode beside Alan. "No offense, but with only one leg, you're of no value to them, and since we both have weapons, they'll likely not risk trying to capture either of us. By God's grace, we'll find a way to get the prisoners free and bring them back to Mastover—if that's what they want."

"And we do all this without getting killed by mangy dogs and their half-wolf offspring?" Alan scoffed. "You have more faith than me."

"And bullets." Eric patted his rifle scabbard by his right knee. "Lots of bullets, if need be."

At the mention, Alan slid his own rifle out. Unlike Eric's bolt action deer rifle with open sights, Alan's weapon was an assault rifle with a scope and a short banana clip of .223 cartridges, the same rounds as Eric used.

By nightfall, they'd ridden farther onto the plain than Eric had ever hiked to hunt for antelope. Throughout the evening, Alan shared what little he knew about dealing with the dogs, and made suggestions for protecting the horses. The lack of antelope certainly confirmed the danger on the range.

"Camping out in the open will be too dangerous after tonight," Alan said. "We'll need to stay in barns or houses each night, and the horses will need to be inside with us, or we'll lose them. In Mongolia, ponies are turned loose to protect themselves from wolves, but I think these horses are too domesticated and skittish to survive a pack of dogs."

They made camp that first night in a low wash they could defend in two directions. Alan slid off his mount and drew out a pair of crutches to hobble about. Eric dug with an entrenching shovel for water before he unpacked the mule, and then collected firewood.

"The doc has some ideas for a prosthetic." Sitting near the heat of the fire, Alan rolled up his empty pant leg to expose his stump. "It feels like it's still there, like I can almost wiggle my toes and everything. Interesting what God will do to a man to humble him and get his attention."

Eric admired the ex-soldier from across the fire. Alan's cool gray eyes seemed to smile as he reminisced on the years when he'd once marched for the most ruthless military force since Pan-Day. But God had brought him low by allowing him to get shot, and Joel had amputated the lieutenant's leg to save his life that winter. There was no regret in Alan's voice, but rather fascination that God had moved so much to draw him from a life of bloodshed and ignorance. Though Eric believed Alan was ready to confront Kelly Morris, he still said nothing of the man being held as a prisoner.

As the fire crackled, they prayed together for God's guidance, for the souls of the slavers, and for the slaves themselves. Alan made some requests of God about the vicious dogs they were about to face as well—that God would drive them to the north, or perhaps cause them to die of starvation before the two of them had to face their wild fierceness.

The next morning, they were in the saddle before dawn, following the trail east that had been left by the slavers on horseback and the prisoners in chains. Eric didn't feel talkative as he rode beside Alan. Although Eric was once again moving in the will of God and not in animosity, his spirit was still unsettled from the few prayerless days he'd spent in gloom. As such, his inner man sensed the lack of ability to clearly perceive God's direction. How terrible, he thought shamefully, that his few days of selfishness had derailed his discernment so significantly!

Thus, when they stopped at noon to change mounts, Eric wasn't surprised that Alan was the one to clear his throat and offer the first insight for their situation.

"I think one of us needs to join the slavers." Alan slid off his horse and stood on his one leg while Eric moved the saddles to the spare horses. "With one of us in their company, traveling with them, and one of us on the outside, we'll have a better chance at success. We need to gather intel, like the spies going into Canaan. Wars are won from gathering intel."

"I didn't bring you along so we could split up," Eric said as they swung into their saddles once again, and started off. "We're gaining on them quickly. I'd say we're only two days behind them now."

But through the afternoon, Eric mulled over Alan's suggestion, and could fathom no other approach to the slavers. The safety of the prisoners needed to be considered as well. A covert action was a good idea, and Eric couldn't imagine another angle for two men to recover twenty-some prisoners from six armed men. Having inside intel on the slavers' party was reasonable, even though daring. Yes, infiltration was the best idea they had so far.

"If I join them," Eric said, "you'll be on your own."

"I can manage with one leg." Alan placed a hand on the crutches. "I'll just move slower with the horses, but if you signal, I'll be ready to help. The slavers probably won't go peacefully, you know. The prisoners are their livelihood."

"I'll have to gain their trust," Eric said, "then get their guns in the night somehow. Joining them with ulterior motives is a good route for us to trust God to work out the details. Or, if I need to, I can simply ride away from them."

"Tomorrow morning, then, you should distance yourself from me. Pack up and ride ahead to overtake them. Hopefully, they don't shoot you or capture you on sight."

"It could happen." Eric nodded thoughtfully. "I'll do some posturing, to make them think I'm like-minded with them."

"You? Like-minded?" Alan chuckled. "Just the thought of you pretending to be like-minded with these kinds of people doesn't sit well with me. You're anything but their kind. You'll need to be real convincing."

That night, they made camp inside a partially-demolished cabin. The horses grazed nearby, but Eric was ready to move their mounts indoors at the first hint of alarm. He packed a bundle of medicine and supplies to place behind his saddle the next morning, to look as if he were traveling alone. Finally, he stuffed his Bible into Alan's belongings.

"Your wife wouldn't be happy that I'm volunteering you to sacrifice yourself like this." Alan frowned at Eric over the fire. "I know some of the stories about you and Mastover, not to mention what you did with those cannibals over the winter. You're always throwing yourself into harm's way."

"We can't help others without making ourselves vulnerable." Eric gazed up at the star-filled sky. "There's something strangely powerful about being willing to give up yourself like that. It's what Christ did, of course, and that kind of love never fails to accomplish something important, something meaningful."

"Well, you'll need some of that kind of power real soon. If this works, it'll be one for the Eric Radner Chronicles."

"The Alan and Eric Adventures." Eric laughed, then felt a seriousness wash over him. He wondered if it was time to tell Alan that his old commander was one of the prisoners. Then, he realized it didn't matter that Alan didn't know about Kelly Morris. Alan was a Christ-follower now, and Eric guessed even if Kelly was the reason Alan had lost his leg, God's compassion would win out in the end. It was best that Alan face that on his own, when the time was right.

At dawn, Eric saddled a single horse and shook Alan's hand.

"Not much about this is real reasonable," Alan said, "at least not as far as our safety is concerned. I'm a soldier. Or I was one. I'd prefer to hit these men with overwhelming force."

"Love is a force." Eric took up his horse's reins. "See you in the distance."

"Or in the clouds." Alan waved. "Hey, if the dogs attack, shoot the leader of the pack. The rest will break until a new leader arises. It was something we discovered when we drove through this region."

Eric turned in his saddle.

"How will I know which one is the leader of the pack?"

"The other dogs will look at him often. They'll watch him for signals. That's how you'll know."

Chapter 4

Eric had enjoyed Alan's company, but solitude had been his companion for years. He relished the isolation of the forgotten landscape of America. Now, he rode alone, with only God as his companion. Deep down, he sensed this was where God wanted him to thrive—outnumbered and forced to lean on God in a desperate way. Only by stepping out in faith could he ever witness His miraculous hand.

And once again, he was riding into a situation that, by all sound reason, he shouldn't survive. Except for the few days of spiritual failure, during which he'd been vexed by his fleshly selfishness, he was naturally compelled by God's Spirit inside him to rescue those in bonds. The Person of Christ within him motivated him to choose a path that placed himself humbly before others, to serve. Choosing his own path—one of self-serving or even vengeance—had already proven most unfulfilling.

Thus, by knowing that God was guiding him in this risky work for others, he was fascinated that he felt no fear. Alan had seemed unafraid as well, though they were still proceeding warily, without recklessness. What greater honor was there than to give one's whole self for others? Eric sensed this place of self-abandon was actually the place of pure living. He couldn't wait to see Kelly Morris' face! The man would certainly think he'd been abandoned by all people and from all care.

Following the slave caravan's trail across the open range was effortless, and Eric sensed even his mount had picked up their direction, plodding directly east on the packed ground of more than twenty people and over a half-dozen horses. He dismounted to walk in front of his horse to stretch his legs and study the tracks of the caravan. They were less than a day ahead now. By the drag marks on the right side of the column, there were signs that a woman in chains continued to fall down, therefore slowing the whole troupe. She wore no shoes and was chained somewhere toward the rear of the line.

Midafternoon, while riding with an eye on the horizon ahead, Eric noticed his horse lift his head and twitch his ears.

"Whoa, there, buddy." He reined his mount to a stop. Though he was no great horseman, he'd spent enough time in the wild to know to pay attention to an animal's instincts.

He stood in the saddle to gaze through his binoculars to the north. The wind was blowing from that direction, and it seemed to have drawn the focus of his horse's attention. Far away, the grass on the range was moving, as if it were flowing water. The grass was mostly brown, but it seemed to be speckled with white and black as well. But it wasn't the grass that was moving. There was something moving through the grass—more than several somethings!

Eric heeled his horse into a trot and began to search for a building in which to take shelter. He'd seen a pack of dogs to the north, numbering in the dozens, he guessed, but not more than a hundred. They didn't seem to have noticed him yet, but on their current heading, they would soon cross the trail he was following. Being caught out in the open was a very unpleasant thought. Now, more than ever, he wished he were in his mountains where there were embankments and at least a few trees to climb to escape wild animals. Out here, there was nothing!

When he pushed his horse into a gallop, his mount didn't object, and Eric gave him his head. The scent of dogs was certain to be in the wind, and the flight instinct came alive in the horse.

Leaning forward, Eric prayed that his mount would notice and avoid all the prairie dog holes, but at that speed, the ground simply rushed by. Stepping in a gopher hole would break a horse's leg in an instant, but caution wouldn't get them ahead of the dog pack. Nor would it save them out on the defenseless range. They needed to find—

Eric saw the town ahead. An old highway angled closer to them on their right. But back and to his left, the dogs broke into a run. Now, it was a chase.

"Come on, boy!" Eric yelled into the wind. He clutched the saddle horn with one hand and the reins in the other. His eyes watered as the wind whistled past his ears and tore at his shaggy hair.

The horse vaulted into the air. Eric thought the animal had lost his footing and they were about to tumble head over hooves in the grass. But an instant later, he realized the horse had just jumped over a barbed wire fence. The town ahead didn't seem to be inhabited, but its structures were still standing, and that meant Eric could stage a defense against the dogs. The trail of the slave caravan was all but lost.

Eric peered under his arm. The dogs darted through the fence without missing a step. The sleeker dogs in front were gaining. He could see them clearly now. Hound crosses and German shepherds, even Doberman-looking canines, though with mangier coats than he remembered for that breed.

The horse altered direction slightly to tear up the ditch beside the highway. Eric peered over the road at the town ahead. Arriving barely in front of the dogs wouldn't offer him much time to find adequate shelter.

When he saw movement ahead, Eric instinctively pulled back on the reins, but his horse was not about to obey him. There was nothing more horrible in the animal's mind, Eric figured, than being hamstrung from behind by ravenous dogs.

The movement before him proved a few seconds later to be anything but adversarial. Two men stood above a blockade of garbage and debris surrounding the town.

One man fired a rifle. Behind Eric, a dog yelped. It seemed that Eric's horse understood where to find safety. Clutching the pommel in one hand and the reins in the other, Eric steered his mount up the side of the ditch and onto the pavement. Another man at the blockade drew back a gate that was as high as a man's shoulders and six feet wide.

Without slowing, Eric and his steed charged through the gate onto the one-street town of thirty buildings, half of which were windswept and falling apart.

"Whoa, whoa!" Eric settled his frightened horse and turned him in a tight circle to cool him down. The dogs were outside, and the danger had passed for the moment.

He hopped out of the saddle onto the dirt-covered street while his horse was still panting heavily. The paved street had been peeled up. Looking back at the barriers at both ends of the street, large slabs of road were reinforcing the blockade around the town.

A stocky, balding man approached Eric while he spoke calming words to his mount, and rubbed his neck. The man wore thick glasses that were held together by black electrical tape in the center and on the sides.

"We saw you coming." The man didn't offer his hand, and Eric was reminded that much of America still feared that the Meridia Virus hadn't yet been eradicated, so human contact was avoided, particularly with strangers. "Usually, we don't welcome travelers past the gate unless they have something to offer."

"Well, I'm thankful." Eric nodded at the barrier at the west of town. "I see you're familiar with the local wildlife already."

"We don't have enough bullets to kill them all. I'd say there's about a dozen packs, some larger, some smaller. We've been forced to begin to eat them now. They've killed everything else within a day's walk, as near as I can tell."

"Dog meat." Eric cringed at the idea of eating Runner, Andy's black Labrador. "I guess we're all learning to survive in new ways."

Eric looked away to survey the town. A people who'd been reduced to eating wild dog meat and peeling up the pavement had also been reduced to scavenging the uninhabited buildings for wood and other materials. Several structures appeared on the verge of collapse. A stagnate trace of sewage lined the street, then pooled close to the center of town.

A woman shrieked and stumbled out of a building, which may have been a tourist shop at one time. It had a decrepit porch that separated the floorboards of the front door from the refuse puddled at the edge of the steps. The woman ran a few steps, then tripped over the fabric of her oversized dress. She landed on her hands and knees in the mud, sobbing and choking on tears. Her hair was short and dark, and even at that distance, she looked bone-thin.

A man emerged from the building and leaped off the porch. He carried a stick and raised it high to strike the woman.

Eric turned away.

"Is there one kind of dog outside the wall and another kind inside?" Eric tried to ignore the sound of blows and the woman's cries for help. "Who's in charge here?"

"I'm Tomblin, and this is the town of Tomblin." The man pushed his glasses farther up his nose. "If you don't like things in Tomblin, you can leave. I suggest you do that even if you do like things here. We can't support any more mouths."

"So, the citizens in Tomblin like the way things are?" Eric noticed other people appear in the doorways of their dwellings to see what all the commotion was. Their clothing was faded, stained, and torn. "He's going to kill her."

"There's no law against it," Tomblin said, moving up beside Eric to admire his town. "There's no law in Tomblin. She belongs to him."

"Belongs to him?" Eric frowned. "You make it sound like he bought her."

"He did. Slavers came through this morning. Sold her to him for his favorite pistol. I think he wishes now he'd kept his pistol. We're short on weapons in Tomblin."

"No law in Tomblin, huh?" Eric checked the setting sun. "Where can a traveler spend the night?"

"The old post office has been gutted for your kind. See the flag pole? But don't expect no welcome. We ain't got but what we need for ourselves."

"That's fine." Eric drew his rifle from the scabbard and chambered a round. "We'll be moving on in the morning."

Eric aimed at the dirt down the street and pulled the trigger. The rifle blast got everyone's attention, especially the man whose toes had been inches from being hit by a bullet.

"What're you doing?" Tomblin shouted. "You coulda killed him!"

"If there's no law stopping him from beating the woman to death, then there's no law stopping me from stealing her from him. Make sense?" Eric chambered another round. "Stay away from the post office tonight. I'm liable to start shooting at anything I think is a wild dog trying to sneak in."

He led his horse down the street, his rifle leveled at the man with the stick. The man took two steps back, raised his hands, and dropped his stick.

Besides being bruised, the woman didn't seem to be badly hurt.

"You're sticking your nose where it don't belong!" the man hissed.

"Tomblin said there's no law in Tomblin." Eric threw the horse's reins over his shoulder and offered his free hand to the woman. Up close, he saw she was older than he'd thought. "I'm just exercising my rights. You should've known better than to buy another human being. I hear you lost your favorite pistol."

"My only pistol." The man's hands slowly dropped to his sides. "And she's worthless, anyway. Too old and weak. Won't even dance for me."

The woman reached out to Eric and he took her hand. The torn skin around her wrists was evidence that she'd indeed been among the slaver's caravan. He pulled her upright and found her to be in her late fifties. The dress she wore clearly belonged to a much larger woman.

"Where's her clothes?" Eric glanced at the woman. "Are your clothes inside? Go get them, and anything else you want to take. There's no law in Tomblin. Hurry now. I'll keep him company out here."

But she didn't hurry, or she couldn't. A tender step at a time, she walked barefoot up the porch and inside. Moments later, she emerged with an armful of clothes and a jug of water.

"Go on into the post office." Eric pointed at the building across the street. "We'll stay the night there. I'll be right behind you."

She walked slowly, as if in a daze, looking around at the town as she moved, her dress dragging in the dirt.

"Get on your knees," Eric said to the man, realizing he sounded gruff and mean.

"Please!" The man hesitated. "I didn't know she belonged to another man! I don't want to die!"

He dropped to his knees and raised his hands as a penitent beggar.

"Don't you know she belongs to God?" Eric scolded. "If I wasn't a man of God myself, I'd put you in the ground instead of just on the ground. Remember this day! Or next time, you might not find mercy for your sins."

Eric heard his own words and wondered where the Old Testament prophet had come from, but his righteous anger had made him bold with godly courage he couldn't stifle.

He turned and walked his horse briskly to the post office. The building's door was open, so he passed through and looked back. No, the door wasn't just ajar; it was missing entirely, maybe having become firewood, or perhaps part of the town's blockade against the wild dogs.

The citizens of the town were out there staring back at him. Like Tomblin, some of them had long guns or handguns, but no one aimed at Eric. He almost recognized this town from years earlier when he'd driven his car west from Lincoln to Wyoming. But the town and the character of its people had been revealed by Pan-Day. They were a cruel and heartless people now, as Mastover had been before its leadership had been shown the hand of God.

As much as Eric wanted to remain in Tomblin and preach the gospel of life and hope in Christ alone, he couldn't. He'd already picked up the abused woman as a travel companion, which would slow him down considerably. Kelly Morris was his main objective.

He moved deeper into the post office. With no door on the building, and the townspeople untrustworthy, he expected it was going to be a long, sleepless night.

Chapter 5

The woman's name was Amber. She made her bed behind the clerk's counter, and Eric unrolled his bedroll in front of the counter. While it was still light, he went out the back doorway, which was also missing a door, and picked grass for the horse. Just inside the front door of the building, he dropped the sweet spring grass for the horse, and the animal learned where his new place was.

If anyone wanted to enter through the front door now, they'd have to crawl under the horse, which wasn't likely without causing some alarm. Across the back door, Eric tipped two metal filing cabinets which wouldn't stop a determined prowler, but the barrier created a blind spot that would cause a cautious intruder to hesitate.

"I remember you," Amber said as she surrendered her raw wrists to Eric's care. He used antibiotic ointment on her wounds, but withheld the little bit of morphine he had for others who might have worse injuries. "Three or four days ago, Smar tried to capture you."

In the fading light from the front door opening, Amber appeared to be a plain woman with brunette hair, but she was so filthy from mistreatment, it was hard to tell. She needed much more than just her wounds cleaned from street grime, but Eric's resources were limited.

"Smar?" Eric dabbed lightly at her skin that had been nearly cut to the bone in places. "The man in the sweater?"

"That's him. He kidnapped me in Oregon. Killed my husband in front of everyone. Now, I have no one. Except you."

Eric glanced up at her face and saw her pleading eyes. She'd been mistreated for so long, she knew how to survive by only one way.

"No, you have many others besides me. You just haven't met them. Your journey isn't over yet."

"Well, I'm not staying here." She shuddered. "I could be your woman. I might look a fright now, but if I wash up—"

"No, Amber." Eric held both of her hands to make his point while looking firmly into her eyes. "That's not necessary. Before God, I'm married. Her name is Gretchen. Nothing is required of you for me to take care of you. I'm your friend, and that comes with no conditions. I'll keep you as safe as I can, and if you want, you can return to Mastover with me, after I free the others from Smar."

"You're going after him?" She withdrew her hands. "I'd rather stay in this town than go back to Smar!"

"Maybe at the next town, we can find a safe place for you to wait for me to return, some place a little more civilized."

"You're going after Smar." She softened. "You just might make it. There's something about you. A confidence I haven't seen in a long time."

"I'm a Christian. If it weren't for the God I follow, I'd be a coward. I was a coward that day Smar found me on the range all alone outside Mastover. I should've done something instead of waiting until now. You could've been spared this further mistreatment."

She looked up at the horse that snorted contentedly over a mouthful of grass.

"Mastover is the town with the swinging bridge? I remember seeing it from the highway. Its streets looked clean. No mud. No garbage."

"It's a nice town. They'll take you in. I have many friends there."

"I'm not a Christian."

"They'll welcome you, anyway." He smiled.

"That sounds nice," she said, and smiled back.

Wearing an extra shirt from Eric's pack, Amber settled down on the other side of the counter and slept soundlessly. Eric dozed while sitting upright, his rifle across his lap.

At the first hint of daylight, Eric rose stiffly and saddled the horse. He cleared the back door of the filing cabinets, then woke Amber. She rose slowly, moaning from her many aches, and Eric helped her into the saddle. He guessed she was the prisoner who'd been hindering the caravan, and her captors had sold her quickly for a single handgun. Although Eric had adopted Smar's nuisance captive, Eric still expected to gain on the caravan since Amber wasn't required to march any longer. Sitting and resting in the saddle, the wounds on her knees and wrists would heal, and he figured she'd be healthy in a week.

Leading the horse, Eric pushed through the town's unmanned eastern gate and left Tomblin with no interference. No one else was even awake that early, and no dogs were visible on the plain. Though he'd wondered occasionally through the night about how Alan was faring on the open plain, he couldn't worry about his companion. Such matters had to be left in God's sovereign hand alone. Alan was resourceful, and Eric didn't doubt the man had found adequate shelter to keep pace on the trail.

Eric picked up the trail of the caravan not far from the town of Tomblin where it left the pavement of the highway to trek cross-country. Although the caravan had armed guards, Eric guessed they were avoiding most largely populated areas because they knew most civilized pockets of America would still object to the idea of slaves or the selling of human beings. Nevertheless, Smar and his caravan of bondage had already traveled across two states, and no one had stopped him yet.

"I thought I would die on that chain." Amber was the first to speak that morning as Eric shared dried deer meat with her. "There were days I wanted to die."

"I hate to make you dwell on your experience, Amber, but I need your help," Eric said. "Can you tell me more about Smar, and what their daily routine is?"

"I can tell you everything. Just promise me this: when you kill Smar and the others, make sure they know it's because of me, that I helped you."

"I won't be killing them." Eric led the horse down a gully and up the other side. His pace was fast on that crisp morning as he hoped to cover twenty miles before the full heat of the sun. "There's something more mighty than death for them to experience."

"Torture? They tortured me. They torture the others, too. Smar wouldn't feed us if we talked at all, or if we disobeyed. That baton in his hand? He would hit us on our shoulders or heads if we walked too slowly. He hit me a lot. He said we didn't need our heads and shoulders to walk faster, so he could hit us there. I still have bruises."

"What happens to us doesn't have to determine who we are or how we'll care for others. We know what they did to you was wrong; it was terrible. But what will become of you now? Will you become a better person for it? It won't be easy."

"What are you, a shrink?"

"No." Eric chuckled. "Just someone who understands the human condition. That's why I'm not going to kill Smar."

"Yeah, you said that. What's so much mightier than killing him?"

"Killing him doesn't reverse what he's done, but leading him through real sorrow for what he's done reverses who he is."

"I've never heard of anything so ridiculous! Smar is a monster. You don't change people like him. You don't know how he allowed his men to treat us."

"Would you rather see Smar lying dead in the grass, or kneeling in brokenness in front of you, asking for your forgiveness?" Eric stopped the horse and removed his binoculars from around his neck. "Don't answer that question right now. Just think about it. Horrible crimes demand justice, but if grace isn't offered, then we've allowed the crime to blind us with vengeance. Here, take my field glasses. You're higher than me. Look all around the range for movement."

"What am I looking for?" she held up the binoculars to her eyes. "Smar?"

"No, Smar is still several hours ahead of us to the east. I'm more concerned about those dogs."

"What dogs?" she lowered the glasses to look at him with concern.

"There's packs of dogs out here. You didn't know? I mean, Smar hasn't crossed them?"

"Smar was a car salesman in California. He brags about it—trading engines for flesh. He has no idea about what's out here. He has one man named Peter who seems competent, but he's just as ruthless. No one in the west knows what's out here. How many dogs are we talking about?"

"Dozens, thousands—depends on the pack. If Smar doesn't know about the dogs, he could be taken by surprise out in the open. That explains why he's marching through this region at all—he doesn't know any better. He could get everyone killed."

Eric didn't stop again until his analog watch showed it was midday. Topping a rise, they saw a large town to the southeast. Smar's caravan tracks curved to the north, avoiding the town.

"I have to leave you here." Eric used the field glasses to study the settlement. "It's larger than Tomblin. Their buildings are in good shape, and they have a six-foot barrier around the whole town, probably to keep the dogs out. I think I even see factories."

"I don't want you to leave me," Amber said. "Please, don't go after Smar."

"I have to. He has a friend of mine."

"You didn't tell me that!"

Eric started walking toward the town.

"I can drop you here, then return in a couple days."

"You're just saying that." Amber scoffed. "I know I'm nothing to you, but don't leave me here. I know you're trying to help me as much as you can, but don't tell me you're coming back for me if you're not really going to. You saved me from the chain. Now you're leaving me to start a new life."

"If that's what you want," Eric said, "but I will come back this way in a few days, and there's no reason why I can't take you back to Mastover with me, if you want to go."

"Listen to me." Amber sniffed. "We've known each other since last night, and I'm already turning into a clingy mother!"

"It's okay. You've been through a lot. It's hard to trust people right now. But if it's in my power to take you back to Mastover, I will. And while you're here, I need you to be diplomatic for us."

"What? I'm only here to wait for you to come back for me."

"No, you're not. When I return with the other prisoners, we'll need supplies for our trip back. You can arrange that with these people."

"A diplomat? Me?" She laughed. "You apparently haven't taken a good look at me. Neither have I, I admit, but I know I'm a mess."

"We're all a mess, Amber. So are the people in this town. They're scared and worried. So, it's our job to bring them comfort, reason, and confidence. They wouldn't be isolated in the middle of Nebraska with a wall around them if they weren't afraid of the world outside."

"I don't have confidence like you do. No, I can't do anything here. You can't ask me to do this. I'm a victim, Eric!"

Eric stopped the horse. They were close enough to the town now to see watchers with rifles on the wall.

"The truth you believe is the life you will lead," Eric said to her. "If you really believe you're a victim, then you'll live in that reality. But I don't believe that's who you are. I believe you were victimized. That's just something that happened to you. Nothing more."

"Who talks like this?" She shook her head. "Who are you? What gives you the right to determine who people are and who they're not?"

"Don't you know that God hasn't abandoned us out here, Amber? Don't you know that it's us that abandoned Him? God hasn't removed Himself, so stop thinking you need to rely on yourself. Hold your head up. Trust in God to move in ways that you cannot, and receive what you're dealt to grow as His daughter."

She blinked twice.

"Seriously? You're insane."

"You're not the first person to tell me that recently." Eric laughed and kept walking. "Your past can't be changed, but your future is up to you. I'm going after Smar. When I return with those people, if our supplies aren't lined up for us, then it'll take longer for us to get back to Mastover. That's all. If you're not comfortable with taking responsibility yet, it's okay. I won't hold it against you. Just think about it."

She didn't speak again until they reached the town's perimeter barrier. A man with an assault rifle and a lopsided beard was flanked by three other gunmen on the wall. The wall appeared sturdy, made of well-cut boards, which were rare in those days, since most lumber was used for fire fuel.

"We're not welcoming any strangers," the lead man on the wall said. Part of his hair was missing above one ear, like he'd been burned or partially scalped. No region of America had escaped hard times. "There's nothing for you here. I have to think of my own people."

"In the last few hours, some slavers passed to the north of you," Eric said, casually resting his rifle over his shoulder. "There were twenty people in chains and six horsemen. You see them?"

"Yeah, we saw them. They weren't any more welcome here than you. At least they had the foresight not to even ask us."

"I don't have that kind of foresight." Eric smiled. "I'm relying on God to give me the strength and wisdom to do what others don't want to do. In this case, that's shutting down those slavers."

"That's your business, not mine."

"Nope, I'm making it your business since they just passed through your front yard and you did nothing. You have a few women in town, I'm assuming. This is Amber. I'll be leaving her here with you as I continue after the slavers. See that she's cared for. I'll be back to get her in a few days. You're God-fearing people, I hope, so I won't mention the degree of discontent that will fall upon this place if she's harmed."

"You talk like you think you have some authority." The man's eyes narrowed. "You have no authority here. Where are you from?"

Ignoring the man's challenge, Eric helped Amber off the horse. She still wore his extra shirt, but he let her keep it, and walked her over to the wall.

"When I return," Eric said, looking straight up at the gunman, "I'll have the spoils of war with me. I expect to do some trading for supplies, then we'll be on our way, all of us better people for caring for our neighbors. We might even share a few stories and catch up on old times like longtime friends."

The bearded man glanced at his friends, then back down at Eric.

"They don't make them like you anymore." He shifted his rifle into his left hand and leaned far off the wall to offer his right hand to Amber. "She doesn't appear to have the virus, so she can stay with us. My wife will love to hear some gossip that isn't already circulating inside Coppertown."

"Comfort and confidence, huh?" Amber said softly to Eric. "You'd better come back for me!"

"I will." Eric lifted her up by her waist to grasp the guard's hand. From there, the stranger and two others hauled her straight up to the top of the wall.

"You're a fool to go after those slavers alone." The man steadied Amber on the wall, then handed her off to someone out of sight. "The dogs will tear you apart, all of you. The only reason we're taking in your lady friend is to spare her the death you seem to be chasing."

Eric swung into the saddle. He was happy to be off his sore feet and to rest his tired legs.

"I have a friend following a day or two behind me. His name is Alan. He has one leg. I'd appreciate it if you could show him the same hospitality, if he stops by."

"A one-legged man traveling alone in this wasteland?" The man frowned. "What kind of people are you out west?"

"When I come back," Eric said, turning his horse, "we can talk more about it."

He waved and galloped away from the town called Coppertown.

Chapter 6

Eric was happy to be out on the open plain alone with God so he could prayerfully prepare for the coming interaction with the slavers. He had received enough inside information from Amber to know that he was joining a cold-hearted crew—if they didn't kill him outright. However, he sensed from God a guarding and guiding hand, which was why he could so easily leave Amber in the hands of strangers. God was intimately involved in his actions, totally aware, and even going before him to prepare whole scenarios.

Regardless of his confidence in God, Eric remained vigilant of his environment. Afternoon passed with a warm breeze, and his horse became skittish, making him wonder if the scent of a dog pack was in the breeze. He picked up the pace and pushed his mount a little harder than he thought was safe. But it paid off as he noticed movement on the eastern horizon. It was the slave caravan.

Sundown swept across the rolling hills covered by brown grass. Rather than ride into Smar's camp weary, Eric climbed off his mount a mile beyond the slavers, and allowed the horse to graze for an hour. Eric laid down and gazed at the darkening sky. Now, he told himself, he would pretend to be a hard-hearted man, maybe even cruel and dispassionate. It didn't set well with him, but it did seem the best route to join such men—to act indifferent to the sufferings of those in chains. As Moses had sent spies into Canaan to conquer the peoples, he was spying out the slavers to claim the prisoners.

Eric rose from the ground and filled a waterproof container from his canteen to water his horse. It was all but the last of his water, but at least his mount would be fed, hydrated, and rested if they needed to flee into the night.

He approached their camp from the south. Anticipation fluttered in his belly at the prospect of seeing Kelly Morris soon—and rescuing the murderer from a fate he certainly deserved more than most.

Three fires flickered on the southeastern slope of a small hill. The placement of the camp told Eric that although Smar may not have been an outdoorsman, someone in his caravan was. They had sheltered from the nightly northwest wind, and positioned themselves to embrace the sun when it would dawn first on the southern slope.

Cupping his mouth, Eric whistled shrilly for the camp to hear him.

"Hello, the camp!" he yelled. "One on horseback coming in!"

A moment passed. Men's indiscernible voices drifted down the hill.

"Come on in!" someone called back. "Keep your hands in sight."

Eric urged his horse forward. His mount's ears twitched as he seemed to sense the presence of other horses. Cradling his rifle across the pommel of his saddle, Eric rode into the firelight of the center fire. The other fires were low and spaced twelve paces from the central fire. They would've never been out there without shelter or high blazing fires if they were aware of the threat of dogs.

Smar, in his same thick sweater, sat at the fire, but his four gunmen stood with rifles or handguns in their hands. The last sixth man with the blue scarf walked in from the dark where their horses were hobbled.

"You again!" one man said.

Eric recognized his red hair and hard face.

"That's right. But I have no interest in seeing you any more than you have in seeing me." Eric studied each of their faces. At the redhead's feet was a length of chain. "But right now, we need each other. We may not even survive the night, but together, we've got a shot."

"I thought you had a camp back near the mountains in Wyoming." Smar holstered his handgun, but the others remained tense. The leader didn't look the part of an ex-car salesman with brutal men flanking him. "What makes you think we need you to survive the night?"

Eric slid off his mount, but kept his rifle in one hand, the reins in the other. Taking his time, he turned and listened to the darkness.

"They're out there, just waiting for us to bed down. That's when they attack, when the fires are low. I'd put more wood on the fires right now, if I were you."

"You're not me," Smar said. "Besides, we don't have much wood. What's out there? We haven't seen anything since we left the mountains."

"Not an antelope or a single deer, I know." Eric let the suspense build as he faced their fire again. "That should've been the first sign. They've killed all the game. Rumor has it, they're Meridia Virus carriers, too. Nothing is safe out here, especially us."

The men glanced about at the mention of the virus, but Smar only smirked.

"You have ten seconds to explain what you're talking about, and then my men will shoot you for your horse. We could use the meat."

"That may be." Eric twitched suddenly, and turned to the dark landscape, as if he'd heard a whisper of sound. "But you'll need my gun. We'll need all the guns. We just have to make it to Lincoln."

"We're not going to Lincoln." Smar used a short stick to stoke the fire. "We'll be passing to the north of Lincoln."

"Then I'll ride with you that far, and peel off. My wife's sick. Lincoln has a huge hospital. Or they did at one time."

"Shoot this idiot," Smar said to his men.

"Wait!" Eric dropped his reins and used both hands to aim his rifle at Smar's chest. "A single gunshot might be enough to set them off. You don't want them attacking any sooner than they would naturally attack."

"What's out there, you blooming idiot?" Smar cursed. "Enough games!"

"The dogs. Thousands of them. You're in the Plains Zone now. Didn't you see the walls around Tomblin and Coppertown? No one is safe. Thousands of feral dogs of all the strongest, fiercest breeds. Only a fast horse saved me yesterday, then I hid inside Tomblin overnight."

"I thought that wall seemed a little low," the redhead said to Smar, "from a defensive standpoint. But it makes sense if it's meant to keep animals outside."

"He's right." Eric nodded at the redhead, realizing he was the one who was probably more dangerous than the others. "It's not built to defend against human attackers, but canines. We're vulnerable out here, and I didn't see any buildings nearby as the sun went down. We'll have to make our stand here."

"He could be telling the truth," the redhead said to Smar. "Back at that creek, we saw a lot of dog tracks. They weren't from coyotes."

"We need to move the fires into a three-point triangle." Eric walked back to his horse and slid his rifle into the scabbard. "We're too spread out. We need to put flames between us and the dogs."

Right then, the hobbled horses just out of the firelight were disturbed and several whinnied and snorted.

"Something's in the wind," the redhead said. "They smell it, even if we can't."

"Well, I'm not dying by no rabid dog!" Another gunman leveled his rifle at the darkness. "Let's do something. All this standing around isn't fixing anything!"

"Peter," Smar said, "can we move everyone into a triangle of fires?"

"We can try." The redhead finally relaxed his gun hand from aiming at Eric. "To make it effective, we'll have to leave the horses outside. If we're attacked, we might lose a couple animals."

"We could slaughter our weakest horse," Eric suggested. "Keep half the meat for ourselves, and leave the rest on the next hill for the dogs. If we're low on wood, not even well-positioned fires will hold those creatures off."

"You're just full of good ideas, aren't you?" Smar glared critically at Eric, then looked to Peter, the redhead. "That one mare is limping, and we need the meat. Do we make a peace offering to the dogs, if they're even out there?"

"We just need to make it through the night," Eric said. "Tomorrow, we can find better shelter."

"We may as well try it." Peter's hand rested on a skinning knife in a sheath on his belt. "Dogs or not, the mare won't get through tomorrow. You—what's your name?"

"Eric."

"Okay, Eric, you just volunteered to help me butcher a horse. Let's see what kind of mountain man you really are. The rest of you move the fires and the prisoners."

"You heard him," Smar said louder. "Get to it!"

As the three gunmen rose to the work, Eric and Peter moved away from the central fire. Peter took the hobbles off a mare that wasn't even grazing. She was indeed lame in one foreleg. Eric looked back at the fires. The man with the blue scarf hadn't moved. Whoever the scarf man was, Smar apparently didn't command him.

Although Eric was anxious to make contact with the prisoners to offer them a sliver of hope, he had to wait for the right moment. He had to gain trust.

From camp, Peter led the lame mare down one hill and up the next rise. Eric held his rifle ready to fire. Regardless of his show of anxiety to Smar about the dog packs, Eric knew better than them all of the reality of that threat. His own mock fear had been contagious, and that had bought him at least a temporary part in the caravan. Now, he had to survive long enough amongst them to discover a weakness to exploit and free the captives.

The mare's life was taken quietly and without cruelty by Peter, and Eric wondered if the redhead's fierceness wasn't but skin-deep after all. Together, they butchered and quartered the animal. The stench was strong.

"Let's just hope this keeps the dogs off of us," Peter said, "and doesn't attract them to us."

Eric dragged one haunch of meat farther away to leave behind, then returned to the carcass to carry a quarter back to camp. He greatly wanted to develop a relationship with each of the men, but these weren't the days when people naturally trusted one another.

In camp, the three fires were brought closer together, and the prisoners were brought inside the triangle of flames. The women captives remained on one chain length, and the men remained on another. From what Amber had told him, Eric understood they weren't allowed to speak, or they wouldn't be fed. The prisoners crowded as close as they could to two of the fires, and Smar and his men faced the darkness from their own fire.

Eric and Peter cut steaks from the quarters as the men prisoners watched in silence.

"We need to cut our losses," a gunman finally said. "I'm not dying for a bunch of slaves."

"This isn't working out the way you said it would, Smar," another said. "We may never reach Chicago now. We've been starving for a week. Whatever price you said we could get for these people isn't worth dying by a pack of dogs."

"Keep your heads," Smar stated calmly. "We'll pick up another ten along the way and reach Chicago before the heat of summer. The prices that trader said we'd get for human cargo in the city hasn't changed. Keep your eyes on that, and you'll be rich men by summer's end. A few dogs won't slow us down. If anything, it'll push us faster."

"I'm selling out my share in Lincoln," the first man said, "and getting back home. This is a fool's errand."

Eric listened to the unrest without looking up from his work beside Peter. So, there was dissension in the ranks, Eric realized, and wondered if he could maximize on it to the benefit of the prisoners.

"We all signed on until Chicago," Peter said. Every man at the fire looked at him. "We need every man to see this through. I'll kill any man who leaves before Chicago."

The discussion seemed to be over, and Eric was impressed at the fear the redhead was able to inflict. He must've committed some horrible acts in their presence to convince them so thoroughly by his word alone.

A dozen steaks sizzled on spits over the low flames, and the men, including Smar, licked their lips as Eric and Peter rotated the meat in the heat. When the first steaks were ready, they ate, and a second batch of steaks was placed over the flames. The meat wouldn't last for more than a couple days, since they'd only kept part of the horse, but Eric hoped it would revitalize the prisoners and lighten the dark moods of their captors.

Then they heard the dogs. It wasn't the playful romping and yelping Eric had heard in the night, but the hungry growling and fighting of snarling canines. The men rose to their feet, firearms in their hands, and stared in the direction of the mare's carcass. They could see nothing in the darkness, so every man's imagination was projected on his face. Only the man with the blue scarf seemed calm, and Eric met his eyes in the light of the fire. Something sinister dwelt behind those eyes, regardless of the man's seeming peacefulness.

Eric chose that distracted moment to nudge Peter's arm.

"Hey, do they eat?" He gestured with a spit of steaks at the male prisoners.

Peter studied Eric's face for a moment, perhaps judging his motives, then nodded.

"Go ahead. Just watch out for their feet. Some of them kick. If they kick, take their food back. But they know that, so I think they'll be still."

Eric didn't wait for Smar or the others to notice what he'd asked to do. He stepped around one of Smar's gunmen, who was staring fearfully out at the range, and found himself in a tangle of legs and outstretched shackled hands. They stank worse than animals since their ragged clothes were soiled, and Eric shuddered at the condition of the sores on their wrists from the shackles, and on their knees from falling.

"One for you . . ." Eric said as he handed one steak at a time to the hungry captives. "And one for you."

The fires were close and everyone was crowded tightly within the area, so faces were illuminated by the flames. However, Eric had to look carefully at the bearded, filthy faces to make out features. In a sudden feeling of panic, he wondered if he were too late to save Kelly Morris. The man didn't seem to be there! Perhaps he'd been too ornery and Smar had disposed of him, especially if he'd been discovered to be the ex-commander of the Lib-Org.

"I just saw one!" a Smar man shouted and aimed his rifle.

"Save your ammo!" Peter ordered. "They'll probably react worse if they sense that we're a threat."

"They're all over!" Smar himself gasped. "The dogs are all around us!"

Eric looked past the nearest fire and saw the darting figures of four-legged beasts, their muzzles aimed at the people, their eyes eerily shining like glass in the dark.

"There's hundreds of them!" another man shrieked.

"Hold steady!" Peter urged. "They're just curious. We left them some food. Let them sniff around."

"The horses, Peter!" Smar hissed. "We're finished without our horses!"

Even as Smar said it, a dog yelped after a heavy thud. Peter chuckled.

"The horses are taking care of themselves, I'd say."

Suddenly, a pair of shackled hands clutched onto Eric's leg. The last steak was offered to this man, and Eric knew immediately who it was. While Smar and his men were distracted, Eric crouched until his face was inches from Kelly Morris' foul breath.

"You came for me!" the man whispered. "I thought you'd left me to die."

"It took me a few days to get myself together." Eric set a firm hand on his shoulder. "Be ready to move when it's time. And no killing!"

"No ki—?"

"No! Remember, I'm a Christian. You're in my hands now!" He stepped away from Kelly before they were discovered communicating, and returned to the fire for steaks for the women.

"I can't stand it!" a Smar man complained. "They're playing with us. They're gonna attack!"

"Keep your head!" Smar thundered. "They're just testing us. Peter?"

"Don't do anything aggressive," Peter said. "It could set them off. There must be eighty or a hundred out there. We could never fight off that many, but they don't know that."

Eric ignored the commotion and the threat. He knew they were in danger, but his heart looked above toward his God. God knew what his mission was—He'd sent Eric to help Kelly and the captives, and He was the Creator of such ravenous beasts. Instead of dwelling on his fear, Eric focused on his calling.

Since Amber had left their ranks, there were only nine women captives remaining, but Eric took them twelve steaks. He gave each of the smallest three women a double portion, and grabbed the upper arm of another woman about his age who seemed healthier. His grasp made her shrink away, but she was shackled between two others, so there was nowhere for her to go. Her eyes were fierce and wild.

"Keep hope!" he whispered. "Don't give up! God is with us!"

It was all Eric could risk to say with Smar and the others so near. He returned to the main fire and continued to busy himself with cooking. While steaks sizzled in the flames, he took up his rifle with the others. But his fear, unlike the others, was tempered by his faith.

Though Smar had a rule of no talking among the prisoners, Eric guessed the captives would often quietly speak amongst themselves. By God's grace, he prayed that his message of hope would strengthen them all.

Chapter 7

When dawn broke, the full extent of the night's damage was revealed. Only three of the seven riding horses remained alive, including Eric's, but the pack horses were too injured to continue. The animal carcasses littered the landscape, and a few stray dogs continued to gorge themselves on the remains, but the pack itself was nowhere in sight.

Eric had suspected that toward morning, as he and the men had lapsed into restless dozing, that someone among them had tried to escape. Now, the evidence of that attempt was on the hillside. The man with the blue scarf was gone, as was one of Smar's gunmen.

"One of them died right away," Peter reported to Smar, who was gazing at the slaughter, "but I'm not going out there to see which one. Even if one of them got over the hill, he couldn't have made it very far on foot."

"The dogs could return," Smar said. "Let's leave this place now. Eric!"

"Yes?" Eric rose from his squatting place by the dwindling fire.

"If you're traveling with us as far as Lincoln, then you'll work like the rest of us. Understood?"

"Understood." Eric nodded at Peter. He felt the two had bonded through the night. They were the only two who had "kept their heads," even though Smar was the one who kept saying it. "Tell me what to do."

"Your horse is the sturdiest mount we have. Pack our priority supplies on him, as much as you can manage. The rest of you make backpacks from the saddle blankets, everything you can carry. We're walking out of here. Peter, see to the cargo. We leave in thirty minutes. I'm never spending a night like this again!"

To add to their sense of defeat, thunder rumbled in the sky to the northwest. Smar led the way on foot, one horse's lead rope in his hand with the women's chain attached to the pack saddle. Eric was ordered to lead his own horse, to which the men's chain was attached. Peter and the two remaining men passed out rain parkas among themselves, then shouldered packs and flanked the weary convoy as it left the hill of slaughter behind.

Within minutes, rain pounded heavily upon their shoulders. The ground turned from dusty earth to slippery mud. Smar and Eric, side by side, slowed to a crawl. Eric didn't mind the slower pace, since the prisoners in chains weren't forced to match a horse's stride that day.

"The dogs won't attack in the rain," Eric said to Smar. "They probably found shelter somewhere."

"You know nature as well as Peter," Smar said, the strength in his voice diminished from the evening before. "But do you know Nebraska? What other perils lie ahead of us?"

Eric contemplated his answer carefully, seeking God's guidance. Indeed, he'd joined a caravan of bondage, but he didn't intend to join Smar in his efforts.

"Between here and Chicago are five hundred miles of the most horrible nightmares known to America. The worst elements of the East and West Coasts fled inland after Pan-Day, and they didn't stop until they reached these lawless lands now called the Plains Zone. Every town has become a fiefdom. Many of them survive now by victimizing travelers. Supplies in every town are scarce, since so few know how to hunt or fish or grow crops effectively. Killing and taking is easier. Four men guarding twenty-some prisoners won't make it to Chicago."

"I'll trade a couple slaves for more horses." Smar slipped, fell to one knee in the mud, then continued. "It's how we survived the winter—trading slaves for more supplies."

Eric made a conscious effort not to think about the horrors left in Smar's wake.

"Who was the man with the blue scarf?"

"I knew him only as Bolture. He joined us on the road when we left California, telling me he could guide us east, where he'd recently come from. He fancied himself a prophet of some sort."

"A prophet?" Eric barely held back a laugh. "Like an old-time Bible prophet?"

"No, he said he hated the Bible. He said it misrepresented the god in all of us, the consciousness in all the things of the earth. The farther east we came, the less he spoke. He guided us through the Rockies, but I was learning to distrust him about the time we ran into you outside Mastover. I'm not sorry Bolture left us. He'd become a nuisance just to have around."

"What brought you into this line of work, Smar?" Eric asked.

"You mean human cargo?" Smar cursed at the sky as the clouds seemed to darken and the rain increased. "Everyone was already stealing and killing. Why couldn't I? I'm not ashamed to do it in the open, either, but everyone else is using each other in secret. It was this way before Pan-Day. Everyone was a slave to their technology or clothes or religion. All I've done is put metal around their wrists and a price on their heads. Everything's for sale, Eric."

Eric didn't want to reveal his personal feelings about Smar's attitude and actions, but he couldn't keep silent about the only truth that could break through Smar's hardened heart.

"Do you ever get to know your cargo?" Eric gestured with his thumb at the prisoners. "Clean them up a little, and I bet they'd look pretty normal. An enterprising guy like you—I bet you could make a better fortune if they were clean and healthy-looking. You know, treat them nicely, and you might get more for your efforts."

"I'm not that sweet, if you've noticed." Smar grunted. "No, I don't want to know any of them. And I don't have the patience to work with people to teach them business, if you're implying that I use them as workers instead of cargo. I'm a salesman. I sell things. That's all."

Eric frowned at his attempt to help Smar care about the prisoners from a human perspective.

"From what you said about Bolture," Eric said, "I wouldn't agree with his idea of everything in creation having a consciousness, but I do believe there is a God. This life will be over sooner than we all want it to end. We'll be judged by that Someone. There's too much evidence in the world around us of a Creator to ignore Him just because man has made a mess of things."

"He might be real," Smar admitted, "but I'm no worse than anyone else. I've seen all kinds of towns in California, when I used to sell batteries after Pan-Day. I'm kind to my cargo compared to how others use them. In the end, in Chicago, all these people will be sold to people who will feed them, clothe them, maybe even free them. Half these people were close to death when I grabbed them up. Some of them might even thank me for giving them a purpose. I gave them value. I'm their god now. If there is a God, He wasn't taking care of them any better than I am now."

"Come on." Eric laughed. "You don't really believe that. What if that was you on that chain and some guy was about to sell you? Would you think of him as a god?"

"What're you trying to say to me right now?" Smar stopped his horse. He was winded from the unaccustomed walking. His rain parka had a hole on the shoulder, and his sweater underneath appeared as sodden with rain as the ground. "You have a problem with what I'm doing?"

Eric realized he'd pushed too far, so he grinned mischievously.

"Maybe I'm just wondering how you deal with your conscience, so if I buy a couple of your people, I can quiet my own conscience."

"Oh." Smar grunted. "The conscience. Right. In this line of work, it's best to ignore that, too. Take what you want, and what you can get away with. And don't let anyone else tell you how to live. That's my motto."

"Words to live by." Eric faced the rain clouds. "We need to head south. We'll never find a town in this low visibility until we can locate a highway. Once the rain stops, the dogs will be out again."

Two miles later, they stomped their boots clean of mud as they stepped onto the asphalt of an east-to-west county highway. Peter wanted to discuss their plans with Smar, so Eric passed his lead rope on to the man, and moved back along the right flank of the captives. The rain had washed off some of the grime from the women's clothing, and though some of them were shivering from the wetness, the air wasn't terribly cold.

He walked beside the woman he'd spoken hope to the night before. She had stout shoulders and a firm jaw, which reminded Eric of Gretchen, except this woman's tangled hair was dark and littered with debris from sleeping on the ground. She glanced at Eric, and he nodded once at her. In the noise of the falling rain and jingling of chains, he could've probably spoken to her in secret, but he couldn't risk it, not with their deliverance so close. It wasn't a coincidence, he believed, that the evil slavers' strength had been devastated since a vessel for God had come into their company. God indeed was bringing Smar and his men to their knees. It was an unmistakable reality that reminded Eric of Israel's commander Joshua who had conquered the Canaanites. God fought for His people when His people sought His purposes!

Through the haze ahead, Eric saw the gray mass of a town, and jogged up to Smar's side.

"We need to dry out," he told the slaver. "The horses need to rest, and we're exhausted. If we don't recover from last night, we may not make it to the safety of the next town. When this rain stops, the dogs will—"

"I know, Eric!" Smar's frustration was wearing thin and about to give way to rage. His knuckles were white as he gripped his metal baton. "Peter, what do you think? Is it too early to stop for the day?"

"This'll all be pointless if our cargo dies just because we want to make a few more miles."

"I'll cover the town," Eric volunteered, and jogged ahead, his rifle in his hands and his make-shift pack jostling on his back. He had no interest in harming any aggressor in the town, but for Smar, he had to keep up his appearance as a team player.

The highway cut through the town of about ten buildings. At a glance, Eric could see that most of the buildings were close to falling down. Hard winters of snow and fierce winds had already toppled a couple of them. There was no barrier or wall around this town, and no barricade across the highway.

He put his right shoulder against the first building and studied the structures for signs of life. No smoke drifted up from any enclosures that might suggest a camp fire or stove. No horses were tethered anywhere, that he could see. The glass in the windows was missing, and the doors to the visible buildings had been removed, probably by travelers seeking wood for their fires.

Smar led the caravan up behind Eric, and Eric waved them forward into the town. They all kept their hands on their guns as they peered into empty, ransacked buildings.

"Here." Peter signaled to the left and led the horses and captives directly through what used to be the doorway of a small diner.

The male prisoners were led to the back of the diner, and the women were directed to the side where several booths still stood upright. Everything else in the establishment that hadn't been fastened to the floor, including tables and chairs, were gone.

"Eric," Smar called, "go find something for a fire."

The captives didn't complain as their chains were released from the lead horses. The men and women collapsed onto the booths and floor. Puddles of water dripped from their clothing, and some shivered uncontrollably. Eric wanted desperately to tend to their needs, to find dry, clean clothes for them, to embrace them with Christ's love, but for now, against his very nature, he needed to continue to act the part of Smar's soldier.

Outside in the rain, Eric looked up and down the street. Where was he supposed to find something to burn in a town that had been scavenged for seven years? They were surely not the first travelers to stop there and search for wood. All that was left of the buildings was metal and concrete. Even window framing and roof edging that may have been wood had been torn or blown off.

Then he saw it, and his mouth opened to praise God. Instead, he closed his mouth and thanked the Lord from within his heart. He wasn't yet overtly expressing his faith in Smar's hearing, even if he had planted a few seeds for the man to consider.

He crossed the street to a bookstore that still had a few letters on its sign on the front, identifying it as Used Books. Eric walked through the open doorway and smelled the musty odor of damp and rotting paper. Books littered the floor, heaps of them, as if someone had spent a winter holed up in the town sorting them into genres. The shelves must've been wood, for they were now gone, and countless books had certainly been taken over the years, but there were still many remaining—more than the casual traveler across Nebraska could read, carry, or burn in a winter.

Eric knelt to pick through a pile of what appeared to be Western dime store novels, sixty years old, when he heard a clatter from the back of the store. He glanced up in time to see the clear shape of a man duck behind the wall. The bookstore had a back door. Someone was in the store with him!

"I'm not a threat," Eric said loud enough to be heard in the back corridor. His words would certainly seem ridiculous to any stranger who'd seen him with a caravan of slaves! "There's enough books for us all. I'm just taking a few armfuls for a fire. We don't want any problems."

Frowning, Eric considered the terrible possibility that Smar would abduct more captives in an instant if it helped his own situation. He would take any food, supplies, or human cargo that he discovered in the town. Eric couldn't allow that!

"Are you alone?" a familiar voice asked.

"Alan?" Eric whispered, and checked the street to make sure no one was outside the diner to witness their conversation. He leaped over a stack of grade school primers and almost collided with Alan on his crutches at the back of the store. "It's not safe for you here. I thought you were far behind us!"

Eric was startled as Alan dropped one crutch, which clattered on the floor, to embrace him tightly with one arm.

"I passed you guys in the night," Alan said breathlessly. "I saw the fires and dogs and decided to push on. But I thought for sure you'd been killed."

He hopped back and Eric picked up the dropped crutch for the one-legged man. A set of stairs leading upward were behind him, and an empty soda machine stood with the door ajar.

"Blood has been shed, but God has preserved me for something more." Eric looked toward the front of the store. "I have to get back to the others. Everyone is near death, but the slaver leader named Smar is too stubborn to give up his plans to sell his prisoners in Chicago. Where are the horses?"

"There's a bank a couple lots up the street. I closed a crash gate to keep the horses safely inside. Those dogs are out there somewhere."

"I've earned Smar's trust, so now I'm waiting on God to unseat him. He doesn't realize how even his own men are close to abandoning him."

"There's no wall around this town." Alan appeared wide-eyed and excited, the soldier in him relishing the tension. "Are you in a defendable position in that diner?"

"Hardly. If the dogs attack, I think we'll be in trouble. There are no doors on these buildings."

"Then let's do it tonight." Alan nodded sharply. "Just get it over with. This Smar guy trusts you. We can't risk the prisoners' lives another day on the plain."

"Okay." Eric paused, praying that Alan still felt the same way when he discovered Kelly Morris was one of the prisoners. "I'll wait for an opportunity in the night, maybe during guard duty. I'll volunteer, then gather their guns. They're all exhausted."

"I'll find a window on the second story of the bank that I can watch the front of the diner and cover the whole street." Alan offered his hand and smiled. "I've heard stories about your adventures, but I never believed trusting God like this would be so exciting!"

"While you're enjoying yourself," Eric chuckled and backed away, "remember to pray for me as I deal with these characters!"

Toward the front of the book store, Eric gathered in his arms a heap of novels to burn in the diner. He glanced back at the rear of the store, but Alan was no longer in sight. Alan seemed like an unlikely partner for such a mission, but Eric believed God was doing a work in the ex-lieutenant. And that work wasn't quite finished.

Chapter 8

The rain decreased to a constant drizzle through the afternoon, but Smar made no attempt to gather his caravan to continue their march eastward. They were a miserable, muddy lot, Eric thought, yet he was anything but miserable. He remained by the front door of the diner, seeming to watch the prisoners within and guard everyone from dogs without. After a dozen trips to and from the bookstore, he'd gathered enough material to burn low fires through the night. In the flickering firelight, he remained alert and cautious.

The stench of twenty-three captives in wet clothing didn't seem to bother Smar or the other three, but toward evening, Eric was getting restless about their condition. The captives remained shackled, a length of chain separating each prisoner. They couldn't take off even their outer layer of clothing to shake off the drying mud from that morning's trek.

In the light of one fire, Kelly Morris' eyes glared at Eric, perhaps urging Eric to strategize, but his options were limited. Smar and Peter both had sidearms in holsters on their hips, besides the rifles that they never set down. Eric thought he might be able to get their rifles away from them if they fell asleep, but not their sidearms. It had to be that night. He couldn't bear pretending to be apathetic any longer. The prisoners, all of them with terrible sores, needed to be helped before their conditions worsened.

Peter brought a horse steak on a page of paper to Eric at the door. Together, they watched the rain fall on the wet street. Eric had tried to identify where Alan had found to hide, but the man had been stealthy, remaining out of sight.

"Your captives will start dying at this pace, under these conditions." Eric chewed on the bland meat. Even in River Camp, they at least had seasoning for their food. "I'm pulling off from you guys in Lincoln, but if you guys are continuing, you'll need to find a whole new system. Maybe get horses for everyone, or something like that. You're killing your cargo."

Peter turned his head and sniffed at the prisoners.

"I don't disagree, but we're all drawn sort of thin here." Peter cursed, then sighed and lowered his voice so Smar and the others couldn't hear. "This was supposed to be our big break. Nobody in California has horses. We were supposed to pick up cargo along the way and trade for more horses and weapons in Chicago. We'd be rich back in California. We all invested in Smar's idea. It seemed flawless, selling people who had no way to defend themselves. Now, I'm not sure we'll make it to Chicago, let alone back to California."

"While you're still alive, why don't you join me in Lincoln?" Eric offered. "Cut ties on this dying enterprise. Return to the mountains with me. It's a good life, living in God's wilderness. It'll put a smile back on your face."

Peter was a hard man, but the thought did bring a smile to the redhead's face. However, an instant later, it faded, and a furrow spread across his forehead.

"No, I made a commitment to Smar and to the others, to guide them. They need me. My family died from the virus. No one else needs me, even if this is the work."

"The prisoners need you." Eric gestured at the coughing and sniffling mass of bodies in chains. "Who cares for them?"

Peter looked down at the floor, then outside.

"I like you, Eric. I didn't at first, but I do now. Don't let that change. Don't cross me. I'm dedicated to Smar. We're going to Chicago one way or another."

With that, the redhead walked away.

"We'll see," Eric said under his breath, and continued watching the street. He wondered if it was raining back in Mastover, if Gretchen was healing well, and if Andy was behaving without his mother and father around. Of course, he realized Andy was fine. Grandpa Hank was seeing to that, and Runner wouldn't allow the boy to get into too much mischief.

#######

Eric woke when Peter nudged his boot. He lifted his head from where he'd been lying on his back on a diner booth. The room was dark except for the low fires of burning books.

"The rain stopped," Peter whispered, his rifle in his hands. "I saw two dogs out on the street."

Sitting up, Eric glanced at the prisoners. Kelly was close to the fire, watching him. The man's face was ashen, but there was a fierceness in his eyes of a general who was demanding results.

"We need to build up the fires near the doors." Eric swung his own rifle over his shoulder. "I'll get more books."

Eric was still waking up as he emerged from the diner and started across the street. He yawned and gathered his thoughts for the coming night. While praying, he'd fallen asleep, waiting on God to direct events that might favor his safe handling of everyone involved.

"Eric!" Peter called.

Stopping in the middle of the street, Eric looked back at Peter in the doorway of the diner.

"Yeah?"

Peter pointed with his rifle down the street. Eric followed the man's gaze, and froze. A pack of trotting dogs entered the west end of town. They were so numerous abreast under the moonlight that the sides of the pack slowed to funnel into the confines of the four-lane street.

They were one hundred feet away when Eric dashed toward the bookstore. Fire was the diner's best defense, and that meant more books. But once inside the bookstore, he glanced around for anything to block the store's doorway. Now he was trapped with thousands of books as over two hundred wild dogs moved into the town! All shelves, tables, and furniture had been removed from the bookstore. There was nothing with which to block the door, and now the dogs had reached as far as the store and diner.

Eric backed into the hidden shadows of the store where he'd talked to Alan earlier that day, where he hoped to wait out the passing canines. They were hunting. Through the front door, a few spied or smelled him, and leaped through the front door and windows. Stumbling in the darkness, Eric scrambled toward the stairway he knew was in back.

He reached the stairs, climbed to the first landing, and looked back. Three growling creatures simultaneously tried to climb the steps. Their jostling against one another for a bit of his flesh bought Eric the second he needed to slip his rifle off his shoulder. He pointed the muzzle without aiming directly and fired the gun.

The blast knocked one snarling beast backwards, but the other two sounded more aggravated, as they barked and snapped. The nightmare would've been terrible enough in the daylight, but in the moonlight, which was diminished inside, Eric wasn't sure what he was actually seeing and what shadows he was imagining. But his ears couldn't lie to him. These animals were killers, and their jaws were inches away!

Using his rifle muzzle, he battered their skulls and managed to finger the bolt action to slide another cartridge into the barrel. Standing on the landing above the two remaining dogs gave him the advantage, but if more dogs joined in the attack, it wouldn't take much for a dog to slip under his waving barrel to nip at his legs. Any injury would prove fatal at this point. Blood would enrage the animals, and a frenzy would ensue.

He aimed low and pulled the trigger again. The lightning bolt of gunfire lit up the back stairway and Eric confirmed no other dogs had joined them, yet.

A dog, about German shepherd size, backed away, confused or frightened by this second terrible noise.

"Get out of here!" Eric growled and snapped his best, backing the remaining dog all the way to the ground floor. He kicked at the dog, connected with its shoulder, and sent it running after the wounded one.

He panted with relief, but only for a couple seconds. A gunshot from across the street reminded him that more than two dozen lives were at stake in the diner.

Cautiously, he edged toward the front of the bookstore, not wanting to catch the eye of any darting canine out on the street. There were over one hundred in sight—all attacking the diner! The dogs climbed over one another as they tried to pass through the doorway, defended by who looked like Peter and another Smar man. The dogs were investigating the low, glassless windows as Eric looked on, but he knew any dog in the street could leap over the windowsill as soon as they figured it out.

But there was no helping the diner from the street or on foot. There were too many dogs. Eric stepped deeper into the bookstore and prayed for help. By God's grace, he wasn't trapped inside the diner with the others—but now what? He couldn't stand aside as two hundred dogs mauled Smar and the prisoners!

He ran to the back of the bookstore and leaned his rifle against the wall on the first stair landing. Then, he went to the soda vending machine and tipped it with effort to judge its weight. Yes, it was heavy enough. Shifting and sliding it, he moved it to the bottom of the stairs, then stood on the steps to pull the machine snuggly against the first step. Except for a couple of inches on either side of the appliance, the stairway was blocked by the six-foot-tall machine. It would have to hold.

Taking three steps at a time, Eric climbed the stairs to the second story and raced to the glassless window that overlooked the street. The mob of canines in the street sounded like something from hell itself. Snarling and barking, the dogs tore at each other for an approach at the front door where Peter fought with his rifle like a club. When the slaver fired into the pack that bit at his legs and threatened entrance into the diner, the sound of gunfire was nearly overwhelmed by the sound of growling and snapping.

Farther to the side of the diner, which Eric could now see more clearly, several dogs used other animals as leverage to leap through the windows. Eric gasped at the terror of the prisoners, imagining them chained wrist to wrist, yet trying to fight off the invading dogs.

The stench of unwashed humanity, no doubt, was driving the ravenous dogs into their frenzy. With so many dogs on the plain, there couldn't have been much food as of late for them all. They were starving, regardless of the horses this pack or another had consumed the night before.

Eric aimed down his open sights at the thickest mob of dogs in front of the door where Peter was trying to defend. Though Eric's backpack with his cache of cartridges was in the diner, he still had thirty extra rounds on him. When he started to fire into the chaos of fur and gnashing teeth, he wondered how a few bullets could make any impact at all. The animals seemed crazed, like some of the wild animals in the mountains, rumored to have been negatively affected by the Meridia Virus. Their natural instinct to fear man, and man's dominion over them, had all but disappeared.

He heard another rifle report from down the street, and he paused for just a moment to surmise it must be Alan, revealing himself right on time. It would take everything they both had to disrupt the pack of attacking dogs.

Inside the diner, the fires that had been used to stay warm were now being used as weapons. The women prisoners were throwing burning books out the windows, apparently trying to establish a perimeter of fire outside the building. At the back of the diner, from what Eric could see of the male prisoners through the windows, a battle was raging. There were dogs inside. Maybe they'd pushed through the back door, or other dogs had leaped through the windows. Men were screaming as fire spread.

Eric reloaded his deer rifle and aimed carefully as Alan, from another angle, fired more liberally with his assault rifle. Dead dogs were beginning to noticeably litter the sidewalk and street outside the diner, but was it enough? Peter fought valiantly at the door, swinging his rifle like a golf club, having no time to reload, but he had to be growing weary. Almost twenty minutes had passed since the first dog was spotted on the street.

Suddenly, Peter was struck from behind and nearly trampled as someone on horseback plowed outward through the doorway! Dogs fell under hoof as the rider urged the horse to wade through the bloody animals. Eric recognized his own horse, but in only the moonlight, he couldn't identify who was on him before the horse and rider tore down the middle of the street. Thirty healthy dogs were in fast pursuit.

Peter rose to his feet outside the door, and Eric fired his last five bullets at dogs around the slaver, to help him recover his position at the door of the diner. The man was visibly bleeding from his arms and legs, his clothing covered in dark crimson. The dogs were beginning to take notice of their diminished numbers, it seemed. Many canines were wounded, whining, and limping away, seeming to break the courage of others. Alan didn't stop firing, but Eric saw the assault dwindling, so he left the window for the stairs.

At the bottom of the staircase, he nudged the vending machine far enough aside to fit through to the ground floor. With his rifle held for striking, he crept to the front door of the bookstore and peered out. Only a dozen dogs seemed to have any fight left in them, but fifty more were still in sight, licking their wounds or lapping up rainwater from puddles. Eric worried that a second assault could be in the making.

"I'm coming to you!" Eric yelled to Peter.

Peter lifted his head, but twenty dogs also turned their attention to Eric as well. He stepped out cautiously amongst the wounded and withdrawn animals. They didn't seem as fearsome spread out as they were, whining like puppies over their wounds. But it would only take one attacking dog to set off the whole lot, Eric realized, so he kept vigilant, his rifle raised over his head, ready to swing.

Alan fired at a Doberman that rose to its feet in front of Eric. Dogs that weren't able to leap away from Eric's path crawled away.

Finally, he reached the door, and Peter fell into his arms. The redhead was bleeding, his clothes torn in patches from dog bites. It was amazing to Eric that the man hadn't been dragged away by the animals.

"Smar left us," Peter mumbled. He dropped his rifle and submitted to Eric. Eric propped the wounded slaver against the inside wall.

The prisoners were all on their feet, except for two men on the ends of the chain. Burning or smoldering books lay scattered across the floor. The makeshift fireplaces that had been sources of heat and for cooking meat hours earlier had been the prisoners' only weapons to use against the dogs that had made it inside. A number of dead dogs lay between the male and female prisoners. The two other slavers were nowhere in sight, and Eric guessed they'd fled on foot out the back door after Smar had abandoned the fight. The two remaining horses snorted and tossed their heads from behind the dining counter, which acted like a stable stall, protecting them.

"Please!" Eric called to the twenty-three captives. Several of them appeared wounded from dog bites and burns from the fire, besides the injuries they already carried from their days or weeks in shackles. "Listen to me. My name is Eric Radner. I'm here to help you."

"We know," the dark-haired, stout woman said. "I've told them what you told me yesterday."

"The dogs may not be finished. We need to get across the street to the bookstore. We'll be safe upstairs and we'll have plenty of books to burn."

"Eric!" Peter cursed as he tried to rise on his exhausted and torn legs. "What're you doing?"

"Only what I came to do, my friend." Eric gently pushed Peter back down to the floor and drew a bulky brass key from the man's breast pocket. He also took Peter's sidearm and stuck it into his own belt. "Do what I say if you want to live."

"Eric," someone weakly called from the back of the diner. It was one of those lying on the floor. "Eric, help me . . ."

"I'm coming." Eric handed the key to the stout woman. "Unlock everyone, then help Peter and the rest of the wounded across the street. Use the chains to fight off the dogs if you have to."

"Help Peter?" The woman yanked the key from Eric's hand. "That devil captured us! Do you know what he—"

"I don't need to know!" Eric stared at all of them. "I know enough to be sick to my stomach about it, but look at him. He's helpless now, and we're not monsters. But we don't have time for this! Get everyone unlocked and across the street!"

"Molly, unlock me!" a woman nearest her cried, and the others crowded near.

At the back of the diner, Eric knelt next to Kelly Morris. By the light of flickering fires, he beheld Kelly's face, blackened and burned. What hair he'd had on his face and head had been scorched off. His facial skin and eyelids appeared melted.

"Eric?" The man trembled in agony, holding up burned and shackled hands. "Is that you?"

Touching the man's shoulder, Eric made his presence known to the butcher of America.

"I'm here, Kelly."

"I fell into the fire, then they fell on top of me. There was nothing I could do. I can't see, Eric. I'm blind. Eric, help me!"

Molly moved through the men, unlocking them as swiftly as possible. She came to Kelly and delicately avoided his blackened hands to loose him from his shackles.

Eric took a deep breath. Kelly's injuries were extensive. His appearance was mangled by the searing heat he'd fallen into. His hands were no better, but it was his eyes that Eric most mourned over for the man. His eyeballs were no more. The fire's heat had been too much.

"Help me, Eric!"

"I will." Eric drew the man into an embrace. It was an embrace that he would never have imagined a year earlier, but now it was the most natural response to this poor soul in front of him. "We'll take care of you, Kelly. I came back for you, didn't I?"

Eric held the man at arm's length, but Kelly couldn't speak through his wailing. Though he made the sound of weeping, he was unable to produce tears any longer. If anyone needed the morphine for pain, which Eric had brought, Kelly did.

The second man on the floor next to Kelly had no pulse, so Eric lifted him into one of the booths and left him there.

"The horses?" Molly asked. She picked up Peter's rifle and checked the chamber. "How do we take them with us?"

"For now, we don't." Eric pointed at the gear Smar and the others had left behind. "Everyone take something with you. We'll need it across the street."

Eric helped Kelly to his feet and supported him with one arm. In his other hand, he picked up his own pack, which was full of ammo, a little medicine, dry clothes, and a little food.

He led the way outside and looked to the left at the dark buildings where he imagined Alan was watching through his rifle scope. And he looked up and mouthed a thank You to the Lord. They weren't alone.

The remaining dogs didn't move as the human survivors hurried single-file across the street. At the doorway of the bookstore, Eric gave Kelly into Molly's hands, then stood guard as the others filed into the store. Lastly, two men supported Peter as he limped up to the sidewalk.

"I thought you were my friend," Peter said accusingly as he moved through the doorway.

"I am your friend, Peter," Eric said. "Right now, you're finding out just how true that is."

Chapter 9

Morning light revealed how terribly wounded the captives were. In the night, they had collapsed from exhaustion on the floor of the loft. By candlelight, Eric and Molly had tended to the worst of the wounded, but their supplies were limited. There was a little antibiotic ointment, enough pain reliever for only a couple victims, and no gauze. Even water was in short supply, so boiling rags for bandages was a challenge.

"I cannot believe Smar abandoned us," Peter said from his place by the window that overlooked the street. Besides Kelly's debilitating condition, Peter's wounds were the worst, mostly to his arms and legs. "After all the miles we traveled together!"

"You're shocked that a man who mistreated innocent people would mistreat you?" Eric scoffed, glad to be free to speak plainly about mankind's true condition. He sat between Peter and Kelly, as Kelly slept on his side, facing away from them. For a while, the morphine helped the man to rest from his burns. "You were blinded by greed, I would say. Men like Smar will always disappoint. I know only One who will always satisfy."

"Who?" It was Peter who scoffed now.

"God has never disappointed me." Eric set his hand on Kelly's slender shoulder. The ex-commander of the Lib-Org had lost so much weight, his shoulder blade and ribs were visible through his shirt. "What He promises for us are not empty promises. I have known His great love, even though I'm an unworthy, imperfect man. Because He is so good and forgiving, I strive to be the same in His name toward others."

"So, the last few days has all been a lie?" Peter frowned. "How is that good?"

"I disguised myself and my intentions to join you for your own good, Peter, not just to rescue the prisoners. I didn't know how God would work it all out. I just knew I needed to be present and available to aid in the deliverance of all of you."

"Do I look delivered?" Peter shook his head at the bandages. "I'm in more pain than I've ever known, and I've lost everything. I went into debt to buy a couple horses for this trip, and now I can't recover my investment because you've let everyone go!"

"You were acting out against God Almighty, and you're surprised your plans blew up in your face? That shows a very basic misunderstanding about your idea of evil, Peter. What you sow, you will eventually reap. It's a fact of life. God makes sure of it, because He is both sovereign and just."

"What are you even talking about?" Peter waved his arms with frustration, then cringed in pain when the movement pulled at his bandages. "Who talks about God? Where has God been? Look at this country. It's a mess. You sound as crazy as Bolture."

"The guy with the blue scarf?"

"Yeah. Over campfires, he used to talk about how everything in existence has a psyche. A rock has a psyche? I don't think so. And your God doesn't make sense to me, either."

"May I make just a basic observation?" Eric asked.

"What?"

"Do you think it's any wonder that you've been bitten by a dozen dogs, and you'll be scarred for life, but the dogs didn't touch me? You think that happened by accident? Chance?"

"You're saying that your God protected you?"

"I'm simply making an observation. My God could've allowed me to be attacked by the dogs, too, and it would've been according to His wise providence. Yet, here we are. I am His ambassador. You've been wicked, and you're covered by bite marks. I choose to submit to God, and I remain uninjured. Like I said, it's just an observation. Think about it."

Molly signaled to Eric from the top of the stairs. He rose and went to her. Two men stood with her, their wrists wrapped with strips of clothing. These were the three healthiest among the ex-captives. The others still moved about weakly. Some of them wouldn't have survived another forty-eight hours on the chain.

"The horses we left in the diner last night are gone." Molly kept her voice low, trying not to cause more alarm for the desperate party. "They weren't killed by dogs, either. There was no blood. None of the dogs are even around, as far as we can tell."

"Someone took our two remaining horses!" said a man with part of his ear missing. It looked like a wound several years old. "Someone is still in town. It could be Smar, or one of the others. We're not just fighting the dogs. We're fighting to survive the chain still!"

"No, the tables have turned." Eric glanced back at Peter. "Even if Smar is still alive, he's ruined. He captured each of you one at a time on his way from California. Now, we're a band of overcomers. He won't try to capture all of us at once, especially since he knows we have a few weapons. What we need to do now is get cleaned up so our wounds can heal, then get as far away from these dogs as possible."

"And go where?" The man with the half-missing ear frowned. The lines of strife on his thirty-year-old face made him appear twenty years older. "We've talked. We're all alone in this world. The little we had was taken by Smar or left behind. We have nothing."

"Not true." Eric placed a hand on Molly's shoulder and one hand on the melancholy man's shoulder. "We have each other, and we have a mighty God watching over us. Let me tell you about a place called River Camp."

For a few minutes, Eric spoke about the refuge by the river in the mountains of Wyoming where a small but peaceful settlement survived off the land. As he spoke, Molly and the two men's tension diminished, and hopeful smiles emerged briefly at the imagery Eric painted for them.

The man with the damaged ear and lined face was named Isaac. He'd come from a family of real estate developers in the Shasta Mountain area of Northern California. When his family had died from the virus and subsequent violence of Pan-Day, he'd hunted and planted around one of his father's old estates. And then Smar had ridden through the property. Isaac had been one of the first men Smar had captured. Peter himself had put Isaac on the chain.

The other man, quieter and older than Isaac, was named Conrad. He was tall with a firm jaw, and whether he meant to or not, his body language and closeness to Molly gave the impression that he was fond of the stout woman in her forties.

"We're civilized people," Isaac finally said, "so we need to execute Peter for his crimes. Then we can move on, heal, and go with you to this River Camp place."

The three waited for Eric to reply, but he didn't respond quickly. He was remembering about the past winter when other victims of evil men had suddenly needed to make hard choices about mercy and justice.

"Peter's a broken man. Look at him." Eric gazed with them at the ex-slaver whose face reflected the pain he felt from his wounds on every limb. "His physical condition is helping him move through the necessary emotions of regret and shame. If he wants to live, he must submit to our care. Nothing is more painful for an evil heart than to humble itself into the hands of kind people. Peter's crimes are many, and they were gruesome. But now we must give his heart time to turn. If we are gracious, we'll win him altogether from the darkness he's lived in, which is why he's done what he's done to you all."

"He'll be a burden to us with all those wounds," Conrad said.

"That's true." Eric took a deep breath. "But this isn't just a time for us to heal physically. This is a time for us to help our enemies heal spiritually. The blind man's name is Kelly. I have adopted him into my care. Someone will need to do the same for Peter. It needs to be one of us. The others are too weak to help another besides caring for themselves."

"I hate him too much," Isaac said. "Talk about God and spiritual stuff all you want, Eric. I won't touch the man."

"I'll help him," Molly said, "if he'll let me. I want to see him in his humility."

"We'll help him together." Conrad put his arm around Molly. "If the snake acts up, I'll belt him one."

"I suppose that's reasonable." Eric smiled. "Now, I'm going to scout around town a little and see who might've taken the horses. Also, we'll need water. Maybe there's a functioning well or something we can use. We also need to drag all the dead dogs out of town. We'll be here for a few days before we're ready to head west. We need to survive."

The gathering broke up, and Eric returned to the window where Kelly lay. He set a hand on the man's shoulder, and the ex-commander stirred.

"It's me, Eric. I'm going outside for a while. Can I do anything for you?"

"Help me sit up." With his hands burnt, he struggled to do anything at all for himself. Eric helped him, and when he was propped against the windowsill, he turned his sightless face toward the sky. "I'm being punished, aren't I?"

"What have you done that would warrant punishment?" Eric had never met anyone who'd done more heinous acts than Kelly Morris, but he wondered if Kelly was able to claim them and experience proper sorrow. The ex-prisoners had been captured and abused by Smar, but Smar's crimes were few compared to Kelly's. The man's blackened face and disfigured flesh would disguise him from anyone who once knew him. And Eric wouldn't call him anything but by his first name, a name only few people knew and could identify as the man who was once Commander Kelly Morris.

"I've done a lot." Kelly bowed his head. "I . . . justified things . . . to achieve a vision. Now, I've reached the end, and my vision—I can't even see."

"Yeah." Eric took the man's upper arm in his grip. "But this isn't the end, Kelly. It may be that God's providence demanded you to be blinded now so you can begin to see in another way. You think about that."

Eric offered his canteen to the nearest lounging man, his beard still bearing the remnants of ash from the burning books the night before.

"If he needs a drink, help him, okay?"

Downstairs, Eric shouldered his rifle and walked out the front door of the bookstore. He stood on the sidewalk and counted the dead dogs. About forty lay still on the street, killed mostly by Alan's marksmanship in the dark of the night. But there were over a hundred dogs still out there, and thousands in other packs that could be in the region. They seemed a formidable force against them. Returning to Coppertown to pick up Amber seemed an impossible journey, let alone traveling all the way back to the mountains of Wyoming. The dogs could attack at any time.

He crossed the street and entered the diner. The floor was scarred from the fires and stained with blood from the overnight battle. The horses were indeed gone from behind the counter. But when Eric crouched to examine the dusty floor, as he'd learned to do as a woodsman, he found little round marks on either side of a single boot print. Such sign would've confused any other tracker, but Eric recognized the one-legged man's presence.

Behind the diner, he found more dead dogs and one of Smar's men who'd tried to escape in the commotion. The slaver had perished.

He kept walking behind the buildings, searching for anything that might help the two-dozen souls in his charge, but the town had been stripped of anything useful during years of scavenging. Even the floorboards of one building had been peeled up and taken away.

At the east end of town, he returned to the street and looked up at the two-story bank building. Alan stood in the bay window, one crutch under his arm, and his rifle in the other. His empty pant leg was tied in a knot below his knee, and he was smiling.

"You think it's safe to be strolling around like you are?"

"With you on over-watch?" Eric surveyed the street. "After last night, I'm fairly confident in your marksmanship to defend me."

"Don't get too confident. I've only got about a hundred rounds left, and I don't think those dogs will let us leave without another fight. I can see them out there to the northeast, laying in the sagebrush, maybe resting up for another attack. I doubt they are focused on moving elsewhere when they think they can get a meal right here."

"We'll need to make a stand, anyway, for about a week. These people are in no condition to march right now. Some of them don't even have shoes."

"Those in worst shape can ride horseback, even double," Alan suggested. "I don't know what you found in that bookstore to keep you safe, but it can't be as good as this place. Someone lived in the bank for a while, even rigged up a cistern on the roof to collect rainwater. I have the six horses locked inside the crash gate here where they're safe from the dogs."

"How're you feeding them?"

"Well, you look able-bodied enough to go pick some grass for them." Alan laughed. "What're you waiting for? I'm sure they're hungry. Go ahead. I'll cover you."

"I'd feel safer if a couple of us covered a few grass harvesters. Can this place house two dozen people? We have no water in the bookstore."

"Bring them down. I'll fire a shot if the dogs start this way."

Chapter 10

It took an hour to move everyone down to the safety of the bank. Its tiled floor was cool and an outhouse had been rigged by the previous residents. Eric supported Kelly along the walk down the sidewalk, guiding him with an arm on his shoulder.

"I'm an invalid," Kelly said. He was the last to reach the bank. "What good am I as a blind man?"

"The question is, what good were you as a seeing man?" Eric asked. "Seems to me you used your sight for evil. Now, God has made you blind."

"God." Kelly scoffed. "There's irony that extends beyond coincidence between you and me, Eric Radner, Mad Man of Wyoming. I remember what I tried to do to you in Mastover."

"You mean when you tried to burn me alive?"

"And now, I'm burned, though still alive."

"Not many receive this kind of opportunity," Eric said. Conrad opened the gate at the front of the bank, then closed it after they entered. "You're still alive, Kelly. Give God some time. You'll find that He still has quite a bit left for you to do."

"Ridiculous." Kelly cursed. "It's no wonder I tried to kill all of your kind. You're filled with pure delusion."

Eric felt stung by the hard man's words. Kelly was too helpless to reach into his own bitter heart and give his broken life any hope. In that instant, Eric wanted only to find his Bible among the belongings he'd left with Alan, and find a quiet corner to be alone and receive nourishment from the Lord.

Before the people settled into their new living quarters, Molly arranged for everyone to take advantage of the cistern of water on the roof. It held many days' worth of drinking water, but for showering, they would need to use it sparingly. But wash they must, Molly insisted, since they all still carried the wounds from Smar and Peter's abuse.

At the mention of his name, Peter shrunk back against the bank wall where he sat alone. His head was bowed and his shaggy red hair hung over his downcast eyes.

In the horse packs near the vaulted crash gate where the horses stood protected behind steel bars, Eric found his Bible and clutched it to his chest. Now, for a place to read . . .

"Eric!" Alan called from his window perch upstairs. "Get up here!"

Taking two steps at a time, Eric bounded to the second story. Molly's showering line was in full swing, but the people hushed themselves as they waited to hear what this new threat might be.

Eric tucked his Bible inside his shirt and joined Alan at the window. Alan handed him field glasses and pointed at the plain.

"Someone's out there on horseback. See to the east? The dogs haven't sensed them yet."

Peering northeast, Eric first acknowledged the dogs on the horizon—over one hundred lay in the sagebrush and grass dotting the hillside. Then, he swung his view gradually to the east where a horse and rider filled his vision. The horse stood still, his head hanging low, and the rider was hunched over, his head bowed.

"That's my horse," Eric said quietly, "and the rider is Smar, the leader of the slavers."

Even as he watched, Smar's exhausted frame leaned to the side and slid off the horse. The horse side-stepped once, then stood still. Smar's form remained motionless on the ground.

"We can't leave him out there." Eric handed Alan the binoculars. "I can get to him before the dogs smell him. He's downwind right now. Can you cover me?"

"It's too far, Eric!" Alan tested his rifle scope by aiming out onto the plain. "It's a fool's errand. The guy is probably already dead."

"Then we need the horse." Eric checked the load on his rifle. "I won't be able to see the dogs from down there. If you see them coming for me, start shooting."

Downstairs, Isaac had assumed the station as gatekeeper at the front door.

"It looks like Smar," Eric said to the man missing part of his ear. "He's in trouble. The dogs aren't far away."

"Don't bring him back here." Isaac glanced at the rest of the people who waited to hear what was happening. "They won't stand for it. Peter is one thing. But Smar?"

"Let me worry about Smar." Eric stepped outside. "Just keep this gate open. I have a feeling I'll be running back with the horse."

Eric looked back at the bank's inhabitants. They were all watching him. Their faces were drawn and worried, regardless of the safety and clean water Alan had secured for them. It was a lot to ask of them, Eric admitted to himself—to forgive the man who had abused them so horribly. But too soon or not, he decided, they would need to adjust. After all, their survival relied on him and Alan.

Jogging out of town, Eric arced first to the south to approach Smar and the exhausted mount on the side opposite the dogs. He knew the dogs were just out of his sight over the next rise. A simple change in the wind would be his death. So many dogs attacking in the daylight would prove hopeless. After all, he had only a bolt action rifle, and he was a quarter-mile from Alan's perch. Striking a running dog at four hundred yards, even by Alan, was unlikely.

"Whoa, boy." Eric held out his hand to his horse. The mount was still saddled and he was bleeding from a dog bite on his left flank, but the animal's legs seemed otherwise free of injury. "Easy, boy. I'm gonna take care of you."

Next, Eric knelt to examine Smar. When he rolled the man in the sweater onto his back, the barrel of a handgun was pushed into Eric's face. Eric froze.

"I should've known it'd be you." Smar's words were fierce, but his breathing was shallow. "Ever since you joined us, we were cursed."

"Don't blame me because you invested in a failed campaign." Eric studied the man's clothing. "You're bleeding. Let me get you back to town. If you pull that trigger, we're both dead. The dogs are just over that hill."

Smar pulled up his torn wool sweater and revealed the gaping wound where it looked like a grizzly bear had taken a bite out of his side. Of course, the wound was from a large dog.

"No, I'm finished." Smar panted and uncocked his handgun and rested his head on the earth, his eyes closed. "I never imagined my life would end so pointlessly."

"It may end, but it doesn't have to be pointless." Eric reached out, drawing from the compassion he sensed God had for this tormented soul. He laid his hand on the man's pale forehead and felt his fever. "Death doesn't need to trouble you, Smar. You've lived wickedly, and you may deserve the worst punishment, but now is the time to receive God's mercy. Don't die in this state of guilt. Accept the forgiveness that can only come from God."

"We're all guilty. I won't ask God to carry what's mine alone."

"Receive His forgiveness, Smar. You must know about Jesus dying on the cross. He was innocent, but He died, so that you could live again, even though you are guilty."

"Shut up, Eric." Tears of pain trickled from the eyes of the once mighty man. "Let me die in peace. What a waste this life has been. So pointless . . ."

"It's not pointless, Smar! Smar!" Eric gripped the slaver's hand, squeezing it. "Come on! Not like this. Oh, God, not like this!"

Eric wept as Smar sighed his last breath. He tried not to imagine the regret Smar felt at that very moment, facing eternity now knowing that he would be judged by his Creator. The man was lost, it seemed, and he had died in his sins. The grief of such a reality left Eric sobbing quietly over the man's bloody and rain-soaked sweater. Life had been pointless to Smar, he realized, only because he didn't know God's purpose for his life. None of the others could be lost like this, Eric determined. He lifted his head at the sound of a shout from town.

There was movement outside the bank. Eric leaped up, glaring with anger through his misty eyes. It was too far away to determine who, but someone was walking slowly out into the plain toward him! How could Isaac allow someone to leave the bank? And Alan couldn't be seen in the window any longer. No one was watching for the dogs! Their keen ears were sure to have heard the shout over the plain as well.

Taking hold of the horse's reins, he drew the weary horse after him. The horse resisted at first, but succumbed to a slow walk. Smar had ridden the horse nearly to death. While dying in the saddle, Smar hadn't realized, apparently, that the horse had returned on his own volition to the dangers of the town he'd left earlier.

Eric let his irritation rise within him, that anyone would allow someone outside the bank, until he realized the person walking hesitantly onto the plain was Kelly Morris! Even as Eric realized it was the blind man, he saw Alan on his crutches, hurrying up the pavement after Kelly.

"Come on, boy!" Eric urged the horse faster, but the animal was already dragging his hooves. "Just a little farther!"

The dogs appeared as they trotted up to the hilltop to the north, and Eric felt his body go numb. He let go of the reins and sprinted toward town. The horse was on his own.

Ahead, Alan had nearly reached Kelly, but Kelly, in what seemed to be a suicide mission, stepped awkwardly but faster away from town.

"Get back!" Eric yelled and waved his free hand at Alan.

Alan froze, looked out at the plain, dropped his crutches, then shouldered his rifle. Balanced on one leg, he fired his rifle rather than hustling himself back to the bank. The dogs were barking as they closed the gap. Eric hoped the sacrifice of his horse slowed them long enough to carry Kelly back to safety, but now Alan was fifty yards from the bank, and in full view of the ravenous canines.

Alan's rifle thundered again and again, its noise rumbling across the plain.

Suddenly, the horse galloped cumbersomely past Eric! Eric looked back. Nothing now separated him from the dogs. They came like a wave toward him, two or three in the front, then the mass shaped like a V in pursuit.

As Eric drew closer to Kelly, he shifted his rifle into his left hand. He barely slowed his sprint before he slammed his shoulder into Kelly, sweeping the man over his shoulder with hardly missing a beat.

But the bank building was too far away, and Eric couldn't carry Alan back as well.

"What are you doing?" Eric panted as he reached Alan.

"No one else would come out and try to save that blind fool!" Alan squeezed off five more shots. "Go! I'll hold them off!"

"Not a chance!"

Eric dropped Kelly to the ground next to Alan, then raised his own rifle as the dogs closed. Together, they targeted the lead dogs. In that instant, Eric recalled what Alan had said about taking out the leader of the pack. As quickly as the thought came to him, he recognized the signal of several dogs on the right as they glanced toward the middle-front of the pack. Guessing the leader was a large mastiff with a brownish coat, Eric fired, and fired again.

The pack broke its stride and split in two. The dogs seemed confused and uncertain.

"My clip is empty!" Alan said.

"They don't know that!" Eric fired in front of the dogs that had slowed to a walk, but were still approaching. The bullets spit dirt into their faces, causing them to flinch away, then stop. "Keep your gun raised. They're catching on that we're a danger to them."

"Aaah!" Alan hollered and shook his empty rifle at the nearest dogs. They paced across the empty ground ten yards away. "Get out of here, Eric! Now's your chance!"

"Nope, we go together." Eric crouched down, keeping his eyes on the dogs, and felt with his hand for Alan's crutches. He handed them to him. "Kelly, get to your feet. Come on!"

He yanked Kelly upright by his arm.

"Let me die!" Kelly cursed and pulled away.

Eric roughly drew Kelly over his shoulder.

"I'm not losing any more people today!" Eric held Kelly with one hand and aimed his rifle with the other. "Just back away, Alan. Come on. That's it. Let them see we're not intimidated by them."

"They're getting behind us!" Alan warned, but they continued to back up toward town.

Suddenly, a ruckus bellowed from the bank. Screaming and yelling erupted, causing the dogs to pause with uncertainty. They seemed unfamiliar with an aggressive enemy in full daylight.

Eric looked back. Conrad and Isaac led a dozen of the healthier ex-captives a safe distance away from the bank. They stood shoulder to shoulder, lengths of chain in their hands. They appeared to be an impenetrable wall of ferocity bearing down on Eric and Alan. One of them caught the frightened horse and led him into the bank building.

The dogs didn't advance further. Several yawned and glanced about. Others sat on their haunches and whined mournfully at a meal gone untasted.

The wielders of chains took hold of Eric and Alan and escorted them onto the street, then the sidewalk, and finally through the bank door. Isaac closed the gate at the door after everyone was inside, and the people gave a collective sigh at reaching safety.

Regardless of his firm hand a moment earlier, Eric gently slid Kelly off his shoulder to sit in the corner against the wall. Kelly held his bandaged hands aloft as he wept quietly at his failed suicide attempt. The poor man, Eric thought, watching the one who had terrorized the nation for years. Everything had been stripped from the commander. Now, he commanded nothing, not even his own senses of sight and touch. It would be weeks before his hands could even be used to tend to his own needs.

"Enough standing around!" Molly chastised the group. "Back in the shower line. We didn't survive this long to suffocate on our own filth!"

Alan nudged Eric's leg with a crutch and signaled to the side. Once the two were away from Kelly's hearing, Alan spoke quietly to Eric.

"You called him Kelly. Is that who I think it is?" Alan eyed the shriveled, blind, weeping man in the corner. "I spent too many years with him not to recognize him, even if his appearance has changed drastically."

"He's the most ruined man here, and you just risked your life to save him." Eric watched his friend closely. "You told me back in Three Lodges that he's the one who shot you in the leg."

Alan nodded, then narrowed his eyes at Eric.

"How long have you known he was one of the prisoners?"

"Since the beginning." Eric tried not to smile in the horror of the week, but it was a moment of triumph. "I had to come back especially for him.

"His army was all he had." Alan shook his head, and tears rolled from his eyes. "Now, he has no one."

"That's true."

"Except us." Alan wiped at his eyes and chuckled. "Our God is some coordinator of circumstances, huh?"

"I'd say so."

"What do we do with him? I mean, where do we take him?"

"We're all he's got. I guess we take him home—to River Camp, or Mastover. The judge thought he might not be welcome in Mastover, so probably River Camp."

"No one else knows who he is?"

"It doesn't seem so."

Conrad approached them. He'd emptied one of the packs of its contents, and had it hung over his shoulder.

"Some of us are making a book run," the tall man said to Eric. "You want to come while the dogs are disorganized? Molly says we need to get a couple fires built up to dry out the clothes we're washing."

"Count me in." Eric patted the man's shoulder. "Let's do it."

Five men rallied together at the door, and Isaac gauged the threat level of dogs in sight. As Eric joined them, his rifle at the ready, he looked back at his one-legged friend.

Alan was hobbling with his crutch over to the corner of the room.

"Mind if I join you for a while?" the one-legged man asked the blind man. The blind man didn't respond, but tilted his sightless head upward. "Yeah, this is just one of the advantages for you and me being crippled. Everyone else has to do all the work."

Eric wondered if Kelly recognized Alan's voice, by the way Kelly moved his head to hear Alan clearly.

"How are you crippled?" Kelly asked.

"Missing my leg. Got shot up last winter. Had to amputate it to save my life. How're you doing? Use some water?"

"You have water?" Kelly held up his bandaged hands. "You'll have to—"

"Don't sweat it, pal." Alan tipped his canteen to Kelly's lips. "I think you and I will be able to help one another. You can walk and I can't, but I can see, and you can't. Yep, we're going to become friends."

Eric grinned at the sight, rejoicing at the way God had brought them all together. Though they were all stranded in a strange Nebraskan town with killer canines all around, if God had done this much, Eric knew He was trustworthy to do so much more.

"Okay, I think it's clear, guys." Isaac the gatekeeper drew the gate back. "Stay on the sidewalk, not on the street. Bring back as many books as you can. "Go!"

Eric led the way outside.

###

~End of *STEADFAST Book Five*~

STEADFAST BOOK SIX

America's Last Days

D.I. Telbat

Prologue, Book Six

Judge Zachary Grayport of Mastover, Wyoming, was mid-sentence in the fourth draft of a letter when his office door flew open, banging on the back wall. He rose to his feet at the sight of Gretchen Radner, Eric's wife. She was pale, sweating, and holding her lower right abdomen. Her fiery red hair was loose and her eyes were wet.

"Gretchen, I thought you were staying at the house today." He moved a metal chair away from the wall and offered her the seat, but she dismissed it.

"I'm not waiting any longer. It's been ten days. I'm going after Eric. He needs me!"

"It's been nine days," he said, "and if you don't rest up, you'll be dealing with an infection we don't have antibiotics for. You just had an appendectomy, Gretchen. Would you please sit down?"

Stubbornly, she plopped onto the chair.

"Something's wrong. Eric should've been back by now."

"The slavers had several days head start on him and Alan." The judge waved his hand. Long past were the days when he expected people to listen to his words without question. He'd learned that those around him appreciated him more when he exercised a softer approach. It was just one of the many things Eric had driven him to apply to his life since Pan-Day. "Four or five days riding east, then five or six days to return with the prisoners—they'll be back within a couple days, I'm sure. Why don't you go back to the house?"

"No. You have to send someone after him."

"Who would I send?" He raised his arms wide. "It's planting season, Gretchen. Everyone's busy working in the gardens and fields. Even the men who once fought in the resistance conflicts, for or against, have picked up seed bags and become farmers. They're not soldiers, anymore."

"Joel would go, if you asked him."

"I'm not sending Joel out into the Plains Zone. You know the stories about what's out there. Sure, it's mostly rumors, but if just a few of those tales are true, it's not safe, especially for a lone man."

"Then send a whole force! He's my husband, Judge Zachary Grayport!" she scolded. "He's Eric Radner, the Mad Man of Wyoming!"

Zachary sighed and returned to his desk. He looked down at the letter and crumpled it up. It had been terms for peace to offer the Pacific States government forces, if they ever reached inland past the Rockies. So far, their influence remained coastal. Eric would know better how to prepare to meet a new government, the judge decided. After all, why make the same treaty twice with another group like the Liberation Organization, which had nearly destroyed them all?

"I'll talk to Joel, okay?" he finally said. "But I can't promise you anything. If Joel can't raise a force of at least ten men to go with him, they have no business going out there and searching for our two men. It even rained a few nights ago. There won't be a trace for anyone to follow."

"Judge, it's Eric Radner. Everyone in Wyoming owes him in one way or another. Joel will find ten men to go, and I'll be riding at the front!"

"No." He shook his head. "You're staying right here to continue healing—even if I have to put you in a jail cell to keep you here. Let Joel handle it. Your husband is a forgiving man, but I don't want to test his forgiveness if I were to allow you to run off and injure yourself."

"Fine." She rose calmly to her feet. "That's all I wanted."

Gretchen closed the door as she left.

Zachary wiped his brow at the thought of Gretchen remaining under his roof—if Eric really did die out on the range. She was too headstrong to have around. Yes, it was best for everyone in Mastover—especially for him—if Eric Radner returned home immediately!

"After you have suffered for a little while, the God of all grace, who called you to His eternal glory in Christ, will Himself perfect, confirm, strengthen and establish you."
I Peter 5:10 (NASB)

Chapter 1, Book Six

Eric Radner sat on the edge of the diner roof in the town his companions had voted to call Refuge, Nebraska. He guessed many such towns had been forgotten in the wake of the collapse of America, then renamed by newcomers. Whole cities had been decimated by the Meridia Virus, and ghost towns now speckled the landscape.

Refuge, Nebraska, had indeed been their refuge from the wild dogs that roamed the Plains Zone. The town of only a dozen buildings had also been a new start for those who'd once been prisoners of Oliver Smar. The wounds from their shackles had begun to heal, and, if Eric was reading them right, a few of the people were being revived by the hope in God that he and Alan had ceaselessly been offering. This wasn't the first time Eric had seen the truth of Jesus Christ transform broken lives. He had himself experienced the new birth years earlier, so he was able to place much confidence in the power wielded by the gospel.

His rifle lay across his lap as he stared northward. The setting sun shone over his left shoulder, and the view of the seemingly endless plain caused him to sigh in contentment, even though he missed Gretchen and his son, Andy. But the next morning, the party of twenty-five would be starting their trek back to the west, toward Mastover and River Camp. He looked forward to witnessing the ways God would use the people of Refuge as they moved into Wyoming. Eric doubted there was a more pleasant Christian community as Mastover in all of

America. There, the survivors of Smar's slave chain could start new lives.

Not far out on the plain, a pack of five dogs trotted east to west, as if on patrol. They were like enemy scouts, keeping the people of Refuge on edge any time they moved outside the town bank. But the bank building gave the people a place to lock themselves and their seven horses behind secure crash gates—the metal accordion-style joints and bars providing them safety.

The main pack of dogs, numbering over one hundred strong, wasn't in sight at the moment, but Eric had learned not to underestimate the predators. They could materialize quite quickly if they sensed the people of Refuge were vulnerable. Twice, Conrad and Isaac had been chased while fetching more books to fuel the cooking fires in the bank.

A sound on the roof behind him made Eric raise his rifle quickly and pivot around. His sudden movement shifted his weight toward the side of the building, and he had to drop his rifle and grab the ledge to stop from falling off.

"I didn't mean to scare you," Molly said as she walked across the roof. The stout woman's face showed amusement as Eric settled himself more securely on the roof edge. "Alan said to come get you before the sun goes down. He doesn't want to try to cover you from the bank after dark."

"That's a good idea." Eric picked up his rifle and rubbed at the new scuff mark on the stock. After years in the wild, the .223 bolt action rifle was weathered and scarred from dozens of conflicts, but it still shot true. "Have the horses been watered?"

"Yep." Molly sat beside him on the ledge, her bare feet wiggling at the spring grass and sage below. Her dark hair blew untethered in the breeze. "We have just enough water to fill our water bags in the morning, and let the horses drink the rest. The tank on the roof will be dry until it rains again."

"Coppertown must have a functioning well," Eric said. "If we can reach them by sundown tomorrow night, they'll resupply us."

"It'll be good to see Amber again. I thought for sure Smar had sold her because she was on death's door. Who knew you were on our trail, huh?"

"One of the many moments we can see that God has been with us the whole way."

"I want to believe that." She tossed her head, closed her eyes, and presented her face to the sky. "How could a good God allow so much evil? Just a week ago, I was chained up and on my way to be sold as a slave in Chicago. Was God with me then?"

"He was. And He is now. Evil doesn't come from God, but from sinful men and the fallen world. God could stop all the evil, that's true. He wants us to choose Him because we realize our need of Him. If anything, the trials of this life should drive us to Him, not away from Him. And that's where faith comes in. And then we shake our heads at ourselves."

"Why shake our heads?"

"Once we come to Him, He reveals to us our safety in His love, and we wonder why we didn't come to Him sooner. No, He's not to blame for this crazy world, Molly. He's the One who is offering the only alternative to escape its tragic end. We were created to commune with Him, to live in harmony with Him. Believing in the truth about Jesus Christ is just the beginning of that adventure."

She was silent for a few moments, and Eric prayed for her to see the truth of her own need. A couple of people in the bank had responded in faith to Alan's testimony of Christ's grace. The others, like Molly, listened with skepticism. Unlike other places when Eric had found himself isolated with others, Refuge had plenty of reading books. Many of the people in Refuge had found contentment in reading novels rather than listening to Eric and Alan's message of reconciliation with God.

"There aren't very many good men left in the world, anymore," Molly stated suddenly. "I'm getting older. Dying alone doesn't appeal to me. My husband was murdered in the Pan-Day riots, and I've just not found anyone whom I thought I'd be happy with. Until now."

"Molly, I—"

"I know it's only been a week, but before someone else comes along, I need to make my intentions known."

Eric clenched his teeth. He was flattered, because Molly was a likeable woman—tough and mild-mannered like Gretchen. But he'd never leave Gretchen.

"I thought Conrad and you were developing some kind of relationship."

"Maybe in his mind, but no. He's not for me. During our marches behind Smar, Conrad complained constantly. We've all seen each other at our worst, and I guess I'm judging by what kind of man he'd be if we were to face difficulty again. But now I've found a man who has known hardship and suffering, yet remains positive. I have to make sure this opportunity doesn't pass me by."

"Molly, this means a lot to me. You seem like a wonderful woman—strong and helpful toward others. But I'm a married man. I've made it known. My wife's name is Gretchen. Alan mentioned days ago that she's waiting for me in Mastover."

"Typical male," Molly said, scoffing and shaking her head. "You think I'm talking about you. I'm talking about Alan, Eric! He has only one leg, but he's twice the man that any of these others are."

"Oh. Alan." Eric felt his face burn with embarrassment, then he laughed it off. "Well, of course! He's a great guy!"

"You guys have a lot of history, right? That's what he said. I mean, you're riding together. You must trust one another."

"Absolutely."

"So, he'd listen to you maybe, if you spoke for me? He hasn't said he's got a sweetheart or anyone back in Mastover."

"Right. Oh, yeah, I think he's single. But Molly, you need to know that he's a follower of Christ."

"I know. That's one of the things I like about him. He's devoted to something besides himself. It gives him a strength I find refreshing."

"That's true, and because of that, a Christian like him knows he's not better than others, but he knows that God wants him to partner with other disciples of Jesus. That includes the marriage department, so that his journey for God is helped."

"But I would help him."

"As a follower of Christ?"

"Well, no." Molly's face lost its light, and she turned away. "No, I guess not."

"But this isn't a deal-breaker, Molly." Eric nudged her arm with his elbow to get her attention. "Coming to Christ is all about change from the old to the new. Recognizing by faith our need for Jesus gives us new life to be much more than we ever were."

"But I don't know that I feel like I need Jesus. He's just a guy I heard lived thousands of years ago."

"Needing Him is recognized by the truth we learn about Him and ourselves. You're a fine woman, Molly, but you need Jesus to bring you into His kingdom of peace. I'll tell you what. You start talking to Alan about this, and he'll guide you to the truth. It'll knit your hearts together more than any natural affection you'd have as lovers. You'll be in harmony in your faith and love for God. Speaking as a man who's married to a daughter of God, I can't imagine a closer union or friendship."

"A daughter of God." Molly smiled as she looked out over the plain. "That does sound like something. When I came up to this roof, I wasn't expecting all this. It's almost as if God is calling me right now to—Eric, look!"

Eric turned his gaze to where Molly pointed. To the west, a horde of about fifty mangy dogs poured across the range toward Refuge. Carefully, Eric climbed to his feet, then helped Molly away from the ledge.

"This is your chance to kill the next leader of the pack!" Molly shielded her eyes from the last sliver of sun. "It's light enough still. We should be able to figure out which one is the alpha male."

Raising his binoculars, Eric studied the dogs in the front ranks. They all walked with tongues hanging and heads low, but after noticing a few gestures from the other dogs, Eric deduced the alpha male was a tall, black and gray Great Dane. Under its thin coat, its sleek and muscular body rippled with power.

"I see him." Eric dropped his binoculars to hang around his neck, and raised his rifle. "A little closer . . ."

He steadied his breathing, trying to relax for the distant shot at the moving target. Everyone knew that the attack the week before had been disrupted by killing the leader of the pack. Alan had assured everyone that the method would work again. A new leader was probably already in place in the local pack.

"No, now's not the time." Eric lowered his rifle. "It wouldn't help anything to take out the leader right now. There'd be another one by morning. But now, we know which one it is. If we need to tomorrow, we'll know exactly which one to go after. Come on. Let's get to the bank before they come down the street!"

Together, they ran across the roof and hung off the ledge until their feet touched the windowsill near the diner's front door. They dropped to the ground and ran across the street. Alan's silent presence above, in the bank's upper window, gave them added security. Isaac, a dependable man in his thirties, who was missing part of an ear, opened the crash gate at the bank's front door. He slammed the gate behind them as the two slipped inside.

The dogs walked into sight and splintered into multiple packs to sniff at the corners and shadows of the buildings. A few wandered up the sidewalk where Isaac stood a few inches from their blood-stained muzzles. They growled at the gate before they moved on.

"We know who the new leader of the pack is," Molly announced to the others who were lounging on the marble floor. "Eric, tell them."

"I spotted him. He's a big male, a Great Dane." Eric smiled, offering them his own confidence. "It gives us an edge for tomorrow. God will watch over us. Get a good night's sleep, everyone. We'll be heading out before dawn."

Chapter 2

Molly and Alan led the exodus out of Refuge the next morning, an hour before dawn. The most frail or wounded in the company, including Peter, Kelly, and several of the women, rode the seven horses. Alan rode Eric's old mount next to Molly as she walked. Everyone else trailed by twos behind the horses, but in a tight formation, since Alan had instructed that their slow, herd-like migration across the plain would keep them safer from the dogs.

Eric walked as the last man. His job was to ensure that everyone stayed in column formation behind the horses. Alan, Conrad, Eric, and Isaac carried the four rifles they possessed, with Conrad and Isaac walking on either side of the column, covering all sides from attack.

There were dogs about as the column trekked out of town in the darkness toward Coppertown, which was a normal day-and-a-half march away. The canines yawned in the morning starlight and watched the column walk away. That morning, the animals seemed more like neighborhood strays than vicious killers, but Eric kept his rifle leveled and ready. The Great Dane didn't show himself as they left, but Eric guessed the fiend was nearby.

The people were in no condition to march, Eric mused, but their water in Refuge was depleted and their food supply was low. Using a saddle blanket and upholstery from a torn sofa in a townhouse, one of the men had cut and made shoes for those who'd been walking barefoot while in Smar's possession. But they were all still weak and malnourished. Only Eric and Alan were operating at full-strength, though the past week in Refuge had forced even them to make sacrifices for the others.

When the sun rose at their backs, Eric paused and looked back at the town that had been the end for so many, and a place of refuge for several others. From that distance, he could see no dogs. He knew they were there, though, lurking and maybe gathering to respond to their natural instinct to chase down the travelers. At the moment, the canines were probably sniffing out whatever trace the people had left behind. Isaac had closed the outer gate to the bank to protect the safety of its interior. Conrad had made sure the cistern on the roof was left as they'd found it, so others seeking shelter would find water where there would otherwise be none.

Two hours later, Alan and Molly called the column's first rest, and Alan rode back to Eric.

"Our first dog sighting since leaving Refuge." Alan gestured at two barely-visible canine heads peering over a nearby hill. "What do you think? Are the rest just out of sight, licking their chops?"

"It's possible." Eric turned and gazed in all directions. "They could come from anywhere, but normally, animals would attack from the rear to take out stragglers. Maybe . . ."

Eric chuckled to himself.

"What is it?" Alan asked. "There are stories in Mastover about the Mad Man Eric Radner. What mad plan did you just come up with?"

"The dogs aren't interested in a fight. They're looking for the weakest member of the herd. I'll limp as I walk and drop off a few yards. They won't attack the column if they're fixated on me."

"That's just asking for trouble."

"I don't see how we can avoid some kind of attack today. But we can dictate from where it'll come. If I look like a wounded calf, dawdling behind the herd, they'll come up on me first."

"It could be swift, Eric." Alan offered his assault rifle. "Your rifle may not repel them if they come suddenly."

Eric had a lot of history with his own rifle, but this was one instance that he realized he needed to submit to reason. He gave up his deer rifle and swapped it for the semi-automatic weapon.

"And don't drop back too far," Alan said as they prepared to start forward again. The man's years as a lieutenant in the Lib-Org showed in his leadership skills. "Hustle up to join us as soon as they start to attack, then we'll all deter them together."

"Got it."

"Gretchen wouldn't be too pleased with me if she knew I let you do this for us, Eric."

Alan returned to the front of the column and they moved forward. Molly verbally passed on the plan from Alan to the others as they walked so the two gunmen on the flanks could remain alert. Adjusting their plan as they traveled, Alan passed the order that at the first warning, the column was to halt and bunch up together, so the gunmen wouldn't have to defend a moving party but a stationary group.

Eric dropped back fifteen feet and began to exaggerate a fake limp, all while holding his borrowed rifle in his hands. After ten minutes of faking a limp, Eric realized that such traveling took more effort than walking normally, or even running! But not a single other person in the column was in any condition to trade places with him. He had to imitate a lame calf, since he was the only one strong enough to react if an attack came suddenly, as they expected.

The first attack came around noon, and only twenty dogs showed themselves. They swept over the hill from the north, and closed on Eric's position at a full run from two points. Isaac, on the right flank, hollered a warning first. Eric lunged on cramping legs to the back of the column as it immediately halted and closed ranks—the horses in the front and the walkers at the rear.

Pivoting, Eric aimed the rifle at the dog in front—a Rottweiler and husky cross. The Great Dane trotted casually in the middle of his pack, and Eric read the situation in an instant. He held his fire as the dogs curved away and slowed to a walk around the whole column.

"That was a test," Eric announced to everyone. "Don't show them any fear. Glare right back at them."

Most of the dogs circled the party of travelers, then sat or laid down on the southern slope of the hill thirty yards away.

"They're like lions," Conrad said. "Look at their arrogance—not even running away. They think they'll wear us down."

"Let's keep moving," Alan said firmly. "Let them see your faces, that you're watching them. Stay together. Eric, this probably isn't the best time to fall back. They're too close."

"I hear you." Eric was happy to walk normally at the back of the column, with a careful eye on the Great Dane as he began to walk parallel with the column.

More dogs wandered over the hill and joined the twenty, until the pack that accompanied the column of travelers numbered close to fifty. Eric admired the people. No one cried out in fear, even though the dogs walked only yards away with their heads low and their eyes daring. The people's courage seemed to keep the horses calm, and the column's pace resumed their steady walk westward.

The afternoon dragged on, and their pace slowed since Alan reasoned against stopping any more. They couldn't risk an attack from the dogs by ceasing to move. A couple people began to grumble as the miles seemed endless, and Eric was reminded of the Israelites in the wilderness. Though freed from their chains of bondage, the Israelites had complained about the discomfort of deliverance. On that day, the people who followed Alan grumbled about the path that led to their safety. As a result, the horses became unsettled, which the dogs sensed. Eric noticed a distinct difference in the postures of the dogs, as they prepared to take advantage of the peoples' shift from courage to fear.

Finally, Eric worked his way up the column to walk beside Alan's horse.

"We have to stop," Eric said low so only Alan and Molly could hear him. "Everyone needs a rest."

"There are only four hours of daylight remaining." Alan gauged the sun's position. "And I'd guess we have a good five hours of walking still to go. We can't be out here after dark."

"Without a rest, we'll be risking the whole group. I've been watching from the back. We're falling apart. We've been walking for nearly twelve hours."

Alan turned around on his mount, and Eric guessed he could see at a glance the downcast, weary faces. All those who were walking were now clinging to the horses that others were riding, lest they all fall to their knees.

"Let's take a thirty-minute break, everyone, but stay close together!" Alan reined in his horse and adjusted the rifle to fire at the animals that panted nearby. "Let's pray their hunger doesn't overwhelm their caution. Four rifles isn't much against that horde. Conrad, Isaac, and Eric, stand firm and visible on each side. Everyone else, stay inside the guards."

Eric took his position at the rear, separated from the column by one pace, and kept his posture firmly planted, his head and eyes lowered like a wary beast of the field. The dogs yawned and lounged on the grass yards away. They rolled against the sagebrush, even wrestled with one another, seemingly oblivious to the terror their presence produced in the humans. Although Eric found little comfort in it, he tried to view them as the lost family pets they'd once been, and prayed for God to restrain the jaws of the animals.

The Great Dane chose to sit on his haunches thirty feet behind and to the north side of the column. When Eric noticed that the giant dog seemed to be watching him alone, he stared right back at the black eyes and square head of the muscled canine. The chest and shoulders of the short-haired Dane were scarred from conflict, adding all the more to Eric's unsettled nerves. In the daylight, the animals were daunting. It was terrifying to imagine facing those fifty after sundown. His memory of the attack against the diner was still fresh. He'd seen it all from outside the diner, the way countless dogs had thrown themselves in a sort of senseless frenzy against Peter at the door, and the way they'd lunged over one another to dive through the windows.

"My hands still work fine," Peter said from atop the nearest horse. He gestured at his handgun tucked into Eric's waistband. "You'll need every gun you can get if they attack."

Eric barely glanced at the wounded slaver, then returned to the staring contest he was having with the alpha male.

"If they attack, none of our guns will matter much." Eric's voice was low, almost a growl, meant for the ears of the Great Dane. "I'm just counting on their inability to figure the odds the way we're able to."

"Don't let me die empty-handed, Eric!" Peter cursed. "I'm not an invalid, even if I am bandaged up. I can fight!"

"You haven't exactly earned back your firearm privileges, Peter."

"Yeah," one of the men said as he passed a canteen to others on the ground, but bypassed Peter. "A week ago, you were trying to sell us, Peter."

"It was just business," Peter mumbled. "None of you would've done any different. We all survive the best we know how."

"There's a difference between survival," Eric said, "and gaining at the expense of others."

The people were quiet for a spell as they ate the last of the horse meat, which had been boiled for the journey.

"What's going to happen to me when we get back to Mastover?" Peter asked.

"Maybe you've heard of Judge Zachary Grayport," Eric said. "He's a personal friend of mine. His security forces pushed the Lib-Org from Wyoming, and the judge's own son is the finest tracker and hunter within a thousand miles. Yeah, justice stands in Mastover, and no one comes or goes from eastern Wyoming without our people finding out. There will be no escaping justice for you, Peter."

Eric waited in silence for the man to respond. He knew he'd put greater dread in the ex-slaver's heart, since his crimes against his fellow man were so great. Despair and hopelessness, Eric understood, had brought people to a place of humility and repentance many times before.

"So, what'll be my punishment?" He sighed heavily, perhaps close to tears. Like everyone, he was exhausted. "What'll that judge do to me?"

"I'll talk to him and see if I can pay the penalty of your crimes myself."

Peter and several others lifted their heads at such a wild suggestion.

"No! What are you talking about?" Peter frowned. "What penalty?"

"You kidnapped a lot of people, Peter, and killed some, it seems." Eric clucked his tongue. "Even in a lawless land, there are some lines you just don't cross. There's a penalty for your crimes. It'll have to be paid. But you're in no condition to pay the penalty. You were nearly mauled to death by dogs just last week. No, you won't be able to endure what will be required of you at this point. I'll have to receive the penalty for you. Maybe along with Alan."

"The penalty for sin must be paid." Alan saluted with his canteen from where he sat on his mount, then he passed the container to Molly. "Justice demands a payment, Peter, which you can't possibly pay. I'm with you, Eric. We came for these people, not just for the good ones, but for the bad ones, too. We'll have to receive his penalty. There'll be no peace amongst us until Peter's penalty has been paid for."

Eric didn't smile, but he appreciated that Alan was indeed speaking the very same gospel that Jesus Christ offered to mankind. And by the confused and pained expression on Peter's face, he was certainly wrestling with what penalty others would pay on his behalf. It was a disturbing thought, apparently.

More dogs from the east merged with the Great Dane's pack, until it numbered nearly eighty.

"This can't go on much longer," Conrad said, his rifle held tensely. "The more dogs, the more pressure they'll feel to attack."

"I hate to quote Smar," Isaac said, "but let's all keep our heads. We still have a long way to go until we get to Coppertown. Eric?"

"Yeah, a few hours, but we can make it."

A few minutes later, Alan roused the others. While the weary travelers gathered their few possessions and grumbled about their sore feet, Eric was surprised to find Molly suddenly at his elbow.

"Alan's concerned about the horses," she said softly. "That week in Refuge weakened them more than we thought."

Quietly, Eric dismissed her without turning his face from the dogs, and without alerting anyone else of the increasing danger. If the rest of their horses were going lame, then those who rode on horses would need to walk, or would need to be carried. Their forward momentum would slow even more. As it was, they wouldn't reach Coppertown until after sundown. The dogs would resist the lure of food for only so long.

The dogs' ears perked up as the column rose to move. Eric chose that moment to move among the people, reaching the stronger mounts that carried small supply packs behind the riders. From four different horses, he drew out a length of chain, each length about three feet long. Fastened at the end of each chain length were two shackles of heavy steel. These were the same shackles that the people knew intimately.

"Let the dogs see you with this," Eric instructed as he gave one length to Molly, then one each to Conrad and Isaac. He kept one for himself. "Let them learn the threat of these chains. They'll hear the sound, and it'll be just one more thing to discourage them from attacking once darkness falls."

Eric slipped his rifle over his shoulder on the sling so he could wield the chain more effectively. He swung the chain and shackles wildly and smashed them on the dusty ground. Several dogs flinched at the ruckus and withdrew a few steps.

The column continued, now at a slower pace. The horses were indeed more fatigued than the people, and Eric hoped the presence of the chains kept the dogs at bay. The dogs, he knew, had a keen sense to recognize a lame animal, and there were very few among them—people or horses—that weren't exhibiting some sort of exhaustion or lameness. Even Eric, at the back of the column, was forcing himself to remain vigilant and give the appearance of strength. The Great Dane watched him warily, trailing confidently behind the pack.

A glance at the setting sun told Eric they would be fighting for their lives in the dark. He did his best to trust the God who had created such animals. The column would need a miracle to survive until Coppertown.

Chapter 3

In the last remnant of light on the plain, Alan and Eric agreed that a horse that had gone lame would have to be left behind. It was Peter's horse. When the column stopped briefly, Eric helped Peter to the ground. The horse seemed to understand its fate, and lay on the ground with a sustained groan. Quickly, to cause the least pain for the animal, Eric opened the horse's neck with his hunting knife.

"Let's go!" Eric urged, and Alan led the column onward from the dead animal as hastily as possible. "Stay close together!"

With his arm around Peter's torso, Eric helped the heavier man settle his stiff limbs into a steady pace. His arms and legs were still bandaged from the dog bites gained in the battle a week earlier. There were no other options except to walk or die, injured or not.

Behind them, the dogs could be heard fighting and snarling over the sacrifice. With his left arm, Eric helped Peter hobble along, and in his right hand, he jingled the chains. The dogs had seen the threat of the chains enough in the daylight to know the sound of them now in the darkness. Since he was aware that the dogs could see better in the moonless night than a human could, Eric swung at imaginary beasts on his heels, hoping to intimidate any of the dogs who were watching him, especially the Great Dane. The carcass left behind wouldn't fill the dogs' hunger for long. It could very well stir within them a need to eat more, and a frenzy could ensue, like sharks in murky water.

"I don't want you to pay my penalty," Peter stated breathlessly as he hustled along in the darkness. "Leave me here. You can't carry us all, Eric. I don't deserve to be helped. No one would blame you for leaving me behind. I couldn't bear it if others received the punishment I deserve for being a slaver."

"I'm a Christian, Peter." Eric said as he swung at the darkness with the chains, sure that there were dogs padding silently nearby. "I don't care about what you've done. I care about who you can be if you surrender to God's will. Jesus Christ died for each one of us, and He did that because He loves us, not because we're loveable."

"You're saying I'm not loveable?" Peter chuckled.

"No offense, pal, but you're not loveable. None of us are." Eric jingled the chain. "Regardless, you were made in the image of God, and I'm not about to abandon my neighbor to the beasts of the field."

"So, you think you're my savior now?"

"Oh, no. Definitely not. I'm just a follower of the Savior Jesus Christ, so I try to live like Him. Since He gave His life for you, then I will give my life for you as well, if need be. Hey!"

Out of the darkness, Eric felt jaws close around his right forearm, then teeth caught in the sleeve of his jacket. The dog ripped and tore at his sleeve, threatening to pull Eric away from the column altogether.

"Stop!" Peter called to the others so the two men wouldn't be left behind.

Within seconds, Eric realized this wasn't one of the larger dogs, only one that weighed about forty pounds, but other canines might be racing forward to take part in the wrestling match. He let go of Peter and shifted the chains to his left hand, then swung with frantic strength at the brute.

The animal let go and yelped into the night. Eric barked and growled after it, and smashed the chains on the ground a couple times before he returned to Peter.

"Forward!" Eric yelled, and felt his knees wobble at the near-death moment that could've gone much differently, if one or two more dogs would've joined the ruckus. "That thing about tore my arm off!"

"There's a light ahead!" Alan announced. "Stay close together—now more than ever!"

"'Yea, though I walk through the valley of the shadow of death,'" Eric quoted Psalm 23 aloud, "'I will fear no evil: for Thou art with me; Thy rod and Thy staff they comfort me.' Please, help us, Lord! Help us!"

"Aaah!"

One of the other walkers toward the back of the column was being dragged on his feet away from the group. By the sound of the growls and grunts, more than one dog was involved. Eric shoved Peter into the arms of the others, then leapt to attack mere shades of black in the darkness. He grabbed onto the upright form of the man, then swung his chain with great thrashing strikes at the smaller shadows.

Another dog brushed past his leg, perhaps in an attempt to move up on the column behind Eric, but he caught the canine with a backstroke and heard the animal run away with a yelp.

Once the shaken man was free, Eric guided him back to the column, which thankfully hadn't continued on without them.

"Forward!" Eric ordered.

He left Peter with the other travelers, and focused on swinging the chain and lunging at darting shadows—half of which he guessed weren't real, but in the darkness, nothing was certain.

"Travelers coming in!" Alan shouted to the lights ahead.

Eric glanced up and saw the lit walls of Coppertown, torches burning and a larger source of light deeper inside the walled settlement.

A dog darted in to bite Eric on the hip, but he kicked at it and smacked it aside with the chain. Ahead, men were yelling, but the column of travelers from Refuge didn't break their momentum as they passed through a gate. Eric stopped in the mouth of the gate between two armed gunmen with thick beards. Together, they looked out at the darkness. There, lurking at the edge of light, where the light met the night, was a wall of fur and fangs. Their eyes shone like diamonds, blinking, but otherwise steady. He wasn't sure, but Eric thought he saw the Great Dane toward the middle.

"We wouldn't have made it another mile." Eric backed through the gate, and the men closed the barrier as high as the six-foot wall. "We were praying the whole way. God saved us."

"God?" One broad-shouldered man scoffed. He wore a white bandana around his neck. "We trust in our own strength around here. There's nothing else out here that's going to keep us alive. How many did you lose?"

"Lose? On the journey? None." Eric laid the length of chain over his shoulder and flexed his hand, which was stiff from hours of holding the heavy iron. "Brought twenty-five from Refuge safe and sound. Well, nearly. I think this is the only real casualty."

Eric chuckled and held up his torn sleeve to the torchlight.

"Twenty-five all that way? Refuge? You mean that ghost town thirty miles east of here? That's impossible."

"What's impossible for man is possible for God." Eric slapped the man's thick shoulder. "It sure is good to see some friendly faces. Are you the one I spoke to a few days ago? I left a woman named Amber here."

"You spoke to Mayor Loggins." The big man offered his hand. "They call me Elk. I was on the wall last week, so I remember you. We never thought we'd see you alive again."

"It seems the Lord has a few more things for me to do in this life." Eric glanced around the torch-lit interior of Coppertown. Its courtyard was wide and the buildings were in good shape. The smell of cut wood was a mystery until Eric realized he was standing on sawdust. "You guys have a sawmill?"

"That's one of our secrets to survival." Elk pointed toward a dark building on the edge of the courtyard. "The sawmill is there. And we have a small refinery on the south side of town. All custom-made."

"A refinery." Eric frowned. "You mean a still?"

"No, oil. Lumber and oil are the life of Coppertown." The man lifted his big head, clearly appreciating the shocked look displayed on Eric's face. "Yep, we're a new frontier town. Someone will show you around tomorrow."

"Right." Eric walked with Elk to the group of travelers, most of whom had collapsed onto the sawdust ground. Even the remaining six horses were on the verge of toppling over. "The night isn't too cold. If you can just point us to a barn or something, we could sure use some sleep."

"Last week, you said you'd be willing to trade for resources. What with the dogs and all, meat has been scarce in Coppertown, and we're tired of dog meat. Those horses would make for some good eating."

"It sounds like we've got something to haggle about tomorrow." Eric laughed, still rejoicing in his heart at having arrived safely.

Elk and a couple other men showed the twenty-five travelers to various sleeping quarters. A few of the ladies from the town took in the women who were accompanying Eric, so they didn't have to sleep outside in a barn.

Eric, Alan, Peter, and the blind man, Kelly, stayed together after leading their horses into a stable with two old draft horses in a back stall. The four men sat on fresh sawdust in one empty stall. Only Alan remained standing with his crutches, adjusting the brightness of a lantern they'd been given.

"Can you imagine what we could do with oil in Mastover?" Alan asked. "They must have a well nearby. And a sawmill? There's not a tree for miles around. Where do they get the logs? They can't travel anywhere with all those dogs out there."

"They said they trust in their own power, not God's." Eric made a pillow out of a horse blanket, laid down, and covered himself with his torn jacket. "I figure they have some system to bait or repel the dogs, or something, so they can travel when they need to."

With his eyelids half-open, Eric watched Alan help Kelly prepare a bed. The blind man didn't speak, only submitted.

"Who's that man to you?" Peter asked Eric, "and why do you and Alan take care of him like a relative?"

Alan heard the question and met Eric's eyes, as if begging him to keep Kelly's identity hidden. The band of travelers didn't need the chaos that could ensue if Coppertown's residents found out that the blind man was ex-Commander Kelly Morris of the Liberation Organization. Eric wasn't even sure that Kelly had realized that Alan was the old lieutenant he'd tried to kill the previous winter.

"He's an old acquaintance of mine," Eric said, noticing that Kelly tilted his head, listening to their conversation about him. "He's like a long-lost uncle, you could say. Once estranged, but now God has brought us together. It's humbling for us, but we'll eventually grow from how God has brought us all together."

"All this God-talk doesn't settle well with people." Peter gingerly peeked under his forearm bandages at his wounds. "Nobody believes it, you know. Pan-Day and everything else proves there's no God out there."

"It proves nothing." Alan set his crutches aside and hopped on his foot twice, then lowered himself to his own bedroll. "Tell him Eric."

Eric smiled, sleep almost overtaking him.

"Pan-Day only proves that man is destructive." His eyes drifted closed. "God will have the final say. You'll see."

Chapter 4

Eric woke rested but sore from the hard march the day before. Alan stirred as Eric tugged on his boots, but Peter and Kelly remained asleep. After checking on the horses, Eric walked out of the stable to view Coppertown in the daylight.

The courtyard was abuzz with activity. Three youths in patched jeans were wrangling a herd of goats across the expanse. A couple does appeared to have full udders, so Eric guessed goat milk and cheese were probably part of Coppertown's diet. On the far end of the courtyard, two sturdy men worked a two-handed saw through a long, 24-inch diameter log. Other logs lay nearby, and Eric stood puzzling over the source of such logs until a blond woman waved at him.

"Eric!" Amber ran from the back of what looked like a school house. The tall woman a few years older than himself, who'd once been near death as Smar's prisoner, was now apparently eating well and growing stronger. She reached him with outstretched arms and embraced him. "I didn't find out until this morning that you'd returned! You brought everyone back?"

"We lost one man to the dogs." Eric held the woman at arm's length. "Smar and his men deserted or were lost, except for Peter. We were able to save Peter."

"Peter! The red-headed guy? Eric, he was the worst of them all!" She stepped back, a pained look on her face. "How could you let him live? He's here?"

"He's back in the stable, injured. He's my prisoner."

"Your prisoner." She frowned. "So, there'll be some sort of justice for him. You'll make sure of that?"

"There will be payment for his crimes, but there's no fixing what damage he's done to your lives. Those are scars we have to leave in God's hands."

"Don't talk about God around here." Amber self-consciously pulled her shirt sleeves down to cover her wrist scars. "These people are crazy about their own self-preservation."

"That's what I'm beginning to realize." Together, they walked toward a two-story building, its door open and frequented by townspeople. "Were you able to line up some supplies for us to trade for? I have four horses I'm willing to give up. That's got to buy us enough food and water for a three-day walk back to Mastover. As soon as I figure out how these people travel without the dogs bothering them, we'll be ready to leave."

Reaching the two-story building, Eric smelled the aroma of hash browns and eggs wafting through the door.

"They are pretty inventive people." She squeezed his arm tightly. "And yes, I've talked to Mayor Loggins about some things for the people you brought back. I still can't believe you came back for me!"

Inside the dining hall, Eric nodded from a distance at Conrad, Molly, and Isaac, who were eating amongst the townspeople, pitchers of milk on the tables in front of them. He accepted a seat at a table, and Amber hurried away to fix the two of them a plate.

As perfect as everything was, or seemed to be, Eric felt uneasy. He hadn't been in any town but Mastover in years. His smile was genuine to the people who came and went, but something was amiss, and he remained open to God's leading to discern what it was. He wasn't against the idea of a small community thriving in the midst of the Plains Zone, with wild dogs surrounding them. However, he had yet to hear of a people who lived well without God in their lives. It made him wonder what terrible secret lurked beneath the facade of perfection around him. Without the Source of joy, peace, and love in the community, Coppertown must have had a dreadful past.

Amber returned, and as he ate delicious cheesy eggs and hash browns, she described the town that had taken her in—as well as the rest of them—when nowhere else was available.

"There's an oil field a day's ride north, they say." Amber hardly seemed like the distraught, scared woman Eric had saved from Tomblin's wicked town of lawlessness. "And two days south, there's a whole forest where they log."

"Okay, but how do they travel?" Eric asked with a mouth full of food. He had to find a way to get a milk goat back into River Camp! "The dogs are everywhere!"

"They put a contraption over and around the horses to protect them. I saw them use it once a couple days ago. They went out to cut grass for the livestock. The horses are protected by the enclosure, even as they walk, and they can pull a wagon with people safe inside. It's not that complicated. Pretty ingenious, actually."

"Sounds like it." Eric leaned over the table. "So, you want to stay here or what?"

Amber glanced over her shoulder and lowered her voice.

"Not a chance. There's something creepy about this place, and I'm not just saying that because Mayor Loggins' head looks like a burnt potato chip. Something's off, you know? The people will look at you, but they won't hold eye contact. There are other things, too. None of the women will visit with me. I mean, we talk about unimportant things, sure. But whenever I bring up how Coppertown got started, or how it's survived out here all alone, they change the subject."

"I don't think they're a cult," Eric said with a frown, "because they seem to reject God. Usually, a cult has some form of religion based on a deity. Does this Mayor Loggins guy come off to you as a cult leader?"

"I don't know." She shrugged. "I just want to go to the town with the suspended bridge."

"Mastover."

"You say the people there are normal?"

"You mean normal as in imperfect and trying to live peaceably in the midst of a thousand challenges? Yeah, they're normal."

"I could live there. I don't want to go back to Oregon. Too many memories."

"Your husband?"

"He's gone, but I don't want to see the people who didn't stand up to Smar when he came through our settlement and kidnapped me. I don't even want to live around them."

"Fear immobilizes some people," Eric said, "and mixed with an identity crisis, mistakes are made that ruin lives."

"Identity crisis?" She rolled her eyes. "Were you a psychologist in your past life?"

"No, nothing like that. What I mean is this: if people don't receive who God says we are, or if they reject their need for God, then they live their whole lives trying to fill a void with nonsense—a void that their Creator designed to be filled only with Him. When we don't know our identity, we have no stability. It's one of the reasons people don't step up to help others, or stand against evil. They don't know who they are or what they were created for. That's an identity crisis."

"You might know what you're talking about," Amber said, "because you seem to have your life together, but I bet you drive your wife crazy with that kind of talk."

"You'll meet her, and you can ask her." Eric chuckled. "Gretchen is at Mastover, waiting for us to come back."

When the two had finished breakfast, they walked outside under the curious glances of the residents. In the dining hall, Eric had been focused on what Amber had been telling him. Now, he acknowledged for himself the strange behavior of the townspeople. Sure, these were citizens who'd been living in an isolated community, cut off from nearby towns by prairie, fear of roaming bandits, and packs of dogs. But there was a sense of suspicion or concern in their young faces that made Eric feel self-conscious. He had invaded their world. Did they think he was a spy for a force interested in their resources? Did they not see that he had a heart for saving people, not to hurt people?

Then, it struck him. He stopped in the middle of the courtyard. Amber stopped beside him.

"What is it?" she asked.

"Just a minute." Eric turned slowly in a circle, studying each bustling person, using his discerning, woodsman's gaze. He didn't want to believe it, but it was unmistakable. "Did you notice that there's no one else your age or older in this town?"

"No, I didn't notice." She looked around. "Pan-Day probably killed off anyone who had a weak immune system."

"No, I think this is something else. Come back with me to the stable. I need to talk to Alan, the man who came with me from Mastover."

They walked in on Alan, Peter, and Kelly as they were rubbing sleep from their eyes and straightening their clothes.

"You don't expect these people to serve us brunch, do you?" Eric joked. "Amber, you might remember Kelly. Can you take him to the dining hall? And Peter—"

"I remember him!" Amber said through clenched teeth. She gave her arm to the blind man, then turned her head away from Peter. "He looks like he can get there himself."

"I don't need her to guide me!" Peter scowled at Eric. "I'm not an invalid!"

"Well, go ahead then." Eric motioned to the front of the stables. "Alan and I need a few minutes."

Alan leaned patiently on his crutches until they were alone.

"You'd better not cost me my breakfast, Eric. I haven't eaten a decent meal since we left Mastover."

Eric made certain they were alone, except for the horses in the nearby stalls.

"You'll eat. There's plenty of food in this place. That's what concerns me. There should be a lot more people living here, but I see maybe two hundred, no more. There are no elderly whatsoever. And all the people are healthy."

"What? What are you talking about? There must be some elderly, even in a town with only a couple hundred."

"I've heard of this happening. Population control. I think they cull their population to conserve resources."

"That's ridiculous." Alan stared back at Eric. "But, I guess it's no more ridiculous than what Kelly and I did to force whole cities to conform to the Lib-Org's standards. We wanted fuel and food, and under his command, we killed thousands for it."

"My first concern is to get our people out of here and back to Mastover." Eric checked the volume of his voice and made sure the stable was still empty. "But we need supplies. I don't see a way around trading four horses with Mayor Loggins and his man, Elk."

"Then we do our trading and leave." Alan shook his head. "That look in your eyes—what are you thinking now?"

"How can we leave without challenging the leadership? I mean, if this is really going on. What if God brought us here to correct this situation?" Eric thought of Gretchen's counsel against him risking his life for others, yet again. "I think we can reach the town of Tomblin in just a few hours of walking. I don't know why, but the dogs don't seem to be ranging much farther west."

"We should all leave, Eric. We can come back here with the power of Mastover to correct or investigate whatever's going on here."

"Yeah, that would be the safest thing to do." Eric winced. "But this is something I sense God urging me to confront right now. In formation and in the daylight, the dogs should be wary of attacking the column, if you lead them out tomorrow at dawn."

"With only two horses? We'll be moving real slowly. The people are still pretty exhausted. Peter can barely walk. Kelly will have to ride a horse, or ride double with me. A couple of the ladies shouldn't be walking far, either, because of the condition of their feet."

"Our options are few. You want to ride back to Mastover and get help now?"

"It would take five days to go and come back." Alan shook his head. "No, that's too long if things go badly here. We're best off to start nothing, Eric. Just get our supplies at a good trade, then we'll all leave peaceably together."

"It's not in me to leave this kind of evil unchallenged. It's like a calling. I have to respond, Alan."

"I know." Alan sighed in resignation. "I was just trying to talk you out of it. God wouldn't have been revealed to me without you and Joel doing daring things, so I know God is with you. If this is of God, I know His will must be accomplished."

"It might get tense. Even violent."

"Then, we'll keep the Lord before us." Alan gestured with a crutch. "Can I go get some breakfast now before they close that kitchen?"

Alan left the stable on his crutches, and Eric checked on the horses and their gear again. Everything remained untouched. He wasn't carrying his rifle around since it would've seemed threatening inside the town's wall. But he was tempted to carry it anyway, just to ward off any potential violence against his people. Nevertheless, he declined since he was intent on showing the strength of God to the town, rather than the strength of man.

Outside the stable, Eric surveyed the courtyard. Now that he knew what to look for, he was seeing it everywhere. The town seemed normal, bustling, and active, but there were furtive glances he now recognized, and men whose heads remained low and guarded, with knife handles near their hands. Elk and Mayor Loggins weren't in sight, but a town that small, with such secrets to guard, Eric guessed the town elders were staying apprised of his every move. Besides, in those days, suspecting strangers kept people safe.

After crossing the courtyard, Eric approached the perimeter's northern wall. A single young watchman walked the boardwalk inside the wall, and Eric waved to him as he stepped onto the boardwalk himself. Gazing out on the plain, Eric saw no dogs, but he knew they were out there, hungry and waiting. The Great Dane himself was probably within whistling distance.

"You're lucky you made it to us last night," a strong voice spoke behind him.

Eric turned and smiled at who he now knew to be Mayor Loggins. Remembering Amber's mention of a burnt potato chip, Eric tried not to stare at the man's burned and scarred scalp and beard from some past tragedy.

"Luck had nothing to do with it, but I'll say thanks all the same."

The two shook hands, which was abnormal between strangers. Mayor Loggins joined Eric on the walkway.

"You're right. It wasn't luck. It was pure preparation and determination. We here in Coppertown were prepared, and your people were determined. Together, those characteristics have kept us alive since Pan-Day."

"I was thinking more along the lines of an all-powerful and benevolent God watching over us all yesterday." Eric leaned on his forearms on the top of the wall. "Determination didn't get us here. I had no control over those dogs. They were held back by an unseen, sovereign hand."

"Your God, or anyone else's god, didn't build Coppertown." Loggins' voice had a fierceness to it. "We've learned to survive on our own. Our sweat. Our blood. Our brains. If we don't manage everything carefully, we'll fall back into the same problems we had before Pan-Day."

"Manage everything, you say?" Eric checked his words before speaking, and found no reason to keep silent. "Is that what you call population control?"

Loggins stiffened and looked to his left. Eric followed his gaze to where Elk lingered nearby. He was about ten strides away, which Eric guessed the sturdy, fit frame could cover in two seconds, if Loggins signaled to him. A handgun and a straight knife in a sheath were attached to Elk's belt.

"Are you accusing us of something besides survival?" Loggins looked back out to the plain. "You don't know what it's been like trying to survive out here."

"Everyone, everywhere, has struggled."

"Here, the winters are devastating. The dogs are merciless. Water is scarce. Nothing grows in this soil but wheat, potatoes, and grass, it seems. But we've learned to adapt. We've even learned to cohabitate with the dogs. We've made the soil fertile. There's a balance here now, but it wasn't always like this. As a town, we've made decisions, and we've preserved ourselves."

"Who decides who lives and who dies?" Eric watched the man's body language closely.

"Who's been talking to you?" he asked quietly as a carpenter with his tools passed below them. "Was it that Amber woman? I knew we shouldn't have taken her in. I should've turned you away last night, too. All we had to do was extinguish our torches."

"No one had to tell me what's been happening here. I just looked around, and God helped me see what's missing. Coppertown isn't as heavenly as it seems, is it?"

"That's what your God showed you?"

"There's a whole generation of people missing from your community. The only question is, what method do you use to exterminate them? I don't see any graveyards around Coppertown. How do you make so many people disappear without upsetting the balance? Everyone in the town must be aware of what's happening."

Loggins glanced again at Elk, and Eric saw worry on both their faces, though Elk probably couldn't hear their whole conversation because they were speaking so low. Eric guessed the town rarely, if ever, had visitors, since the dogs kept them at bay. A stranger like Eric asking questions was sure to upset the townspeople—they would want their dark secret to remain a secret.

"We live by our own code and our own strength here. We have no help." Loggins swore. "What has God done for us? We were abandoned by everyone after Pan-Day. We had to establish a system to bring in new life. To preserve life, those who are a burden on the community have to be given up."

"Given up?" Eric noticed a small troupe of dogs trotting across the plain. "How? To the dogs? Is this why the dogs seem to gravitate around Coppertown? You feed your sick and elderly to them?"

"It's survival!" Loggins spat over the wall. "We all know the score. We all know that our survival is on a razor's edge. We're all willing to accept that life has no purpose except to coexist for the good of the people. The many are preserved by the sacrifice of the few."

"History is full of tyrants who have said the same thing." Eric rested his hands on the wall. "I don't envy your responsibilities, Mayor, but giving up on people who seem to be a burden is forgetting that God gave us burdensome people to teach us while we care for them. Throwing away the burdensome only breeds more selfishness. Tell me: when it's your time, will you let them give you up to the dogs?"

"You have no say here." Loggins rested his hand on a knife handle on his hip. "And your God can do nothing for us. We survive on our own out here. We, not God, devised a way to stay safe. We travel outside these walls in security to get oil and timber. God doesn't do that for us. We are the answer to our survival. Our strength. We are gods, and nothing will change that!"

"No, you're wrong." Eric faced Loggins more directly. The mayor was a larger man, but Eric knew from Scripture that God had used the lesser to defeat the greater more than once. The good name of God was at stake in the eyes of an evil man. "My God is greater than your strength. You do indeed live on a razor's edge here, Mayor. One mistake, and your whole empire falls apart. Those who live for God need to fear nothing, because He is our strength."

"Prove it."

Eric blinked in surprise.

"What?"

"Prove it." Loggins smirked at Eric's hesitation. "Exactly. You can't prove it. Your God is imaginary. I can show you my strength, my ingenuity, and my authority. Your God won't do anything."

Eric felt an anger rising up within him. How could he allow someone to speak like this against his God?

"My God created the heavens and the earth. He suspends galaxies in space and holds the earth on its cycle. That's proof enough of His power."

"And you say you fear nothing?"

"I fear nothing—because God is my refuge."

"Then walk out there and show me." Loggins gestured to the plain where the dogs were trotting across. "Show us that your God is mighty. If He's mighty, you have nothing to fear from the dogs. Go ahead. Hop over the wall!"

"Okay." Eric swallowed, and felt a drop of sweat trickle down his back. "But if it's my God against your strength and ingenuity, we both walk out there. You supposedly have some invention to keep you safe. Let's put it to the test. And all the people will watch. God against man—a man who claims to be a god."

"You're an idiot. We go out there all the time. It's nothing."

"Prove it," Eric challenged. "And if my God proves Himself, then Coppertown reforms its methods of preserving life."

"And if I have my way," Loggins said, stepping closer, "you'll be dead, and your horses are mine."

"Then it's agreed." Eric backed away, then hopped off the boardwalk. "At dawn, the whole town will see whose God is real—the God of the universe, or you!"

Chapter 5

Eric was hiding in one of the stalls, feeling like a fool, when Alan found him. The ex-military lieutenant set his crutches aside and sat in the sawdust next to Eric. Silently, the two watched one of their mares swish her tail at flies a few feet away.

"Nice day outside," Alan finally said. "Nice day for everyone to be running around, talking about us. It'll probably be a nice day tomorrow, too, when you get yourself killed trying to prove something that needs no proving."

"I don't know what got into me." Eric rested his head on his fist, his elbow on his knee. "It just sort of tumbled out of control. The next thing I knew, I was Elijah on Mount Carmel, challenging a false prophet to a face-off."

"It could be worse. There could be hundreds of rabid dogs surrounding you, trying to kill you. Oh, right—there are!" Alan scoffed. "I get it. I get that you want to prove to these people that God is real, but this is ridiculous. You have to get out of the challenge!"

"Believe me, I would if I could." Eric lifted his head and stared at the rafters. "I've been in here a couple hours, begging God to show me a way out that allows me—and me alone—to be the only embarrassment and coward. But I can't do that. I've involved God's name, so I can't back down without bringing shame to Him."

"God is a big God, Eric. He can handle it. He's invincible. But you're not! Did you really wager our horses? All of them? That's what the mayor is bragging about to everyone. How're we supposed to get Kelly back to Mastover, and the others who can hardly walk? How am I supposed to travel at all? On crutches?"

"Well, I'll just have to win the challenge, that's all."

"But you can't win. The dogs will kill you!"

"But our God is the God of Daniel. And He is the God of King David. And He is the God of Moses. I definitely can't win this contest, or challenge, or whatever it is. But God can win this! He can shut the mouths of lions. What's a few wild dogs to Him?"

"You and your steadfast faith." Alan was silent for a moment. "Do you know the town is turning this into a celebration? They're celebrating their own genius and achievements. Instead of humbling these people, you're doing the opposite. They're becoming bolder and more proud. That mayor is boasting about it to everyone. This is such a mess!"

"I'm not doing that to them, Alan. I think you're missing the whole point. All of this started when I confronted Mayor Loggins about killing off the elderly. If I prove God is greater, Coppertown will stop killing its people to conserve their resources. God has brought us here to stop the killing and to reveal to them the God of the Bible."

"Oh, I get it. So, you give your life, and they're supposedly going to think twice about their custom of death?"

"No, my idea involved only risking my life, Alan, not dying." Eric elbowed his friend lightly in the ribs. "And you're not helping my confidence in trusting that God can deliver me."

"Now I understand why there are stories about your wife scolding you for putting yourself in harm's way to make a point. Joel thinks you're a hero. God knows you had a hand in saving my own life, but right now, you just seem like a fool, Eric. Don't get me wrong—I'm on your side, but don't ask me to approve of your methods."

The crunch of footsteps on the sawdust grew louder as someone out of sight walked into the stable. Suddenly, Amber came around the corner of one wall and stopped. Her hands went to her hips, which drew up the arms of her long-sleeved shirt, exposing her scabbed wrists.

"So, there you two are!" Her eyes were full of fire. "Are you going to tell me what all this is about? I'm out there defending you, and you're in here sulking?"

"I'm trying to talk him out of this nonsense," Alan said. "He's more stubborn than stories give him credit for."

Amber dropped to her knees in front of Eric.

"Eric, you saved me from the people in Tomblin. And somehow, I'd like to think you miraculously rescued everyone else from Smar and the dogs, then brought them here. You're crazy enough to show that monster Peter some mercy, so now even I am feeling sympathy for him! You've been talking about your God to the rest of us, and to these people. This town is all twisted if they're really killing off their citizens. Just do what you've been doing the past week and a half."

"What have I been doing?" Eric asked.

"Well . . ." Amber shrugged. "You've been trusting in your God, right? Can He keep you safe?"

"He can," Alan said. "The question is, will He?"

"I'm talking to Eric." Amber cast Alan a critical glance. "And you should go find Molly, Alan. There's a half-dozen men trying to woo her into staying in Coppertown when we pull out. Does she mean something to you or not?"

"I know when I'm not wanted any longer." Alan collected his crutches, rose to his foot, and left the stable.

"Amber, you're not even a believer." Eric smiled. "Are you encouraging me to go through with this challenge?"

"I know only two things. One, something is seriously wrong with this town. And two, something is seriously right about you. If what is right about you is your God, then I believe it. But, do you believe it?"

"I do." Eric smiled.

"Why are you smiling?"

"You remind me of my wife."

"What? She's an old lady trying to find meaning in this crazy world, too?"

"Oh, no. She's a fiery redhead who isn't afraid of tough odds . . . like you."

"Do you have a plan to beat these people at their own game?"

"No." He frowned. "I mean, well, yes. Something just came to me. Gather everyone you can find from Refuge. Get them to the courtyard."

"You want to talk to them out there? In front of everyone?"

"Yes." Eric took a deep breath. God was refreshing him with renewed zeal. "It's time to raise the stakes even more."

"You are a little mad, aren't you?" She chuckled and held out her hand. Together, they rose to their feet. "Your wife must be some woman to keep a guy like you in line."

"She is. You'll see. But first, we need to leave Coppertown. All of us."

After Amber left to gather the people from Refuge, Eric had a few minutes alone with the horses to consider the older woman's words. She'd revived in him the priority of what God intended through this situation. This was about bringing people out of the bondage of darkness and into the freedom of light. God was greater. Man's strength and a dog's bite were unremarkable to a sovereign God. A woman who had never believed before was now believing something about God. There were miracles already happening!

Eric wiped his eyes and stretched his hands and arms toward heaven. Yes, he'd seen God do mighty things in his life, and this would be the greatest, he decided, since rescue, deliverance, and safety seemed so unlikely.

When his heart was settled upon God's love and omnipotence, he walked out of the stable and stopped at the edge of the courtyard. Men and women from Refuge were gathering, but so were the people of Coppertown.

Something was afoot, they surely sensed, and the town in which there was little for people to do wasn't willing to miss a moment like this!

With her arms crossed, Amber stood at one side of the Refuge gathering. She nodded sharply, defiantly, at Eric. Alan leaned on his crutches nearby, a worried look on his face. Peter appeared confused and concerned, as he studied the townspeople. Kelly's face was turned toward the sky, as if to feel the noon-day sunshine. His head tilted slightly this way and that as he listened to whispers and hushing sounds.

Eric walked stiffly into the empty space and stood in front of the twenty-five Refuge people.

"You may think I'm a stranger to this land, but I'm not." Eric's voice felt strong. The words came naturally. "I grew up a few miles south of here. You may think I'm a fool to face this danger, but I'm no fool. He is no fool who gladly faces danger to rescue people from evil. He is no fool who trusts in the Creator of heaven and earth over the created animals, plants, and insects.

"The fool is the one who serves and bows down to the creation, as if it were a god. The fool is the one who trusts in his own strength to control what only God Almighty can control.

"People of Refuge, listen to me! You've been brought through the horrors of slavery and captivity. You've seen the slaughter of dogs. And you've known for a week the safety that comes from the strong arm of the Lord. I'm not that strong arm. I'm just a man, like you. But I'm a man whose life belongs to the God of all things. And I know He will strongly support me at dawn tomorrow, when His strength is tested against the strength of Mayor Loggins.

"Make no mistake! This is not a competition between two men! This is a contest between God and man, and I assure you, God will prevail! He always does, in His way, and in His time.

"Why is this happening? I will tell you so all things will be in the open. Coppertown is locked in a death struggle. As in other communities since Pan-Day, frightened people have thought so little of life, to the point that they have chosen death for others. In Coppertown, this has come in the form of the extermination of the elderly and the disabled. Look around you! These are the faces of a people doomed to be executed by their leaders, as soon as they reach a certain age. Or, if they are injured, or become ill, a similar fate is set for them.

"You can be assured that every man, woman, and child present is now accountable for this terrible crime. Provisions have become more important than people in Coppertown, and everyone here is responsible for what happens next. But Coppertown doesn't need to live like this! Two days' ride to the west, there are mountains and forests rich with game. The rivers are full of fish. There are dangers, yes, but there are no wild dogs. When we leave tomorrow, after the challenge, any who desire to leave the dread of Coppertown will be welcome to go with Alan.

"But beware! Beware of Coppertown's policies. The world out there will judge Coppertown's leaders for their inability to manage provisions. The world will learn about the wickedness of Coppertown's mayor, because now we know! We know, and we will tell the world. Every traveler will hear about Coppertown and the sacrifice of life so others can take more. Coppertown will become a curse word on the lips of Americans. Unless Coppertown and its people repent. Turn from your ways, my friends! Reform your policies. Let go of fear, and challenge the terror in which your leaders hold you!

"Tomorrow's challenge is no small matter. Light and darkness will clash. If I lose, it will mean I have died at the hungry mouths of wild dogs, and I have promised the mayor the reward of all our horses. But if I win, then Coppertown will reform its practices, and the untimely death of many at the hands of men will no longer haunt this part of the Plains Zone.

"I ask you only this, people of Refuge—those who best know my heart and dedication—pray. Pray for me, pray for God to show Himself mightily tomorrow, and pray for yourselves. Since the mayor has heard these words, and since he has killed often and many, he won't hesitate to kill again to keep his secret from the outside world."

Eric stared at Mayor Loggins, who was flanked by Elk and other elders, a couple who held rifles. Even the two men who usually stood sentry on the wall had moved closer to listen. For a moment, Eric thought Loggins would have words of his own for the crowd, but instead, the man turned and marched away. His entourage went with him, but Eric didn't miss their hateful glares as they parted.

Amber hustled up to Eric.

"You just put everyone's lives on the line!" Amber grinned. "That was brilliant! Loggins will have to back down, or slaughter us all. You're right. If we leave Coppertown like this, the whole country will learn of their atrocities."

"Sadly, every town in the country has its own atrocities." Eric cleared his throat. "But the pressure was intended for Loggins, so maybe we can bring a peaceful end to all this."

"But the challenge has to go on, right?" Amber sounded hopeful. "You have to prove that your God is better than Mayor Loggins' system of survival."

"Yeah, it may come to that." Eric locked eyes with Alan as the one-legged man hobbled up to him on his crutches.

"Okay, you have us all beside you after that." Alan looked back at the people of Refuge. "We should keep them together tonight. No one should be alone. I can only imagine all the methods a people such as these might use to abduct people in the night who go against the leadership.”

“And we can’t leave the town with all the dogs out there,” Amber said. “Not safely, anyway. You’ll show them tomorrow, Eric! You’ll show them.”

Chapter 6

Alan, Amber, Molly, Isaac, and Conrad were keeping a close watch over the people of Refuge. Eric was content to leave the people in their able hands so he could focus on the challenge he would face the next day. Those who wanted to join them were moved into the stable where they would feel safer. There wasn't much that Alan could've done with only four rifles if the townspeople did attack, but Eric knew Alan wouldn't shoot to kill anyone, anyway. They were trusting in God's hands.

Approaching from the back at one end of the stable, Eric climbed onto the roof near dusk and sat cross-legged, staring at the setting sun. Far to the west, a forest fire must've been burning, since the sunset was a hazy orange and red. The God who kept the sun in orbit, Eric considered, was the God he worshipped and served now. This was what he needed to focus on if he were going to survive the following day.

Below, the townspeople filtered in and out of the dining hall for dinner, but Eric didn't feel like eating. His portion that night was God and His all-sufficiency. Sitting alone on the roof, he could almost forget the town was down there. The sound of their voices rose as they talked quietly about the event coming the next day. But Eric wasn't interested in conversation. This wasn't a party or a celebration. A fierce spiritual battle was taking place, and lines would be drawn during the challenge. A split could even occur amongst the people of Coppertown, and Alan might need to lead more than just their own Refuge people west.

"You're not making this easy on me, brother," Alan said as his head appeared at the edge of the roof. "Could you give a one-legged man a hand?"

Eric braced himself and took hold of Alan's arms. The man leaped from his precarious footing on a fence post, trusting Eric to draw him the rest of the way. Though Eric was lighter in weight, he managed with strain to roll his friend onto the roof.

"To get down, someone should pile up some hay for us to fall onto," Eric said, "because there's no way you're leaping off here into my arms below!"

"Someone said you'd come up here." Alan's voice was serious as the two sat side-by-side to watch the sky darken. "I figured you wanted to be alone for a while, so I gave you some time, but we've got to talk."

"I agree." Eric closed his eyes and meditated on the very presence of God that was promised for all believers. "Whatever the outcome tomorrow—whether you have the horses or not—you need to lead the people west. It's only a few hours of walking for a healthy party. It might take you all day with the injured, but you'll reach Tomblin long before dark. In the daylight, the dogs shouldn't be too problematic."

"And you think Tomblin will take us in?"

"A man named Tomblin runs the town. They're hungry and lonely and afraid. Share with them, and they'll embrace you. There's probably only thirty or so people there, surviving mostly on dog meat. Amber was there for a couple hours more than me, so she might be able to tell you more details."

"And what about you?"

"If I survive, I'll stay here a few days and sort out the leadership, as well as the dog issue. If I die, you don't need to worry about anything except getting our people back to Mastover."

"You realize that the dog problem in this area is perpetuated because of this town. These dog packs can't be sustained by the occasional sacrifice of human life, but it certainly isn't helping."

"Yeah, I know." Eric turned his head to acknowledge an armed man walking past an oil-burning torch on the perimeter wall. "They must call the dogs somehow when they want to feed them. A town this resourceful could've eliminated the dogs already if they'd wanted to. A month of poisoning would decimate their numbers. Even a box of ammunition and a couple sharp-shooters on the wall could've diminished the threat level."

"But they keep the dogs," Alan said, nodding. "The people use the dogs, and the dogs use the people."

"It seems so. And the line between the two is fading." Eric peered over the edge of the roof. "Our people are resting?"

"They're bedded down in the stalls. Your stand against this town has them rooting for you, believe it or not. Amber's even told a few of them to pray for you."

"Maybe that's all God wanted through this." Eric smiled at the stars above. "A display of confidence in Him that attracts others. I don't want to die, Alan, but if this is how it ends, with others coming to God, I can't complain."

"Well, Gretchen will complain. And there's others who won't be happy with me that I let you do this. Judge Grayport will probably ban all one-legged people from Mastover. All of Wyoming would mourn over you, Eric."

"I don't want to be mourned over, Alan. Just point people to God. I'm only willing to die because I know God is real. He lives inside me. Death holds no sting. It isn't the end."

"I'll tell them. But somehow, I keep thinking God just might do a miracle tomorrow."

"I could live with that," Eric said, and the two men chuckled.

Alan laid a hand on Eric's shoulder, and prayed. However, it wasn't a prayer about Eric, but a prayer about their God. The God of whirlwinds and galaxies, who moves stars as easily as He moves insects, who calls forth hail and thunder through storms, who feeds every creature, who keeps the world turning and alive—it was a prayer of worship. By its conclusion, Eric felt both humbled and empowered. God was indeed with them!

Eric climbed off the roof first, and he guided Alan down to the fence post without much effort. The town was asleep and most of the torches had been extinguished as the two men made their way toward the door of the stable. Although Eric had come to know other believers since Pan-Day, he felt a special bond with Alan, who'd been a believer for only a few months. But those were the days of quickening through hardship, and in the humbling of losing his leg, Eric knew the man had been particularly open to God's filling. His very prayer for him spoke of his true heart, Eric believed, and any caution the man had voiced about the following day's challenge had merely been Alan caring for Eric. His one-legged friend clearly had firm convictions about God's power and goodness.

From the shadows under the awning of the stable, men clothed in dark shirts emerged into the starlight. Eric glimpsed five men with clubs before he could cry out. He raised his hands to defend his head, and Alan threw up both crutches at once, but these were hearty men. Determined men. Violent men, who'd perhaps committed similar ambushes toward other travelers or townspeople alike.

Eric was unconscious before he hit the ground.

#######

When he woke, Eric's head was throbbing from pain. The rumble of wagon wheels and jostling over hard ground didn't help the agony pulsing between his ears.

A rag had been stuffed into his mouth, and his wrists and ankles were bound tightly. His brow was against buckboard siding where he could see daylight through a crack in the wood. Glimpses of the grassy plain flashed in his vision as the wagon thumped over the terrain.

He turned his head and squinted up at blue sky through a wooden cage. The cage encompassed the whole top of the wagon, even the driver, whose back was three feet away. Eric recognized the shoulders and frame. It was Elk, one of the leaders of Coppertown.

The wagon stopped, and Eric forced himself to focus one eye to see through a crack in a board. There were no dogs outside the wagon. At least, for the moment, he wasn't being fed alive to the dogs.

A chain rattled—iron against wood. It was a gate of some sort. The wagon rolled forward a few yards, then stopped again. Elk climbed back into the wagon and unlatched the sides of the wooden cage, then lifted it away. The strong man avoided Eric's eyes and roughly dragged him to the back of the wagon and rolled him out onto dusty ground. Eric tumbled out and groaned through the rag in his mouth. From other merciless treatment through the night, he could feel his many bruises and scrapes.

Eric lay there on the ground watching Elk lift the cage from around one draft horse—like a protective shell that had sheltered the animal from the dogs on the plain. Elk unharnessed the horse, then turned it loose in a narrow corral inside a small walled complex. And that smell—it was oil! This was Coppertown's oil pump. Of course, they had needed to build a wall around it to protect occasional workers. A shack stood silent and dark next to the lonely remnants of a donkey pump, its joints long-ago rusted.

Once the horse was cared for, Elk dragged Eric feet-first into the shack and left him against a wall. Eric took in the interior as Elk lit a lamp and stocked shelves from provisions he'd brought in the wagon. Apparently, they were staying for a few days.

Resting his throbbing head on the floor, Eric prayed, his eyes half-open. Weariness was close to putting him to sleep again. How could this be God's will? This wasn't victory. This wasn't triumph over a self-determined and violent people!

"Let me have that back." Elk knelt and waved dirty fingers in front of Eric's face. "Give it to me. We'll be here alone for a while. I'll let you talk as long as you don't try anything."

Eric relaxed his jaw, and Elk wrestled the rag from Eric's teeth. He moved his jaw and felt his swollen lips with his tongue. While unconscious, he'd been beaten by his kidnappers. But at least he could breathe easier now through his mouth.

"This isn't the way I expected today to turn out." Eric felt the calmness of God, as strongly as the night before on the roof. "What happened to Alan, the man on the crutches?"

"He's gone." Elk pumped an old cast iron water pump at the sink, rinsed the rag out, then tied it around his neck. "The usual way."

"The dogs." Eric took a deep breath. Alan was gone. He had two legs again in heaven, at least. "He was a good man. He was a man of God."

"Maybe, but not like you are." Elk sat on the edge of a twin bed, adjusted the sidearm on his belt, and drew his knife to cut at a chunk of goat cheese. "We voted, and all agreed we should kill you. But not right away."

"So, you fear God?" Eric scoffed. "You would kill one man and not another?"

"Your Alan friend wasn't challenging Mayor Loggins or Coppertown's authority. You were."

"You knew I would prevail, with God's help."

"We couldn't risk it." Elk spoke around a mouthful of cheese. His beard was bushy and untrimmed. "The survival of Coppertown is too important to us to see life interrupted by some traveling prophet."

"I'm no prophet, but you're wise to fear the God I serve. Don't you fear Him now, that He'll be upset since you've kidnapped me?"

"I think we can come to an understanding." Elk pointed his knife at Eric. "You threatened our normal way of life in Coppertown. That needs to be reversed. You need to reverse it."

"Reverse it? I was only upsetting your system of death, not life."

"It's the same thing out here. When new life comes, old life must go out."

"God teaches that He can give life from death." Eric cleared his throat, his clarity returning. "The fear you have, Elk, is misplaced. Coppertown can survive without killing its people off. God will show you how. He will support you as much as He supports me. You can become a man of God and understand these things as well."

"Not true. I don't know anything about any God out there. Most of the people were just celebrating the challenge. Nothing too exciting happens in Coppertown. There's unrest underneath it all. You made citizens question Mayor Loggins. You, a stranger, gave them boldness. That's how rebellions and insurrection starts. The one who planted that seed will now return to Coppertown and say you were wrong. You know what's out there on the plain. Coppertown is the most bountiful town you've ever seen, isn't it? Like no other?"

"It is bountiful, but at what price?"

"Any price!"

"You can't be serious!" Eric frowned. "You seriously expect me to disregard my God-given convictions and speak for you instead of against you?"

"Yes."

"What if I don't?"

"The dogs are always hungry."

Chapter 7

That night, Eric slept uncomfortably. His hands were numb and his shoulders were sore from being strained. Dried blood matted his hair and despair threatened his faith. He feared he wouldn't see Gretchen and Andy again. Or worse, that Gretchen would wander out into the Plains Zone looking for him!

Elk's snoring caused Eric to focus on the broad-shouldered brute on the bed. Obviously, mere knowledge of an almighty God hadn't brought change to the man's heart. It would be a great task, but somehow, Elk needed to be converted. It would require a miracle from God Himself.

At the thought, Eric wept repentantly. He'd been striving so hard to show God's might in a miraculous way, that he'd overlooked the greater needs of the souls around him. And Eric knew instantly that his priorities had been backwards. He should've been striving hard to show God's mercy in a miraculous way. Elk and the townspeople were already frightened. They didn't need to be challenged, but to be loved dearly. Of course, that love would require some sure correction within the ranks of the town's leadership, but mercy was the answer! However, how could he possibly show this man mercy?

As quickly as Eric turned from his old thinking and determined to promote God's love, he felt Elk slice away the bonds around his wrists and ankles. The knife he used was so sharp, the tethers fell away like grass.

"Thank you," Eric mumbled to his captor in the dark room. Then, he suddenly realized that Elk was still sleeping and snoring on the bed a few feet away! Grinning, touched by God's presence, he corrected himself with widened eyes. "I mean, thank *You!*"

Painful minutes passed as the blood returned to Eric's hands and feet, so he rejoiced in God's perfect timing and favor. This was it! This was how he would begin to show his enemy the mercies of God!

Eric rose to his feet and leaned across a counter to gaze out the shack's only window. It faced south, and far to the left, a reddish glow lit the horizon. Dawn wasn't far away.

As quietly as possible, Eric worked the lever on the water pump and washed his wounds. His scalp was painful to the touch, but even the little sleep he'd gotten had revived his strength and diminished his headache to a dull throb.

From the food stores, Eric found bread, more cheese, and chicken eggs cushioned in cartons of grass. He primed an old stove and found a pan to cook breakfast. About the time the eggs began to sizzle, Eric lit the lantern and turned it up brightly. Elk's sleeping face twitched as his senses began to relish at the smell of food.

He found a jar of something that resembled chicory, perhaps from the forest reportedly located to the south. With delicate fingers, Eric drew Elk's knife blade from his belt, washed it, and cut slices of cheese and steamed the chicory for a weak brew.

"Wake up." With a loud thump, Eric stabbed the blade tip into the bed's headboard. "Breakfast is ready."

He turned down the lantern as daylight shined brighter through the window, then leaned against the counter to watch Elk wake up.

Elk was slow to gather his wits. He blinked away his sleepiness, acknowledged Eric standing feet away, then scratched for his knife on his belt. But his knife wasn't in its sheath. Turning pale, he realized it was stuck inches from where his sleeping head had been moments earlier. Then, Elk noticed his sidearm on the counter where he'd set it before going to sleep the night before. He could see that Eric hadn't touched it.

"Egg and goat cheese sandwich okay with you?" Eric set a tin plate in Elk's hands, then returned to his place at the counter. "Lord, we thank You for always providing for our needs. You are so faithful, even though we are simple-minded and uncaring. We accept Your correction, and we ask You to guide us throughout our day. Thank You also for new friendships and fresh perspectives. In Jesus' name, amen."

When Eric looked up, Elk was wide-eyed, studying the situation, the plate still in his hands.

"The rope." Elk frowned at the remnants of twine on the floor.

"Yeah, I thought you had cut me loose earlier this morning."

"I didn't cut you loose!"

"Oh, I guess it was the hand of God then. Eat up while it's hot." Eric took a giant bite and held the fierce gaze of Elk. Neither man flinched as Eric chewed loudly. "I'll eat yours if you don't like eggs over-easy. Something about traveling far from home makes me hungry. You?"

"I'm eating." Elk took a bite, then yanked his knife out of the headboard and slid it into the sheath on his belt. Then, he shoved his sidearm into his hip holster. "You could've killed me. Why didn't you?"

"We're just getting to know one another. Why would I want to kill you?"

"Because I'm supposed to kill you, if I can't make you see things the Coppertown way."

"How many days will you need to try to make me see things the Coppertown way?"

Elk swore, set down his tin plate, and went to the wall. He crouched down and picked up pieces of the twine that had been Eric's binds.

"These weren't cut." Elk stood, one piece still in his fingers. "These were torn apart. No one is that strong. You tore these apart yourself?"

"Now, do I look like a man who could tear through that kind of stuff? Don't give me credit for something when you know the credit belongs to God."

Elk backed away to sit on the bed and nibble at his sandwich.

Eric could read the dilemma on the man's face. He was expected to do a job for his friends, but Elk had been shown mercy at a moment when he knew he deserved wrath.

"How many days do they expect you to be gone with me?" Eric asked again.

"Two or three. At my discretion."

"And my friends?"

"Loggins is holding them in Coppertown. You scared us when you said you'd tell the world about us. The world can't know, you know, what we've been doing."

"The world doesn't matter right now. What matters are the lives under your and my immediate influence. It's time for change, Elk. That's why I'm here. Are my friends in danger?"

"No. I mean, just the one-legged guy. He fought back and one of the men killed him. Loggins is telling everyone you and the cripple deserted them. You got afraid about the challenge and ran away in the night. There were no traces of you two left behind."

"My people will never believe I left them." Eric set his tin in the sink. "I went through all this danger to rescue them from slavers, and then I abandon them when a confused town is hiding a secret? No, they'll see through the lie."

"It's the Coppertown citizens who needed convincing. You're the only one who's ever challenged us, so they'll think you admitted your error when you and your friend ran away. Things are slowly being restored."

"Your deception is just a piece of the problem. An entire regional armed guard from Wyoming will mobilize for me. We cannot allow a war, Elk!"

"An army? Why am I not surprised? You're valuable to them?"

"I'm just a man like you, Elk." Eric held up his hands. "What makes me different is that God is in my life. When I finally surrendered to His will and received His forgiveness, my whole life became free to live in His power. I think you've seen something of His power."

"I've never seen anything like it. I was sleeping right there the whole time. I didn't notice a light or anything."

"There was no light. God is subtle like that sometimes. There and gone. We have to pay attention."

"Well, you'll need Him to be not so subtle if we're going back to Coppertown."

"So, we're in agreement that it's time for Coppertown to change?"

Elk sighed and looked at the twine on the floor.

"We're in agreement." He shook his big head. "I'm not sure what you'd do to me if I didn't agree. I have a family who depends on me. I don't want to die."

"Come on, Elk. You're almost twice my size. What could I possibly do to you?"

"I misspoke. I'm afraid of what God would do to me."

"The Bible says that fearing God is the beginning of wisdom, so I'd say you're on the right path."

"But it'll still take a miracle to avoid a war." Elk took off his bandana and wiped his face. "Mayor Loggins and the others are more stubborn than me. They founded the town before me. I'm just the muscle."

"God will sort it out if we submit it to Him."

"If I go back with you alive, Loggins will think you came to some sort of agreement with me."

"I'd say we have come to some agreement." Eric offered his hand. "Haven't we?"

"I'm going to regret this." Elk groaned and shook Eric's smaller hand.

"No one who genuinely repents from a path of sin and wickedness regrets it. Otherwise, it's not true repentance. Shall we talk about the particulars?"

"Do I have to get on my knees or something?"

"I don't think the position matters much, Elk." Eric smiled. "But it would be good for us to humble ourselves like that this first time."

Eric painfully tried to kneel. His many injuries from the mistreatment from Elk caused him to twist sideways and he lost his balance. Elk caught him and eased him down to the dusty floorboards.

"What do I do now?" Elk's large frame dwarfed Eric's bruised body.

"It's not about doing something, Elk. It's about giving in. It's about acknowledging who God is, and trusting in His Son Jesus as your Redeemer. He's bought you back from the brink of destruction. Talk to Him about the forgiveness you need and the deliverance you want. Go ahead. He's listening."

"This is foolishness! I'm not a praying man." Elk awkwardly lifted his burly arms and clasped his hands. "Just talk to thin air?"

"He's here. Believe it."

"Uh, God, it's Elron McKinney here. I'm new at this, but I think maybe I've been on a road to meet You sooner or later, so it may as well be now, while I'm confused because of Your guy Eric here. I'm all disoriented, God, and maybe that's the point. Looking back, I admit to, well, um. Hmm."

Elk went silent, and Eric looked up into his bearded face.

"You were doing fine, Elk."

"I get it." The larger man's chin trembled, and he glanced at the door. "I think I need to be alone. You know, to talk about the rest. Unless you have to be here."

"Oh, no, I don't have to be here." Eric used Elk's shoulder to climb to his feet. "Take your time. I'll just be outside."

Eric walked outside and closed the door to the shack. The late spring day was warm, and Eric stretched his battered limbs toward the blue sky. His heart was soaring from God's obvious hand in all that had happened. He no longer felt disappointment at having missed the challenge the day before. Elk placing his faith in God was worth all the bruises and welts he carried.

Through the thin walls of the shack, Eric heard Elk sobbing and mumbling incoherently. Eric remembered his own conversion on a mountaintop. Fear and uncertainty had stolen all hope, but God had stepped in and saved his life and his eternal soul.

Moving from the shack, he walked around the wagon they'd brought from Coppertown. The protective wooden cages, one for the horse and one for the wagon, sat on the ground nearby. They appeared heavy enough that two men would need to lift them on and off, but Elk was stronger than the ordinary man.

The draft horse nuzzled Eric through the corral fence as he walked into a hay shed and offered the animal an armful of hay. Directly behind the shack was the oil well, which had somehow been rigged to operate for the people of Coppertown. They apparently powered the well when they needed more oil in town. It really was ingenious, but the mayor's hatred and scorn of God was far greater than their accomplishments. Coppertown had merely adapted to their circumstances, and in their pride and fear, they were slowly killing themselves to preserve their resources.

The shack door opened behind him. Elk walked out and stopped to face Eric. The big, bearded man had slept the night before in his clothes, so they were wrinkled. His eyes were red, and his hair and beard were askew. He appeared about to speak, to explain what had happened to him, but then seemed at a loss for words. Maybe there were no words, Eric thought, to explain what miracle had occurred inside him. Instead, Elk gestured to Eric's clothes.

"You're a mess. We should get you cleaned up."

"I was about to say the same about you." Eric chuckled, his body's aches seeming to evaporate. "You first. The horse trough isn't big enough for the both of us at once."

"No, you first." Elk sighed, solemnly. "I owe you. I owe you everything. And when we get back to Coppertown, you're telling my family about God, and I'll owe you even more."

"No, brother, you owe me nothing. We both owe God. You and I were just fellow sinners. Now, we're brothers and saints together. That's who we are. And now, to honor Jesus Christ, we live like it."

Chapter 8

The following morning, Eric climbed into the wagon as Elk harnessed the horse, then the Coppertown resident lifted the wooden cage over the horse to protect him. Finally, he settled the other cage over them and the wagon as he seated himself beside Eric. Though both men had talked late into the night, they were excited to see how God would bring about peace and change to Coppertown.

Riding beside Elk, Eric felt honored to have been the one God had used to bring conversion to the father of two and husband of nine years. Although Elk had wanted to talk primarily about his new life in Christ, Eric was able to beg a few details out of the family man about the community that was called Coppertown.

Elk shared that the town had become a ghost town after Pan-Day. Families who were traveling on the highway began to gather in the remote town, which was called Coppertown due to the appearance of copper-colored grass on the rolling hills nearby. A clean water supply and functioning well had convinced many to stay.

An engineer had helped build the small oil refinery, once the oil well miles to the north was discovered. Another group of men hauled an old sawmill into town. Recognizing the rarity of what they'd built, laws had been established to keep the oil refinery a secret and to maintain their meager food production.

With the coming of the dog packs a couple years later, the town was further isolated from the outside, and travelers on the highway ceased. The town's rules became stricter as its twelve elders determined to conserve their resources, even at the expense of its citizens.

The previous mayor had died in a refinery fire. Loggins had been horribly scarred in the same fire, but was later elected from among the twelve to be mayor. The twelve were those in charge of keeping a balance between food and life. A strict limit on mouths to be fed needed to be enforced, they believed, to survive the circumstances of the Plains Zone. Morale in town had plummeted as obsession with their own laws caused more and more loss of life. Instead of promoting life in the town, Elk admitted that the people had consistently become more depressed, mechanical in their duties, and suspicious of the twelve leaders.

As such, the twelve had withdrawn more from interacting with the townspeople, and the "culling" of the population when a new child was born was accomplished in the dark of night, much like Eric had been abducted. No townspeople complained aloud, lest they be removed by the twelve.

"I'm even one of the twelve!" Elk cursed, then apologized for his language. "I've been a trusted Officer of Preservation for six years, ever since bringing my family from Omaha to Coppertown. Until you came along to challenge us, I haven't cared much about what happened to the people we decided to put down."

Eric held onto the cage above his head as the wagon wobbled over uneven ground. The track across the range was filled with weeds since it was infrequently traveled.

"How do you decide who lives and who dies?"

"The twelve have a ledger of everyone by age and health status. A health condition raises that citizen's consumption rate of Coppertown resources, so that citizen may rise to the top of the list for removal. Your blind friend would be at the top of the list, as well as your friend Amber, who you left with us when you went after the slavers. Amber's the oldest person in town, if you haven't noticed."

"The word barbaric comes to mind," Eric said. "Sorry, but even a systematic method that seems logical doesn't mean sound judgment is being used."

"I'm seeing it all from the outside for the first time." Elk held the horse reins lightly, expertly, allowing the horse to manage its own plodding pace. "It seemed perfect at first; so simple to stay alive. Gradually, like a frog in water, the heat was slowly applied. And we didn't even realize how bad everything was becoming."

"There are alternatives to killing off citizens for conserving resources."

"That would require risky expansion from Coppertown across a dangerous region, but I see now that it has to be done. Believe me, even as a system, I knew it was being abused. Members of the twelve would alter their family members' health ratings, or even their own ages in the ledger, to keep loved ones safe. My family is young, so I didn't have any need to do that, but I saw it happen more than once."

"And innocent people were killed instead?"

Elk didn't answer. He didn't have to.

Eric changed the subject to talk about terms in the Bible that referred to the spiritual life that had taken hold of Elk—terms such as redemption, substitution, reconciliation, and propitiation. As the wagon rolled southward, and the noon hour approached, Elk listened and asked questions about certain truths. Though they had no Bible with them, Eric knew the basic doctrines well enough to quote from memory God's very Word.

Suddenly, Elk reined in the horse. Eric stopped speaking and waited for an explanation. A small pack of dogs rose from the grass amongst sagebrush where they'd been laying.

"Coppertown will be within sight in the distance as soon as we go over this last rise." Elk's eyes pleaded with Eric. "God is big enough to fix this mess we're in, right?"

"He is. We just need to be open to His leading, not our own feelings or reasonings."

"If I have to leave Coppertown, let me and my family come with you to Mastover."

"You would be welcome to join us, Elk." Eric shook the man's hand. "Let's just take things real slow once we're back in town. It'll work out."

"They'll think I turned you, since we're coming back together. You're still alive. That'll be unexpected."

"I understand."

"And . . . they would've disposed of your one-legged friend since we left. I'm sorry."

Eric nodded, thinking fondly of Alan.

"I'll miss him, but I knew Alan. He would've gladly sacrificed himself if he knew it would lead to the repentance and faith of others."

"Alan suffered a substitutionary death?" Elk raised his eyebrows. "So I wouldn't die in my sins? Sort of?"

"Sort of. But his suffering is over. We'll remember him. Okay, let's do this."

Elk slapped the reins as Eric prayed aloud—and louder as more dogs came into sight.

The plain opened before them, and Eric beheld the town of Coppertown from an angle he hadn't seen before. It seemed like a Western fort, totally walled and contained by its own cut wood. Instead of Indians, hundreds of dogs surrounded the town, many more than Eric had seen a few days earlier outside the town.

"There's a bell on the north wall." Elk pointed at the town. "The dogs know they're about to be fed something when they hear that bell. We've trained them this way."

"Fed something? Or someone?"

Elk encouraged the draft horse down the slope and into the midst of the assortment of mutts. Eric searched for the Great Dane, but the tall dog didn't seem to be on that side of the town.

For the first time, Eric witnessed the effectiveness of the cage around the horse in motion. The cage hung a half-foot off the ground, anchored across the broad back of the horse. If the six inches of space below the cage tempted a smaller canine, lengths of old tire had been nailed to the bottom of the cage. The lengths of tire occasionally dragged on the ground, but offered no resistance for the horse drawing the wagon forward.

The nearest dogs trotted up to the cage, growled, and sniffed at the cage as it rolled forward. Elk loosened his sidearm in its holster in case he needed to offer additional defense. The horse snorted at the nearby dogs, but otherwise held his gait up to the town gate, which opened without making them wait. When gunmen appeared at the open gate, the closest dogs scattered away, as if they were familiar with the weapon in a man's hands.

The wagon stopped in the courtyard, and the clamor of the townspeople and surprise at the sight of Eric was apparent on their faces. Eric steeled himself with God's courage as the courtyard was filled with people seeking news.

The cage was removed from the horse first, then men lifted the shell from the wagon. Elk hopped down to the crowd. Eric was slower, since his injuries from the last three days were still healing.

"Hi, there." Eric smiled at faces he didn't know. But he didn't see his friends. "Elk, I'm going to the stable."

"The mayor will want to talk to you," he said with a look of warning. "Right away."

Eric nodded and pushed through the crowd. Seeing no familiar faces concerned him immensely. If his friends had all been executed to keep Coppertown's secret, then he'd returned with Elk for no reason.

At the stable, a man with a sidearm started forward with concern on his face.

"It's okay." Eric greeted with a wave. "I just returned from the oil well with Elk. Are my friends inside?"

The young man in homespun clothes glanced toward the center of the courtyard, perhaps seeking Mayor Loggins. For all Eric knew, this man was one of those who'd jumped him and Alan a few nights earlier.

"I'm not supposed to allow anyone out without permission," the man said.

"And you should obey that order. But I'm going in. That's not against orders, right?" Without waiting for the man's approval, Eric lifted the light beam away from the double doors and handed it to the gunman. "You can even block the door once I'm inside. I'll tap three times when I'm ready to come out. Thanks!"

Eric swung one door open, just enough to slip inside the dusty interior. Weary faces from inside the stalls peeked from behind walls and piles of hay. Amber was the first to rush forward. After her came Molly, Conrad, and Isaac. Peter and the others came more reluctantly, though once they were close enough to touch, Eric embraced each of them as if they were close relatives. Only one person was missing.

"What have they done with Kelly?" he asked, accusation in his voice.

"I'm here." The blind man weakly stepped from one stall, his hands outstretched. "Is that you, Eric Radner?"

"Yes, it's me." Eric walked over and embraced the old commander. The man's body was rigid at first, then he relaxed. "I'm glad to see you're safe, my friend."

"Where's Alan?" Molly's face was red, and her eyes were wild. "Why isn't Alan with you? They said you and Alan abandoned us. Eric, where is he?"

"The other night, when they kidnapped me," Eric shook his head, "they killed Alan."

"We knew you'd never leave us." Isaac handed Eric his pocket Bible. "We found this on the ground the next morning. We read it while you were gone."

"Thank you." Eric slipped the Bible into his outer jacket pocket.

"They won't let us leave," Conrad stated, his arm around Molly's shoulders as she wept against his chest. "Those things you said made them suspicious of us.

They're afraid we'll tell the world about them if we leave. And they took our guns!"

"They're suspicious and afraid because they're ashamed." Eric said. "Their secret sin has been exposed. But God has been working. Everything seems hopeless right now, but I believe victory is before us. Continue to pray and trust God. He'll see us through."

Both stable doors opened. Four gunmen flanked Mayor Loggins as he stepped inside. Elk's larger figure hovered in the entrance.

"Eric," Loggins called, "I understand we've come to some understanding?"

Realizing he was being summoned, Eric moved beyond his friends and strode confidently toward the mayor.

"An understanding between me and Elk has been reached." Eric stopped feet away from the men. "We should talk somewhere. And my friends should be free to move about the town."

"I'll decide when that happens." Loggins smirked, wrinkling his burnt forehead. "Follow me."

Chapter 9

On one edge of Coppertown's courtyard was a two-story lodge, the finest building Eric had seen in the town. He was led up the stairs by Mayor Loggins, followed by eleven other men, including Elk. To Eric, it felt more like an execution squad, and the whole town in the courtyard had turned out to see what would happen. Men, women, and children stood silently below, perhaps better aware of what awaited him than he knew himself. With all his inner strength, he reached out for God's presence, and his faith grabbed hold of the only hope he needed right then. God was with him.

On the second floor of the lodge, Eric walked across a carpeted suite of luxury. A stuffed antelope stood against one wall, and a large stuffed dog stood against another. It looked like a German shepherd, but it had a longer snout that made Eric wonder if it was a wolf cross.

A round table stood in the center of the grand room, surrounded by twelve chairs. Beyond the table and the two ornate side walls was the distant wall in which was placed a magnificent picture window. The view overlooked the eastern plain. About fifty loitering dogs were in sight on that side of the town, but Eric knew he was safe inside Coppertown—at least from wild dogs. Not even Mastover had such a room or furnishings like this!

The twelve men seated themselves, as if assigned to specific chairs, but there was no chair for Eric. He guessed this was by design. Whoever was in the presence of the elders was supposed to feel subordinate and uncomfortable.

"The sanctity of Coppertown must be upheld," Mayor Loggins said, as if speaking to statesmen who didn't already hold his views. "We have all made sacrifices, and those sacrifices have paid off. Because of our own efforts,

Coppertown has never been richer, its citizens better fed, the work more productive. Our labor has produced everything we need and have."

Eric stood at a table close to the south wall. He faced Loggins directly, and glanced at Elk, who didn't look up from his slouched position. The big man was picking at a thumbnail. Surely, he was worried as to how the day would develop, Eric guessed, and if it would end with them both being fed to wild dogs.

"The coming of these strangers is not a terrible situation," the mayor continued. "There is good stock among them. Some are craftsmen, and several women are of child-bearing age still. For the good of Coppertown, we welcome the right citizens, of course. The question we are here to decide is, what should be done with those whom we don't want to stay and those we don't want to be part of our bloodline? How we decide, interestingly enough, is in the hands of this Eric—Radner, isn't it?"

"Yes, sir." Eric cleared his throat.

"You had a fine, defiant speech the other day, Eric. It stirred up all kinds of unrest. That was irresponsible of you to go against those who've been your deliverers from the wild dogs. Perhaps your time with Elk has softened your position regarding our need for security and preservation."

All twelve men watched Eric closely, so he didn't react outwardly to the man's words. He surveyed the men's faces, wondering which of them had attacked him that fateful night, and which of them had killed Alan. It could've been Elk, for all he knew, so he pushed his one-legged friend's memory aside for the moment.

"Yes, Elk and I had some very convincing conversations up at the oil well. I'm absolutely humbled by all I've seen here. I hope to offer nothing more than what Elk and I have agreed is true and right for Coppertown."

Elk frowned and squinted his eyes, as if trying to read between the lines of his cryptic message.

"And, where do you stand in regards to your God?" Loggins asked. "And our own might? Will you give credit to the people, to the men at this table, for our town's survival?"

"On that, your elder, Elk," Eric emphasized, "has made it very clear for me. Elk and I have had a connection, you could say, and our hearts are knit together on the whole issue of the might and power of Coppertown's people."

"Why, Elk!" The mayor chuckled. "It seems we have underestimated the power of your persuasive reasoning over the power of your brute strength!"

The men at the table laughed and thumped the table with their fists. Elk turned red-faced.

"If I may say so, sirs." Eric took a step forward. "The transformation that occurred up at the oil well was heartfelt and real. You need not fear me. My heart and Elk's heart are the same now. I want the best for Coppertown."

"Well!" Loggins rocked back in his chair, seeming to be very pleased with himself. "Then there's no hard feelings? This was easier than I thought it would be. But would you be willing to speak to the people once more? Share about this 'meeting of hearts' you've had? The injuries from a few days ago need to be healed."

"A few days ago," Eric nodded solemnly, "matters were left unresolved. To address everything, and to make sure that all these matters are settled—I would be honored to speak plainly to your people. Perhaps my fellow travelers could be there as well? I will convince them very quickly that what Elk and I discussed at the oil well is indeed the way we all must proceed, or risk our very lives."

Mayor Loggins looked to Elk as the other men mumbled their approval.

"Elder Elk, would you recommend this man trustworthy to speak once more to the people, to correct what has been left confused?"

"I would, uh, recommend it, yes." Elk sat up straight in his chair. "Although Eric is an outsider, he may be able to put things into words that we ourselves haven't considered. I see no harm in having his own people attend as well."

Loggins looked to the other elders, and each gave their consent by a nod of the head. Eric knew that Elk had further tied his fate to Eric's by his words of approval, but Eric thanked God in his heart that the muscled brute at the elders' table had so thoroughly come to see the light. God could indeed reach the rest of the elders, too!

The meeting was adjourned, and the twelve men emerged from the lodge's great room to appear on the balcony outside. The people below hushed themselves for whatever proclamation was to be made. Loggins raised his arms, smiling like a benevolent lord.

"Someone bring our guests from the stable. Our friend Eric Radner here has an announcement that will lift the hearts of Coppertown like never before." He turned to Eric. "Give them a few minutes until everyone is gathered. Then, the floor is yours. We're counting on you."

"I'll do what's right." Eric nodded reassuringly, but knew he was about to disappoint the man terribly.

For a few moments, Eric was alone to pray. Off to the side of the balcony, he rested his hands on the wooden railing and bowed his head. The God of Daniel, and David, and Elijah was his God. He would not be afraid!

Someone brushed up beside him. It was Elk.

"Is this your plan?" Elk mumbled. "How are you going to do this? I don't think God would like it if we backed down and conceded to the elders' demands."

"Oh, don't worry. I'm not backing down." Eric sensed a peace within himself, a peace from the same God who had shown Himself mighty in a dozen other monumental moments. "It's about to get very lively inside Coppertown. If you know of some safe place to hide, I'd go there now, with your family. I don't know how, but God must prevail today."

"And you want me to hide and miss everything?" Elk scoffed. "Just tell me your plan. I'll stand for God with you."

Eric looked Elk in the eyes.

"I'm going forward with the challenge from a few days ago. The elders need to be beat once and for all in full view of all the people."

"The challenge?" Elk turned pale. "With the dogs? That's crazy! Or you've got faith like I can't imagine."

"No, we've got a God who's going to blow imaginations!"

Eric saw his friends escorted through the throng in the courtyard. Molly held Kelly by the shoulder. Conrad, Isaac, and Amber were all there, peering up at him. He hadn't known them for long, but he'd come to love those people who'd once been slaves. By God's great favor, he would live to see them freed from this other type of bondage as well.

"My friends!" he called. The crowd hushed themselves. "Townspeople of Coppertown, elders, and travelers from Refuge, it is an honor to speak to you a second time. I want to thank the mayor for another opportunity to pursue what was once interrupted."

Eric turned, smiled, and gestured to the mayor, who waved and grinned at the people.

"While Elder Elk and I were up at the oil pump house," Eric continued, "he told me of the rich and even tragic heritage of Coppertown. I'm moved to say that you have all endured so much to be standing here today. You have worked hard. Coppertown is truly an oasis amongst a devastated land. On every side, there is danger, and yet, here is a flower in the Plains Zone, that even wild dogs cannot destroy."

Eric paused for his words to sink in. Elk stood at his right elbow, almost stone-still. And beyond him, the eleven other elders glowed and took credit.

"While we were at the oil pump house, Elk and I witnessed three miracles! First, the bonds with which I was tied fell off my wrists and ankles in the night. Second, God's Spirit moved me to care mercifully for Elk as he slept. Even though he took me up there to kill me, instead of killing him, I made him breakfast. And miracle three, Elk's heart was softened and we spoke for almost two days about how change needs to come to Coppertown!"

The elders were now in an uproar, jostling for position to interrupt Eric, but Elk, with his sidearm drawn, stood in their path. While he had the floor, Eric figured he'd better keep talking.

"People of Coppertown, you live in fear, and you tell yourselves that you are victorious. You murder each other in the night and call it preservation. You feed your own people to the dogs and call it security. This must end! Before I was kidnapped by the elders a few days ago, Mayor Loggins and I were going to prove who is greater—God or man. I see no reason why the same challenge cannot go on today, right now, before all these witnesses!

"What do you say, Mayor? Are we finished with the theatrics? Can we show the people what they came to see? Do you fear me so much that you will keep these people in the grip of death rather than life? You and me, Mayor. Right now. Do you accept?"

Loggins elbowed his way clear of his fellow elders and stepped to the railing of the balcony. With one hand, he swept at his wisp of tousled hair.

"I . . . accept!" Loggins shouted and pointed a crooked finger at Eric. "I will show that our strength and ingenuity is greater than the wild fantasies of the past! Let's do this and be rid of this charlatan! Bring me the exoskeleton! To the west gate!"

Chapter 10

The bell on the north wall of Coppertown tolled ten times as the townspeople waited on the wall and at the closed west gate. Eric wished Alan were there with him, but God had given him a mighty armor bearer named Elk, and all around him were the people he'd rescued from Refuge. Not one had mixed with the people of Coppertown or turned aside their loyalties. Even Kelly was there, being apprised of everything as Molly whispered the description of the scene before them.

"I told you," Elk said softly. He hadn't holstered his sidearm since the balcony speech. "The dogs are trained. That bell tells them there's a meal to be had."

"Don't frighten him!" Amber scolded. "Eric, you're not afraid, are you? Dogs smell fear. It's a chemical we put off, and they smell the emotion."

"No," Eric said, "I'm not afraid. I've invested everything that God has made me into for this very moment. Somehow, we will prevail."

Curiously, he glanced to the right where several of the elders were strapping Mayor Loggins into a wooden exoskeleton. A harness over his shoulders, which was also supported around his waist, carried what looked to be a fifty-pound load of wooden bars, joints, and braces. The invention was meant to allow the man to walk slowly onto the plain, and not be attacked by dogs.

"We use the exoskeleton," Elk said, "for brief errands outside the wall. You can see, it's like a bird cage around his whole body. No dog has ever gotten through the exoskeleton. I don't think I've ever seen Loggins use it."

One of the older elders climbed onto the wall's ramparts and hushed the crowd.

"When the gate opens, both men will walk out together. Eric, you walk out to the left, and Mayor

Loggins, you walk out to the right. You will each move away from the wall one hundred yards, turn, and stop. When the bell tolls, you will return. Let the challenge begin! Good luck to you both."

"Whose side are you on?" Loggins hissed at his fellow elder. "Just open the gate!"

Several men with assault rifles approached the gate to protect the people. One man drew back the iron bolt.

"Remember what our God can do," Elk said, and patted Eric on the shoulder.

Eric stepped away from his friends and up to the gate. Loggins—now inside his wooden shell in the shape of a man—came and stood beside him. Through the poles of the exoskeleton, which extended above Loggins' head, Eric could see the man was already sweating.

"A nice warm day for a walk," Eric said. "Now, the people will learn that God is greater than what you've designed and preserved."

"Keep talking." Loggins laughed. "You're about to be eaten alive."

"God is my refuge and my shield. My people have walked through fire, slain giants, tamed lions, and conquered nations. That's the God I serve!"

The gate swung open. Hundreds of dogs sat or stood expectantly, some of them licking their chops.

Both men walked side-by-side through the gate, then angled away from one another. Above, on the wall, there was a whisper of movement as the townspeople shifted to observe the challengers now outside the gate.

"What do you hope to achieve by your death?" Loggins asked. "You're just giving us more evidence that you and your God are weak."

"My God created these animals," Eric responded. "You'd best watch your footing while carrying all that weight."

Both men covered the gap of empty land between the wall and the dogs. The canines nearest Eric seemed almost apprehensive about the meal they didn't have to fight for.

"Get out of the way!" Loggins snarled at several dogs as he laboriously stepped farther away. "Get!"

"'The Lord is my Shepherd,'" Eric prayed, speaking softly to the dogs as they parted before him. "'I shall not want.'"

Their ears perked at his voice, and he raised his hands about waist level, palms open and revealed.

"'He maketh me to lie down in green pastures; He leadeth me beside the still waters. He restoreth my soul; He leadeth me in the paths of righteousness for His name's sake. Yea, though I walk through the valley of the shadow of death, I will fear no evil, for Thou art with me.'"

Eric's palm grazed the head of a mangy Husky with red-stained jowls. The animal whined at the touch and raised a wet nose for further attention.

"'Now I know that the Lord saveth His anointed,'" he continued from Psalm 20, "'He will hear him from His holy heaven with the saving strength of His right hand. Some trust in chariots, and some in horses; but we will remember the name of the LORD our God. They are brought down and fallen, but we are risen, and stand upright. Save, O LORD; let the King hear when we call.'"

The dogs stopped moving aside from Eric's path, and he found he had to step around them. One, he even had to step over as it lay on the spring grass. He was a lamb among wolves, and yet the wolves were docile, as if they'd lapsed by instinct into their old domestic state rather than their wild state.

There was commotion and swearing to the right, and a few dogs barked and growled from that direction, but Eric continued on his line. Calm. Trusting. Surrendered.

He reached a point that he guessed was one hundred yards from the town wall, and came to stop face-to-face with the Great Dane. It was as if the Great Dane had been standing there, waiting for him the entire time. For just an instant, Eric wondered if the devil had sent the Great Dane for this moment, to disrupt what God was proving to the people. After all, this was the leader of the pack that had chased them from Refuge to Coppertown!

"Come here, boy." Eric patted his leg as he turned to face the town. The bony head of the battle-weary dog nuzzled under his hand. The alpha male turned his head to feel Eric's touch behind his ears, as if the dog remembered another human owner from ages past, caring for him so. "My boy has a dog who likes her ears rubbed that way, too."

The dogs nearest the Great Dane moved closer to be pet as well, some jealously vying for attention. Eric started to laugh as he knelt and his face was licked by one with rancid breath.

"I'm as far as he is!" Loggins yelled back at the town.

Eric judged the distance with his eyes. The mayor was clearly short of one hundred yards by a tenth of the way. The dogs around him were becoming more aggressive, pawing and gnawing at the wooden exoskeleton. Loggins jabbed a stick at the dogs through the bars but his wrath only upset the dogs more.

The Great Dane turned to look at Loggins and growled, but Eric shushed him gently and stroked the animal's neck.

The townspeople on the wall and at the gate were motionless, silent.

"Father, accept their silence as praise," Eric prayed aloud, "and their stillness as worship. Move through this town as You did through Mastover. Give me their ear, Lord, and I will preach Your gospel until every soul who wants to be saved from their sins is in the fold."

"Get away!" Loggins scolded a bear-sized St. Bernard. The dog received the abuse upon its head from the mayor's stick, and rammed its head against the exoskeleton. "You cursed animals! Back . . . off!"

Suddenly, all two-hundred pounds of knotted fur and muscle of the St. Bernard leaped up and rested its forelegs on the exoskeleton about shoulder height on Loggins.

The bell on the wall tolled. It was time to return to the town.

"Loggins!" Eric yelled "Get out of there!"

But the weight of the heavy dog was too much for Loggins. He staggered sideways, trying his best to keep his exoskeleton upright, but the St. Bernard's hind legs kept pace, walking forward, leaning heavily.

Slowly, stubbornly, with cries of desperation from within, the exoskeleton tipped over onto its side. Like a turtle's underbelly exposed, Loggins kicked at the feral dogs as they closed in. He cursed God and screamed. The exoskeleton was only effective while it remained upright.

A half-dozen dogs dragged the mayor out of the bottom of his protective wooden cage. Eric moved toward the helpless man, but two dozen more dogs darted in for a piece of flesh. Then, it was over.

Eric took a deep breath. These weren't tame dogs by any means. God had protected him for the face-off, and there was no sense in taking advantage of that protection. He patted the Great Dane on the head and walked away, toward the gate. Walking calmly, he didn't look back. The gate had remained partially open with armed men visible. Those armed men now backed away as if Eric were on fire.

He sensed their awe as he moved through the gate and stopped on the edge of the courtyard to face them. They remained on the wall, now gazing inward. They looked at him in silence, as if he were a god.

"What's happening?" Kelly asked Molly. The two stood nearby. "Tell me!"

"Nothing," she said. "Just listen."

Amber was beaming with pride, her hands clasped in front of her, and Elk wept openly, one hand wiping away the tears, and the other arm around a plain woman who Eric guessed was his wife. The rest of the Refuge people were there as well, and their awe was as apparent as it was from the people of Coppertown.

"I'm just a man," Eric stated loudly. "What you've seen here today is the power of our Almighty God. He alone can take your wild hearts and tame them. He can take what is wicked and evil and dead, and give you new life. You have only to repent of your sins and trust in Jesus Christ, the Savior who died for you."

Eric wondered what he should say or do next, and realized he'd been at this point before—when hurting, shameful lives needed a shepherd to guide them forward to new pastures.

"Elk, please step forward." Eric waved at the husband, father, and elder of Coppertown. He set his hand on the taller man's shoulder. "This is Elron McKinney, a six-year citizen of Coppertown. You've known him to be harsh, I think, but God has given him a new spirit and a new heart. That's what Coppertown needs now. A new spirit and a new heart—a heart that cares more for life than provisions. In Loggins' place, I nominate Elk as the new mayor, and the expansion of Coppertown should begin immediately.

"No more will there be secret disappearances in the night hours when the population grows too large. There are other towns nearby, forgotten towns that people can inhabit. There are enough resources for everyone to live without resorting to taking life unnaturally. It will take work and patience to decide what to do to preserve all life, not just some life. Coppertown doesn't need to be a blemish on Nebraska's range. Become the town that leads other towns to productivity and care, even Christian care.

"My friends and I will be leaving Coppertown tomorrow, but now that we know you're here, Mastover will most certainly establish trade with you. That means the dog population will need to be eradicated, not used as a means of erasing your victims. God will guide us all forward, and Elk will trust in God to direct you, if you confirm him as mayor. That's all."

Chapter 11

After the face-off with Mayor Loggins and the speech of hope to the townspeople, Eric retired to the stable. He wasn't especially tired, but he felt he needed to get out of the spotlight and allow the town to begin adjusting to its new agenda—if indeed they would accept his suggestions.

All of the people of Refuge joined him in the stable and celebrated their victory with cries and laughter, though Eric continued to direct their gratitude toward God. As the twenty-four settled in and found places to rest, Eric noticed Amber crying alone in a stall. He knelt next to her, his hand on her shoulder as she faced the wall.

"It's just too much," she sobbed. "I can hardly believe it all. God is so real! How could I have lived my whole life and not know it? Now I'm an old woman. What can God do with me now?"

"Listen, listen." He took her hands in his, tenderly touching the healing wounds that peeked from under her sleeves. "We can't concern ourselves with all the years we were without Christ. Just rejoice that He has provided a way at all. Do you believe Jesus died for you?"

"I do. God is so real. I've seen something of Him in you. I believe He loves me, like you've said."

"Then you are His daughter, whether you feel old or not. A new life is before you, and I'm confident, even if it's not filled with as many years as you'd like, they will still be years of caring activity as you yield yourself to His direction."

"Will I see you again?" She wiped her nose on a sleeve. "After we get to Mastover?"

"Well, I live out in the woods with my wife and son, but we come to Mastover once in a while."

"I bet you're a celebrity." She shot him an accusing look. "I bet your wife has to use a stick to keep the available women off you!"

"Well, no." He felt himself blush. "I think a celebrity would need to bathe and shave a lot more often than I do—"

"And probably stop risking his life for all kinds of causes."

"Lord willing, you'll meet my wife and son, Andy, someday."

"I'll really be accepted in Mastover?" She shook her head. "With my past . . ."

"We all have pasts, Amber. What's important is that God has forgiven us, and given us a new future."

"Eric!" It was Kelly. He blindly felt his way along the wall and into the stall. "Eric, keep talking so I can find you. Where are you?"

"I'm right here." Eric guided the man by the hand to his side. "How are you doing, Kelly?"

"Frustrated. That Alan man had committed to guiding me. He promised he'd see me to the end of the trail, back to Mastover, or wherever you might take me. But these cursed people killed him!"

"I'll miss Alan." Eric sighed heavily, then lowered his voice. "Kelly, it's time you knew who Alan really was."

"What do you mean?"

Eric firmly gripped the man's upper arm.

"He was your Lieutenant Alan Tesh. You shot him last winter. He had one leg because Judge Grayport's son had to amputate it to save his life."

"No, Tesh died in the—" Kelly raised his head. "No. There are many Alans in this country. It can't be."

"I'm sorry. He was a good man."

"But, if I did that to him, why did he promise to . . .?"

"It was the love of Christ." Eric looked at Amber, believing she would keep their conversation secret, then he turned back to Kelly. "You tried to kill him, he said, but he cared for you instead. That's the kind of beauty that God brings out of hatred and selfishness."

"No, but—" Kelly shook his head. His lips formed words that didn't come right away. "But I was blind. He could've done anything to me. Why didn't he kill me, or take revenge? Why? Why didn't he tell me who he was? Why did he have to die? Now I can never tell him . . ."

Eric couldn't bear the man's despair any longer. He pulled him into a tight embrace, and Kelly Morris, ex-commander of the Liberation Organization, wept like a child on Eric's shoulder. Amber joined the men, embracing them both from the side. She whispered encouragements like a mother soothing a broken-hearted son.

That evening, Elk brought some of the townspeople to the stable to speak to Eric. They carried Bibles with them, and they asked him questions, since he was clearly a spokesman for God. Elk remained attentive through the conversations, and when it was late, the people left, but Elk stayed behind. Just the two of them stood at that end of the stable.

"I feel like I'm living in a new world," Elk confessed.

"It's not the world that's different, Elk," Eric said. "It's what—or Who—is in you that's different. God lives inside you now. Listen to Him, and He will speak to you through the truth of the Bible. You'll feel differently about the world around you because greater is He that is in you, than he that is in the world."

They stood silently, contentedly listening to the quiet conversations of the people of Refuge at the other end of the stable.

"Negotiations have begun." Elk scratched at his beard. "Some people want to leave Coppertown. Others want to stay. But some still want what Loggins wanted."

"Still?" Eric frowned. "How many?"

"Three elders. They represent only their own families, I think, but they are stubborn men who loved the attention of leadership and power. Everyone else in town has agreed to change. We'll remove the dog threat once and for all, and maybe expand to Refuge. That name has a nice ring to it."

"The bank in that town has a cistern on its roof, but you'll need to dig a new well. We couldn't find one."

"Noted. So, tomorrow you leave, huh?"

"Yeah, I need to get these people situated. They've been on the move for too long."

"I'll have to come look for you, one day." Elk's voice broke slightly. "Always favored mountain living."

"You'd be welcome at River Camp, Elk. Any time."

"Who would've figured you and I would become friends, huh?"

"Or brothers!"

They laughed, shook hands, clapped each other on the back, and parted ways. Eric would miss Elk. He reminded him of a young Hank Worcester, his father-in-law, though not as ornery.

In the morning, after a hearty breakfast in the dining hall, many citizens gave gifts to the travelers, mostly clothing or tools. Eric became concerned that they would have too much to travel with. Their rifles were returned to them, and no one objected to Eric saddling all their horses but one, which was old and ready to be butchered.

"Are you feeling well enough to walk?" Eric asked Peter, whose dog bites had been healing well.

"Yeah." Peter glanced up at a woman from Refuge sitting on his horse. "Strange how God works things out sometimes, right?"

"His ways are mysterious." Eric gave him a wink. "The heart has a way of its own, too!"

"Do you still have to see to my punishment when we get back to Mastover?" The ex-slaver pursed his lips. "I mean, if I'm healthy enough to walk on my own, I'm healthy enough to receive the penalty for my own crimes."

"That'll be decided by the judge." Eric adjusted his rifle over his shoulder and studied the line of riders and hikers still in the stable. "Everyone ready? Okay, Peter, let's move them out. I'll bring up the rear. We've done this before. If the dogs attack, I'll call out, and you stop the column."

Barely had the column of travelers moved into the courtyard when three men with shotguns intercepted them. The people halted and Eric stepped up quickly next to Peter. He guessed that the two of them standing broadside could protect everyone behind them if they received all the buckshot from the barrels at that distance. The three gunmen looked familiar. They were the three elders, Eric figured, who were giving Elk a hard time about change.

"Ivan!" Elk shouted from the side where the well-wishing townspeople were gathered. "Put it down! Let them leave! Lower your weapons, men!"

Eric held Peter back, remembering that Peter, when healthy, had stood in the doorway against a pack of wild dogs. The redhead didn't seem frightened about three gun barrels aimed at him, either.

"You ruined our lives!" the elder named Ivan said to Eric. "And we're here to ruin yours!"

"I gave you back your lives," Eric said.

"Mayor Loggins, too?" a younger elder squawked. His gun barrel shook in his hands. "Did you give him back his life?"

"He chose his own death. I didn't. If it were my choice, Mayor Loggins would still be here, too."

Eric saw the men's eyes widen, as if their resolve was giving way to murder, when suddenly, the air was filled with a rumble. It was dull at first, like distant hail pummeling the barren ground. But it grew louder. A man on the wall pointed to the west.

"Riders coming in!" he shouted. "Lots of 'em! And fast!"

Eric contemplated jumping the three gunmen and disarming them, but their barrels were still aimed at him.

"Are they armed?" Elk asked.

The people of Coppertown who'd stood in the courtyard dropped everything and scattered. Some ran to the wall where they were tossed rifles. Others hustled children toward doorways.

"They're armed, all right," the sentry replied. "Too many for us, Elk!"

"It's Mastover," Eric said to Elk. "No one else can man a cavalry in this region."

"Open the gates wide!" Elk ordered. "And hold your fire!"

The rumble in the air was now discernibly horses' hooves. A few seconds later, they poured in by twos through the gate. The first ten reined in their horses around Eric, Peter, and the three elders with shotguns. Another thirty riders splintered off throughout the town, and aimed assault rifles at the men on the six-foot-high wall. Their horses were lathered, as if they'd been ridden hard for hours. The men were stone-faced, brandishing bandoliers and additional weapons tucked into their belts. These were Mastover's defense forces, some of them left-over resistance fighters, and some of them the judge's personal security.

In the front was a man with no gun at all, just a bow and quiver of arrows strapped to his back.

"Since you're still alive," Joel Grayport said with a half-smile, his front tooth missing, "I guess I'm not too late."

"Your timing seems about right." Eric chuckled. "I thought Gretchen would be leading the assault, though!"

"She wanted to, believe me." Joel's horse pranced sideways. "The doctor didn't advise it this soon after her surgery. She hadn't even gotten her stitches out when we left two days ago. Are these the people you came for?"

Joel nodded at the column on foot and horseback.

"What's left of them. Alan was killed. Others were lost. But new life was borne, if you know what I mean. Here's one now. His name is Elk, a new brother in Christ."

"A pleasure." Joel nodded sharply at Elk, then focused on the three elders tirelessly holding shotguns on Eric and Peter. "How about these boys?"

"Just three men who are fighting change, down to their last breath, if need be."

Joel dismounted.

"Don't you men know who this man is?" Joel approached the nearest gunman.

"Don't come near me! I'll pull the trigger! He ruined all our lives!"

"Did you?" Joel asked Eric, but didn't wait for him to answer. "That doesn't sound like Eric Radner. Let's just point this at the sky for a moment."

Joel, from the side, used his hand to direct the nearest shotgun barrel upward as he walked in front of the men, putting himself between the three men and Eric. He moved to the second and third man, until all three shotguns were aimed at the blue sky. He did it so quickly and casually, it hardly seemed like an aggressive move at all. Elk was immediately in their midst, yanking the shotguns out of their hands. Face to face, no one could resist Elk's brute strength.

Peter sighed with relief by bending over and resting his hands on his knees.

"Get up to the lodge!" Elk ordered the three elders, who scowled and walked away. "Eric, have a safe journey, but I need to tend to things of my own here."

"Go on, Elk." Eric waved. "We'll see ourselves out. Thanks for everything!"

Joel and some of his men dismounted to walk or ride double as the travelers from Refuge were each given a mount.

The forty horses, plus Eric's own five, passed through the gate of Coppertown. Eric and Joel followed at the rear on foot.

"Seems like a nice enough town, huh?" Joel turned around in the courtyard. "Prosperous, it seems. I thought this area would be more like the Wild West."

"I'm sure it has its moments." Eric smiled, and waved at the watchmen.

"All looks clear, Elder Eric," a young Coppertown sentry stated from the wall. "Not a dog in sight, sir."

"Thanks, and God bless."

Outside the gate, Joel threw his hands into the air.

"Okay, I have to ask. Elder Eric? I don't get it. I thought you were just chasing down slavers. How did you become an elder of a town in just a few days?"

"I'm sure it's just an honorary thing." Eric shrugged. "Wait. Hear that?"

The bark of a dog raised the hair on Eric's neck, and he started to unsling his rifle, but then noticed the only dog in sight was the Great Dane, bounding awkwardly on his long legs from over the hill to the north. Eric slapped his thigh and knelt as the battle-weary canine collided into him. Eric received a tongue in the face and he ruffled the dog's short hair in return.

"And you now have a pet dog?" Joel laughed. "Or should I say, by the size of him, a pet horse?"

"Leave him alone. You see all these scars? He just needs some love. Like we all do."

"You know," Joel said, surveying the countryside, "I thought there'd be more dogs out here. I'd heard rumors, but I guess they were false."

"Let's stay up with the others," Eric said, jogging ahead with the Dane, "or we're liable to find out how true those rumors are!"

Chapter 12

Eric sat on a boulder at the edge of the shallow but wide river that ran through River Camp. The dry summer heat had come with no wind to the mountains of Wyoming. He watched dragonflies dodge drifting spider webs in the afternoon sunlight.

A woman's laughter from River Camp reached his ears, and the voice of his wife telling a story he couldn't quite hear made him smile. A little to the south, young Andy, soon to be eight years old, led a handful of youths on an adventure. When they weren't hunting turkeys, they were fishing, or trying to outsmart the wily wolverines behind camp to the west. Runner, Andy's black Labrador, pranced proudly next to her master, and the boys turned into the forest on a deer trail below the nearest ridge.

Dane yawned loudly on the ground next to the boulder, and arched his boney head up to look at Eric.

"It's a good life, boy," Eric said over the rippling water of the river. "Much better than the Plains Zone, huh?"

The dog lowered his head back onto his paws to rest. The alpha male was old, and Eric wanted to make sure his friend was comfortable during his last days on earth. Everyone in camp knew what the dog meant, or at least represented, to Eric. Stories from the Refuge survivors had circulated—they'd been first-hand witnesses of God's mighty hand against a horde of vicious dogs.

In the middle of camp, on a stump that had become his perch, Kelly Morris blindly braided rope for the camp's use as Hank Worcester spoke to him in low tones. Hank had once been a resistance fighter, but now he and the ex-Lib-Org commander found commonality in conversation as well as a cabin they shared. Few in camp knew who Kelly really was, and Eric aimed to keep it that way. The man would die there, Eric guessed, since his life would be in danger anywhere else. But in River Camp, the man was loved, and he seemed to have no reason to leave now.

Joel and Peter emerged from the woods above the ridge, each burdened with the end of a pole between them from which hung a doe. They were a strange pair, Eric thought, but they'd become friends on the return trip from Coppertown. Joel was a woodsman and a husband to a mute woman who sometimes didn't seem to know he was there. Peter was an ex-slaver, intent on a new life as a Christian, preparing to marry a woman from Refuge. And Peter had given up all firearms. Like Joel, the redhead had taken up archery, and the hunting pair, Eric decided, would be good for River Camp.

Eric had been true to his word, and Peter had stood before Judge Grayport for his crimes. Aloud, the judge had considered a public lashing, and even facial brandings, just to watch Peter squirm. But, in the end, the judge relented to Eric's private recommendations, and sentenced River Camp itself to deliver ten deer to Mastover before winter. Peter's heart had been further endeared to Eric through it all, and he'd assured Eric he would make full restitution. Joel, it seemed, didn't mind helping his new friend meet the quota, and an important lesson about grace had been learned.

"What are you seeming so satisfied about?" a familiar voice asked.

It was Amber. After meeting Gretchen in Mastover, Amber had insisted on going to River Camp instead of staying in town. After a few weeks, she'd even stopped looking crossly at Peter, though she still wore long sleeves to cover her scarred wrists.

The older woman stroked Dane on the head, then hopped onto the boulder with Eric to watch the hidden canyon.

"Just counting my blessings," Eric said, his eyes on Gretchen near their cabin. "For a little while, everything seems as it should be."

"It's not perfect," Amber said, drawing her knees up, "but I'm learning that being a Christian isn't about perfect circumstances. It's about resting in Christ in the imperfect circumstances."

"Spoken like a true sage," Eric said.

"The wisdom of Hank Worcester. He's a rude man, but I like him."

"He has his moments." Eric chuckled.

They watched the river sparkle with the sun's reflection for a time.

"What's next for us?" she asked. "What will God do with River Camp now? Do you know?"

"No, I don't know." Eric closed his eyes and lifted his face to the sky. "But I know this country is in a state of anxiety still. The West Coast and the East Coast are developing governments. The Plains Zone is anything but tamed. It would be okay with me, if God wills it, that I raise my son in peace and continue to teach new believers about Jesus."

"But?"

"But, I know my God." Eric opened his eyes and looked down at his hands. "He will send more challenges our way, to test our faith and refine our character. It's for the best that we learn along the way."

"So, we wait for God's next move?"

"We grow in Christ," Eric said, "and yes, we wait. For His calling, and also for His coming. It won't be long now. We just need to be steadfast in faith until the end."

~End of *STEADFAST Book Six*~

APPENDICES

Steadfast Character Sketch

Alan Tesh - As a lieutenant in the Liberation Organization, he is a career soldier, now in his thirties, devoted to a fault to the military.

Amber - As an ailing captive of Smar's chained cargo, this fifty-year-old from Oregon will need a hand of mercy to survive.

Andy Adkins - The young son of Joyce, Andy was born since Pan-Day, and has been trained by his father how to carry a rifle and how to be a man in an unfriendly land. Beside his trusty dog Runner, Andy is as asset even at his young age.

Commander Kelly Morris - Commander of the Liberation Organization. This brutal general will stop at nothing to destroy those who oppose him, especially Christians.

Conrad - In his forties, this tall and direct man favors Molly, whom he met as a fellow prisoner of Smar.

Elron "Elk" McKinney - An elder in Coppertown, this sizeable "Officer of Preservation" will hurt anyone who might threaten his town.

Eric Radner – This man in his mid-thirties was once a blogger, traveled America, and lived a luxurious life. Now, he has run to the mountains of Wyoming to hide as the Meridia Virus sweeps the nation. With no survival skills, he must learn to stay alive in the wilderness. Though his greatest cravings are for his own safety and solitude, he knows since he's a Christian now, he must set his own desires aside to help those in need.

Gretchen Worcester - In her mid-thirties, this fiery woman has earned the nickname "Grim" for her no-nonsense attitude. When armed with her hunting rifle and skinning knife, she may be the best ally for the mountain survivors.

Hank Worcester - As a native of the town of Mastover, Hank is a fierce defender of what America once was. His mood swings and rough disposition make him a prominent resistance leader against America's newest challenges.

Issac - As a prisoner of Smar, this thirty-year-old appears much older, and bears the facial marks of past violence. However, his dedication to help his fellow captives is without measure.

Joel Grayport - Once a popular student in Mastover, this native of Wyoming has taken up his bow to provide meat for his small family. If he can lose his father's reputation, he might become a welcome party to the resistance.

Joyce Adkins - As a young mother and wife, she is independent and determined to carve a life out from the rural landscape with her small family.

Judge Zachary Grayport - The tyrant who rules the town of Mastover. His dark eyes seem to dare the boldest resistance fighters to attack his town—and suffer the consequence of hanging or being burned at the stake.

Mayor Loggins - As the Mayor of Coppertown, he is determined and stubborn. From a refinery explosion, the hair on his face and head has been replaced by burn scars. His goal in life is to show how great his town is in the midst of the nation's chaos.

Milton Pickford - As the older brother of Sheriff Leo, big Milt is protective and ornery. He becomes leader of the resistance.

Molly - With a stout figure and firm jaw, this prisoner of Smar has an eye for survival and good men. In her forties, she carries the scars of abuse. She becomes an asset to Eric in the aftermath of great turmoil and pain.

Oliver Smar - Once a car salesman in California, now this brute in a wool sweater traffics in human cargo.

Peter Nelson - As Smar's right hand, this redhead has enough survival experience to make him dangerous to any defenseless traveler whom he wants to kidnap for a convoy of prisoners.

Talia Wiseman - Now in her eighties, this traveler from Seattle is in the fight for her life against racial prejudice and an outbreak of the virus.

Wendy Sullivan - A woman in her mid-forties, she outlived her brothers in Montana during the early years of the pandemic. Her hunting skills make her a valuable asset at River Camp.

Steadfast Glossary

Appalachian Federation - An East Coast government that spans from New York to North Carolina

Lib-Org - This nickname for the Liberation Organization is the label by which the rogue military unit is known as it sweeps across Western America, in the name of freedom. Their leader is Commander Morris, and their forces, dressed in black and gray uniforms, number in the thousands, complete with vehicles fueled by confiscated fuel.

Pacific States - A West Coast government organized from its capital in San Diego, headed by President Criswell.

Pan-Day - Panic destroyed and killed as many Americans as did the pandemic (the Meridia Virus) when it swept across the continent. When more cities were under quarantine than not, all banks had closed, and civil panic reached its peak—that day became known as Pan-Day. The pandemic and panic prevailed from that day forth.

Plains Zone - The no-man's land of roaming armies and barricaded towns between the Pacific States and the Appalachian Federation.

The Resistance - Fighting against thousands, these survivors in the woods number only three hundred fighting men, each wearing a red, white, and blue armband over their patched clothing. But in the midst of their combat against the Lib-Org, they are burdened with one hundred women, children, and wounded.

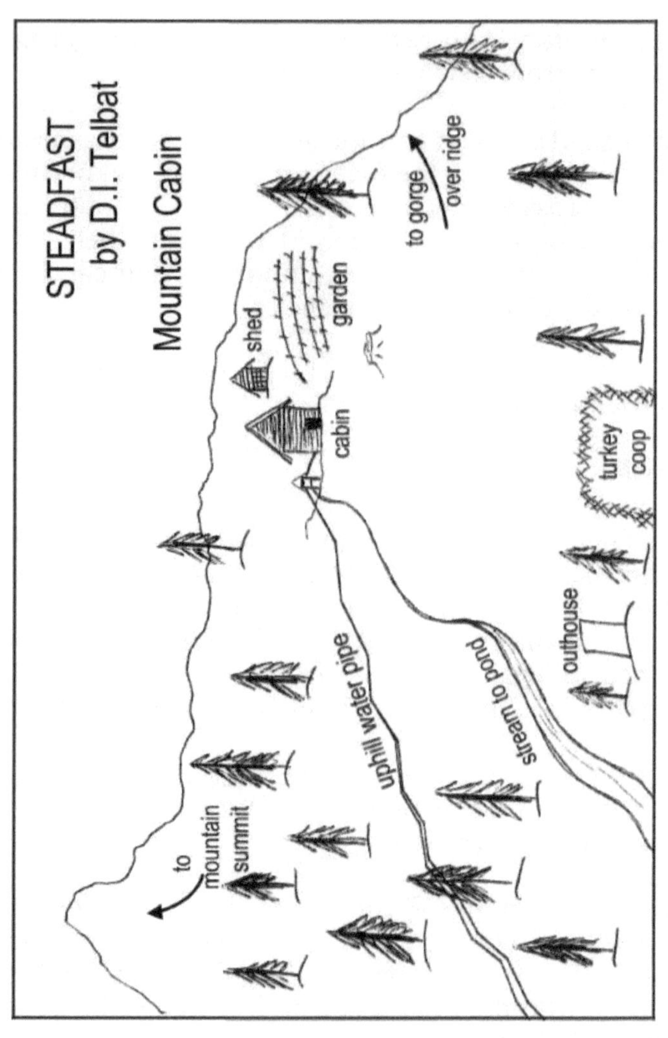

STEADFAST
by D.l. Telbat
Mountain Cabin
shed
garden
to gorge
over ridge
cabin
turkey coop
outhouse
uphill water pipe
stream to pond
to mountain summit

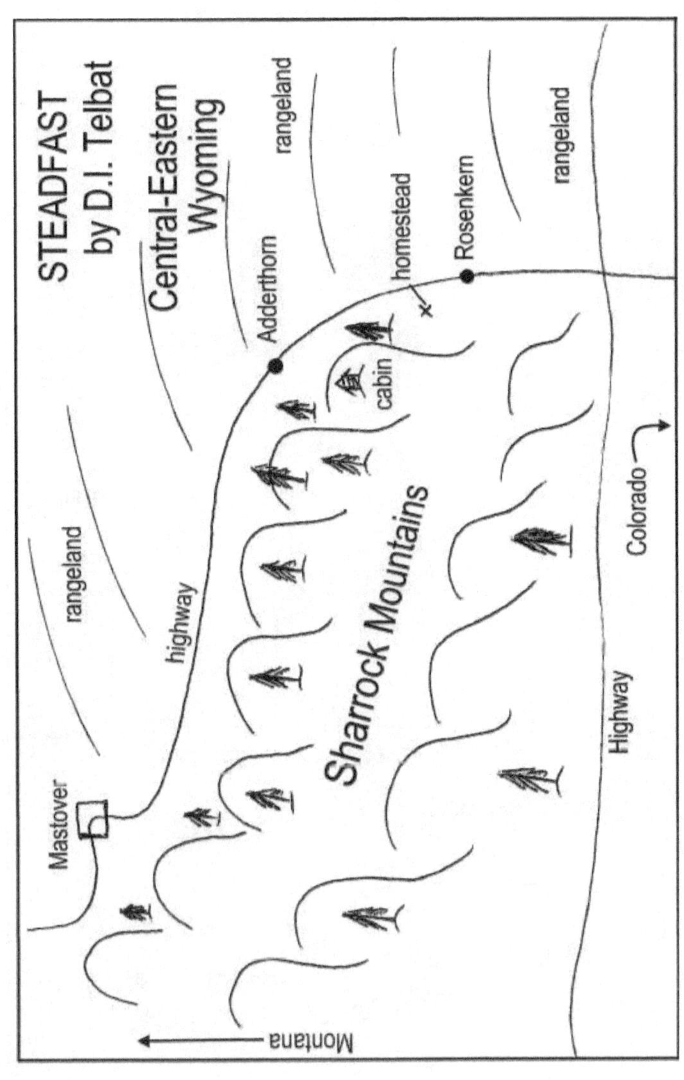
STEADFAST
by D.I. Telbat
Central-Eastern Wyoming
rangeland
Adderthorn
rangeland
homestead
Rosenkern
rangeland
highway
Sharrock Mountains
cabin
Mastover
rangeland
Montana
Colorado
Highway

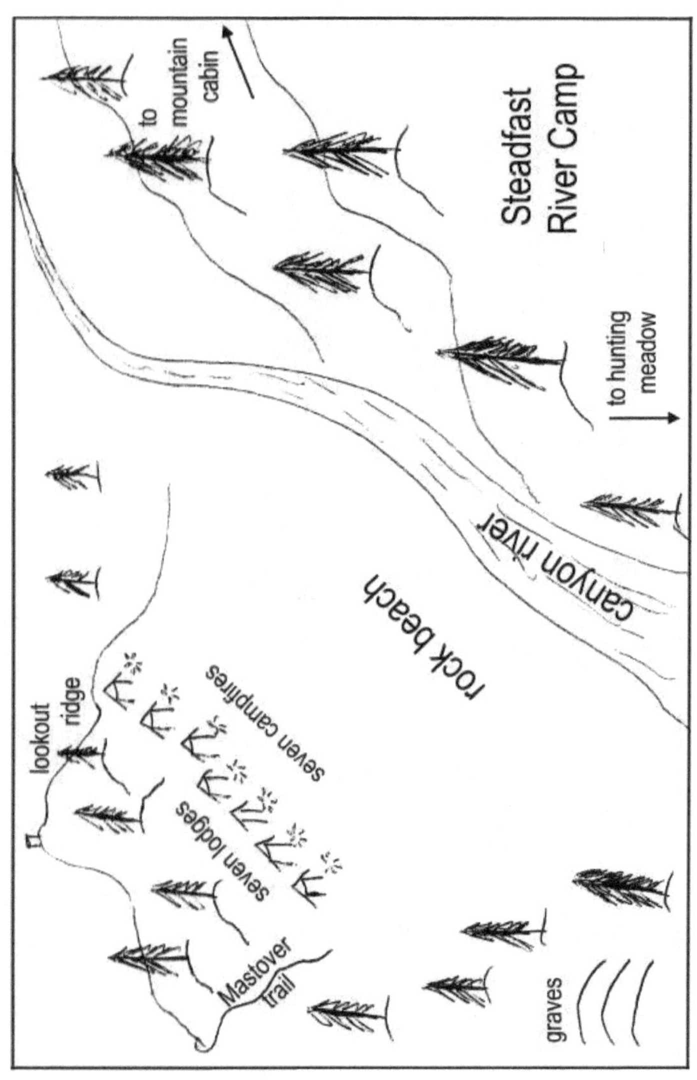
to mountain cabin
Steadfast River Camp
to hunting meadow
canyon river
rock beach
lookout ridge
seven campfires
seven lodges
Mastover trail
graves

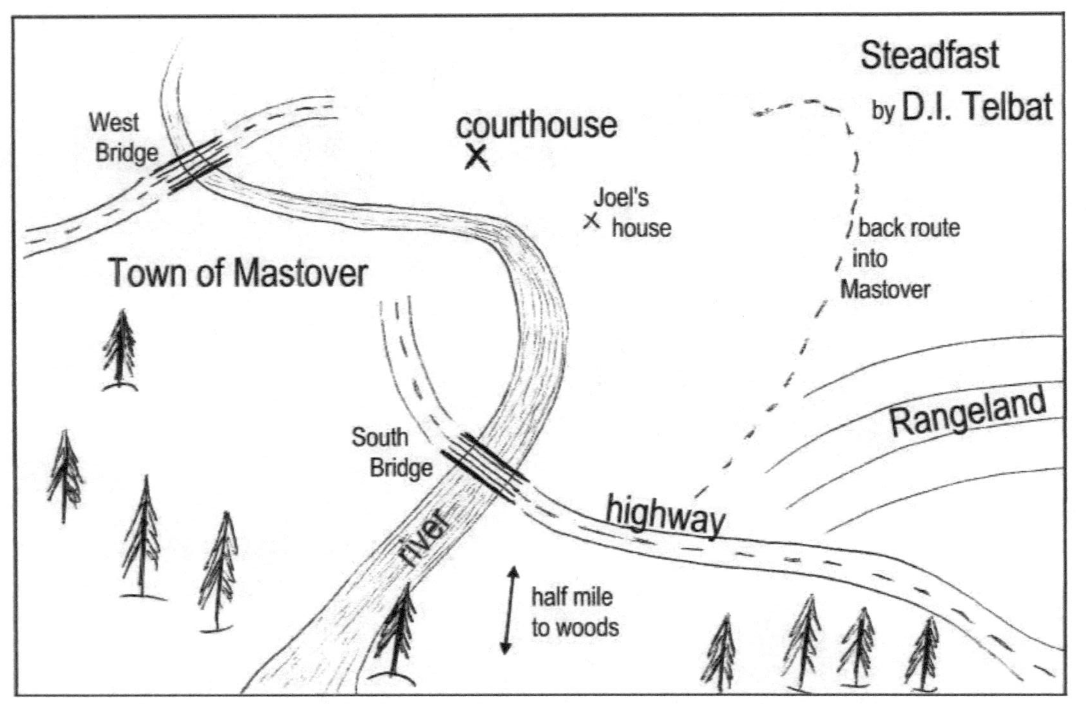

Steadfast
by D.I. Telbat
West Bridge
courthouse
Joel's X house
back route into Mastover
Town of Mastover
Rangeland
South Bridge
river
highway
half mile to woods

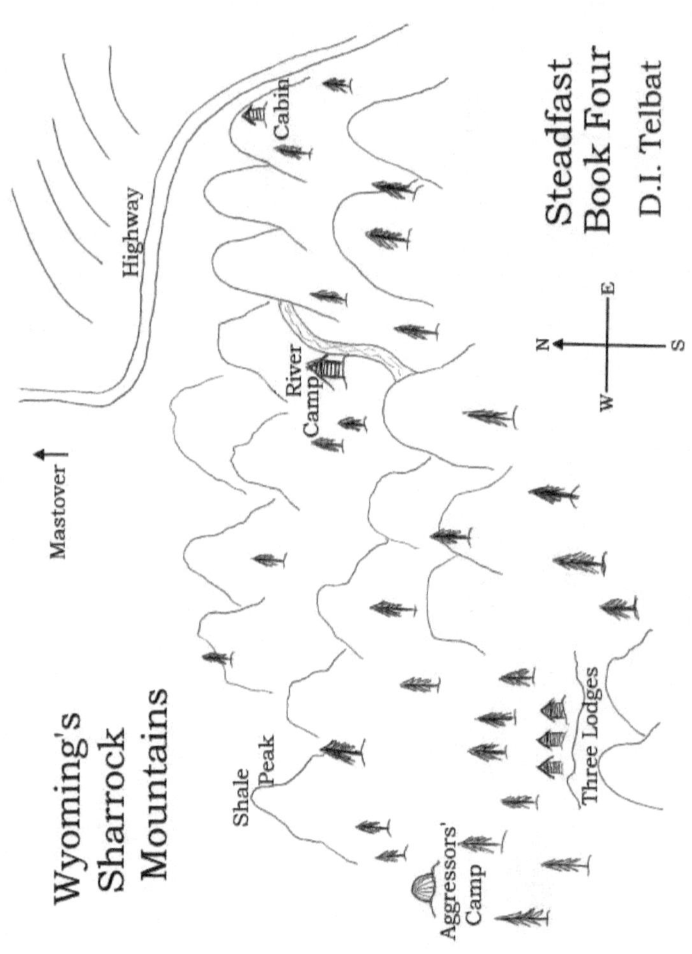
Wyoming's
Sharrock
Mountains
Mastover
Highway
Cabin
River
Camp
Shale
Peak
Aggressors'
Camp
Three Lodges
Steadfast
Book Four
D.I. Telbat
N
W   E
S

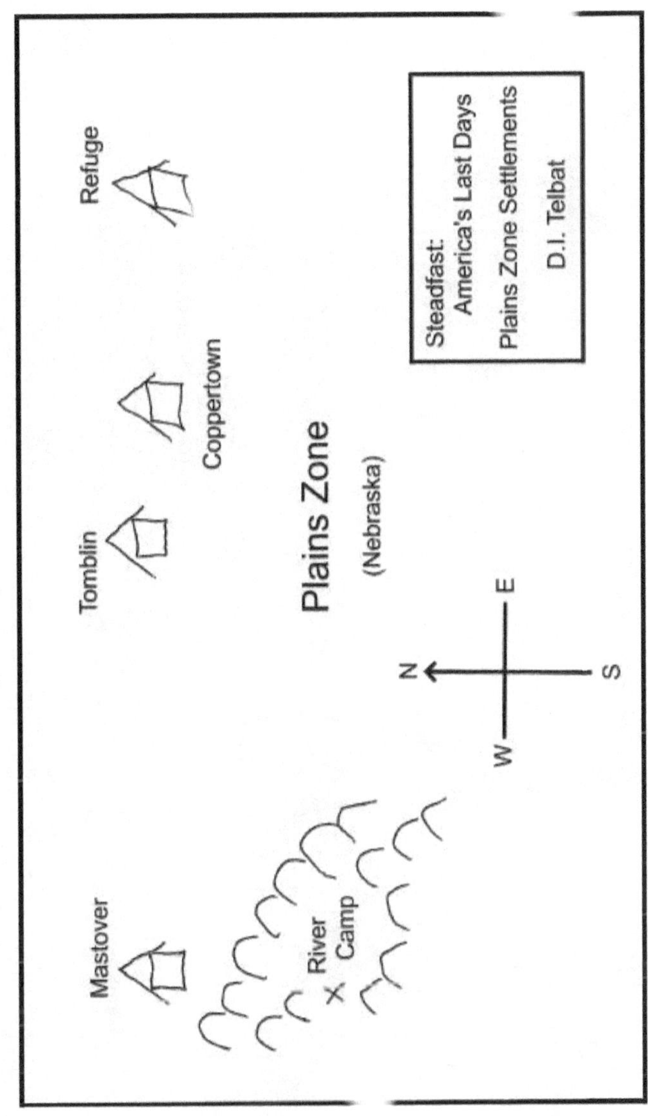
Refuge
Coppertown
Tomblin
Mastover
Plains Zone
(Nebraska)
River
Camp
N
E
S
W
Steadfast:
America's Last Days
Plains Zone Settlements
D.I. Telbat

Coppertown Settlement Map

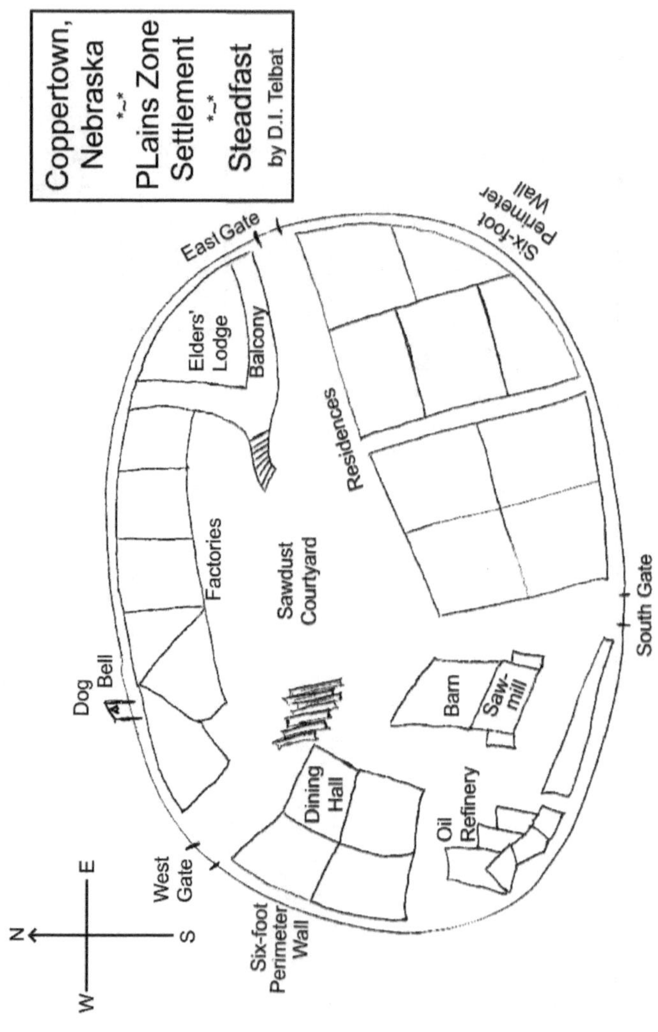

BONUS: STEADFAST SHORT STORIES

America's Last Days is told through the eyes of Eric Radner in the series, but there are other characters who wish to offer their perspectives as well. The following characters share with us stories of steadfast faith in the midst of turmoil. It's my prayer that the fuller truths embedded in the stories will be recognized as principles from the Bible. In these last days in America, let's remain steadfast examples of Christ when we relate to others. Enjoy these extra adventures!—*David Telbat*

Lonely Days

A Steadfast Short Story
D.I. Telbat

Forty-five-year-old Wendy Sullivan stared at the deer through her rifle scope. She needed the meat, but she didn't know who was in the area. The sound of a gunshot on the open plain would carry for miles, and she wasn't prepared to fight with someone over food.

Two does joined the buck in her scope, and the temptation to shoot the smallest doe was overwhelming. Wendy didn't want much meat, just enough to keep her moving southwest. Sundown was an hour away. People would be less likely to confront her over meat if it was dark. They wouldn't know if she was alone or with a party of hunters. But if something went wrong, Wendy had no plan. She was alone, and had been for a long time.

The family hunting cabin outside Billings, Montana, had been a safe haven for her and her two adult brothers for the first months of the collapse of America. Vic, the eldest, had been the bravest. He had dared to hike into Billings for supplies, before that first hard winter. From somewhere, he'd picked up the virus, but he'd made it back to the cabin. He died a week later.

Wendy and her younger brother, Bud, had survived the virus, even through caring for Vic in his last hours. Then, Bud had died two years later. She'd buried him after an infected axe wound to his foot had killed him. In those days, there were no hospitals to rush to. Medical care was limited to whatever knowledge the caregiver had

For the last three years, Wendy had been alone. The seclusion of the cabin had kept her safe, but she couldn't stand the silence any longer. She couldn't tolerate not being around people. She needed to know if the virus had passed, and if pockets of civilization had stabilized. For years, she'd heard nothing. The cabin had no electricity, no radio, no company. Her journey southward had begun that spring.

As Wendy stared through her rifle scope, she wondered what the distance was to the buck and two does. She guessed they were around two hundred yards away. Vic had taught her how to shoot years earlier, and Bud had taught her how to carve up the meat. Such memories seemed like a lifetime ago now. She missed them. She missed everyone.

If the deer were still out in the open at sundown, she decided, she'd take the shot. Until then, she'd wait and watch.

By trade, Wendy was a long-haul truck driver. Against her father's wishes, she'd avoided college and gotten her Class A trucking license. For ten years, she'd traveled the country, from El Paso to International Falls, from Baltimore to Coos Bay. Trucking had its highs and lows, but the money was good, and she'd always used her radio to stay in touch with humanity. There'd been lonely days on the road occasionally, but nothing like this. When the virus had truly become a pandemic, Wendy had driven to her childhood home in Eastern Montana. For safety's sake, she'd listened to her two brothers and hid out at the cabin with them.

"Even the deer aren't alone," Wendy mumbled as her cheek rested against her rifle. She'd noticed a year earlier that she'd been talking to herself more frequently. Why not? There was no one else to talk to. "If there were only two of you, I wouldn't have to shoot. But there are three, so when I take one, I won't be leaving any of you alone." Even for the animals, she refused to sentence the survivors to her same lonely fate.

Dusk settled, and storm clouds rolled in from the northwest. Though she'd been on the move for sixty days, she could only guess where she was now. Somewhere in

Wyoming, maybe. Several times, she'd seen other hunters at a distance, but she hadn't liked the looks of them, and chose to press on. When she came upon highways, she crossed quickly, though the roads were always deserted.

That evening, Wendy welcomed the rain. It meant people would be less likely to investigate her gunshot, if anyone was around.

The deer had grazed closer to a small stand of fir trees, but Wendy could still see them in the last rays of light. After a final glance at the empty plain, she sighted on the smallest doe and fired. The buck and larger doe ran away as the sound of the gunshot rolled across the plain.

"Maybe they'll think it was thunder," she said as drops of rain fell on her shoulders.

Rising to her feet, Wendy clutched her pack and jogged to the fallen deer. The sky was completely dark now, and she couldn't possibly gut the deer without starting a fire for light. The stand of trees was twenty yards away, so she ran to the thickest, tallest tree and set her pack against the trunk. By the time she returned to the deer, the rain had increased, but even in those summer months, Wendy wore a hunting cap and a weather-proof coat.

With effort, she dragged the deer to the tree, then gathered wood for a fire. She still had matches from her Montana cabin, so the fire sparked to life in minutes. The air wasn't cold, so she didn't need a huge fire for warmth, only for the light.

Drawing a short but sharp skinning knife, she started on the carcass. Mentally, she counted the minutes since the gunshot. It wasn't wise to stay in the same location for long. Once she got enough meat for cooking and drying, she'd run into the storm to hide under her tarp on the open plain. By nightfall, she guessed she'd be in the next mountain range, within sight of the southwest. Then, she could take her time and scout out safe company. She had to make contact with someone!

Suddenly, she stopped cutting on the deer and gazed into the darkness. Her small fire burned low, hissing briefly when the occasional raindrop made the journey from the sky through the tree branches all the way to the coals. Something had moved or made a noise out there in the night. After years in the wild, Wendy's senses were tuned to the barely perceptible noises and smells.

She continued on the deer, briskly cutting away meat to last a few more days. The wild dogs or wolves on the plain could have the rest of the deer, as long as she got enough to get her to the mountains and—

A branch broke nearby. Wendy glanced at her fire. Whoever was that close had already seen the light of her fire, she guessed, so she didn't bother to throw dirt on it. Instead, she lay two more thick branches on the flames, then clutched her rifle and darted into the dark woods. No way would she remain a sitting victim of strangers when she could be cautious and lurk in the darkness.

From behind a thick fir tree, she watched as two bearded men prowled into the firelight. They both carried assault weapons, not hunting rifles. Their clothing was wet, and they had no packs. That probably meant they hadn't come far.

The larger of the two men knelt over the deer as the smaller one examined Wendy's pack. She cursed to herself for not taking her pack with her. If she had it, she could've run onto the plain and been gone. Alone, but safe!

"Blood's still warm," the first man said as he touched the deer. He had a Southern drawl, maybe New Orleans. "I think she's alone."

The two men snickered together in such a way that Wendy was tempted to run away, even without her pack. Meeting these two men wouldn't end well.

The smaller man set his rifle against a tree and rubbed his hands together as he surveyed the forest. Wendy wondered if she was tough enough to take the shorter man, if he were alone, but there was no way she could fight off both of them.

"Come here, little lady," Shorty called. "Come on, now. We'll keep you warm tonight. We got your thingies here." He crouched and untied her pack. "What's this?"

He yanked out a flannel shirt and tossed it over his shoulder onto the ground. His partner drew his knife and continued what she'd started on the deer.

Wendy raised her rifle. She'd never killed anyone before, but if it was them or her—

"Hello, the camp!" a loud voice shouted from the tree line.

"Who's that?" The two bearded men squinted into the darkness and fumbled to aim their rifles, half-turned away from Wendy. "Who's out there?"

Licking her lips, Wendy eyed her open pack. If she could sneak up behind the two scavengers and grab her pack, she could be gone in seconds. But she'd never be able to survive and start over without her gear. Whoever else had been attracted to the gunshot, could fight over the deer with these two.

But while she was still contemplating, her window of opportunity closed as a brown-haired man and a blond boy, about five or six years old, stepped into the light. The newcomer carried a hunting rifle with no scope.

"We heard the gunshot." The new stranger stopped just inside the ring of firelight. His voice was clear and friendly. Though he was bearded like the other two, his eyes had a gentle and even casual look about them, like he couldn't be upset by much. "You boys from Mastover or Adderthorn? Got yourself a deer, huh?"

The two first-comers aimed their rifles at the man and his boy, but the stranger didn't seem to care. The boy patted his leg. A young Labrador trotted from the darkness, but she looked too friendly to be an attack dog.

"Come here, girl!" The boy's eyes were big as he and his dog acknowledged the two bearded men.

"Yep, we got us a deer," the larger of the two said. "We're fixing to have us a little party, and you're interrupting."

"I see." The stranger and his boy looked at one another. Wendy heard no communication, but something passed between them, for the boy turned and walked straight back into the woods with his dog. After the boy was gone, the stranger focused again on the two Southerners. "Yeah, I see a lot, actually. One of the things I see is that pack hardly seems like it's a fit for either one of you."

"I said you're interrupting!" the larger one said.

"Oh, it's my intention to interrupt. You see, I know you two didn't shoot that deer, and that isn't your pack. It seems Andy and I were watching the same woman as you two this evening, as she hiked in from the north, right?"

"Hey, where's that kid of yours?" Shorty snarled at the darkness. "Tell him to come back out here with his dog!"

"I've got to tell you two something," the stranger said. "You are the bravest men I've ever met. Look at you! Taking a gal's deer, and sorting through her pack like this. And there she is, somewhere out there, probably aiming her rifle right at you. Yes, sir, you're pretty brave."

"What?" The larger man ducked his head. "She's out there?"

"Well, sure! And we already know she's an expert markswoman, bringing down that deer with a perfect heart shot. Yeah, you two have nerves of steel. I mean, if I were you, I'd begin to back away real slowly, just in case she fires. I wonder which one she'll shoot first if you stick around. She's out there in the dark, and you're very visible here by the fire. Pure courage, on your part; no fear at all!"

Wendy couldn't help but smile as she listened to the stranger. Instead of confronting them violently, he was using reverse psychology to encourage them to leave without a fight.

"Now, we don't want no trouble, missy!" Shorty shouted and raised his empty hand in surrender, while he still gripped his rifle with his other hand. "We were just looking for some fun. We're leaving now, see?"

"Yeah!" The other man took deer steaks and stuck them raw into his jacket pockets. "We're done here. No need for any shooting."

The two men backed away from the fire.

"It'd be a good idea," the stranger said, "if you two stayed in your tent on the other side of the trees for the rest of the night. What a tragedy to be mistaken for a bear in this storm. Might get yourselves shot, right?"

"Might. We're going now."

In seconds, the two men were gone, and Wendy lowered her rifle. An instant later, she shrieked aloud as the lab sniffed her leg.

"Don't do that!" she whispered to the dog and ruffled the canine's ears. "Don't sneak up on me like that!"

Hesitantly, Wendy approached the fire and the stranger. The man shook out her discarded flannel shirt and stuffed it back into her pack. He looked up when she appeared. Up close, he was visibly younger than her by about ten years.

"Clever," Wendy said quietly, wondering if she could remember how to talk to people after so many years alone. "You made them leave."

"Well, I figured they needed to leave before you and I could meet." He held out his hand. "I'm Eric Radner. This is Andy."

Wendy sheepishly shook the man's hand. The boy held out his hand like a little man as well.

"I'm Wendy." She shook Andy's hand.

"This is Runner." Andy rubbed under the dog's chin. "She likes it when you do this."

"You guys were really watching me today?" Wendy asked.

"We saw you approaching mid-afternoon. Andy and I were out hunting." Eric set more wood on the fire. "Usually, we stay in the mountains, but we spotted those deer out here, so we set out around noon. You beat us to them."

"Do you need some meat?" Wendy drew her knife again. "I can share. I don't need much."

"We do have a few mouths to feed. Thanks." He frowned at her as she continued to work on the deer. "It's a little strange to find a woman all alone on the range like this. Are you lost?"

"No, I just . . . got tired of being alone up north." She looked up suddenly. "I don't think we're supposed to shake hands! What about the virus?"

"People with the virus nowadays aren't out carrying packs and hunting for deer. Besides, for the sake of being neighborly, we have to be a bit vulnerable ourselves, right?"

"You know, you have a natural way about you." Wendy smiled, and liked the way it felt on her face. She handed him a deer steak. "Are you for real, or has everyone up in the mountains gone bonkers?"

"What's bonkers?" Andy asked, then pulled Runner back from sticking her nose into the deer.

"Where are you headed, Wendy?" Eric asked. He stabbed the steak through the middle with a tree branch, then handed it to Andy to hold over the fire. "You've been alone for a while?"

"For years. I was going insane." She felt herself blush. Talking to actual people was weirder than she remembered! "You're with other people?"

"A small settlement. We call it River Camp." He thrust another steak onto Andy's stick, and Andy laughed at his bowed branch as he struggled to hold it above the flames. "That's the real reason Andy and I sat and watched you and those deer today. You seemed lonely, and maybe a little too cautious. That's no way to live life. I've been there."

"Caution is bad?"

"Oh, caution is good." Eric nodded. "But I've learned that, well, we can isolate ourselves to the point of silliness. At River Camp, we relax a little. And, of course, the Lord has a way of watching over His people."

"The Lord? You're religious?" Wendy felt herself draw back at the thought of fanatics. "Wasn't religion one of the problems with the world before the virus?"

"Sure, people have always used religion to commit all kinds of atrocities or to justify evil. But we at River Camp are just simple followers of Jesus. No religion, Wendy, just kindness."

Wendy stared at Eric for a moment. She'd never heard anyone speak like him before, but she'd witnessed his kindness already in action—the direct but caring way he'd dealt with the bandits, and now how he so effortlessly made her feel at ease. Whoever he was, she hoped there were more like him left in the world!

Andy giggled as he was about to lose the battle with the steaks on the stick.

"So, do you think you have room in River Camp for one more person?"

"River Camp would be happy to have you, Wendy." Eric scowled playfully at Andy. "Are you done playing with those steaks, young man? Runner and I are hungry!"

They all laughed. And for the first time in years, Wendy wasn't alone.

~End of "Lonely Days"~

Bicycle Bandits

A Steadfast Short Story
D.I. Telbat

Ben Lawrence pedaled his mountain bike faster. Sweat poured into his eyes—not from the exercise, but from the terror. After remaining cautious for so many years, highway bandits were now about to kill him!

He ceased pedaling for an instant and peeked under his arm at the road behind him. Heidi, his wife of seventeen years, was falling back. During the first winter after the virus had swept across America, Heidi had lost too much weight, along with her stamina. Now, with five robbers on bicycles chasing them, Heidi was faltering when she needed to pedal for her life!

"Keep going!" Ben yelled ahead to his sixteen-year-old daughter, Annette. She had been only ten when panic and the pandemic had left one hundred million dead. Pan-Day had changed everything.

The teenager didn't look back, and Ben was glad. Her parents were about to be massacred; she didn't need to see that. The bandits surely wanted the supplies hc had in his little low trailer behind his rear tire. Provisions for survival were more valuable than gold those days. But the bandits would be disappointed, he knew. All he had was a small wall tent, a few cans of food, and three sleeping bags.

Leaving Denver and heading north that spring didn't seem like such a good idea now. But the violence in Colorado had reached a dangerous pitch. Six years after Pan-Day, food and resources were short. It was just a matter of time before Ben was killed, maybe along with Heidi—and Annette would be forced into an unwanted relationship. Ben had seen it the year before. Families were worried about their progeny, but forced marriages and shot-gun weddings had ensued.

It was supposed to have been safer outside the city, fleeing to the north, but Ben realized he was drastically unprepared for the problems that day.

Ben risked capture by touching his brakes and slowing down for Heidi to catch up. He couldn't leave her behind.

"Push it, honey!" he screamed. His own leg muscles cried for relief, but he couldn't stop and rest. His family's only chance of escape was to outrun the five bandits. "Faster! Come on!"

For the first time in ten miles of chasing, the enemy was close enough for Ben to see them in detail. The nearest one was only one hundred yards back. He wore goggles to ward off bugs, and tight clothes that didn't hinder his movement. The distinct barrel of an assault rifle poked over the man's shoulder. Since they hadn't used their guns yet, Ben guessed they had some dreadful plans for them before killing them.

Heidi flew past him. She was breathing hard, gasping for air. Ben stood up to pedal, straining to get his speed up again with the heavy load on the back of his bike. Now, the bandits would probably catch him easily!

From far ahead, Annette screamed. It was a chilling sound that made Ben tense and growl simultaneously. He shook his head violently, whipping the sweat from his brow, and peered ahead. His daughter was coming upon two more gunmen standing on the roadside. Their rifles were in their hands. It was an ambush! The bicycle bandits had chased them into a perfect trap.

Up the highway, Annette tried to make a sharp U-turn, but her speed was too great. His daughter stuck out her leg to skid the back tire in a drifting turn, but her balance was off and her strength was spent. Annette went down on the highway pavement, only feet from where the two gunmen stood.

Ben stifled a sob. There was nowhere to go. Wide open range land spanned to his right, and thick mountainous forest stretched to his left. He looked back, realizing he had only seconds to decide what to do. Heidi skidded to a stop next to their daughter and climbed off her bike to help the injured girl. The two gunmen on foot were moving toward Annette.

For a moment, Ben had a clear view of the two killers ahead, so he reached into his jacket and drew his revolver. He had only four bullets left, after many failed attempts at hunting with the small caliber handgun. But if his family was to escape, it would be by continuing forward, not back. Killing two enemies had to be easier than trying to kill the five coming up on him.

Heidi huddled over Annette. Since they were so close to the two gunmen, their survival seemed unlikely, but Ben had to try.

He gritted his teeth as he steered with one hand and aimed the gun with the other. After squeezing the trigger four times, he glared disgustedly at his gun. Though he was no marksman, he'd expected to hit at least one of the gunmen at that distance! Instead, the two, apparently unharmed, reached his wife and daughter, and crouched next to them.

There seemed no hope for Ben to rescue his family. He threw down his empty gun and steered off the highway. He'd try his luck in the forest. On the edge of the highway, the ditch was deep and steep. His front tire hit the bottom of the ditch and stopped. The rim folded in half. Ben went airborne over the handlebars and landed on the other side of the ditch, facing the sky. Dazed, he rolled to his knees.

Before he'd completely gained his senses, he crawled through knee-high grass into the bushes, then the forest welcomed him into the shade of heavy branches. From the shadows of the trees, he watched as the five bandits rode past his gear and broken bike. Suddenly, a gunshot, then another, split through the mid-morning air. The two gunmen with his family had fired into the sky!

The bandits on the bicycles slowed to a stop only forty feet from Ben's family and the two gunmen. Quietly, the bandits discussed something between themselves, then turned and pedaled south, from where they'd come. After ten miles of chasing, they were suddenly gone!

Ben staggered from the forest. What had happened? He tried to understand what had seemed like a stand-off between the two gunmen and the five bandits. He'd thought they were together, but now it was clear they were indeed separate aggressors.

Rather than witnessing a massacre, he saw his wife standing over their daughter as one of the gunmen knelt next to Annette, who was still sitting on the ground. Ben traversed the ditch past his bike, and reached the highway. At a jog, he approached the two gunmen and his family.

However, he slowed to a walk as he realized the gunmen held only hunting rifles, and the one who was tending to Annette wasn't a man at all, but a redheaded woman in her late thirties. Her companion was a broad-shouldered man with an otherwise medium build, and he wore a beard.

"I just want my family," Ben said, his empty hands held wide, "and we'll be moving on."

"You crashed your bike pretty bad back there." The man's voice was friendly. Even at a time like this! "And your daughter could use more water than we have in our canteens to flush gravel out of her road rash. I'd say you'll need to rest a little before moving on."

"What?" Ben frowned, then remembered the five bicycle bandits. He shielded his eyes and looked to the south, but saw no one as far as he could see. "You mean us no harm?"

"She'll be fine," the redhead said to her partner as she stood. "They look a little hungry, though."

With Annette still seated between them, the four adults studied one another. Ben didn't know whether to pick up Annette and walk away, or tackle the strangers for their guns. His family had ridden through whole towns wiped out by rampaging soldiers and looting civilians. No one could be trusted! It was hard to figure what form of brutality this couple had in store for them.

"Well, I'm Eric Radner." The bearded man stepped abruptly forward, smiling, and held out his hand. His hand was calloused and tan. "Welcome to Wyoming."

Ben took a half-step backwards.

"I . . . don't shake. The virus." To emphasize his point, Ben hid his hand behind his back. He tried not to think about the redhead already touching his daughter. "The virus is still around, you know."

"Of course." The man dropped his hand, but the friendliness remained in his voice and on his face. No one was this friendly. America was in utter ruins! "There's a stream coming down from the mountain over here. Your daughter can get cleaned up there. Gretchen?"

Together, the redhead and Heidi helped Annette to her feet.

"No! Don't touch her!" Ben reached out, but stopped before making contact with anyone. They looked at him for a moment, then he dropped his arm to his side. "I just want to be cautious. The virus, you know."

"Well, I don't have the virus," the redhead said, then nodded to Annette. "Can you walk a little ways? Take it slow."

The women started off the highway, and Ben hung back with the bearded man who had called himself Eric Radner.

"We have a settlement back west about twenty miles," the stranger said. "We watch out for virus carriers, too. I don't blame you for being careful."

"I thought you guys were with those bandits." Ben ran his fingers through his hair, trying to relax, but found himself still shaking. "I could've shot you!"

"Come to think of it, I think you tried!" The man actually laughed. "But no, a few warning shots into the air sent them away. We came to the highway at the end of a hunt. The deer seem to have pushed south of us, but we like to meet travelers on the highway occasionally to hear the news. We'll say this wasn't a wasted trip, huh?"

"You . . . meet people?" Ben frowned. "Are you mad? No one purposely meets strangers anymore. It's too dangerous!"

"If I avoided everyone who might be dangerous, I wouldn't meet any pleasant people on the highway."

"But this day and age—" Ben hesitated. "Oh, you're talking about us. Well, you almost got shot by us pleasant people!"

"Tell me," Eric said, "where are you and your family headed?"

Side by side, they walked back to Ben's wrecked bike and trailer.

"We heard the Liberation Organization might have pulled out of Wyoming, that it might be safe to live up here with a teenage daughter."

Eric swung his rifle on the sling over his shoulder and lifted the front of the bike.

"You're going nowhere on this, even if you hammered it out." He set the wheel down. "Adderthorn is a few miles up the highway, but it's not real safe since it's right on the highway. Mastover is a day's hike farther northwest. That might be a good place for you. Do you have a skill to offer?"

"Not really. I was a day trader before Pan-Day." Ben sighed, expecting the same pity he usually received when he confessed how he'd once spent his life. A day trader had little value in those days. "You know, the stock market, numbers, and investments. I guess that explains why I can't shoot a gun too straight."

"Why, because you had a desk job?" Eric swatted at the air. "God saw to it that you couldn't shoot straight. He kept me safe. That had nothing to do with your being a stock analyst. Truth be told, our settlement could use a good actuary."

"What? How?" Ben scoffed. "I mean, nobody's cared much to have me around before. I've barely survived and kept my family alive by scavenging."

"You know how to measure risk and dangerous investments, right?" Eric shrugged. "That's all we do nowadays—measure risk for this and that. I think you probably haven't had the right friends who knew your value. Until now."

Ben stepped away from the strange man and the bike. He looked up and down the road, then at the forest and high mountains that threatened to turn the sun into a shadow. This was Wyoming. Perhaps this was what he'd come to find, he thought—a simple man with a friendly voice, who spoke to him of value where Ben felt none.

Finally, Ben turned back to the man.

"I tried to shoot you, and you're inviting me to your home?"

Eric smiled.

"I've learned a lot in the last six years. Maybe the most important thing is that God prefers to use men and women who think they're not useful anymore. He allows us to get torn down, and then He begins to rebuild us. So, tell me: you narrowly escaped a band of murderers and nearly murdered me and my hunting partner. Have you been torn down enough yet for God to rebuild you?"

Ben glanced at the empty revolver on the road. He'd bought the gun in the early days of the pandemic when he guessed there'd be unprecedented crime across America. Now, he stood before a man who had saved his life, a man who spoke of God, and usefulness, and rebuilding.

"She'll live," Heidi announced as she walked up with Annette and the redhead. One of Annette's elbows was wrapped in cloth. It wasn't any cloth Ben recognized, so it had to have been provided by the woman. "We can ride double, or you can ride her bike and Annette can ride on the trailer behind you until we reach the next town."

"There won't be any next town." Ben inhaled deeply, and looked into the eyes of Eric. Oh, to have the confidence and friendliness he could sense in this man! "I think we've reached the end of our journey, if Mr. Radner will take in a man who can't shoot straight—or ride a bike too well."

Eric laughed with the others.

"It's a good thing we have use for your other skills, right?" Eric clapped Ben on the shoulder. Ben didn't shrug away at the man's touch this time. "We'd be glad to have you at River Camp, but your bikes won't make it on these trails. There's a burned-out homestead up the highway. We can hide your bikes there, if you'd like."

Heidi moved close to Ben so they could speak privately. Annette and the two strangers chatted casually as they unfastened the trailer of gear from the ruined bike.

"Are you sure they're safe?" Heidi asked Ben.

"You mean, safer than sleeping in a tent in strange fields and running from bandits on bicycles?" He felt his heart beat with anticipation. He took her hand and held it to his chest. "Do you feel that? I can't remember the last time my heart beat like this."

"Benny, you were just about killed. Of course your heart is beating fast!"

"No, this is something else." He gazed up at the mountain. "It's something that man has. It's in the eyes of the woman with him, too. It's God. I think. Don't you see? They aren't just surviving. Whatever this River Camp is— we have to go there. The whole world may be coming to an end, but here, we've found something resilient. Or maybe, He found us!"

"Okay, okay!" Heidi laughed. She hadn't laughed in years. "We're with you. We'll go to this place. I hope it's everything you want it to be."

"I don't just want it to be something, Heidi." He took her hand and walked after the others to the functioning bikes. "With God, I think it's more about faith."

~End of "Bicycle Bandits"~

Sudden Accomplice

A Steadfast Short Story
D.I. Telbat

Red Fisher used binoculars to scope the Sharrock Mountains to the west. After the war zones he'd passed through in the east, Wyoming looked inviting since it was green and seemed secluded. The ruggedness was nothing like what he'd known in the Appalachians. Though he wasn't geared-up for forest survival, he only had to find someone who was. Red was an expert at taking what wasn't his.

"We've just got to get through the winter, Bonnie," he said to his Blue Tick hound. She had long legs and a sleek body—perfect for outrunning the wolves and wild dogs of the plains. "The snow will be deep, girl. You sure you want to stick with me?"

As if in response, Bonnie yawned and licked her jaws.

"Really? No, I don't think you stay with me because I feed you well." Red picked up his walking stick and started forward again. "If we get through the winter, we might reach California next year. There'll be plenty of people there. Where there's people, there's food for the taking."

For six years, Red had been moving west, doing his best to avoid cities and armies, but not small settlements. Anyone he could steal from made his life easier. In this way, his existence after Pan-Day was the same as it had been before Pan-Day—since he'd been a criminal then too.

By mid-afternoon, Red reached a highway bordering a steep mountain blanketed with thick forest. The mountains jutted up sharply from the prairie, but the highway at Red's feet seemed more inviting. It stretched out of sight to the south as far as he could see, and to the northwest, the cracked pavement curved around the mountain. Which way should he go?

From his waistband, Red tugged a worn-out map and unfolded it. Bonnie whined and lowered her head at the looming mountain peaks.

"Don't be a chicken." Red scoffed at the hound, though he quickly forgave her. He didn't really expect the dog he'd rescued as a puppy from a Kentucky alley to have the heart of a lion. "Just be my nose and ears, and I'll take care of the rest."

Red frowned at the weathered map, which he'd stolen from a Nebraskan trader the year before. He'd never heard of half these towns, being born and raised in the east. Weighmouth, Rosenkern, Mastover, Adderthorn? Adderthorn was to the northwest, maybe just a couple of miles.

"We didn't get this far by wandering into strange towns, right? And south, there's nothing for miles."

Bonnie whimpered in response, and Red shaded his eyes from the setting sun to see the top of the mountain above them. All he wanted to do was get to sunny California and live like a king. His whole life, he'd heard how California was the breadbasket of the nation. Pan-Day couldn't have changed all of that. He was tired of starving.

Instead of walking up the highway in either direction, Red crossed the ditch and headed into the woods. The mountain was steep, but Red was in no hurry. It had taken him six years to get this far. Besides, he'd found that moving slowly, he would most often see other people before they saw him. If they were friendly, he would steal from them when their guard was down. If they weren't friendly—he had no qualms about running away. Cowards lived longer, he told himself.

That evening, Red made camp beside a deep gorge that held a creek. The walls of the gorge were too steep to climb down to fetch water, but he had enough water in his canteen for now. Over a small fire, he heated the last of their canned food and split a biscuit with Bonnie. It was all that remained of the food he'd stolen from a family two days earlier.

The next morning, he followed the gorge on its northern edge for a mile to the west before he veered away to easier ground. Twice that day, he and Bonnie came upon deer. Though he needed the meat, Red didn't draw the pistol from his hip. He was no hunter or marksman. That was why he didn't carry a rifle. His gun was for protection only. After he stole from people, he needed to protect himself from them.

Toward the end of the day, he was cresting a wooded ridge when Bonnie's ears perked up and her tail stopped wagging. Red unclipped his gun holster and crouched behind a log.

"What is it, girl?" he whispered.

But true to Bonnie's nature, she whined fearfully and moved behind her master.

"Fine, you chicken." Red sighed. "You did your job. Now, I'll do mine."

He crawled forward, through the bushes, hoping to find the campsite of a family hiding in the wilderness. Maybe they had a pack of canned beef or fruit cocktail! It wouldn't have been the first time he'd picked clean the gear of Pan-Day survivors while holding them at gunpoint.

But through the bushes and over the ridge, Red discovered a small canyon below filled with activity. Seven log cabins sat on the bank of a winding river. Men carrying axes walked out of camp to the south. Others with rifles approached from the west, one holding what looked like a coyote pelt. Children threw rocks in the river, and a black dog barked as a youth pulled in a fish flopping on the end of a line.

Bonnie pushed up next to Red's elbow at the sound of the dog's bark.

"We're better off avoiding this lot, girl." He frowned at the few who had hunting rifles. "They look like they're a little tougher than the people we're used to relieving of their property."

Red was about to retreat into the foliage when he noticed a camper butchering a fresh deer on a block of wood. As the man cut steaks, two women seasoned and draped them over wooden racks to smoke-dry over a fire.

Bonnie licked her jaws.

"Exactly my sentiments," Red said. "But we'll have to wait until dark to take what we want."

Red pulled back into the trees and worked his way off the north side of the ridge. He waded across the river upstream from the settlement, carrying Bonnie through the cold water since she wasn't fond of the chill. Though she was an unlikely companion for a thief, Red saw much of himself in the little hound. Because of her cowardice, he'd never had to tie her or shush her when he was on the prowl. She either hid or joined him as he'd elbow-crawled up to snatch a camper's meat.

But stealing food from an armed settlement? It went against all the cowardice in their bodies. However, hunger had a way of making even Red more courageous than he wished he were.

While it was still daylight, Red prowled behind the settlement's seven cabins then waited on his belly in the bushes with Bonnie. His handgun was in his hand, ready to fire a warning at anyone who walked up on him. In the fading light, he studied his approach into the settlement and up to the racks of drying meat.

Before he finalized his plan, the bushes behind them rustled. Red glared critically at Bonnie for not warning him of some creature behind them. But, as always, he forgave her. She'd been as focused on the mission in front of them as he was.

Without rising, Red twisted around and aimed his gun at the bushes. He expected one of the settlement's mischievous dogs, or a wayward porcupine. But instead, a bearded man's head appeared! Red was so shocked to see a man seven feet away that he didn't pull the trigger or speak, and Bonnie seemed no less confused by the intruder interrupting their quest for a meal.

The bearded man held up a finger to his lips. Red frowned and lowered his gun. Much to his consternation, the stranger crawled with determined stealth right up next to him, and surveyed the settlement from their hidden vantage point.

Bonnie looked at Red, and Red looked at her, neither knowing exactly what to do about their sudden accomplice.

"What do you think?" The bearded man narrowed his eyes at the settlement, his gaze measuring the angles. "These people won't miss what we take, huh?"

"Excuse me?" Red preferred his thieving ways to be a secret—strictly between him and Bonnie. "I work alone!"

"Sorry. The name's Eric Radner." The man shoved his hand at Red so abruptly, Red could do nothing but shake his hand. "I was out in the woods, saw you sneaking up on this place. Figured four hands are better than two, right? We going after their meat?"

Red growled under his breath, realizing there was no easy way to dismiss the stranger, not without drawing attention from the settlement. He and Bonnie would have to tolerate him for now, if they wanted to eat that night.

"Yeah. They have enough to share." Red lowered his head. "Just keep your voice down. This only works if they discover we were here long after we're gone."

"Hey, I'm as hungry as you are," Eric said. "You guys come far?"

"East coast."

"Wow. That's some trek. You always make ends meet like this? By stealing?"

"More or less." Red shrugged one shoulder. "Can't trust people enough to do anything else but steal from them."

"How much are you taking? I mean, how much do you need? How far are you going?"

"What is this—an interview or a robbery?"

"I'm just saying," Eric pointed at the settlement, "if you don't need too much, maybe we could just ask them for some food. Maybe they have extra."

"That kind of defeats the purpose of hiding in the bushes, doesn't it?" Red scoffed. "Look at you. Why didn't you ask them? Then you wouldn't be hiding here with us, risking our lives with dumb questions!"

"They look nice enough." Eric glanced up at the sky. "It's almost dark. It'd be a shame to approach them in the dark and get shot at. They have rifles, I see."

"They're just for hunting. I think." Red put his arm around Bonnie to comfort her as she trembled. "I don't see any assault rifles. They're hiding out here like everyone else is doing these days."

A few minutes of silence passed, both men studying the route to the meat racks.

"It'd sure be a waste if we stole what we could just have if we talked to them." Eric clucked his tongue. "I'll talk to them if you will. We can go together."

"I'm not talking to them!" Red lowered his voice. "I'm here to steal some meat! As much as I can carry!"

"Yeah, but why steal what could be a gift? What's the worst that could happen?"

"Well, they could ask questions."

"Why, you have a past?"

"Yeah, and I don't like nosy people."

"We all have pasts. Maybe these people know that and they'll just accept us."

"It's my experience that people judge first," Red said, "and ask questions to find out your real faults second. Bonnie and I are too smart for that."

"Well, you don't mind if I go ask them, do you?"

"Are you dense?" Red gritted his teeth. "We can sneak in and take the meat in a couple hours. We never even need to speak to them!"

"But, aren't you hungry now?" Eric nodded at Bonnie. "Your dog sure looks hungry now. Listen, you stay here. I'll ask them if we can have some food. If it's safe, I'll signal you."

The bearded man moved ahead on all fours, then stood upright.

"No! Wait!" Red aimed his handgun at Eric's back, but decided against shooting the man. Of all the luck—a perfectly good caper was being spoiled by a stranger who was so simple-minded, he was about to ask for food instead of stealing it! Didn't he know that no one shared food anymore? Since Pan-Day, stealing and hoarding was the only path to survival.

Red watched as Eric walked calmly between two of the cabins and nearly bumped into a redheaded woman. Her arms were full with a bundle of deer skins. To Red's amazement, Eric spoke to the woman Red figured was in her late thirties, perhaps explaining his plight and requesting some meat. But when Eric pointed out at the woods in Red's direction, Red hid his face against the forest floor, not caring that pine needles were poking him in the forehead.

"The fool!" Red hissed to Bonnie, who continued to tremble under his arm. "He just gave us away. This is why we never work with partners, girl. They have no sense for the way the world is now. I'd be surprised if we live out the night."

"Hey! Hey, buddy!" It was Eric, yelling at Red in the woods. "They say it's okay. Come on in and get some food. There's even bunk space for the night! You hear me?"

Red didn't move. He'd been so careful to avoid making contact with people. It was harder to steal from folks when he knew their names. And he definitely didn't like people knowing about his past.

Bonnie whined. She was hungry.

"I hear you, girl." Red closed his eyes. "Well, we do need somewhere to spend the winter. It's been a hard few months."

Red slid his handgun into its holster and climbed slowly to his feet. To his humiliation, about ten people, settlers of all ages, stood with Eric, and watched him emerge from the bushes. He couldn't remember ever being caught so red-handed, prowling up on potential victims. He was exposed.

"They're fixing some stew right now," Eric said as Red reached the gathering crowd.

"And we have extra," the redheaded woman said. She reached out and took Red's arm. "Come on, now. You look like you've been on the road awhile. Let's get you cleaned up."

"You know, they call me Red," he said as she marched him away to a wash basin of steaming water. It had been a long time since he'd visited with anyone but Bonnie. "So, you understand, I'm partial to pretty redheads."

"If that's a pickup line, Red," the woman said, handing him a bar of soap, "you're several months too late. I'm spoken for. Eric's my fiance. The one you met in the woods."

"Eric?" Red accepted the soap and glared back at the bearded man. "You mean he's from around here?"

He shut his mouth. A boy of about six years old ran into Eric's arms and Eric threw the boy over his shoulder like a backpack, while tickling the youth. The black lab Red had seen from the ridge had already stolen Bonnie's attention. Red clearly understood he'd been had.

"Don't feel sore," the woman said. "You're not the first one Eric's lured into having dinner at his campfire. It's for a good reason, though, right?"

"What's a good reason? I told him I try to avoid people!"

"Most of us here in River Camp have witnessed God do miracles inside us, changing our whole perspectives, even though our circumstances remain the same. Jesus Christ lives inside us, teaching us how to live for Him. Doesn't that sound like a good enough reason to mingle with some friendly people?"

"You mean, Eric was pretending to be a thief like me, and it was all to get me in here to talk to me about God?"

"Are you hungry or not? Take off your gun and wash up."

Red dipped his hands in the water and splashed it on his face. He'd always thought he was so crafty, and everyone else was the fool. But he'd been taken captive by a forest settlement who offered him soap, food, and a bed, even though they knew he'd intended them harm.

Maybe it wouldn't hurt to stay in River Camp and find out about their God. After all, Bonnie certainly seemed at home already.

~End of "Sudden Accomplice"~

The Red Scarf of Hope

A Steadfast Short Story
D.I. Telbat

It had not been easy raising a family after the collapse of America. Karl Sibley and his wife Brooke knew that God had shown them favor while hiding for years in the safety of the woods of Northern Colorado. If his three children had been younger, or if he or Brooke had caught the Meridia Virus in the first years, the outcome would've been different. But after seven years of isolation, Karl was feeling a tug to take his family elsewhere.

Karl used his binoculars to scope the north-to-south highway far below. Their family cabin was set high up in the mountains where even hunters rarely ventured over the rugged terrain. The few woodsmen who Karl had come across over the years had been passing through, and after a few words in conversation, Karl never saw them again. It was those short conversations with strangers that continued to gnaw at his conscience. Some had told him that pockets of civilization had been restored, and Karl had begun to wonder if keeping his family in hiding was still necessary.

A party of four travelers were moving down the highway below Karl's mountain range, and for twenty minutes he watched them draw closer as they moved at a slow pace toward him.

There were three classes of people now in America, as far as Karl was concerned. There were those who had preferred to survive like rats in the cities. Then there were those who had run into the wilderness to hide. And the third class were those who constantly moved around, looking for hope or resources—or victims.

Karl saw himself in the second class—a person who had fled into God's creation to live off the land. But after seven years in the wilderness, his oldest boy, Jacob, was now fourteen. His middle boy, Isaac, was eleven, and his youngest boy, Joseph, was nine, born two years before Pan-Day. Brooke was content to keep their boys hidden from the world, but now Karl wasn't too sure he was doing the boys, or the world, any favors.

Growing boys needed to interact with other people to grow socially, Karl had been privately thinking, and to be tested in their faith. Protecting them from potential dangers that might exist had been necessary while they were young. But now they were maturing. Jacob could hunt, track, and hike as well as a grown man. Karl didn't want to keep the youth at the family cabin longer than the boy wanted to be, even if Jacob hadn't said anything about leaving yet.

The four travelers on the highway below left the cracked pavement to kneel at the water's edge of a stream that cut across the landscape. Karl could've called out to them from his place on the forested ridge, but he continued to watch them instead. Discerning who was a threat and who was simply another survivor in America's last days wasn't always easy. This party seemed to be made up of two men and two women. The men carried rifles and packs. The women carried only packs. All four seemed tired, and were lacking in vigilance, Karl noticed, as they all were dipping their faces into the water. Even Karl's sons knew to always leave one person as a lookout in all circumstances—familiar or unfamiliar situations— so no one could surprise them.

While the four travelers were distracted and drinking from the stream, Karl slipped out of the trees and down the ridge to the grassy plain. He moved all the way to the stream close to where the travelers knelt. They were drinking from one side of the stream, and he approached on the opposite bank. There, he crouched and watched them only yards away. But they still hadn't noticed him.

Being this close, Karl could see they were a weary lot, but not without resources. Their clothes were weathered, but not patched, and their boots appeared almost new, maybe even factory-made.

Movement thirty yards to his left startled Karl and he flinched to the side. He saw the form of a slender man also crouching on Karl's side of the stream. Peering a few seconds into the mid-morning sunlight, Karl recognized his own son, Jacob, and guessed the youth had followed him from the cabin. Although the family had rules about hiking to the east like this, Karl knew that he couldn't keep his boys caged up forever. Besides, those rules had been for when they were younger and needed more guidance.

Jacob gestured to Karl, directing his father's eyes back toward the four travelers, and Karl felt a welling sense of pride in his son's caution. The boy had probably come down from the trees to watch over his father, so that any interaction with strangers didn't go awry. They both had hunting rifles, though Karl had taught his boys to never take an animal's life unless they intended to eat it. And there would never be a time to take a man's life, since man was created in the image of God. As far as Karl knew, this was Jacob's first interaction with strangers since Pan-Day.

Across the stream, the eldest of the two women glanced up and noticed Karl crouching there. She alerted her companions, and all four rose to their feet, their eyes open wide. Only then did they realize there was a second person farther to their right. But neither Karl nor Jacob rose from where they crouched. Nor did they aim their rifles at the strangers.

Karl tensed as he watched the uncertainty wash over the travelers' faces. They'd been caught by surprise. The two men with rifles seemed as if they would raise their own guns, but instead, they slid their weapon slings over their shoulders. They weren't interested in aggression, which was strange to Karl. He thought that most people would try to kill others before they were killed.

The younger of the two men raised one hand in greeting. He then slipped off his stocking cap so his face was more easily seen. Karl looked into the eyes of a man no older than twenty, he guessed, and any initial fear the young man may have had was now gone. In its place was confidence and even friendliness. These weren't enemies, just fellow Americans.

Karl rose to his full height of six feet and glanced at Jacob. The boy remained motionless at the side of the stream.

"We're messengers from the town of Mastover," the young man said. "My name is Ross. This is my wife, Amy, and my father-in-law, Hal, and his wife, Nina."

For a moment, Karl continued to study them. He hadn't kept his family alive this long by being hasty. This wasn't the first time he'd spoken to strangers on the highway. Usually it was just for a little news of what might be happening in the country. And he'd always been extremely careful about how he'd done so. He'd never taken Brooke to speak to strangers, but he'd returned from his excursions to whisper to her any news he'd discovered. Rarely had he returned with positive news. However, now Jacob was involved, and his brothers would be curious as well as to what might lay beyond the woods of their upbringing.

"Messengers of what?" Karl asked.

The four strangers exchanged glances, then the older man raised his head.

"This country has never needed the message of hope and peace more than now. We're messengers with the gospel of Jesus Christ."

"You mean, you're missionaries?" Karl frowned. "I've never heard that Mastover survived the collapse."

"Mastover didn't survive the collapse," young Amy said. "The town rotted and died in the years that followed Pan-Day. The Lib-Org saw to its demise. But then a man stood up and offered his life for us all. His name was Eric Radner. From him, we learned about Jesus Christ in the Bible, and we started to print Bibles on an old printing press. The Bible had been banned from Wyoming months before."

"The Bible was banned?" Karl shook his head. "I didn't know that."

"So, Mastover has been reborn," the woman continued. "For the last couple years, we've been studying the Bible and growing in the Lord. We've been living in the contentment and joy of our salvation, but we knew we couldn't do that indefinitely with a clear conscience."

"What do you mean?" Karl asked.

"There are many across America who don't know the peace that Jesus has graciously given all people. They need to be told to turn from their sins and believe in Jesus Christ."

"It's too dangerous." Karl gestured to the highway. "If I were a bandit, I could've killed you a dozen times since you left that highway. None of you should be traveling on the open road—not without an armed escort, at least."

"God will provide," Ross said with a shrug. "We know we're going to places that will be dangerous, but we can't keep our mouths shut. We were raised in cities, and though there are no cities left, we still have to go to what is left. People are lost, and they need to know the way to life."

Karl sighed and looked at his son, who still hadn't moved. Jacob was wise for his age, and Karl wondered what the boy thought of the four foolish travelers. Although he and Brooke had raised their three boys to be well-versed in the Bible, Karl had never taught them to be careless when it came to risks. He hadn't needed to introduce them to dangers outside the woods to warn them of what might be out there.

"Well, where are you going?" Karl asked. "You don't look like you have much on you. Do you expect to meet up with people in the next town? How far are you going?"

"Just south, to start with." Ross smiled. "We're looking for people who haven't heard the gospel, or if they have heard it, to help them understand it. Do you know, sir, that Jesus died for your sins so you might have eternal life?"

"Yes, I'm already a believer. My whole family is." Karl shook his finger at Ross. "Don't change the subject! You don't know what you're doing out here. You have two women on a highway that's known for violence. You have no escort, and you're ignorant about the towns to the south. Your confidence won't keep you from being killed for this foolishness! You need to go back to Mastover and get properly set up for a journey like this."

"No, we're the four that Mastover chose to send, and we're prepared enough. We're willing to die, if God wills it, to speak the message." Hal tilted his head. "If you know so much about what lies to the south of us, and you're a believer, why don't you come along?"

"Yeah, right." Karl scoffed. "I have a family, and I've heard what's out there just waiting to rob us of everything I've kept safe all these years."

"It's by the grace of God you didn't get the virus," Amy said. "That wasn't you protecting your family. That was God. We can't control what we can't see or know. That's why we trust God."

"Dad?" Jacob called.

Karl turned to see his son signaling him to the side. Stepping away from the stream, Karl set a hand on his son's slender shoulder, their heads inches apart.

"They're Christians, Dad. We have to help them."

"There's no helping them. Listen to them. They've been living in Mastover where they've been safe. They have no idea how to live in the wild or how to travel along highways like this. By the look of them, they've probably never even hunted deer. They won't listen to reason. They're clearly going forward with or without our help."

"Then we help them go forward." Jacob raised his eyebrows. "I've memorized the maps of all the towns and roads to the south, as far as the Mexican border. You've taught me how to be careful, to observe, and to track. I can go with them for a few days, just to make sure they find good company."

"Jacob, you're fourteen years old. It's out of the question."

"If I was with them, would it help them?" Jacob asked. "Do I know enough to help them, Dad?"

Karl scowled at the grass and looked back at the four travelers who were speaking quietly amongst themselves. Brooke would never forgive him if he let Jacob go with strangers.

"You know the wilderness as well as any person I've ever heard of, Jacob, but what lies to the south is more than wilderness. There's burned-up cities and bandit ambushes, wild animals, and crooked traders."

"And you've taught me all about those things."

"Yes, but you've never crossed them."

"Dad, I don't mean to argue with you, but neither have you. We've all been in these mountains for years."

Karl felt his shoulders droop. His son was right. He knew only rumors and potential dangers. He'd never actually been to a looted city or burned-out town since Pan-Day. But he was a man, and his son was just a . . .

"You've become a man while I wasn't looking," Karl admitted sadly. He watched his son's countenance brighten with hope, and Karl envied Jacob's sense of adventure and even his yearning to do and go where few would dare. "Your mother won't rest until you make it back safely."

"If I'm more than a week, I'll send word with people traveling north up this way." Jacob drew a worn red scarf from inside his jacket. Even though the spring weather was warming, the boy had been taught to always be prepared in the outdoors. "I'll give this scarf to someone traveling this way. You'll see them wearing it, and you'll know they have news from me."

"Well, at least you have your pack on you." Karl nudged his son's pack, which was about half-full. "You have clean socks? Take care of your feet."

"I know, Dad."

"When you scout ahead, stay off the beaten path. You won't see ambushes, otherwise."

"Okay."

"Keep yourself safe and healthy, or you won't be able to protect others."

"All right." Jacob was grinning, but there was sadness in his young face as well. He threw his arms around his father. "I won't let you down, Dad. Tell Mom and Isaac and Joseph that I'll pray for them every night."

Karl squeezed his son tightly, then held him at arm's length.

"It's just a few days, son, but things can happen quickly in the world. If you come to the end, remember the Lord. Finish your race with courage. I'm proud of you, and I'll be watching for that red scarf."

When Jacob bounded across the stream to the four strangers, Karl didn't go with him. Instead, he remained where he stood, allowing the tears from mixed emotions to fall from his eyes. He watched as Jacob explained to the ignorant travelers that he would guide them south, since he was a trained outdoorsman and hunter. The party welcomed their young guide, and after filling their canteens at the stream, they waved at Karl and headed back to the highway.

Karl sighed loudly as the five travelers walked out of sight beyond the trees. His melancholy was short-lived, however, for he remembered that Jacob wasn't only his child, but he was God's child. Jacob wasn't alone. For a little while, he and Brooke had raised up the boys in the solitude of the mountains, but it was clearly time to now offer them up to the trials of the world. Their faith would be tested. They might experience some failure and suffering. But ultimately, they were in God's hands, and he didn't need to be overly cautious about their protection any longer.

He started up the ridge toward the cabin that had been his family's home for seven years. The news that the town of Mastover was a center for Christian learning and ambassadorship was interesting. Such a place would be a good first step for his young family to visit. Besides, he wanted to meet the man who the travelers had called Eric Radner. Maybe America, even in its last days, still had some good people in it after all. He felt he was ready to meet them.

~End of "The Red Scarf of Hope"~

Other Books by D.I. Telbat

Suggested Reading Order

The COIL Series, FREE Prequel + 5 Books
eBook, Paperback, Audio
*

The COIL Legacy, FREE Prequel + 3 Books
eBook, Collection in eBook + Paperback
*

The Resolution Series*: America's Last Days*
4 eNovellas; Collection to Come
*

The Steadfast Series*: America's Last Days*
6 eNovellas; Collection in eBook + Paperback
*

Last Dawn Series*: America's Last Days*
4 eBooks; Paperbacks to Come
*

The Leeward Set*: Where Christians Dare*
2 eBooks
*

Arabian Variable, eBook
Called To Gobi, eBook, Paperback
God's Colonel, eBook
Soldier of Hope, eBook

D.I. Telbat Short Story Collections

COIL Extractions, *COIL Short Story Collection*
FREE eBook
COIL Recruits, *COIL Short Story Collection*, eBook
*

Father's Day Short Story Collection; 20 Stories
eBook, Paperback
Mother's Day Short Story Collection; 20 Stories
eBook, Paperback
*

VISIONS of COURAGE: *Short Story Collection*
31 Stories; eBook, Paperback
VISIONS of FAITH: *a Christian Short Story Collection*
31 Stories; eBook, Paperback
*

Books to Come

Never Lost Series
3 eBooks, Paperbacks

About the Author

D.I. (David) Telbat is a Christian author best known for his clean, **Suspenseful Fiction with a Faith Focus**. This includes his bestselling and award-winning *COIL Series*, *Steadfast Series*, *Last Dawn Series*, and other Christian suspense and End Times novels. He wrote his first book at age 14, and he hasn't stopped since!

David studied writing in school and worked for a time in the newspaper field. Getting into serious trouble with the law as a young man became a turning point in his life. The Lord used that experience to draw David into a personal relationship with Him. Re-focusing his life for Christ, he now seeks to honor God with his life and writing by doing what he loves most—writing and Christian ministry.

Though D.I. Telbat is currently living on the West Coast, he has kept his home office in the Northwest U.S., where his assistant, Dee, lives and helps with his research and editing needs.

Subscribing to his free, biweekly newsletter will give you one of his Christian short stories, or an Author Reflection, or his Novel News Update. Also receive exclusive subscriber gifts such as his *Three For Free*—three novels in one volume! Discover his books and subscribe to his newsletter through ditelbat.com or books2read.com/DITelbat.

There is no redemption without sacrifice.

www.ingramcontent.com/pod-product-compliance
Lightning Source LLC
Chambersburg PA
CBHW031946130726
47904CB00012B/22